Kataza

Kataza

Andy Stewart

Kataza
Copyright © 2019 by Andy Stewart

Content Editor: Klancy Hoover
Copy Editor: Amanda Clarke
Editor-in-Chief: Kristi King-Morgan
Formatting: Kristi King-Morgan
Cover Artist: Elizabeth Dubos
Assistant Editor: Maddy Drake

Printed in the United States of America

ISBN- 978-1-947381-26-1

www.dreamingbigpublications.com

To Dad: My role model, my friend, and a thoroughly good man. May you rest in peace. I wish that more men were like you!

To Mom: A beautiful person and a beautiful human being. Intelligent, artistic, compassionate and talented: your support has always been invaluable. I wish that more women were like you!

To Alison: Wherever and whoever you may be: I look forward to meeting you.

To Tai: a wonderful person and a treasured friend.

To Klancy Hoover and Amanda Clarke, both of whom helped edit this novel, my admiration and gratitude for their insights, astute observations, patience and professionalism.

"FEED THE WHITE WOLF"

PART ONE

PROLOGUE

Kataza is a Matabele word meaning 'worry' but, for me, *kataza* means the bush, warm tranquil days, balmy nights, loving parents and friendly neighbors. It is laughter, conversation and the warm people of Southern Africa, for whom I care so much. *Kataza* is the name of the farm where I grew up.

CHAPTER 1
900 CE: KATAZA

In the distance, a lone man fell to the ground.

"He's dead," a young woman whispered. He lay inert, then picked himself up and shuffled forward. With a burst of energy, he lurched onward but struggled to keep his balance. Again, he crashed into the dirt, his body trembling as he retched black bile onto the earth. He leaned forward on shaky arms, swaying uncertainly while he mustered his last remaining energy. Once more, he picked himself up and tottered ahead, spume trailing down his chest. Once more, he fell. People started to gravitate toward one another, forming a crowd. There is safety in the herd.

"He's one of our kind," shouted an old man.

"I'll fetch water." A teenage boy ran toward the circular stone wall behind them, his grey cotton tunic swirling. Bright colors were reserved for those with more status. As he dashed away, the young woman called after him: "Bring ointment, he is bleeding." Although her cool cotton robe was drab, she looked quite regal, the material flowing gracefully down to her ankles, drawing admiring glances from some of the men. Her long black hair was braided with beads and glistening, saturated with scented oils.

"Fetch the healer," a tall hawk-faced man instructed, pointing at a boy. The crowd parted as he strode out toward the stranger. By now, the entire village had congregated together in macabre curiosity, watching from a distance.

"Make way." The youth returned with a calabash of water. He knelt beside the prostrate figure, placing the gourd to his cracked lips.

"Drink this slowly."

"Thank you," the stranger rasped, his throat raw from running. He took a sip of water and winced. It was painful to swallow.

"Who are you?" the hawk-faced man inquired, kneeling.

"My name doesn't matter," the stranger wheezed, panting for breath. "You must abandon this place."

Ignoring his words, the concerned woman began smearing a sticky medicinal poultice of honey and crushed herbs onto his arms. Cuts and scratches covered his limbs, and his feet were a mangled mess of blood and blisters. Pulling his arms away impatiently, the exhausted outlander tried to stand, but the hawk-faced man placed a restraining hand on his shoulder.

"Hold on my friend, let me help you."

"They're coming," the stranger warned. "Leave now."

"All in good time," the hawk-faced man smiled. "You're safe with us."

"You don't understand," the man gasped, glancing fearfully behind him. "They are like locusts, consuming everything in their path; we will all be killed." He lumbered to his feet and limped forward, leaning on the hawk-faced man. His cotton kilt was torn and shredded, yet he paid no attention to it, as he shuffled toward the crowd.

Fascinated bystanders demanded to know what was happening. Voices competed to be heard and dogs began baying, but above this din rose another sound, like the far-off roar of flooding water. Uncaring slaves watched on from the fields; this was not their concern.

*****

Jaban was in his alcove when the commotion began. Engrossed in his work, he was the last of his village to react. Faint whispers filtered through the stone corridors to his small enclave, his retreat. At first, they fell on deaf ears, but gradually he became aware that something strange was happening outside. Jaban was one of the few who lived within the protective stone wall of the small town; most others dwelled in mud huts. But Jaban had always been a man apart. Jaban carefully added his name to the clay tablet upon which he had been working a self-indulgent vanity. He set his stylus down with care, parallel to the rectangular tablet, and stretched his thin, angular body. Running his fingers through his carefully coiffed long brown hair, he straightened his robe before turning and weaving his way through the maze of granite.

The afternoon shadows were lengthening across the tall grass when Jaban emerged and the runner staggered into view, stumbling with fatigue. The stranger had discarded his helmet, but his shield was still slung across his back, as was his iron sword. Jaban was just in time to see the exhausted stranger collapse and the crowd close in, like jackals. As always, Jaban hovered on the periphery. No one noticed him; he was on the fringes of life, seldom involved. All that was about to change; life was preparing to devour him. Gasping for air, the man heaved out an ominous warning: "The dark ones are coming. The great city has fallen. Prepare yourselves. The black warriors are close behind me. Abandon this place. Flee." As he spluttered, a blanket of rust-red dust hugged the horizon, presaging the advance of a mighty Bantu army. The indistinct smudge in the distance was accompanied by a faint thrum, like the rumble of thunder.

*****

The villagers stood in hushed torpor until spurred to action by a strident command:

"Lock the slaves away," the hawk-faced man blurted. "Prepare for battle." People started to panic, clamoring for the safety of the wall—and the intervention of their gods. They needed all the assistance that they could summon. The slaves were herded into the confines of the wall and corralled within a large enclosure; their loyalty could not be trusted.

"The gods must be appeased," a woman shouted. The village demanded blood. Jaban did not join them as they rushed inside; instead, he paused to think. This was not his fight. Jaban was not made for courage and had no appetite for action. He took one last look at the magnificent circular stone wall that had harbored him for so long. It was not a mighty wall, but it was impressive still. At ten feet high, six feet wide at the base and three feet wide at the summit, it was not insurmountable, but it was ornate and this pleased him. A decorative row of granite slates had been integrated into the masonry near the summit, the attractive herringbone design making the wall look almost delicate.

As the crowd hastened toward the temple at the center of the enclosure, the village priest burst into the slave stable, flanked by armed acolytes.

"That one," he screeched, pointing to a suckling child. An acolyte snatched the wailing child from its mother, one of the many Khoisan slaves. Ignoring her pleas, the priest hurried to join his congregation massing in the center of the sacred enclosure and, as he did so, he withdrew a curved dagger from its scabbard. Hoping to please the pagan gods, the community chanted prayers as they huddled around the altar. The sacrifice was swift and sure: the throat of the innocent infant was slit with one deft slice, the baby's blood gushing into a ceremonial bowl and splashing onto the stones below. The limp body was tossed onto the beckoning fire for the gods to feast on. But the anger of the gods did not abate.

*****

Jaban's mind was churning as he threaded his way through the throng of people. The mighty stone heart of the kingdom had been torn asunder, and all hope was lost, yet he had to survive. As he slunk toward his enclave, he was ignored by his preoccupied neighbors: an invisible man. Recognizing the futility of fighting, and fearing for his future, Jaban filled

11

the pockets of his blood-red robes with his prized bangles and two bone-white ivory statues that he had recently carved. He stuffed a sack with whatever might be useful: clothes, preserved edibles, knives, leather, and twine. On a whim, he snatched up the clay tablets, so recently inscribed, and scurried away into the twilight. Darting through the back entrance of the confining stone walls, he melted into the wilderness beyond.

*****

As dusk approached and Jaban slipped into the night, the mighty Bantu army reached the hamlet, their progress halted by the stone wall. This was a small outpost, with only a few hundred citizens; the rest were slaves who tilled the fields, worked the nearby mine and performed the menial tasks. They would provide no more than token resistance. The Bantu army began to encircle the outpost, hungry for the killing.

*****

As the dark hordes prepared for their onslaught, the fearful villagers made their own plans. the men armed themselves as best they could, preparing for the fight to follow, while the women started to boil cauldrons of oil to pour over their attackers from the comparative safety of the stone walls. But few of these villagers were warriors; most were merchants and farmers, grown soft and lazy through inaction, forcing their minions to work on their behalf. They were no match for the Bantu warriors from the north. These Bantu invaders hated them; they detested these men for enslaving their people and sacrificing their children. The callous Bantu would show no mercy.

*****

Jaban was frightened and confused; he did not know where to go or what to do. His race appeared to be doomed, and the cities of his people had been vanquished. There was nowhere to go. Flitting nervously from tree to rock to tree, anxious to avoid detection, he made his uncertain way to a rocky hill some distance from the village. The kopje was so steep and overgrown that he was forced to climb it on hands and knees. He crawled, crept and clawed his way up the sheer side of the hill until he reached a small cave near the summit, where now he cowered. He cut some branches from nearby trees and placed them at the entrance of his cave to obscure it.

*****

Instead of attacking, the Bantu occupied the deserted huts, wanting to recuperate before annihilating the scourge: they sought time to intimidate the enemy. Some of the warriors began to light fires, while others approached the stone wall and hurled threats, taunts and insults at the invisible long-haired Arab half-castes hiding within. The Bantu regarded these foreign intruders as vermin, the progeny of Arab fathers and reluctant Khoisan mothers, who worshipped the ungodly gods of their forgotten forefathers. This cruel mongrel race had enslaved Bantu and Khoisan children to service their venal designs, and they sacrificed children to their avaricious gods. They were a blight to be eradicated.

The Bantu warriors were a fearsome sight, each of them adorned with a headdress of ostrich plumes. Their biceps were girded with colorful feathers, their loins were covered by animal skin and many of them had either a leopard or lion skin draped over their shoulder. The cumulative effect was to convey an impression of immense size and strength. The psychological warfare did not end there: every warrior wore an ankle rattle and, as the army advanced, jogging, never walking, the 'shuck-shuck' of thousands of rattles was amplified, sounding like distant thunder.

They were armed with an eclectic array of weapons. Long-shafted assegais, knobkerries, battle-axes, and daggers were obligatory, but many of them were also armed with swords, spears, helmets, and shields of foreign design, pillaged from their previous conquests. Notably absent were bows, which the Bantu abhorred, believing it cowardly to kill another man from a distance.

As night descended, the warriors took turns rattling their assegais and knobkerries against their shields and whispering soft war chants, the sinister sibilance both terrifying and relentless. With dawn approaching, the cadence of the chanting quickened, growing louder and louder still as they all contributed. Suddenly, the chanting ceased and there was silence. Then, with wild howls, the irrepressible Bantu warriors launched themselves toward the stone wall, like ravenous ants swarming to a carcass. As they flooded forward, an ineffective volley of arrows was fired at them, harming no one. When they reached the entrances, they found that they had been plugged with rocks and rubble. Finding their progress barred, the Bantu army concentrated their efforts on scaling the stone barrier. Ladders were balanced precariously against the wall, and warriors swarmed upwards like ants on a stick. The first wave of warriors was unfortunate: boiling oil was poured from above, and a man screamed as scalding liquid blistered his back and the skin slid off, exposing raw meat.

The villagers resisted valiantly, but they were too few and the enemy too numerous: they could not prevent the intractable enemy from breaching the walls. When only a few of the warriors were ensconced on the narrow parapet, the fate of the villagers was sealed. The battle-hardened Bantu relied on axes and daggers, relishing the cut and thrust of personal combat, wanting to feel the metal pierce flesh and to hear the wound suck air as the blade was withdrawn. There was something oddly intimate about close combat, connecting the killer with the kill. One enormous warrior was particularly impressive, consumed by bloodlust. Mounting the narrow parapet, he confronted one of the armed defenders. Hooking his shield behind that of his enemy, he ripped, swiveling as he did so. With his enemy pulled off balance and the ribs exposed, he plunged his long dagger into the man's chest, hilt deep, penetrating the heart. Bellowing triumphantly, he hurdled his fallen adversary and leaped to the ground, charging at an elderly man: the priest. Smashing his shield into the terrified man, he struck, slashing the priest's throat. Just as the infant had died, so too perished the priest: divine justice.

The slaves were liberated, celebrating their freedom with wild ululations and by helping to massacre their former masters. For a brief time, there was an orgy of killing as the Bantu warriors bludgeoned, hacked, cut and slashed, sparing no one. Women screamed, hysterical mothers clutched babies to their breasts and old men pleaded for mercy: to no avail. They were all butchered.

When the carnage was over, corpses lay everywhere, in pools of dark blood. The black warriors moved methodically from corpse to corpse, laying them on their backs, slitting their bellies from groin to sternum, and pulling the intestines from the body: the ultimate desecration. In fact, it was the only act of compassion shown; the belly was slit open to allow the spirit to escape and seek the company of the ancestors.

*****

Jaban had prayed to Shem, to El and to Athtar with feverish conviction, but his pleas had been ignored. Perhaps their time too was ending, or perhaps it was divine indifference. He had trembled as he listened to the dark, godless savages sound their warning to the village below: the sound of thousands of assegais beating rhythmically in unison against the hard hide shields had churned his stomach with terror as had the sound of thousands of warriors whispering, *"uSuthu, uSuthu"* in soft harmony, over and over again. In the morning, he had listened to the screams of his people as they were butchered, never daring to venture out.

When the screaming subsided, Jaban mustered enough curiosity to slip from the safety of the cave and hide behind an enormous boulder to witness the destruction of his civilization. Over a thousand years of history were torn down in a day. He watched with horror as the corpses of his people were disemboweled. He could do nothing as the dark men stood on the stone walls and threw every stone into the wilderness. The high walls shrank shorter and shorter still, until finally there was virtually nothing left of them, merely stunted remnants of their former grandeur. Jaban slunk back into his refuge, pulling the branches behind him. He slept only fitfully that evening, cold and afraid. In the morning, he made a decision: he would travel south to the great river and then he would walk even further south to the fertile mountains beyond. Having a new purpose, a sense of calm embraced him; he would move at sunset. Jaban prepared a trench at the farthest end of his cave, lining it with loose granite using random pieces of flat granite were strewn all around, the result of eons of weathering. He wrapped his tablets, his bracelets and his carvings in leather parcels, bound them with twine and sealed them away in the cavity; they were all that marked his existence. Placing a thin granite slab over the trench, he then replaced the soft earth and compacted it, shoveling small rocks on top. He would not need these possessions anymore; they would be an encumbrance in his travels. As Jaban pondered his future, the branches concealing the cave were flung aside. He caught sight of the sun shining on steel and a dark form, black as midnight, crouched at the entrance of his crypt.

CHAPTER 2
2005: BEITBRIDGE

"Bruce Savage." The customs official enunciated my name slowly, as though he was chewing on rubber, as he scrutinized my passport. He did not deign to look at me. I smiled inwardly; another small man gaining status through situational power.

"In the flesh," I rallied, artificially cheerful. I did not want to antagonize officialdom. I had been here for five hours and was exasperated by interminable queues and the bored indifference of the officials. But this, too, would end.

It had been an interesting day, packed with incident. I was already weary when I reached the customs buildings; five hours of night driving will do that to you. After unraveling and stretching my grateful legs, I joined the queue, which snaked away from the building and along the road. Before long, I found myself wedged between Atholl, an investment banker from Johannesburg, and a family from nearby Musina. We made some introductory small talk to pass the time and had shuffled up to the outside steps when there was a blur of movement. A young Black man sprinted down the street, panic in his eyes. A shrill blast of a whistle saw police officers converging on the young man, trapping him. One police officer struck him on the shoulders with his baton; another hit his legs with a sjambok, causing him to jump and scream. The police officers grabbed him and hauled him away. I got one last look at the criminal before he disappeared. His eyes were filled with tired hopelessness. I turned to Dirk, the farmer from Musina: "Another one bites the dust," I joked. "I wonder what he did wrong."

"He was probably caught pilfering. These guys are too lazy to get a proper job and are happy to steal from decent hard-working people," said Atholl.

"That's rich, coming from a banker," I joked. He did not appreciate my humor. It amuses me to ruffle the feathers of people who take themselves too seriously.

"He is probably more honest than the policemen who arrested him," chimed in Dirk. "I'm willing to bet that he is one of the few people here who is not stealing from the public."

"Pray tell," I encouraged him. Happy to act as an authority, Dirk explained:

"Beitbridge is a cesspool of corruption. Many of these officials are on the take and those who are not are complicit because they tolerate it and say nothing. To be fair, anyone who did speak out would be ostracized, and nothing would be done to solve the problem: too many people are benefiting from bribery. Over a hundred people are arrested daily because they don't have the necessary papers or the money to pay the bribes."

"So, the phrase 'customs duties' takes on a whole new meaning here," I said.

Dirk smiled: "A great many people from Zimbabwe and Malawi cannot find employment and they seek work in the south. Bureaucratic ineptitude is such that it can take years for a passport to be issued, so these people arrive here with no papers, hoping to buy forged documents. Touts in Zimbabwe will sell them a fake passport and charge a small fortune for the photograph. Customs officials on both sides of the border will backdate their stamps, for a fee. Most of these illegal immigrants seek safety in numbers and travel by bus or in mini buses. Sometimes they don't even require papers because the drivers have forged relationships with a partner in crime and the whole bus is signed off on without inspection. These 'commuters' pay a lump sum to the driver for his protective services. If the trafficker is tardy with his payment, the officials punish him by forcing him to wait for hours."

"I suppose this explains why it is so easy to smuggle contraband, such as cigarettes, through Beitbridge," I observed dryly.

"You're right," Dirk said. "People are processed like commodities, and commodities have a price." We were almost at the counter, ready for processing, when one of the officials was summoned away, presumably to back-stamp a passport and to fatten his wallet.

"The guys I feel most sorry for are those who cannot afford to play the game. Those with no money are forced to run the gauntlet and risk their lives. They sneak around the border post to the bridge and climb up underneath it, crawling along the trusses to the other side. One slip and they are dead: if they fall into the Limpopo River, they are snapped up by crocodiles. Crocodiles around here are very well fed," Dirk explained.

"It serves them right," Atholl interjected. "They are parasites: leaching off society and stealing jobs from our people by being willing to work for virtually no pay." He really was full of himself. Dirk and I ignored him.

"How is it that you know so much about this?" I asked Dirk.

He smiled: "My cleaner, Lucy Maseko, is Zimbabwean and often takes groceries back to her family. Because Musina is so close to the border, she can return there often. She has South African papers but is familiar with people who don't. A round trip will probably cost R500 for someone with no papers."

"That's a lot of money for someone who is unemployed," I commented. "In fact, it's a lot of money for someone who is employed."

"I earn more than that in an hour," boasted Athol. He was beginning to grate a little. I turned to Dirk.

"So, what happens to these people when they are caught?"

"If they are apprehended on the Zimbabwean side of the border, they are simply sent home and told to come back again when they have the money. If they make it to the other side of the border before they are caught, then they will spend a month inside the Lindela detention center contemplating their failure. They will eventually be deported and told to try again."

"So, the young man we saw earlier is probably too poor to pay bribes. Instead, he will have to pay the penalty," I commiserated.

"At least he will be fed for a month," remarked Atholl the rude man. "It's nice to know that my tax money is doing some good." I did not appreciate his sarcasm. I struck back: "Atholl" I said quietly, "your parents named you well." I looked him squarely in the eyes and smiled. Some people are not worth knowing. Dirk was chuckling to himself and I commented happily, "What rhymes with banker?"

After clearing customs on the South African side of the border, I was halfway across the bridge and paddling my feet in a cocktail of tepid disinfectants, when I noticed a flock of people on the walkway parallel to the road. They were scrambling to squeeze themselves through the narrow space between the concrete pillars lining the bridge. My heart went out to them because now I knew that they were risking life and limb in the hope of a better life.

Having dried my feet, I was certified as free from 'foot and mouth' disease and my passport was stamped again—free of charge. As my car was nudging forward, I watched the Limpopo River raging east toward Mozambique and the Indian Ocean. Early rains meant that the river was flowing strongly, its muddy waters replete with crocodiles and hippo pods. Angry voices startled me. On the other side of the road, the driver of a taxi was arguing vehemently with a policeman. I could not hear the words clearly, but the pantomime was superb entertainment. Hostile words were exchanged, interspersed with wild gesticulations and pained expressions as the passengers watched helplessly. These two rogues were brazenly negotiating a transaction.

As quickly as it started, it was over: a deal was struck, sealed with a handshake and smiles—the passengers relaxed.

The Zimbabwean customs offices were bedlam: a chaos of confused people milled around aimlessly, waiting for instructions, and the customs officials, the wardens, were struggling to keep pace with the workload. Outside the building was a host of hawkers, peddling their wares, just as people, too, were being peddled. The searing heat was almost unendurable, and the air was rank with the smell of fetid fruit and human sweat. As I meandered toward customs, a voice rang out:

"*Mngane, wena funa lo makaza manzi?*: Friend, do you want cold water?" The old man was seated beneath a large flamboyant tree, hogging the shade. He was looking in my direction, but his question was addressed to anyone and everyone. The elderly entrepreneur was selling T-shirts, handbags, soap-stone carvings, snacks, and beverages. I decided on a ginger beer and was just starting to drink it when one of the officials began inspecting a bus choked with people traveling south. He was laughing and joking with the bus driver, enjoying the power he wielded, but the bus driver looked very apprehensive and tightly wound.

"Remove the luggage from the bus," the official demanded. The passengers removed their suitcases from the side of the bus and he rifled through their passports, making a show of it.

"Dube. Patrick Dube," he called, perusing the crowd. A young boy, hardly more than fifteen years old, stepped forward uncertainly. The customs officer lobbed the offending passport to him, but he failed to catch it. The boy's hands were shaking as he picked it up. No one tried to help him, not wanting to make a target of themselves.

"Go and stand over there," the official ordered, pointing to a police van nearby. Patrick Dube was escorted to the van by a waiting policeman.

"Linda Ndhlovu." He selected his next victim. Linda was a slender middle-aged woman, who had presumably not paid sufficiently. The malicious official decided to make an example of her too.

"Open your luggage." She searched through the pile of suitcases until she found her sports kitbag, which she handed to him tentatively. The official removed its contents with complete disregard for her privacy or feelings, displaying her clothing and private effects for the crowd to see. Then he jammed them all back in again and handed the bag to her, leaving her standing as he drew the bus driver aside.

"I will send every one of these people back to where they came from unless they each pay me R10 more." He had demonstrated his authority and now he needed to profit from it. The bus driver gathered his flock around him and explained the situation, apologizing profusely. Perhaps the situation was contrived, but they all started contributing money, collecting the deficit. I calculated that nearly R700 was harvested before the bus continued south. Corruption is good business. Disgusted and depressed, I aimed myself toward immigration.

*****

All that was behind me; I was now confronted by a deliberately obtuse official. My patience was frayed by a string of inane questions: "When last were you in the country? Where will you be staying? How long will you be staying for? What is your profession? When did you emigrate? Why did you emigrate? Do you have any relatives in the country? Were you ever in the military? What regiment did you serve in? Are you in possession of any contraband?" I had answered them all with good humor, and then he suggested that my car be searched, and my luggage examined.

"Are you serious?" I despaired.

The official looked me squarely in the eyes, inscrutable—then he grinned. He had been toying with me: "My cousin, Fasika, works at Kataza. I have been there many times, and it is a wonderful place."

"You rogue! You've been pulling my chain for the last ten minutes." I smiled, enjoying his joke, and relieved that the tension was broken.

"Fasika is very fond of you and your father. Please give him my regards." I examined his name tag, noticing that his name was Philani Mathuthu.

"I will Philani, and I hope that I will see you when next you visit Fasika. He's a good man." Philani smiled and gave me the thumbs up.

"Welcome home." He was right: even though I resided elsewhere, Kataza would always be home.

*****

It was December 10, 2005, and I was on my annual pilgrimage to see my dad. Distance, and the demands of work, meant that I only got to visit Dad once a year. After the weariness of driving all day and the bedlam of the border crossing, I felt my spirits soar as I reached familiar territory near the little town of Esigodini. From here, Kataza was only seven kilometers east. I remember feeling a wonderful sense of anticipation as I crossed the bridge over the Ncema River, and I made a conscious decision to soak in the scenery, recognizing at a subliminal level that I may never come this way again. To my right lay the purple spine of the Mulungwane Mountains, to my left lay the Blue Hills. The tall amber grass undulated gracefully in the soft breeze and patches of bright yellow dotted the landscape: the African wattles were in full flower. They looked magnificent. It all seemed so perfect—not a soul in sight. I truly was back in the solitude of the wilderness.

I turned left onto the dirt track that led to Kataza and after another five minutes of slow driving, the car rattling over the corrugated and stony road, the homestead came into view. I drove through the gates into a veritable oasis, awash with color. The lawn was emerald green and fringed with large shade trees. In one corner, the water sprinkler had attracted a flock of yellow weaverbirds, enjoying the last light of day. All around were the ubiquitous grey louries: go-away-birds. The flower beds surrounding the lawn were resplendent with masses of orange gladioli, purple irises, ivory arums, and pink hydrangea and, in the center of this paradise, lay the regal old lady, our home, with white walls, green tiled roof and an enormous veranda which encircled the house. The bougainvillea had grown since last I was here and now embraced the home with crimson clutches. Standing on the veranda was my dad, waiting anxiously for my arrival. He waved me in with a delighted smile, dressed in his familiar faded khaki longs and blue shirt, the sleeves neatly rolled to above the elbow. Merlin and Madam, his two Jack Russell terriers, stood faithfully beside him, tails wagging frantically. His silver hair was neatly parted. With his right hand, he was waving to me while his left hand held his walking stick. I felt elated and relieved to finally be home, but shocked to see how frail Dad had waned. Little did I know that this would be my last ever visit to Kataza.

After giving each other a hug and exchanging pleasantries, we went inside the house, with its spacious rooms and comfortable furniture. Dad poured me a cup of coffee, and we sat and chatted well into the night, catching up on all our news. It felt good to be home. I went to sleep in my old bedroom, surrounded by all my old treasures, truly contented and peaceful for the first time in a year.

CHAPTER 3

Almost all my memories of Kataza are happy ones, infused with mellow sunlight, joyful curiosity and the aromatic, herbal smell of the bundu. A few of these imperfect memories are less pleasant: recollections of the war and of the occasional reprimand from my parents. But these are bitter-sweet memories, tinged with affection and humor. There is one sinister recollection that lingers darkly in the recesses of my mind. I can picture it with vivid clarity, although some of the finer details are murky. I remember my dad answering the telephone and his normally calm demeanor changing into one of concern.

"What's wrong, honey?" my mother asked.

"The police are on their way to the compound," Dad replied absently. "Apparently the new guy, Meshach, is blind drunk to the point that he doesn't even know his own name. He has vandalized the dairy and, from what I can gather, there has been an incident of domestic violence. He has hit his wife and his son."

I was not surprised. Meshach was a relatively new addition to the village and he was a man with a grudge against the world, resenting his wife, his son, his lowly position in life, his employer and the European colonialist exploiters. The community had not taken kindly to this surly, sullen man and had shunned him from the outset.

"Can I come with you, Dad?" I asked expectantly.

"Not this time, chap," replied Dad. "This is not going to be pleasant."

Dad snatched his keys from the coffee table and rushed out to the Land Rover, his FN rifle tightly gripped in his left hand. With the war on, our rifles accompanied us everywhere we went—just in case of an ambush. I watched the Land Rover rumble out of our yard and toward the village, feeling a mixture of trepidation and excitement. As the dust was settling, I set off in pursuit, leaving my mother alone in the kitchen, the smell of bacon and freshly baked maize bread permeating the house.

The Land Rover disappeared behind a twist in the road, and I decided to take a shortcut, veering to my left onto an indistinct game track through the bush. Sprinting along the narrow path, I hurdled rocks and roots, handed away low branches and ducked beneath solid boughs. The track was so overgrown that it was barely visible for the high grass and dense bushes and, as I careened through the undergrowth, my face was whipped by grass tassels and stung by thorny twigs; I loved it! After about ten minutes of running, the path emerged onto the soccer field bordering the compound. The field was fringed by tall mukwa trees and aloes, providing me with cover as I skirted toward the action.

Dad was standing with our foreman, Henderson, and two young men. Henderson was a wise, calm, old man with ash-grey hair and a gentle sense of humor. He and Dad had a remarkable connection, trusting each other implicitly, and they stood side by side as one of the young men amused them by recounting Meshach's transgressions. I noticed that Meshach was a short distance away, sitting on a log with his head cradled in his hands, muttering loudly and then gesticulating. A couple of men sat beside him, alternately laughing at him, restraining him and reasoning with him. Beside them, an audience had congregated. Dad and Henderson were grinning broadly, despite the situation, because the young man was acting out Meshach's actions with gusto: he staggered around, rolled his eyes, muttered and mumbled, wiped spit from his chin, pretended to push people and took a swipe at an imaginary object—all the time he was narrating. Then he pretended to smash our dairy, and Meshach's wife and son, and the smiles disappeared. By now I had crept to within a few meters of the action, hidden by a large aloe.

Just then, the police Land Rover arrived; it snarled and shuddered to a halt before three men got out. I recognized them as a recent appointment, James O'Connell, and the familiar regulars, Tendeka Khumalo and Gift Mpofu.

"Hello, Ian. Hi, Henderson." James shook their hands. "What's the palaver about?"

"Nothing too serious, Jim. Meshach over there has had too much Chibuku and is causing trouble. He has inflicted some minor damage to the dairy and needs to be locked away until he sobers up and is no longer a danger to anyone. More importantly, he has assaulted his wife and kid, but they are not badly hurt."

"Alcohol brings out the worst in some people," Jim noted.

"Unfortunately for him, this has cost him his job," Dad said. "I feel desperately sorry for his family, but he is no longer welcome here; the community wants him to leave."

Tendeka and Gift walked across to Meshach, each of them grasping an arm. He reacted violently, shoving Tendeka away and taking a wild swing at Gift, who simply stepped aside and grabbed the arm, twisting it into an arm lock.

Meshach was handcuffed and shoved into the back of the Land Rover, his drunken eyes seething with rage: perhaps he had consumed more than mere alcohol because his eyes were frosted and unfocused and his angry rantings were incoherent. As he was manhandled into the van, his despairing wife was standing and watching, her top lip swollen and bleeding, surrounded by the concerned community. Standing in front of her was her young son, Abednego. Her protective hands rested lightly on his shoulders, as though restraining him. I had only seen Abednego a few times and had never talked to him, partly because he was a few years older than I, and partly because he kept to himself. His body was taut with anger: his fists were clenched, white-knuckle tight, and his face was contorted with rage as a small rivulet of blood from a cut above his left eye dried and hardened on his cheek. What really disturbed me was the intensity of his hateful glare and the fact that it was not his own abusive father who he glared at with such moldering, consuming hatred: it was mine! I had a peculiar feeling that our lives would intersect in the future.

As Meshach traveled into obscurity, Dad, Henderson, and a few of the other men sat on the ground to chat, passing a gourd of Chibuku beer around. My attention was focused on Abednego, who was still glaring at Dad, his lips quivering and muttering dark words as his mother tried to shift him. I was transfixed by the tangible hatred. When I looked back at Dad, he seemed to be staring straight at me, faintly amused. Perhaps I was not as clandestine as I had thought. Dad looked away, smiling, and lit a cigarette, cupping the flame with his hand, before passing the packet to Henderson. In hindsight, I believe that Dad stayed with his people not to savor the beer and the pleasant company, but to allow me time to get home and pretend my innocence.

*****

It was while I was basking in the comforts of home, relishing a few lazy, languid days, that something happened which would change my life forever, although it took a few years to manifest. I was sitting one evening with Dad, having spent much of the day exploring the vast wilderness that is Kataza. Kataza is an enormous property and I was physically exhausted, yet I felt invigorated; my soul was replenished. We had been chatting relentlessly, discussing politics, life, love, women, books, and movies, and a comfortable silence settled upon us. I was looking around the living room when I noticed something that I had never seen before, perched inconspicuously on the mantelpiece above the fireplace. I stood up and walked up to it. It was a small falcon carved out of ivory. Yet the ivory was mustard yellow with age. This was obviously not a tourist's trinket.

"Where did you get this?" I asked Dad.

24

"Oh," he responded. "One of the young kids found that somewhere near the old walling, close to Three Fingers kopje, I suspect. A couple of them were exploring the area, and apparently, they stumbled upon that. They brought it to me, hoping for some cash and so I paid them for it. I think I may have been a little generous because the next day they brought me another statuette. If you look to the left, you will see a little crocodile."

Both the falcon and the crocodile were beautifully carved and both looked indelibly old, as though they had been weathered by time and nature.

"Would you like to take them back with you?" Dad inquired graciously.

I gave it some thought. "No thanks Dad," I responded. "Perhaps next time I'm up here." I think I was keeping the door of possibility open, desperately hoping that there would indeed be a next time. But I also knew that the chances were slim. Dad was living in a state of constant dread, knowing that Kataza had been targeted for redistribution. Some five years previously, it had been decided by the government that all white-owned farms were to be returned to their rightful owners: the people. Kataza was one of the few farms to have escaped this fate, but we both knew that it would happen sooner rather than later.

There was a typical pattern to this repossession. The farms were never turned over to the people who had lived on them and worked the land. In fact, I think Dad would have been quite happy for that to happen, as he had an excellent symbiotic relationship with his workers, a relationship based on mutual respect, and he sincerely wanted the best for them. Instead, busloads of 'war veterans' would be transported in and the farmer would be given a few short hours to gather his possessions and hastily leave. In many cases, these farmers had been brutalized and their innocent pets killed. These 'war veterans' were the subject of much dark humor: the vast majority of them were youngsters, in their teens or early twenties, and since our bush war had ended twenty-five years previously, hardly any of them had even been born when it had been happening, let alone old enough to contribute to the fighting. Nonetheless, armed with pangas and machetes, they were not to be trifled with.

I asked Dad which of the youngsters had found these beautiful statuettes, and he mentioned two names that I was not familiar with; Thabani and Senzo.

"Who are they?" I asked.

"Do you remember young Solomon?" Dad responded.

"Vaguely. It's been a long time since I last saw him."

"Well, he's grown up now. He got married about fifteen years ago, and Thabani and Senzo are his young boys; really good kids, but naughty as hell," Dad said with an affectionate chuckle. "They are constantly getting into trouble. There is not an ounce of malice in either of them, but they are typical boys; curious and mischievous. A little like you were," he said with affectionate nostalgia, allowing himself an inward smile.

I think I must have been a bit of a handful growing up, constantly exploring and pushing boundaries. Quite honestly, not much has changed since then. I always wanted to play out in the bush, or swim in the river, or climb the kopjes on the distant fringes of the farm. All of which were good healthy fun, if not for the fact that there was a war on, and my parents wanted to know exactly where I was and what I was doing at all times. The war itself, the Chimurenga, was always an abstraction for me—not quite real—despite the fact that we were technically in a red zone, a dangerous area riddled with enemy combatants. I was constantly coming home with scraped knees, covered in scratches and bruises: happy. I did not think it at all abnormal to carry a sub-machine gun around with me, although the absurdity of it now amuses and amazes me. That was simply the world that I grew up in, and I took it all for granted. Despite this, I never felt unsafe or threatened. Although I slept with an Uzi next to my bed, my bedroom door, which opened out onto the garden, remained ajar almost every night in summer. I was vulnerable and exposed, yet never felt that my safety was at risk. The arrogance of youth! I was far more afraid of snakes than I was of terrorists slithering into my room.

"I want to have a chat with these guys," I informed Dad. "Where will I find them?" I asked.

"Solomon has a house in the workers' village, painted yellow. Where his kids will be, I don't know, but you'll probably find Solomon in the maize fields. If not, he may be working in the dairy." Dad obviously didn't really know where Solomon would be, but he didn't want to admit it.

The next day, I traversed the track down to the workers' village, admiring as I went the lush maize fields, the beautiful, wild bush and the fat, contented cattle. The walk took me half an hour until finally, I reached the little village with its neat, but small, houses -- cottages really -- each surrounded by a little vegetable garden. Solomon's abode was not difficult to find, being conspicuously yellow, but it did take me considerable time to reach it. Every few steps seemed to be punctuated by conversation with the workers and their wives, all of whom I knew and many of whom had known me since I was just a little *umfaan*: a little boy. Their uninhibited joy to see me was humbling. It made me realize just how far I had strayed from the real world with its sincere people, to the false reality of the city and its artificial people, where everyone is your friend until you need them. Eventually, I found Thabani and Senzo helping their mother tend the vegetable garden.

"*Conjane*, Mama," I greeted the boys' mother, Miriam, with the traditional Matabele salutation. "How are you, good woman?"

"*Lungile, Conjane wena Mziki?*" she responded exuberantly with a broad smile, surprised to see me. "Fine, thanks. How are you?"

When I was a little boy I had been affectionately labeled 'Mziki' after the Reedbuck, a small antelope that makes a whistling sound. I have always loved music and used to whistle tunes wherever I went.

"Do you mind if I talk to your two boys?" I asked her.

"What have they done now?" she asked, cautious and fearful. "Have they been naughty again?" Her exasperation and limited patience were palpable. Already I liked these kids and I hadn't even met them yet.

"They've done nothing wrong. Don't worry. All I want to do is to meet them so that I can see how Solomon's sons have turned out and to ask them where they found two little carvings. I promise you that they are not in any trouble," I reassured her, amused and intrigued. I was looking forward to meeting these two young rascals.

Miriam called them over and hovered as I squatted on my haunches so that my eyes were level with theirs. They appeared shy and embarrassed, looking at one another for reassurance.

I looked up at Miriam. "You have two fine young boys," I complimented her. This seemed to delight her. She was obviously very proud of her children, mischievous as they might be. Turning to the two boys I looked them squarely in the eyes. "Do you remember that little carving of the *nYoni*: the bird?"

"*Yebo Baba*," they meekly responded simultaneously.

"Where did you find it?" I queried. Neither of them uttered a word, looking very sheepish. They obviously wanted to keep it a secret. Then it dawned on me that they did not want to confess the location in front of their mother. I asked Miriam if she minded whether I spoke to the boys alone. She retreated a little, cautiously, and I asked the boys again.

"Three Fingers," they responded in unison. It was now obvious why they had been reluctant to talk in front of their mother. Three Fingers kopje is so named because of three enormous boulders on the summit; it is one of those hills that is sacred to the Matabele. It was at the far extremity of the farm, a considerable distance away. There are some hills in the Matabele culture that are so sacred that they may not be pointed at, nor climbed, for fear of incurring the wrath of the ancestors. Three Fingers was one of those hills, and these young lads would be in deep trouble were their parents to know that they had been anywhere near it.

"Did you go to the top of Three Fingers?" I asked the question calmly and without any recrimination. I did not want the two boys to think that they were in any trouble—which they weren't.

"No *Baba*," Thabani—the taller and, I assumed, the older of the two—responded, taking the lead. I found his defiant tone funny and endearing. He showed spirit. Good for him!

"We were playing near the old wall," he admitted. I knew exactly what he was referring to. To the side of Three Fingers lies a section of ancient wall built entirely of stone blocks. It runs for approximately a hundred meters and stands a paltry half meter high. Strange as it may seem, this is not an unusual occurrence; the country is littered with thousands upon thousands of these ancient walls and Matabeleland is particularly rich with these antique dwellings. Not far from Kataza lie three magnificent ancient megalithic towns constructed entirely of rock: the Dananombe Ruins, the Naletale Ruins, and the Zinjanja Ruins, each of them spectacular in their own unique way.

These particular walls were unspectacular and of little apparent interest to an archeologist. They must once have been large though, as their base was about two meters wide and around the walls were the old rocks from which they were once built. It is as though they were deliberately destroyed; torn down by hand, so that no vestige of them remained.

"*Nyabonga*, Thabani." I thanked him, and, on impulse, I decided to give each of the lads five US dollars—a veritable fortune at the time. I said goodbye to Miriam and made my way back to the farmhouse, filled with conflicting thoughts. I wanted to go out to Three Fingers to investigate, simply to assuage my curiosity, but, on the other hand, I had only one night left of my holiday and I wanted to spend as much time as I possibly could with Dad. The solution was simple: I stayed at home with Dad.

That evening was one of the most pleasant and memorable that I have ever spent. I played with Merlin and Madam for a while until I was exhausted. Then Dad and I sat out on the veranda and enjoyed a sundowner, eating dried cabanossi and biltong, waiting for the sun to set.

*****

There are times when you will be in the bush and not see any game for weeks on end, but there are those special moments when nature rewards your patience and provides a rare and wonderful treat. This was one of those precious moments, as though Kataza herself was bidding me adieu. The garden was a flurry of colorful motion: the glossy teal of the cheeky starlings; the long brick-red tails of the paradise flycatchers fluttering gracefully and the shimmering green, purple and scarlet of the nervy hummingbirds, so fond of the honeysuckle. We heard the distant yelping of a solitary jackal and were blessed by the company of a tribe of cute little meerkats that waltzed across the lawn, constantly standing alertly to attention. Kataza presented a memorable spectacle that evening: a wonderful farewell performance, albeit a melancholic one. It was a particularly glorious sunset, fiery red, and as the curtain fell and night approached, a couple of shy, nocturnal bush babies—small, delicate lemur-like apes with large innocent eyes -- observed us cautiously from a tree. This lavish display was the perfect parting gift. I savored the moment.

I then set about the business of lighting a fire for the barbecue. We were having impala for dinner; one of our neighbors, the Mylne's, had culled an elderly buck earlier in the week. Dad and I both got a little merry and a little emotional as we talked of the past and we hoped for the future. Floating gently about us was the mellifluous voice of Dusty Springfield, one of Dad's favorite artists. We spoke about every issue under the sun, we ate a fine meal and we listened to music: for Dad Dusty Springfield, Dean Martin, and Shirley Bassey; for me, Bob Seger, the Eagles, Rod Stewart, Dire Straits, and JJ Cale. We stayed up well into the night, neither of us wanting this time together to end, avoiding tomorrow, but — tomorrow came.

I rose early in the morning to find Dad already awake and the percolated coffee steaming on the stove. We hardly said a word but "goodbye" as I got into the car with a heavy heart and started my long journey back to my ordinary existence in the city. The drive back to civilization seemed to endure far longer than the trip to Kataza had taken me.

*****

Some five months later I received a despairing phone call from Dad. The dreaded moment had finally arrived: he had been evicted from Kataza. He had been out in the fields with Henderson when they had been accosted by a group of 'war veterans', who told him that the farm was now their property and that he must pack his bags and leave. Dad always planned ahead; his bags were already packed, as they had been for a few months. He had long since said his goodbyes to Kataza and to his people, considering every day at Kataza to be a gift.

When I received his phone call, he was firmly ensconced in our small town house in Bulawayo. He had been allowed to leave peacefully and with some measure of dignity, but the injustice of it bit him to the bone. He feared for his people on the farm. What was to become of them? Where would they go? What did the future hold for them? Dad knew that he would be fine: he had a place to live and enough money to get by on but gone were his days of wide-open spaces: now he was limited and constrained. Yet he was alive and relatively healthy. Trust Dad to always look on the bright side of life and to be more concerned about others than himself.

CHAPTER 4
2005: KATAZA

"We're going to have a good crop this year." Dad was proud: Kataza was flourishing and life seemed perfect, for once. Running a farm is always a case of crisis management. Henderson nodded indulgently. The maize stalks towered over Dad and Henderson, patrolling Kataza while planning the weekly work.

"What will happen to the farm when you retire?" Henderson had never broached the topic before, but they were now two elderly friends concerned about their futures and Dad was becoming too old to manage on his own. After all, there was always the faint hope that the property would not be expropriated.

"I had always hoped that Bruce would inherit it, but that is unlikely to happen because the land issue is so contentious. I believe that Bruce wants to work the farm one day, but he loves academics and teaching. Thank goodness he has options!"

Henderson smiled patiently, waiting for an answer to his question. The truth was that Dad did not have an answer, because the question would be decided by politics.

A sound of chanting echoed behind them and Dad pivoted toward it too quickly. His foot caught on a clod of earth and he sprawled to the ground, his walking stick skidding into the maize field. Henderson picked him up, concern sketched on his face. At this age, a seemingly minor slip could have serious consequences.

"Are you all right?"

"Yes, thanks Henderson. Old age is not for the meek." Dad smiled weakly: he had just turned seventy-six yet felt sprightly and sharp-witted. The mind was willing, but the body was not. Just then Edward shot out from between a row of maize, breathing rapidly and sweating profusely.

"Boss ... Ian." He couldn't speak, panting for breath. "We must ... get back ... to the house ... quickly. We are being ... invaded by ... war veterans."

Henderson gripped Dad's arm and steered him gently toward the Land Rover moored at the edge of the field.

*****

31

A large bus had parked at the farm gate, the driver unwilling to risk Kataza's dirt road. About fifty young men disgorged from the belly of the iron beast and began dancing and chanting their way toward the homestead, leaving a plume of dust in their wake. A couple of intrepid enthusiasts had armed themselves with pangas, but the majority sported sticks—and brand new ZANU T-shirts, resplendent with the image of Robert Mugabe. Loyalty is bought cheaply when people are mired in poverty.

*****

By the time Dad reached the homestead a phalanx of war veterans was massed beside the gate, screaming slogans and threats at the empty house and at Madam and Merlin who were valiantly defending the property. A small sampling of curious workers was huddled on the periphery, anxious and afraid. They too were intimidated by the war veterans, whose anger seemed feigned, but whose propensity for violence was not; they appeared to relish an outlet for their pent up frustrations.

As the Land Rover growled up to the gate, the barrage began. Sticks lashed the chassis and a brick was hurled at the windscreen, narrowly missing Henderson. It landed on the back seat, leaving a gaping hole in the windshield and a spiderweb of smashed glass. Dad was both scared and angry. Hemmed in and surrounded by an unruly mob, he reversed the Land Rover, changed gears and began to rev the engine. Fearing that Dad was about to accelerate into the mob, Henderson placed a calming hand on his shoulder. His voice was tinged with sorrow:

"Calm down, Boss Ian. We knew that this day was coming and have prepared for it. One moment of anger could ruin the rest of your life. This will soon be over, and no harm will come to you or the dogs."

Before Dad could do anything rash a voice bellowed from the right: "Stop this. Give the old colonialist scum some room to move. Let him in!"

Parked beneath the shade of an old Olea tree rested a sleek black Mercedes-Benz with tinted windows and a portly figure, immaculately attired in a dove-grey suit, leaning casually against it, polishing his spectacles. He glanced contemptuously at Dad, and with a flick of his wrist, instructed him to drive forward. When the Land Rover was safe beside the homestead it was this man who opened the car door for Dad to get out.

"Mr. Savage: welcome to my humble abode. My name is Ngwenya and this property now belongs to my employer. I'm eager to inspect my new lodgings."

"Please don't hurt my workers or my dogs," Dad pleaded.

"I'm not a stupid man. I'm not going to do anything that will antagonize my future laborers—not unless I have to."

The rooms inside the homestead seemed cavernous, gutted of all but the most spartan furnishings. It was bleak and soulless.

"I see that you have been expecting me."

"You, or someone like you." Dad's voice dripped with insolent disdain. "You have thirty minutes to collect your belongings and leave."

Ignoring Dad, Ngwenya strutted proudly around the house, mentally refurnishing it, while Edward shut the dogs in the study, out of harm's way.

Accompanied by Henderson, Dad scavenged through the house, collecting those small items that were not already packed: the coffee percolator, some mugs, some clothes, the laundry, and toiletries. Everything else was already in suitcases, lying on the bedroom floor. Edward grabbed two of the suitcases just as Ngwenya sauntered into the bedroom.

"Leave those alone. You do not work for this white scum anymore. He will carry his own *impashla* to the car." Accepting the challenge, Dad stared at Ngwenya before he lifted the suitcases and marched to the Land Rover, careful not to betray any signs of effort. The suitcases were deposited at the back of the Land Rover, accompanied by wild ululations and threats from the crowd: "Go back to England, you colonialist scum."

The youthful veterans wanted action, and a slow chant began to gain volume: "*Jumbanja. jumbanja. jumbanja.*" Jumbanja: the Shona word for the farm invasions.

Dad turned to go back to the house.

"Mr. Savage—you have made a mistake. That vehicle is farm equipment and belongs to me. You can take your other vehicle." Ngwenya was enjoying himself, putting on a show for his flock. Dad tried manfully to rid his face of emotion as he deposited the suitcases in his old Datsun 120Y, Henderson watching helplessly from the veranda. Returning to the house, Dad said his farewells to Henderson.

"Goodbye Henderson, my friend. I'm grateful for all the years that we have known each other. It has been an adventure and a privilege working with you. Good luck and good fortune. Say goodbye to everyone for me and wish them luck. I think they may need it." Dad hugged Henderson, who said nothing—words were unnecessary. With Madam draped over Fasika's shoulder and Edward cradling Merlin, they walked solemnly to the car.

As Dad drove out of Kataza for the last time, the sound of jeers and jibes following him all the way to Bulawayo.

*****

Each December for the next five years I visited Dad in Bulawayo, relishing his company and admiring his knowledge and wisdom. Dad was a veritable fountain of information, full of pithy advice. He always seemed to be in good spirits, cracking jokes and making witty remarks, yet something precious had been lost. His cheerful bonhomie disguised the scars on his soul. Losing Kataza was the second great tragedy in Dad's life—the greatest tragedy had been losing that which he loved more than life itself: my mother!

My mom was another remarkable person. Like Dad, she was fiercely independent and highly intelligent, but, whereas Dad enjoyed the solitude and space of Kataza, my mother yearned for company and friends. My parents each perceived their marriage differently: Dad regarded it as contented companionship; Mom as emotional detachment. They had divorced while I was still at boarding school and, as hard as it hit me, it hit my dad far harder. I knew that it had taken courage for my mom to leave both Kataza and my dad, and to start a new life for herself teaching disadvantaged children. The divorce came close to destroying him. I watched this proud man pine for his lost love, overwhelmed at times with self-recrimination. Eventually, he had recovered, but he was changed. Gone was the extrovert, replaced by a calmer man, slow to judge and quick to praise; thoughtful with his advice; more eager to listen, less anxious to be heard; more considerate of others. I had always loved Dad, but I liked this new version of him more than the previous one. I became closer to him, to the point where he was not just my father but was also my friend and confidant.

This new tragedy changed Dad still farther. He became introverted and melancholic without sliding into depression. There was a resignation about him that disturbed me, as though he had simply accepted the injustice that life had thrown at him. He was imbued with a sense of fatalistic pathos; he could always console himself with the knowledge that he had once had a better life than most people, and that being able to live at Kataza for so many years had been a gift beyond price. Dad never grew bitter; he was too much of a man to allow himself to become a diminished individual. But a lot of the fight had been knocked out of him, replaced by a sense of resigned acceptance.

Added to this burden was his deteriorating health. Dad was a smoker, and emphysema was gripping his lungs and it was not letting go. Every breath became a struggle, and Dad became attached to the umbilical cord of an oxygen tank, yet he never complained, often joking about his disability. I felt guilty that I could not visit him as often as I would like, and each visit became an exercise in futile frustration and trauma. I hated the fact that I could do nothing to ease his suffering. Always, I remembered that last holiday at Kataza with its wide, open spaces, beautiful people, and my magical, last evening there. Now, each holiday with Dad was spent sitting in his cozy little living room, looking out at his enclosed little garden, while we chatted to fill the silence with small talk, or watched the small screen television. Life had become mundane and boring for him, altogether lacking in purpose: life for him was painful.

I suppose we grew closer still over those short, infrequent visits, never lost for issues to discuss and talk about; often our conversations would turn to the two small statuettes, and to speculation and wild imaginings about who might have carved them. I postulated that some Rozwi villager from the old Mwenemutapa kingdom was responsible, although I did not discount a later craftsperson. Dad was more prone to speculate suggesting Sabaean Arabs, Phoenicians, and even Indians. It became a harmless game between us, suggesting implausible and often ridiculous answers. I now know that he knew more than I.

CHAPTER 5
2011: RANDBURG

At 10 o'clock on the morning of August 18th, 2011, I was sitting at my desk in my home in Randburg, preparing notes for my history students, when I received a phone call. It was from Linda Robinson, a friend of Dad's. She was distraught, but still managed to tell me in a calm, compassionate voice, that she had arrived to visit Dad earlier that morning and she had let herself into the house when there was no response to her knocking on the door. She had found Dad sitting on a couch; the television was still on, but he was not watching; he was dead. The doctor diagnosed that it was a heart attack, induced by coughing. Feelings of shock, anguish, and disbelief flooded me as I struggled to compose myself. I abandoned what I was doing, phoned Mom, who now lives some twenty kilometers away from me, and the two of us flew back to Bulawayo to pay our last respects.

The funeral service was small, solemn, and intimate, most of Dad's friends having either died or emigrated. I delivered a eulogy that I hope Dad would have been proud of, were he there to hear it. Perhaps he was! Mom and I enjoyed time together, consoling one another, reminiscing and immersing ourselves in nostalgia.

Besides having to contend with our grief, there were practical issues to deal with: Dad's estate and the executors. We were informed that the estate would take considerable time to wrap up, something to do with a pension fund from Britain and that the town house would need to be sold. Also, Dad's finances would need to be consolidated. All in all, it would take at least a year. Thank goodness for Linda. She promised to look after Dad's meager possessions until the estate was wound up and they could be shipped to me in Randburg. I asked her to donate his clothes, linen, and kitchen utensils to charity, and to take for herself anything that she needed.

Linda offered to put Dad's furniture into storage. She went out of her way to help us: cooking meals and keeping us company. It was the little things, like buying us groceries, that we appreciated the most. Small kindnesses are often the most genuine. Mom and I were grateful to Linda for her invaluable help.

I got the feeling that she had loved Dad, but that it had not been fully reciprocated. Dad was a one-woman man, and he had never stopped loving my mother: she was irreplaceable. I think that a part of Dad always hoped for reconciliation, despite the fact that Mom had remarried, and had a fulfilled life with a good man. Ironically, Mom and Linda had liked each other from the first time they met and formed a bond of mutual understanding and empathy.

We returned to Randburg feeling emotionally drained and unfulfilled, as though a dark cloud was hanging over us. Every few days I would get a phone call from Linda informing me about the status of the estate, but it took an interminably long time to consolidate: it was only finalized in July 2013. Dad's will had been short and simple; he left everything to me, with the stipulation that any items that my mother wanted, and which were reasonable, should go to her. He trusted me to honor his wishes and I did.

In September 2013, a Stuttaford's van delivered Dad's material possessions to me. They comprised some furniture, photographs, and a few boxes of books and ornaments. I have never been motivated by materialism, considering the penchant for possessions to be a character flaw, but I was grateful for the photographs and books: they were the essence of Dad.

It took me the better part of a day to rearrange the furniture and to unpack the multitude of books. One of the first boxes that I unpacked contained all of Dad's old vinyl records and his antiquated portable record player, still in perfect working condition. I listened to his old records and Dusty Springfield as I placed all his treasured possessions in their new home, feeling melancholic. The last box that I unpacked held a gift-wrapped parcel and a Christmas card. The card read:

Dear Bruce

Wishing you a Merry Christmas and a Happy New Year!
I'm not sure that I will be around to give you this Christmas present in person, but I hope that it brings you pleasure and that in some small way it will continue to remind you of me. I'm proud of what you have accomplished in life and I love you dearly.

Your loving father

Ian

The card was dated July 2011. It had taken over two years for me to read it, but I was grateful and touched. Dad had obviously believed that his death was imminent and had taken the time to give me one last Christmas present. What a present it was! Inside the parcel were the two ivory statuettes that we had admired and discussed so often. But there was a third item, carefully wrapped in old newspaper, and to it was attached a note. I unraveled the shroud to find a beautifully carved, anatomically correct, circumcised bone phallus and a clay tablet about the size of a laptop screen covered in line after line of indistinct writing that had been pressed into the clay when it was still soft. I did not recognize the script, but it looked vaguely Arabic. I read the note:

Bruce, I'm not sure what to make of these two enclosed items. The one, I know, will provide some amusement value—a great many carved phalli have been found in the ruins so close to Kataza—but it is the tablet that is cause for some speculation. I have the feeling that it could spell trouble, if you pardon the pun. I have no idea what type of writing this is, but it is certainly writing of some sort. I have done some research on the internet and it looks as though it could be an old Arabic script, called Ge'ez. Apparently, it was used by both Sabaean Arabs and Phoenicians. I don't think it would be prudent to start suggesting that either of these two cultures had anything to do with the old walls on Kataza. That could cause unpleasant repercussions. Be careful.

Love, Dad

I had no idea what to do with the phallus. It is not the sort of ornament that I wanted to display on the wall unit in my living room! Accordingly, I wrapped it up, placed it in an old shoebox, and buried it at the back of my wardrobe, hoping that my cleaner would never find it. I decided to have the clay tablet mounted and framed, not knowing what else to do with it. So, it was proudly displayed on my living room wall, becoming yet another ornament: a topic for polite dinner conversation. That is, until Alison swept into my life.

CHAPTER 6

From the moment I cast eyes upon Alison, I was enchanted. She was exquisite. I met her at a dinner party hosted by mutual friends. When first I saw her, she was oblivious to me, engrossed in conversation with friends. She was laughing uninhibitedly, and her joy was infectious.

"Who is that?" I asked the host, Dylan. He smiled. "She's lovely, isn't she?"

I grinned awkwardly: "Stunning. Is she married?"

"No. She's a little suspicious of men, but whoever wins her trust will be a very lucky man. Come, Bruce, let me introduce you to her."

Nervous, I allowed myself to be steered toward my destiny, and we hovered in the background until there was a lull in the conversation.

"Alison, I'd like you to meet Bruce Savage."

"Hi Bruce," she said. Our eyes met, and there was an instant attraction which I like to believe we both felt. I felt electricity. She had bewitching topaz-blue eyes, honey-blonde hair, and a beautiful, seductive mouth. Her face was tanned and her body athletic. I don't know if it was recognition of a kindred spirit, or simply lust, but I could not break eye contact with her. The attraction was overwhelming.

I spent the rest of the evening talking with her, spellbound, making only perfunctory conversation with everyone else. I suppose I might have been a little rude, neglecting others, but I could not get enough of Alison. I found out that she had a doctorate in economics and lectured at the University of the Witwatersrand; her father was English and that her mother was Afrikaans. I learned that she loved to read, to garden and to hike. She was interested in politics, art, history, and astronomy.

Alison had been married once, but the union was loveless and childless (her ex-husband had had wandering eyes and wandering hands) they were no more than intimate strangers. She had been divorced for many years now. It was clear that we had a great deal in common and, when everyone else had departed, I asked her for her phone number. She smiled and gave it to me, saying expectantly: "I hope you will call me soon." She needn't have worried on that score.

I met her twice in the following week, taking her to my favorite restaurants. We never seemed to run out of conversation and neither of us was guarded or in any way inhibited. We each instinctively trusted the other, and I found her captivating and nourishing. Alison was everything that I admired in a woman: she was a symphony of harmonious and rare qualities. She was highly intelligent, competent, well-organized, and efficient. She was relaxed, confident, and independent. She was caring and compassionate. She did not need other people to validate her. She was neither vain nor ambitious. She loved knowledge and learning for its own sake. She was both creative and analytical. People's opinions mattered to her, but people's opinions about her did not. She preferred comfort to cosmetics, jeans to dresses. She was a homebody who loved to entertain, but preferred small groups of friends to large groups of friendly strangers. She hated bars. When she smiled, she lit up the room, and her laughter was joyful and contagious. She had a delicious sense of humor, with a whimsical sense of the absurd. She loved nature and despised any form of bigotry or malice. Every inch and every ounce of her was pure, unadulterated woman: Alison would never be pushed around by anyone. I found her beguiling, intoxicating, and invigorating. In short, I admired, respected, and loved her.

It was not long before I introduced Alison to my home and my dogs, Buddy and Jessie. They took to her instinctively, and this seemed to validate her even more. When Alison saw my house, she was smitten, captivated by the verdant plants and the privacy. I lived on a large plot in a thatched converted chapel with stained glass windows and surrounded by indigenous trees and plants. She found it hard to believe that I was so close to the city and yet so remote and removed. We listened to music and drank a few drinks together, enjoying each other's company and, for the first time since I had left Kataza, I felt as though I had a real family.

The next time that Alison visited was for dinner. I had prepared something simple yet tasty: chicken casserole and a potato bake. After the meal, we went inside and Alison seemed to notice every picture, book, and ornament in the living room. She was impressed by the paintings, admired my three Persian swords—wanting to know their history—and wanted to know which of my books were worth reading, but she was particularly taken with my ivory statuettes.

"Where did you get these?" she asked.

"They were found on our old farm, Kataza," I explained. "At the far extremity of the farm is a massive kopje, and adjacent to that kopje is a section of old walling. I don't know exactly where they were found, but it was somewhere close to that old wall."

"Interesting," she responded. "So, these are genuine archeological pieces, not something you bought in a shop?"

"They are," I said proudly.

"I wonder who could have made them. They look as though they are at least a hundred years old, judging from the weathering."

"There's something else I'd like to show you," I said. "Take a look at this and see what you make of it" I took her hand in mine for the first time, tingles running down my spine, and guided her to the framed clay tablet. I gripped it with both hands and gently laid it down on my coffee table.

"This was found in the same place, and I believe that there is some historical link between this and those two little carvings." My tone was speculative rather than authoritative. I did not want to feed her my own opinion but wanted to know her thoughts.

"I'm sure you're right. If they were found in the same vicinity, then there must be some causality." She wasn't so much responding to me as she was articulating an internal dialogue. She obviously found this intriguing. She looked me in the eye.

"Who do you think crafted them?"

We were both hunched over the clay tablet, our faces almost touching. Her proximity to me brought a flush to my face. I found her almost irresistible. Yet resist, I did. I returned her gaze.

"I'm not sure. The clay tablet puts a whole new complexion on the statuettes. I can only speculate, but I believe that they are a lot older than a hundred years." Alison and I were almost nose to nose, eye to eye. I felt myself being drawn toward her by her personal magnetism.

She smiled knowingly. "Where's that drink you were promising me?" she asked, diluting the tension. I poured us each a drink, Jack Daniels with ginger ale, and we passed the rest of the evening in banal but pleasant conversation. Mission accomplished: I knew that she would want to continue seeing me.

In time, Alison started to spend weekends with me. We would sit on my veranda and enjoy our sundowners and eat our meals and listen to music. Occasionally I would go over to her place, which was about ten kilometers from where I lived, but she felt more comfortable in my home than I did in hers. By her own admission, Alison was not too fond of her town house. It was small, and she was constantly surrounded by other people. She felt hemmed in and claustrophobic, but she lived there for the security. There were high walls, fences, burglar bars, and armed guards; but she felt that it was not so much a home as it was a base. Over time, Alison spent more and more of her time with me, and my house became a home for her. Finally, I had a relationship that mattered.

I remember one weekend with vivid clarity—it is strange how seemingly random and inconsequential events can have enormous repercussions. With hindsight, the dull and banal events of this weekend were to launch us on an adventure that we had not foreseen. To be accurate, it was not events so much as the conversations and the ideas that were planted and germinated over the course of a couple of days which set in motion a series of life-altering events. It all started on a Friday afternoon: I was sitting at my desk marking, and Alison was in the living room listening to me engaging with the student essays.

"I think the only time I ever hear you swear is when you are marking history essays," Alison laughed sympathetically. She walked through and sat on my knee, draping her arm on my shoulder; I grimaced in mock anger.

"I love these kids to bits, and some of these essays are brilliant, but if you read the last two, then you would fear for the future. Sometimes I despair for humanity when I mark this drivel."

"You should read some of the tripe that I have to mark," she comforted me.

"If I were one of your students I'm sure you would think that my work was tripe too," I joked.

"But I would still give you good marks," she reassured me and gave me a kiss. Alison wanted company and she suggested that I abandon my marking and join her on the veranda where we could listen to music and relax.

While we were sitting on the veranda enjoying beer shandies and snacking on dried cabanossi, I confessed to Alison that I believed my little statuettes had been carved, not by Bantu, but by an earlier people. She was astounded.

"Such heresy!" she exclaimed with good humor. "You should be burned at the stake, you heathen!"

"I'm serious," I responded. "I just don't see how Horus and Sobek could have been created by a culture that did not deify animals." I had given the statuettes names now, based on their Egyptian mythological equivalents. Mentally, I had already given them a different lineage and heritage.

Alison was unconvinced. She adopted her didactic tone, as though she was lecturing one of her students, not one of her brightest students either. She tried to put it simply so that I could understand and digest the information.

"You know as well as I do that there is no way on Earth that any culture other than the Bantu could have carved the statues or built any of those ruins. It is simply not possible. You need to accept reality. They are lovely, beautiful carvings, but they are not the key to any great mystery. They are not going to change anyone's view of history. Just accept them for what they are. They are already extraordinary." She leaned over and ruffled my hair playfully. "I love you to bits you silly, stubborn man." She stood up. "Would you like another shandy?"

"I would love one," I responded, deliberately sullen. "Thanks."

When Alison returned she had our drinks and some more cabanossi. "Why don't we go down to the dam and immerse ourselves in nature for a while?" Alison suggested. I liked the idea, relishing the opportunity for a change of scenery. At the edge of my property there was a small, exquisite small dam, fringed with bushwillow trees, combretums, and surrounded by delicate wildflowers. Patches of waterlilies floated on the surface of the water and many were now in bloom. It was a beautiful, serene setting allowing us to be alone without distractions. We left Buddy and Jessie in the garden and walked the fifty meters down to the dam where we reclined on the lush buffalo grass which covered the dam wall. For a while, we talked about trivia, interspersed with comfortable silences until I resurrected our conversation about my statuettes. I suppose I was petulant, slightly annoyed at having been dismissed so easily, and so conclusively, earlier in the afternoon.

"Why are you so adamant that those two little statuettes are not archeologically significant?" I challenged Alison. She looked at me thoughtfully, realizing now that the issue was more important to me than she had given it credit. She answered patiently and considerately.

"Bruce, honey, I didn't realize how important the statues must be to you; I apologize if I upset you by dismissing them too easily." Her beautiful blue eyes were shining with sincerity and I felt guilty about having brought the issue up again. I gripped her hand, giving it a gentle squeeze, and smiled.

"Don't worry; we all make mistakes."

Alison extended her middle finger, smiling weakly. "I'll be the judge of that."

"Those little statues are rather like you, Alison: an intriguing mystery. I want to know more about them. I don't care where the knowledge leads me, but I am curious to know what their history is!"

"Well, they are obviously old. I know that they will have considerable historical value, but I would surmise that they are trade goods from an altogether different culture, possibly India or China, and that they simply reinforce the notion that the old Zimbabwe kingdom had extensive trade relationships with Asia and with the ancient kingdoms of Central West Africa. Yes, they are valuable and yes, I would love to know their story, but we never will, and we must be content with the mystery," she placated me. Then she smiled: "I think I prefer them to retain an aura of mystery; it adds to their appeal." In some ways, I wish that the mystery still remained!

We stayed at the dam for another half-hour and when I was truly relaxed, Alison informed me that she had invited two of our friends over for lunch the next day. She timed her announcement carefully, waiting for the most auspicious moment possible—when nothing could disturb my calm. Doug Williams was one of my oldest friends and I liked the man, but this would be a sad occasion. Doug and his wife Sarah had decided to uproot themselves and join their children in Australia, leaving behind all that they once held dear. They feared for the future and were gambling that Australia would provide them with greener pastures. This would be the last time that I would ever see Doug, and I felt the loss already. I detested Doug's wife Sarah. I liked to think of her as Doug's bitter half. Sarah was a vapid, pallid, and rather poisonous raven-haired woman, whose idea of good conversation was to slander her friends, family, and colleagues, and whose idea of wit was caustic sarcasm. She had once been a beauty, but constant anger had made her face tight, and ugly. Now her only redeeming qualities were her slender figure and her firm breasts, of which she was exceptionally proud! Doug was a great hairy bear of a man with broad shoulders and a beer belly.

When first I met him, Doug was a hale and hearty, larger-than-life character, who smiled easily and whose broad smile was a joy to behold. His immense physical strength belied his rather simplistic and childlike approach to life. He was ruled by emotion, and decades of exposure to the toxicity of Sarah had scarred him. He had become morose and cynical; his joyous smile, and his contagious good humor, now seldom seen.

Small choices have indelible consequences. I accepted Alison's revelation with as much good grace as I could muster. Still, it would be good to see Doug one last time.

CHAPTER 7

Alison cooked an early breakfast the next morning with a little unwanted help from me. Before I knew Alison I never used to eat breakfast, but she insisted. We started the day with hot coffee, scrambled eggs, and bacon, followed by a bowl of yogurt. At about 10 o'clock Doug and Sarah arrived, parking their car just outside the garden fence. Already I could hear that they were bickering, and I knew that departing for Australia was never going to solve their problems. Alison welcomed them with her usual calm good grace, ever the thoughtful hostess and, once we had dispensed with the necessary salutations, Doug and I extracted ourselves and went into the garden to light the barbecue, armed with our drinks and accompanied by two excited dogs.

Doug was profoundly serious and I could tell that he was weighed down by the irrepressible nastiness of Sarah. I don't think he even realized that he was depressed, it had become so ingrained; I was saddened by the fact that this likable man had been so eroded by life. I tried to lighten the mood as best I could, encouraging him to talk by asking as many pertinent questions as I could think of, but he always brought the conversation back to his personal tragedies. I needed to find some way to cheer him up and take his mind off his problems. Walking into the house to collect some slabs of meat, I discovered Alison and Sarah standing beside the clay tablet in animated conversation. Here was the opportunity I sought and, walking out to the veranda, I called to Doug:

"Hey Doug, there's something here that I'd like to show you. Come and have a look."

As it turned out, there were hidden depths to Doug of which I was previously unaware; he was a conspiracy theorist at heart, and surprisingly knowledgeable about ancient Sub-Saharan history. I had found a topic of conversation that would take Doug's mind away from quotidian problems, but in so doing, I had opened a can of worms! Doug was fascinated by the clay tablet and his reservoir of enthusiasm began to fill—and overflow.

"The script on this tablet is amazing," he enthused, "and it is very similar to other writings found locally. It is a pity that the script is so indistinct."

Gathering up the meat, everyone went out to the barbecue and began preparing lunch. Doug continued excitedly: "I know that conventional wisdom would have us believe that the old megalithic cities were built by the Bantu, but there is a slew of evidence that would suggest otherwise. I want you to imagine how large this ancient kingdom must have been. It was an area about the same size as Western Europe. It stretched west from the coast of Mozambique all the way to the Okavango Delta, and it stretched south from the Zambezi River to a few hundred kilometers south of the Limpopo River.

"Then I want you to imagine how many of these ancient cities there were: approximately twenty thousand of them, differing in scale and magnitude. The sheer plenitude of them suggests that they would accommodate a large population. That assumption is supported by the presence of vast irrigation terraces designed to facilitate water-intensive crops. The terraces in the eastern highlands of Zimbabwe cover over one hundred and twenty thousand square kilometers. The population they serviced must have been enormous."

I grinned discreetly, enjoying the spectacle of Doug coming back to life.

"But Doug, all the evidence suggests that the ruins were built by the Bantu. What makes you think otherwise?" Alison asked, tempting him to answer.

"I'm glad you asked," he responded gleefully, with a broad simian smile; he was starting to enjoy himself. "A great many things. Firstly, the Bantu did not farm water-intensive crops. They have always grown drought-resistant grains, such as sorghum and millet. I know that this is circumstantial, but the accumulation of circumstantial evidence is overwhelming.

"The second reason relates to dating and demographics. Only one organic item has ever been found in the actual construction of the Great Zimbabwe ruins, which means that there is only one artifact that can be carbon dated. That item is a length of tamboti timber which was used as a reinforcement beam and may well have been added after the original construction. The piece of timber was originally dated to 700 CE, long before the arrival of the Bantu. The Bantu simply were not present at that time for them to have been the architects of this large civilization"

Alison could not allow this to go unchallenged. "Please correct me if I am wrong," Alison interjected, "but hadn't the Bantu penetrated as far south as the Limpopo River before 1000 CE?"

As Alison asked the question, I glanced toward Sarah, who was sulking silently on the sideline. Sarah never could see the value in any conversation in which she was not the focal point. I felt sorry for her and tried to involve her.

"How are you doing Sarah?" I asked politely.

"I'm fine, thanks," she responded, dismissively. She glanced away, deliberately ignoring my efforts. Her choice. She was a woman who delighted in taking the 'special' out of special occasions and the 'joy' out of joyous moments! So, I left her to sit and pout. Doug railed on.

"Many estimates claim that the main advance of the Bantu migrations south from central Africa occurred about 1200 CE. The vanguard of the Bantu migration south may well have occurred before 1000 CE, but that would only have been a trickle of people. Certainly, there would not have been enough people to have sustained a large civilization. Remember, I've been quite cautious with my figures, but a former professor of archeology, in fact, the head of the Archeology Department at Wits University, Professor Mason, suggests that there are over one hundred thousand stone ruins, covering an area of well over five hundred thousand square kilometers. He also speculates that this civilization would have had a population well in excess of one million people. The Bantu simply weren't present in large enough numbers." Doug had the bit firmly between his teeth and was clearly happy to be valued. He looked smugly satisfied, like a cat with a feather in its whiskers.

I decided that I wanted to have my own say.

"These people were also very skilled miners," I interjected. "Even modern-day miners are impressed by the skill evident in many of the old mines, with fairly sophisticated ventilation and drainage techniques. They mined iron and gold in abundance. There are over eighty thousand ancient mines in this area, and the Bantu were not a people who placed much measure in gold. Knowledgeable estimates say that huge quantities of gold were extracted from the gold mines. Where is it? Only a few gold trinkets have been found at these sites. This was obviously a trading empire, and traders need to keep records of trade. You cannot simply trade and not keep track of the exchanges. Where are the records? No Bantu civilization had writing."

"You're very perceptive," Doug praised me.

"Not really. I'm simply stating common knowledge." Doug smiled. "You're a modest man."

"I hope that I'm humble, but I'm certainly not modest." I retaliated. Alison chortled, but Sarah looked confused:

"I don't get it," she complained. Patient as always, Alison explained. "Modest means not amounting to much."

Sarah started to say something, but a warning glare from Doug silenced her. She didn't need to speak; I knew the gist of what she wanted to say. Alison grinned at me, quietly applauding my restraint.

"By the way," I added, "the most famous gold artifact was found at Mapungubwe, just south of the Limpopo River is a figurine of a rhinoceros made of gold plate.; it is very beautiful, and it was skillfully made. But what is curious, is that it has only one horn. African rhinoceroses have two horns. It is only in India that the rhinoceros has one horn.

"Another thing that I find very curious is that this trading nation needed to transport goods over enormous distances, yet the Bantu did not have the wheel, nor carts. How were these goods transported? If they were carried by people, using baskets and pots, a huge population would have been needed simply to carry things."

Alison glanced at me scornfully; perhaps she thought that Doug and I were ganging up on her. Never one to shrink from combat, she went on the offensive. "All that the two of you have presented me with thus far has been pure, undiluted sewage," she said dismissively. "You have not presented a single solitary scrap of evidence that has any verifiable substance. Every quantifiable piece of evidence found thus far corroborates a Bantu origin for these ruins. Every artifact, every shard of pottery, every skeleton, every ancient hearth, and every preserved grain of food explicitly supports a Bantu genesis of this magnificent culture. I know that the two of you are arguing devil's advocate, but all you have to offer is empty conjecture!"

Sarah grinned. Determined not to be outdone, and thoroughly enjoying the opportunity to be heard and validated, Doug interceded. "Also, the architecture of all of these ruins requires some explaining. They are all built in the same manner, with the same decorations, and with similar floor plans as the ruins in Arabia and the Mediterranean. They are remarkably similar in design, building techniques, and decorative stone walling to the nuraghe of Sardinia. The Great Zimbabwe itself has a floor plan, and size, that is identical to the temple of Ma'rib in modern-day Yemen, where the Queen of Sheba is reputed to have come from. This is not a coincidence. Things like this simply do not happen in isolation. There are simply too many anomalies in the Bantu builder theory; there are too many inconsistencies for me to be convinced by the present narrative."

"This all sounds very romantic and exotic. It seems to me that you are suggesting a biblical link to the ruins. Are you suggesting that this is the mythical Ophir from where King Solomon got his gold?" Alison was a little incredulous and very skeptical.

"I'm not suggesting anything at all. All I want to do for now is to lay all the conjecture out on the table. Certainly, Southern Africa would tick all the boxes: Ophir was supposed to be a land of gold, jewels, peacocks, sandalwood, and apes; Southern Africa has vast stores of gold. When it comes to jewels, there are substantial diamond deposits in Southern Africa. Southern Africa is famous for its emeralds, rose quartz, amethyst, and tiger's eye. If we assume that peacock is a generic term for brightly colored birds, then Southern Africa certainly fits the

48

bill—pardon the pun. Sandalwood is a scented wood, and again, Southern Africa has many indigenous trees with scented wood, and of course, apes and monkeys are common throughout Southern Africa. Besides which, the ancient kingdom of Saba is known to have controlled much of Eastern Africa, and the word *Ophir* is the same as *Afer*, from which the word Africa is derived. The old kingdom of Saba was famous for its irrigation terraces, which are remarkably similar to those at Nyanga." Alison did not respond, but it was not because she was lost for words. I knew her well enough by now to know that she was consciously allowing Doug to have the final say, recognizing that he desperately needed his spirits buoyed. That is Alison: ever gracious, ever considerate, ever wise.

By this time our steaks were cooked, and we adjourned to the veranda. I was feeling rather ashamed of myself for having such latent hostility toward Sarah, and I hoped that she had not detected it. Knowing that my feelings were irrational and childish, and realizing that these feelings were caused by a desire to protect my friend Doug, I seated myself next to Sarah and made a conscious attempt to reconcile with her. I inquired about her job, her health, and her history; her responses were polite, but cursory. I joked with her, and she giggled, but always the emotional distance remained. At long last dessert was served. Tucking in heartily, I complimented Alison.

"This trifle is no small matter."

Alison smiled and gave me the thumbs up, but she alone caught the joke.

It was only when I asked Sarah about her imminent departure to Australia that her guard finally came down; her eyes welled up with moisture, unable to repress the emotion. She confessed that she was terribly worried about the future and was overwhelmed with fear, knowing that she would never return. For the first time since I had known her, I felt compassion for her. It appeared to me that her brittle exterior was a shield, defending her from attack. When people admit to their own vulnerabilities, they always become more human and more likable. Alison was strangely subdued, lost in thought, as our conversation meandered from topic to topic. It was early evening when Doug and Sarah finally left, each of them a slightly larger personality than when they had arrived. Bon voyage!

Alison and I washed the dishes, tidied the house and played with the dogs before flopping onto our settee, exhausted. As I hugged her close to me, she leaned in and wrapped her arms around my waist.

"I really enjoyed seeing Doug and Sarah," Alison said. "It was wonderful to see Doug getting enthusiastic about something positive."

"He's a very good man and has been a great friend to me," I responded. "I've never really taken to Sarah, but I think we finally connected this afternoon. At heart, for all her quills and barbs, she is really just a frightened little girl."

"I must say that I'm now more intrigued than ever by the history of your statues and their origin. You and Doug really got me thinking this afternoon," Alison confessed. "For the first time, I am beginning to think that it may not have been the Bantu who created the local ruins. My mind is now more open to suggestion. I still believe that it was the Bantu who built the megalithic cities, but I'm not as adamant as before. I want you to convince me I'm wrong!"

"I have every intention of convincing you. But not tonight. Why don't we sit on the veranda, enjoy a drink, watch the sun set, and listen to some music? I don't know about you, but I'm feeling rather drained and I simply want to sit and enjoy your company."

"I think that would be a lovely way to end the day," Alison concurred.

"By the way," I added hopefully, "you said that you were open to suggestions and I would like to suggest a truly … elegant way to spend the evening." Alison smiled knowingly.

CHAPTER 8
GONAREZHOU NATIONAL PARK:
SOUTHEAST ZIMBABWE

Skulking shadows in the afternoon light, the hunters stalked their prey. Flitting furtively from thorn bush to thorn bush, the five men crept with practiced precision, crouched low, careful to keep downwind of their unsuspecting targets. The fallen mopane leaves were crisp and dry; the slightest sound could betray them. Scurrying soundlessly through the dense grass as tall as them, they closed in for the kill. This bush was dangerous: not because of the animals it sheltered, but because it was so arid that one misplaced step could herald their presence. Approaching their prehistoric prize, they sneaked forward, apprehensive. Ahead of them were their intended victims, a mother rhino and her calf, grazing contentedly apart from the small herd. As its placid mother moved a few paces forward, the doting calf followed in the safety of her shadow: easy prey.

With grim determination, the lead hunter knelt when the complacent rhino shifted position, presenting him with a perfect side-on view. Resting his elbow on the raised knee, he steadied his rifle and took aim, focusing on the area slightly behind and below the shoulder muscles: the heart. With telescopic sights, it would be hard to miss the granite slab in front of him, but he was anxious for a clean, swift death; they needed to move speedily before the Rangers could react to their intrusion. When it came, the shot sounded like the crack of a whip, but its effect was fatal. A fine spray of blood erupted from the mother rhino's side. She staggered, and then her front legs collapsed beneath her so that she too was kneeling, as though in prayer. Then she rolled onto her side, spouting frothy blood from her nostrils. Her lungs were ruptured. Confused, the distraught calf nuzzled his fallen mother, seeking the protection that she could no longer. Confident now, the men approached the rhinos to complete their deadly duty, the bemused calf gazing at them expectantly. When they were almost within touching distance, one of the men opened fire and the little calf crumpled.

There was something incongruous about the motley group: they were all dressed in rags, their shirts were dirty, faded, and torn. Their trousers were tattered. They were wearing sandals cut from old car tires. Yet their equipment was new and expensive: high-velocity rifles, telescopic sights, radios, and chainsaws. They did not celebrate their good fortune prematurely, working silently and seriously. One of them started his chainsaw, effortlessly cutting both horns off the mother rhino. She was barely alive as he sliced the precious cargo from her, her beady onyx eyes dimming in death. Then he turned his attention to the lifeless body of the calf. At least their deaths would not be without purpose; somewhere in China flaccid men would become hard for a fleeting moment— maybe two. Damn them to hell.

Wielding the chainsaw with expert ease, large chunks of meat were cut from the flanks and legs of both warm carcasses; the meat from the youngster would be particularly tasty, and these desperate men sorely needed meat. Their impoverished families would be delighted, both with the food and the income—their employer would be happy with their harvest. The meat was flung unceremoniously into a large plastic dustbin bag, while the four horns were carefully wrapped in newspaper and placed tenderly into a canvas sack; the horns were their meal ticket. Turning their backs on the two dead rhinos, the hunters walked away without a backward glance, leaving devastation behind.

The five hunters followed the course of the parched Guluweni River upstream, heading back toward the park border. Another of their companions was waiting in a concealed utility vehicle beyond the boundary fence, ready for a long journey ahead. Gonarezhou is a vast wilderness, and the hunters never worried about being discovered because one of their contacts within the park had informed them by radio that the highly efficient Park Rangers were not in their vicinity. As they trudged north toward safety and transient wealth, they were presented with an unexpected gift: a magnificent bull elephant with enormous tusks presented himself for their financial benefit. As he browsed on the tasty leaves of a Combretum tree, the gentle giant was oblivious to their presence and his impending demise.

Almost two hours had passed since the slaughter of the rhino, and they had walked nearly ten kilometers, yet still, they were grateful that they were downwind of the old bull. Elephants have an acute sense of smell and he would have smelt the rhino blood and fled were they not. At least the smell was muffled by the plastic bag, and the horns were wrapped in newspaper. The hunters placed their precious cargo on the ground and huddled together behind a thorn bush, whispering and gesturing animatedly.

Crouching low, one of them circled behind the solitary tusker, while two others slunk in the opposite direction, creeping cautiously toward it. The two who remained next to the rhino horns started to crawl slowly toward the majestic giant. When they were near enough, one of them stretched out and braced himself on his elbows. Nesting the rifle to his shoulder, He steadied the weapon and took careful aim at the elephant's head. Very gently, he applied soft pressure to the trigger, exhaling completely as he did. When the shot rang out, it was lethally accurate: the old bull was dead before his body hit the ground. Startled birds took flight, and the bush fell silent, apart from the delighted yelps of the hunters who now converged on the unexpected kill. Using their machetes, the opportunistic killers hacked and hewed the stubborn tusks from the elephant's head and continued back toward the park boundary, grateful for the detour. Death was such rewarding business.

The dying day was bid farewell by a wan, listless orange sunset as the scruffy scavengers cleared the boundary fence and trekked toward their team leader waiting patiently in the utility vehicle. Now they were comparatively safe, beyond the jurisdiction of Park Rangers and under the protection of their powerful patrons. When they reached their vehicle, they started to celebrate.

As they smiled and laughed and cheered, and the warm Chibuku beer refreshed their gullets, the team leader radioed ahead to inform their protector that they were on their way. It was reassuring to know that they had official sanction and were guaranteed safe passage from that point onwards, impervious to police inspection and inoculated from prosecution. Corruption is good for some. Hardly troubling to conceal their trophies, throwing only old blankets on top of them, the five hunters sat in the back with their prizes, exposed to the elements, as their leader and driver started the engine and their long journey toward the town of Chiredzi.

Nearly two hours later, in the blackest of black nights, the vehicle slowed down to turn left and, as it did so, the headlights shone on a signpost: "Jabulani Farm 3 kms". *Jabulani*: joy in the Matabele language, which is precisely what the hunters now felt as they drew closer to their pay. It had been a long hard day, but at least it would be rewarding. When the vehicle finally slowed to a halt, they were confronted by an ordinary house and the enormous figure of a rotund gentleman wearing a dove-grey suit adorned with gold jewelry and wearing glasses: the boss.

He greeted them with effusive pleasure, slapping them on their backs and shaking their hands, congratulating them on their courage and efforts. as he did so, he handed each of them a sealed envelope with their money. The hunters took their cash meekly, looking timid, subservient and scared.

"*Nyabonga gakulu*, Mr. Ngwenya," said the driver, speaking on behalf of the grateful group.

"Thank you too," Mr. Ngwenya replied jovially, "you have made me a very happy man, and my superior will be grateful. What a wonderful day this is!"

The driver smiled cautiously, knowing that Mr. Ngwenya's benign demeanor belied a cold, calculating saurian brain. "Mr. Ngwenya, sir, we have some meat in the back of the car. Do you mind if we take that with us?"

"Not at all."

The hunters grabbed the black dustbin bag from the utility vehicle and carried it behind a nearby shed where an old Peugeot sedan was parked. Placing the meat in the boot, the six men squeezed themselves into the low-slung car and wound down the manual windows.

"*Shahla gahshsle, Baba,*" the driver called out as he started the reluctant engine.

"Travel safely and have a pleasant journey home. *Hamba gahshsle,*" Mr. Ngwenya said in friendly dismissal. Slowly and tiredly, the Peugeot strained away into the enveloping night.

As soon as the hunters were gone, four men emerged from the shadows, immaculately attired in police uniforms. Two of them carried the ivory tusks and horns away behind the house, where a police truck was parked and waiting, while the other two took the rifles, radios, machetes, and chainsaw into the shed, ready for the next hunt.

Once the trophies were removed from the utility vehicle, one of the policemen took a garden hose to it, washing and scrubbing all traces of blood away. The tusks and rhino horns were sprinkled with lime and disinfectant to prevent rotting and were then carefully wrapped in muslin cloth and placed in the back of the police truck. The four policemen accepted their envelopes from a smiling Mr. Ngwenya and started their long journey toward Bulawayo, safe in the knowledge that they were impervious to any repercussions.

At about 11 o'clock at night, they pulled into an isolated warehouse on the outskirts of Bulawayo where they were let in without question by the expectant night guard. They eased into the grounds and parked in front of the warehouse entrance. As they did so, the headlights illuminated a corroded sign leaning against the warehouse. The signage was badly weathered, the paint peeling, but the lettering was still clear: 'GUMEDE ENTERPRISES'.

CHAPTER 9
RANDBURG

"A great many of the architectural features also need explaining," I said with conviction. We had both woken late, and I had prepared breakfast in bed for Alison. We were now sitting in the garden beneath the shade of a large pompon tree, the pink blooms of which had just opened. Alison listened patiently, cupping her steaming coffee mug with both hands, while Buddy and Jessie lay beside us, each gnawing on a piece of dried rawhide. The songs of Van Morrison's *Wavelength* wafted softly across us.

"There is evidence that the doorways had hinges for doors, yet the Bantu never had hinges."

"Circumstantial," said Alison, smiling.

"Another thing I find intriguing is that some of these ancient ruins were carefully astronomically aligned. This suggests an advanced knowledge of astronomy, which is seldom achieved without a substantial mathematical background. The Bantu did not have mathematics.

"The ruins are obviously temples of some sort, and because of the precession of the equinoxes, and the wobble in the Earth's rotation, a fairly accurate estimate of date can be calculated; and the date that has been established for many of these ruins is remarkably similar is astonishing: 1100 BCE. If that date is even remotely accurate, then there is no way on Earth that the Bantu constructed these ruins."

"Circumstantial," said Alison, baiting me.

"This, of course, would fit in very snugly with the oral tradition of the Bantu themselves. They claim that they did not build these ruins and that they are so ancient that 'they were built when the rocks were soft.' Credo Mutwa, the famous *sangoma*, is quite explicit. Not only does he state that the Bantu absolutely did not build these ruins, he also identifies quite clearly the people who did: Phoenicians. He is insistent. He describes the builders as evil people who were eventually subsumed by the Bantu in their migrations south from central Africa. He claims to have physical evidence of this in the form of Phoenician artifacts."

"Hasn't Credo Mutwa fallen out of favor?" drawled Alison.

"I suppose he has," I answered, "but that doesn't mean that he is wrong. It doesn't mean that anyone else is wrong either, but what it does do is give an alternative opinion: it encourages debate and I think a lot

55

more debate is needed." Even though I was pleased that I was giving a convincing argument to the contrary, to some extent I was still arguing devil's advocate. My mind was certainly not made up.

"But wait—there's more," I playfully mimicked the well-known advert.

"Heaven help us. No more please." Alison teased me. She wanted to have a little fun at my expense, probably enjoying the fact that I was getting quite passionate about the subject.

"A wooden bowl, with the signs of the zodiac clearly carved into it, is amongst the artifacts found. Certainly, the Bantu are not associated with astrology. Then there is the fact that many of the molds used to pour the molten copper, gold, or iron into are of a very peculiar shape, exactly the same shape as that used by the Phoenicians. Nowadays we use a mold that is rectangular, which would seem to be the obvious choice. They used a mold shaped like an X. To have two cultures so far apart from one another having so many similarities, some of them quite strange, must suggest that there was at least some cross-pollination of ideas."

"Hearsay and conjecture. I admire your enthusiasm and conviction," Alison taunted mischievously, "but you do realize that what you are presenting is a mixture of circumstance, coincidence, speculation, and wishful thinking. It is an aromatic brew, but it is pure liquid, completely lacking in solid substance."

"I know that," I retorted, undaunted, "but the cumulative circumstance and coincidence are still pretty convincing. I'm not so sure that I am thinking wishfully, though. I really don't care one way or the other who built the ruins."

"I'm sure you don't," Alison sympathized, "but what you are saying is asinine; it has the stench of racism."

"I know it does, but only because the issue itself is inextricably entwined with racist overtones of eugenics. I despise the colonial logic which maintains that these magnificent constructions could not have been built by the Bantu peoples simply because the Bantu people were incapable of creating a sophisticated civilization. It angers me. But I also despise the equally racist notion that simply because the colonial logic was saturated with bias, the culture must therefore have been Bantu in origin: that logic is flawed.

"These conclusions must be based purely on empirical evidence. I want to completely eliminate race from the issue, but to even suggest that Africans did not build these ruins immediately makes one the target of accusations of racism. Truth is truth! Emotion needs to be subtracted from the equation. The truth is obfuscated farther by the imprecise term, 'African'. Academic tomes refer to 'African progenitors', but who are these Africans? Are they the original Africans, the Khoisan, or are they Black Africans, the Bantu, who migrated here from Central Africa? A great many of the skeletons found at the archeological sites are of Khoisan people. I consider myself as African as anyone else and take great pride in African history and the achievements of African people, but that doesn't mean that I must blindly accept the old narrative. All I care about is the actual evidence. And I just don't think that the evidence is conclusive."

"But nothing you have said is very convincing either," Alison chided me. "The concrete evidence is all pointing in the same direction: away from you."

I think she was inviting and encouraging me to give her more evidence—to somehow convince her. She was looking for a reason to believe me, despite her better judgment.

"Remember that 'the absence of evidence is not evidence of absence.' The reason the Bantu builder theory is accepted so universally is simply that there is no evidence suggesting any other possibility. That is until recently. In the last few years, incredible evidence has, in fact, been unearthed, and from a very unlikely source." I was asking her for her tacit permission for me to continue.

"Go ahead," Alison said patiently.

"There is a Bantu tribe, the Lemba people, that claims that it was their ancestors who built Great Zimbabwe and all the other ruins. Not only do they say that their ancestors built these ruins, they also say that their ancestors were white—but only through the male line. They claim that their forefathers were Semitic and that they came from a foreign land across the sea. Their culture certainly confirms some Semitic links: they have a ceremony of the New Moon, similar to Jewish tradition; they only eat kosher food; and will not eat pork or fish without scales, as instructed in Leviticus. They believe that one day of the week is sacred, and their prayers include Semitic words. In fact, there are many Semitic words in their language. They are reluctant to marry outside of their tribe, and they are reputed to have introduced the practice of circumcision to southern Africa. All the stone phalli found in the ruins were circumcised. By the way—what is the plural of phallus? Is it phalluses or phalli?"

"I'm not sure," said Alison, "but either way it is spelled with a p for pleasure!" She grinned broadly. "Tell me more about these naughty, African Semites."

"When they bury their dead, the Star of David is placed on the tombstone. Furthermore, they bury their dead in an extended position, whereas most Bantu bury their dead in a curled position. All the skeletons found at all the ruins are buried in an extended position.

"Once again, all of this is circumstantial, but some twenty years ago their claims were put to the test, and their DNA was examined. It was found that more than half of the Lemba Y chromosomes were of Semitic origin. This itself is extraordinary, but it did not end there. Many of the men carried a certain haplotype, the Cohen Modal Haplotype, which is particularly prevalent in rabbis. While this is obviously not conclusive, it is very convincing. The Lemba are of Semitic blood.

"It would seem there is some considerable substance to the claims of the Lemba people. they claim that their pale forefathers came from overseas and took local wives. They also claim that their forefathers were here with the specific intent to mine gold."

Alison appeared to be impressed, but unconvinced. "The fact remains that all your incredible theories lack any foundation, and when I say incredible, I mean 'not credible'!" Alison admonished me patiently.

"I know. A year ago, I would have said the same thing. I would have ridiculed these ideas and had a good laugh. But a year ago I did not know what I do now. You should also know better because now we have the evidence that changes our perspectives. I would expect you to be more open-minded." I returned the rebuke.

Alison stood up abruptly, brushed the dried leaves off her rump, and went inside to the living room, leaving me to ponder whether or not I had upset her. I needn't have worried; she is too resilient to be upset by a trivial remark. She returned with Horus and Sobek and placed them gently on the grass beside me.

"So, you think that these two little guys are the key to a mystery? A mystery that didn't exist until you created it." Alison's atonal voice was completely serious.

"I honestly do," I replied. The events of the previous day still resonated with me: Doug and Sarah's tarnished marriage made my relationship with Alison seem more precious than ever. We elicited the best in each other. Having wrestled with my conscience, I made a spontaneous decision of trust.

"Come with me," I said, "there's something else I would like you to see." I stood up, whisked the leaves off my khaki shorts, and reached for Alison's hand. I led her into the house and through to our bedroom.

"If you're going to show me what I think you're going to show me, I'd rather have a drink first," Alison joked.

"Don't worry, you're not in any danger," I reassured her.

"Damn," she laughed, "I was rather hoping ..."

Alison sat on the bed while I opened the cupboard and knelt.

"I've heard of people coming out of the closet, but never going into it. I like the view," said Alison mischievously. I ignored her, secretly quite pleased, and scratched around the cupboard. I withdrew a cardboard box and handed it to her, unopened.

"Have a look inside," I said.

Alison opened the box and unwrapped its contents. I was watching her intently, waiting for her reaction. Her curious expression changed to one of incredulous astonishment, then to one of pure delight. She laughed with uninhibited mirth.

"You dirty devil. When I said you were going into the closet, I had no idea!" she could not complete the thought, because she was crying with laughter.

"Oh, if you only knew all my dark secrets," I teased. "You have no idea what I have been hiding from you!"

"I shudder to think," she laughed, gaining control of herself.

"With anticipation, I hope."

Temporarily gaining mastery of her emotions once more, Alison pondered the ancient dildo.

"I suppose this also came from Kataza?" Alison queried. She was brandishing it like a weapon; I winced in sympathy.

"It came from the same place as the other three. Up until now, there has been no evidence of the ruins being built by people other than the Bantu, but these change all of that. They were all found in one site, and that site is equidistant to the five major ancient cities around Bulawayo— in the center of them all. The phallus that you are holding so fondly appears to have been carved from animal horn."

"Horny devils," quipped Alison, her giggles resurfacing.

"They worshipped that," I laughed.

Alison examined the phallus intently. "I don't know why; these guys were obviously not very big people," she reverted to giggles again.

"I tell you what," Alison said, wiping her eyes, "I'm going to speak to a colleague of mine, and see if she can offer any insight. She works in the Archeology Department at Wits University."

CHAPTER 10

The next day, Alison returned home at about 5 o'clock, beaming triumphantly. I welcomed her home with a kiss and a hug and carried her briefcase inside for her. Once the dogs had calmed down and Alison was seated on the veranda with a Jack Daniels and ginger ale, her legs stretched out and resting on mine, she intoned in the most nonchalant voice she could muster: "I spoke to my friend Tabitha Govendar at Wits today, and she would love to see your phallus." She said it mischievously, her eyes twinkling with merriment.

"I would love to show it to her," I joked, "but unfortunately, I am a one-woman man."

"Which woman would that be?" Alison teased.

"Ah, that would be telling," I responded, "and a gentleman never tells!"

Alison leaned over and kissed my forehead: "But you are no gentleman."

Tabitha is very intrigued by your Kataza collection and thinks that it should be examined," Alison informed me, her tone more serious. "She is making no promises but wants to have a look at it. She seems to think that there may be some Indian influence because there was trade with both India and China, and these items are certainly not Chinese.

"Could you bear to be apart from your precious collection for a week or two?" Alison was obviously doing this to please me, and I felt a swell of gratitude course through me.

"Thank you." I gave Alison a warm hug.

"Good," she smiled. "Maybe we can get some answers, even if they are not the answers you are hoping for!"

We spent the evening watching television together, warm and content. I was amazed at how Alison had changed my life and how comfortable and secure I felt when she was around. I believed that she felt safe and protected with me around.

The next morning, I wrapped up my Kataza collection, placed all four pieces in a briefcase, and entrusted them to Alison. These were my most precious material possessions and I was relinquishing control, placing them in Alison's care.

When she returned from work that evening, Alison informed me that she had handed the collection over to Tabitha and that Tabitha had been surprised. She had not expected there to be much credibility to Alison's story, and as soon as she saw the tablet and the figurines she had recognized that this was a significant discovery.

"Tabitha was amazed by the figurines," gushed Alison, "but when she saw the clay tablet she was astounded. She could not believe it! She stood there transfixed as though she had seen a ghost." Alison was excited as she recalled the moment.

"Maybe you were right," exclaimed Alison. "Maybe this is something extraordinary." Impulsively, she hugged me tightly; so tightly she almost shook me.

"Tabitha wants to ask a favor of you. She wants to carbon date the figurines and your magnificent phallus." Again that naughty provocative smile from Alison: "Do you mind if she takes a very small scraping from each of them? Just a tiny sample will suffice. You will hardly notice the difference." Alison pleaded with me.

The moment that I had handed the briefcase to Alison, I had committed myself to this journey.

"Of course not," I assured her. "That's why we are doing this: to find the truth."

"I have another request," said Alison. "The clay tablet cannot be carbon dated because it is not organic, and Tabitha would like another professor to have a look at it: Professor Cameron. Apparently, he is an expert in ancient languages and may be able to identify the language. With a bit of luck, he may even be able to translate it. I've never met the man, but I'm sure it will be safe. Would you mind?"

"In for a penny, in for a pound," I responded without enthusiasm, allowing my precious collection to be even farther removed from me. If only I had known then, what I know now.

CHAPTER 11

The next ten days passed uneventfully. There was a new pattern to our lives. My holidays were over and I was spending my time marking essays and lamenting the education system while Alison was spending the weekdays at her town house and her weekends with me. I was continually trying to convince her to move in with me permanently, but she refused. I suppose she wanted to cling to her independence; her town house was far closer to her work than my place, and she wanted to avoid the heavy traffic.

On a Friday afternoon, Alison arrived home at about 4 o'clock. She parked her car in the garage, and I welcomed her with a kiss and a hug.

"How are you? It's good to see you." I was happy, now that she was here. She was in a jubilant mood.

"It's good to see you too," she said. "I've got some really good news for you."

"Great. What is it?" I asked.

"Let's go inside first," she said. "I've had a long day and I just want to relax with a cup of coffee for a minute or two first."

"You don't want something harder?" I speculated hopefully.

Alison grinned: "Maybe later." She hugged me. "In fact, most certainly later," she promised.

We went to sit on the veranda.

"The university has gone and made casts of all your ornaments," Alison told me triumphantly. "You're going to be a daddy," she smiled.

"That's fantastic," I responded. "When do you think I'll get my collection back?"

"Possibly in a day or two, maybe Tuesday or Wednesday next week," Alison guessed. "They poured molds of your collection, creating duplicates that look almost identical. They even used colored dye to make them look authentic. They did the same for the clay tablet, and I swear if you look at them, you cannot tell them apart. It's only when you hold them that you notice the difference. The plastic models weigh a little less, but most people wouldn't be able to tell. How nice is that?"

Alison was delighted that the university felt these objects were significant enough to make copies of. It seemed to validate them, and hence the two of us. We had a wonderful weekend together, spending the Saturday afternoon at one of our favorite local haunts, a rustic outdoor garden bistro, and the Sunday with friends for a barbecue. It was all very domestic and very pleasant.

On the Wednesday evening, I made my nightly call to Alison, and she informed me that the university did not need my collection anymore and had given it back to her. She would bring it over on Friday afternoon. I felt relieved, knowing that I would soon be reunited with my treasures which reminded me so much of Dad.

True to her word, Alison brought the Kataza collection back home and, once again, my narrow world seemed complete. We spent another unremarkable but comfortable weekend together, and Alison dutifully went back to work on the Monday morning.

That Thursday evening, I was about to eat dinner and had just put away another batch of unexciting marking, when I received a frantic telephone call from Alison.

"What's wrong?" I asked nervously. Her voice had a hint of panic to it.

"I arrived home this evening," she said, "and I found that my home had been broken into. What really troubles me is that it was hardly noticeable at first. My security gates were all locked, my windows were closed, and my doors were locked. Someone must have used the master key to get in. The only reason that I know that people were in here is because my ornaments are slightly out of place, my CDs are in a different order, and all my drawers have been searched through. I can see that my clothes are not neatly folded anymore. Nothing is broken and, as far as I can tell, nothing has been stolen. But someone has definitely been in here." I could detect anger in the timbre of her voice.

"Hang on; I'm coming over," I promised.

*****

I drove over to Alison's town house and let myself in. She was sitting on her couch, seething.

"I know it seems stupid," she explained, "but I feel violated. Someone has been in my personal space—uninvited. I feel angry and helpless and frustrated!"

"Don't worry," I reassured her. "Everything will be fine. I'm here now and no one is going to hurt you." I was not confident of my boast, but I wanted Alison to feel safe. "I think you should come back to my place; you'll be safe there."

"Thanks," she said gratefully. Then she looked me in the eye. "I'm so glad you're here. I know I can depend on you."

63

"Let's get some bags packed," I suggested. "I think we should take as much of your stuff to my place as we possibly can." Alison did not object and moved into my home on a permanent basis.

The next day Alison returned from work with more depressing news. "I was talking to Tabitha today. She said that some ominous looking people were in her department—some very serious men. They were not advertising the fact, but they all had guns underneath their jackets. They were there in an official capacity.

"Apparently, everyone in the Archeology Department was taken into a back room and interrogated. No one was hurt, but they were asking questions about your collection. They wanted to know who I was. They wanted to know where I had gotten the clay tablet from. They wanted to know where I live. I think they must have been the ones that broke into my house yesterday. They could easily have found out where I live from university employment records.

"They also quizzed Tabitha's professor friend, the linguist. Tabitha claims that he has managed to decipher the tablet. She does not know what is written on it, but I think that the clay tablet is at the center of all this."

I felt uneasy, and a little insecure. Making a spontaneous decision, I reached for my cellular phone. I had an old school friend whom I did not see often. His name was Johan Nel, and he had a small holding out near Hartebeesport Dam, about forty-five kilometers north of me. I phoned Johan and asked him if he could meet me the next day, Saturday. Then I went through to the living room and, once again, packed my collection into their briefcase.

I departed home at about 9 o'clock the next morning, leaving Alison with the dogs. I had a bad feeling that I would soon be having unwelcome visitors, but I was sure that these men did not yet know of my relationship with Alison. It was simply a matter of time before they did, though, and I wanted to take the necessary precautions. At 10 o'clock, I met Johan at Mango's, close to Pecanwood estate. They serve excellent steaks and hamburgers, with generous helpings.

When I arrived, Johan was already sitting out on the sundeck. He had probably shaved that morning, but his tanned face already had what appeared to be two days of stubble on it. Typical of Johan, he was dressed in khaki shorts and hiking boots, but no socks. He was wearing a red, sun-faded T-shirt that must have been ten years old.

"Howzit?" he said. "Long time no see."

"Count your blessings," I responded.

Johan smiled: "What can I do you for?"

"I'll have a beer, thanks, Johan. I don't want to eat on an empty stomach. How are you?" Johan proceeded to tell me.

I do not think that I had seen him in the past two years, but Johan spoke as though it were only yesterday. Johan told me of the damn weather, the damn labor force, his damn children, the damn electricity supply, and the damn crop prices. When he had finally purged himself, I bought us both another beer.

"Enough of me, I'm boring myself. Tell me about you," Johan instructed in his brusque, forthright way.

"I think I'm in trouble Johan. I want to ask for your help if you don't mind."

"What sort of trouble? I know you, and I can't see you breaking the law—speeding perhaps."

"I inherited some ornaments from my dad. They are very old and may be quite valuable. I think that someone wants to get hold of them.

" I've got a lovely new girlfriend, whom I would love you to meet someday. She works at Wits and she took them to the university to have them tested. Since then, her house has been broken into, but nothing was stolen, and colleagues of hers have been questioned about those ornaments. All I'm asking is that you hold onto them for a while; take them home with you and keep them safe. No one knows that you and I are friends, and I doubt that anyone will ever come knocking on your door."

Johan digested this information for a moment or two. "Sure. Fine. I'll do it."

We went out to my car, and I handed Johan the briefcase. He didn't even want to look inside.

"Thanks, Johan," I said. "I owe you one."

"Sure," he conceded. "Next time you buy all the beers."

Thank goodness for my trusty intuition. When I arrived home nearly an hour later, I found a sleek black Mercedes-Benz with darkened windows parked outside my gate. As I got out of my car to unlock my gate, three large young men emerged from the car.

"Are you Bruce Savage?" the oldest of them asked. He was tall, tanned, and dressed in a black suit.

"Yes, I am," I answered. "How can I help you?"

"We need to have a short, informal chat you and I," the man insisted. I resented his abrasive manner. Normally I would invite someone to chat in the comfort of my living room, but these men made me nervous and I knew that Alison was waiting for me inside. I did not want to bring these men into her company.

"You need to listen very carefully," I was instructed. "Where is that block of stone that was at the university?"

"I don't know what you're talking about," I said with calculated insouciance.

Pain shot through my body and I was suddenly unable to breathe. The muscled monster to my left had punched me in the solar plexus with enormous power. I was doubled over, struggling to get air into my lungs. I looked up and he was standing there with his hands clasped in front of him as though nothing had happened, his face dispassionate and expressionless. He stood over me like a malevolent monolith. I was not a small man, and I was fit and strong, despite my years. In my youth, I was pretty wild, and I do not intimidate easily. But I had been an enthusiastic amateur; these were hardened professionals. I knew that any one of them could take me apart in a minute flat without breaking a sweat or feeling any remorse. I was not going to encourage them; I had grown wiser with age. I partially straightened up, leaning on my knees, sucking in air, and gasping for my dignity.

"Hitting me won't change the fact that I don't know where it is," I gasped. I knew that I had to lie. "I had them in a briefcase in the back seat of my car yesterday. I went shopping and I must have left the car unlocked. When I came back they were gone." I knew that they knew I was lying, but if I kept to my story there was nothing that they could do about it. Thank goodness that Johan had agreed to look after the collection. They were not going to find anything in my home, and if they could not find anything, then there would be no evidence; not that I had done anything wrong.

"Where did those little carvings come from?" the leader asked again.

"I inherited them from my Dad," I rasped, deliberately evasive. "Where he got them from I have no idea," I lied. At least I was starting to breathe normally. But I did not want to be hit again.

"If you do have them, and if you know what is good for you, then you'll go inside and you will give them to me." He spoke softly, but his voice was the more menacing for it. I have met some scary people in my life, and I could recognize that this man was particularly scary. I did not want to trifle with him. But then again, I was not going to be truthful with him either.

"I know you don't believe me, but I don't have them. I can promise you that you're not going to find them in my house. They are not there."

"If they were stolen, why have you not filed a report with the police?" the man asked me, gripping my bicep and helping me to stand upright.

I looked him squarely in the eyes. "It only happened yesterday, and I was thinking of doing it either later today or tomorrow. Besides, I know that the police will never get them back. It is a waste of time."

That much he believed. "Let me tell you what is going to happen now," he said. "Every move you make will be watched, and if we find out that you have been lying to us, then you're going to be in deep, deep trouble."

"At least I'll have additional security," I joked defiantly, but my heart was racing. He chuckled without amusement:

"Goodbye my friend," he said gently, his soft voice unnerving and menacing. "I'm sure we are going to run into one another again soon."

I did not relish the prospect, but I did not tell him that.

CHAPTER 12

Alison went to work again on Monday, and her day was uneventful but stressful. On Tuesday evening, Alison returned home looking serious and perturbed. When we were comfortably settled inside she told me about the day's events. Someone had broken into the Archeology Department and stolen all four plastic casts. Alison speculated that whoever had stolen them probably thought that they were the original artifacts simply because they looked identical to the originals. She told me that she had stopped in at her town house and that it had been burgled yet again, this time without finesse. Her drawers had been overturned and emptied of their contents; the couch had been tipped over so that it was resting on its back, and some of her ornaments and lamps had been broken.

She swore blind that a black Mercedes-Benz had tailed her home, and that it had parked outside her town house complex. She said that it was probably waiting outside my gate right then. I could hear the trepidation in her voice: she was frightened, and she was uncertain about what to do. She was looking to me for help, but I had absolutely no idea what to do. My own day had been dreadful. I had been followed to work, also by a black Mercedes-Benz, but the two occupants had taken no effort to avoid me.

They had followed my car, and every time I stopped at a traffic light, they had stopped uncomfortably close to me. Everywhere that I went I was followed. They waved at me. It was obviously an attempt to intimidate me: and it had worked. I did not want to tell Alison, she had enough on her plate. Adding to the paranoia wasn't going to help the situation. Not only did I fear for Alison, but I was also worried about the safety of my dogs. Quite honestly, I was beginning to fear for the safety of anyone who knew me. Anticipating more trouble, I decided to do something that I absolutely dreaded. I put the dogs into my car and delivered them to my mom for safekeeping. I know it sounds silly, but my dogs were like children to me, and I hated to be without them. Although I tried to reassure Alison, she was inconsolable.

For the next three weeks, wherever Alison or I went, we were tailed. As our watchers ran out of patience, they became more and more brazen in their actions. They sat at the back of the lecture theatre while

Alison taught, and they drank coffee in the cafeteria in plain sight of her. My experiences were similar: wherever I went, I was followed. At no stage did they try to make contact; they wanted to instill fear, and they succeeded!

In retrospect, I believe that our mutual ordeal brought Alison and me closer together: it served to cement our relationship, rather than to break it. Even though the house felt like a morgue at times, without the energy of the dogs or the company of friends, Alison and I were focused on each other and had no distractions. We each learned to trust the other more. Alison became my emotional anchor, and I hers. With Buddy and Jessie now gone, we only had each other to hold onto, and we held on tightly.

One evening Alison returned home, looking drained and fatigued. She had news:

"I think I know why we are in so much trouble," she informed me. "Apparently that silly old professor managed to translate the tablet. I'm not sure of the details, but from what Tabitha tells me, they are mundane records of trade which is quite exciting! It records transactions of the sale of gold, copper, ivory, and birds. The professor was so excited that he could not contain himself; he simply had to share with someone. Possibly he wanted to boast and to boost his image a little. So, the silly fool phoned a friend of his, a colleague at the University of Zimbabwe. It simply amazes me how stupid people can be—even intelligent people."

Alison mused, obviously tetchy: "This is where the story becomes more complicated. Apparently, this colleague in Harare is well-connected. He phoned a friend of his, a government minister. This government minister was outraged, claiming that your collection must be fake and fraudulent. He also claimed that you have no right to it: it is the property of the people of Zimbabwe, part of their heritage. So, he phoned a friend of his, his counterpart here, and now our government is involved. This daily harassment that you and I are experiencing is emanating from the highest levels of government, and the guys tailing us are probably state security. Don't you think it would be wise to simply hand over the collection to the authorities and to be done with it all?"

"Alison, honey, I know you want this to end, so do I, but those things are part of my own heritage. My dad gave them to me. It is not simply a matter of ownership; I can live without them. It is also a matter of truth, honor, if you will. These artifacts have a story to tell. If we simply hand them over now, I think the truth will remain buried; it is simply too unpalatable."

"But why are these things so important? I do not understand why there's so much trouble over these artifacts," Alison said, confused.

I pondered her question. "I've given that question a lot of thought over the last few weeks and it seems to me that the answer is twofold. Firstly, I think that there are a great many reputations at stake. I think that some very influential people could have their reputations tarnished, and I think that those people have friends in high places: friends of politics and power. I think that some of these people could be using their influence to protect themselves and that they are closing ranks. But I don't think that that is the most important reason.

"This is an issue of identity, of one's place in history. If these findings ever came to light, the old racist colonialists would be vindicated, and that is simply untenable. I think that this strikes to the core of Bantu identity. This is about an issue of self-worth, which resonates loudly in this country. Not only does this change orthodox history, but it also portrays the Bantu in a very different light.

"For the last three centuries, white colonists have taught that it was they who brought civilization to Africa and that the Bantu have no history of any worth. The old apartheid education system spent very little money on Bantu education, and the Bantu were simply prepared for a life of menial servitude. This had a deep and profound psychological impact: if you're told often enough that you are not worthy, then you will come to believe that. It is a self-fulfilling prophecy.

"When Rhodesia became Zimbabwe, new interpretations of history emerged with a flood of more scientifically minded, less racist, archeologists. Their findings were simply based on empirical evidence, not on self-serving racist theories. They were adamant that the Bantu built these ruins because that is where the evidence led.

"During the tumultuous years of apartheid, a new ideology evolved, influenced by the civil rights movement in America and by the Black Consciousness Movement. Steve Biko was a courageous young intellectual who managed to galvanize his people, and who was murdered for his beliefs. He became a martyr.

"He taught that the Bantu had a credible history and that they were in every way equal to whites, and I agree. He helped to create a proud and distinctly Bantu identity. I think that these artifacts could be perceived as a challenge to all that. The Bantu people point to these ruins with pride: as evidence of their past accomplishments, an edifice of their glorious history. These ruins prove that they have value, that they have an identity, and that they have a proud and glorious past.

"Now we come along with our little trinkets and threaten the foundation of Black identity. It strikes to the very soul of the Bantu people. I can understand that we are a threat, and I do not want to undermine Bantu identity in any way; but that does not mean that we shouldn't acknowledge the truth—whatever it may be. We cannot change history by ignoring it and pretending that it never happened."

"But that doesn't mean that we go on floundering in the past," said Alison. "We all live in the present, the here and now. I don't think that we should be mired in the mud of the past. We all need to look to the future."

"I agree. But the past impacts on the future and, in this instance, it gives Bantu people a sense of identity."

"The past informs the present, but the future should not be captive to it. I just don't understand how we can pose a threat to anyone."

"I don't think we pose a threat in the sense that we were going to topple the government, or even that careers will be ruined. I think our threat is a little more insidious than that. It strikes at the core of the Bantu persona. If this knowledge ever comes to light it will be an embarrassment, rather than a catastrophe. Careers will continue, with a shrug and a smile. The deeper threat is to pride and self-worth."

"I just don't think that the issue of ancient history should have much bearing on the present. After all, Bantu people have accomplished many other great things. They have so much to be proud of in any case. Why should this be so important?"

"Look, I'm only theorizing. This is all conjecture on my part. But I do believe that the issue of national identity and self-worth is a big part of our present situation, even if it is at a subliminal level."

"Well, whatever the reason," Alison insisted, "I've had enough of this. I honestly do not know how much more of this I can take. Our lives have been made a misery. We are constantly harassed and threatened. We do not really have much of a life anymore, and I don't feel safe. I hate living in fear."

"I do too," I sympathized, "but if we can just get through the next few days, I'm sure that this will all blow over."

How wrong I was.

*****

Alison returned to work the next morning, only to find a note in her staff pigeonhole that she was to report to her head of faculty. She had to run a small tutorial group, and after the tutorial was over Alison reported to Professor Endersby. The old gentleman was contrite and apologetic, but said that her performance had been under review by the university administration and that they were disappointed by her inability to publish sufficient articles. He mentioned that there was a possibility the terms of her tenure might be revised and that there had been reports that some of her comments were politically unacceptable; some of her tutorial students, including the students whom she had only just finished teaching, complained that she did not devote enough individual attention to them. Professor Endersby also intimated that the university was under pressure to promote more people of color to senior positions, hinting that Alison's job might be at risk. Alison was not inclined to shirk confrontation; she gave him a piece of her mind, using her most colorful language.

"The poor man looked so uncomfortable," she later explained. "He didn't know where to look. I don't think he knows what half of those words mean."

She laughed sourly. "I know that it was an impulsive mistake, but I couldn't contain myself."

Alison was devastated and communicated her fears to Tabitha, who commiserated with her but voiced the suspicion that there was a lot more to this than Alison's inability to perform. Alison herself believed that she had published more than the stipulated number of articles and knew that her students responded well to her: it simply did not make sense! Tabitha confessed to Alison that she herself had been interrogated and was warned not to associate with Alison. It appeared that Alison was to be shunned.

My experiences in the next week were similar. On Tuesday morning, I was summoned to the headmaster's office and the bad news was delivered to me: The Board of Governors was debating whether or not to continue offering history as a subject at the school. History, sadly enough I was told, is a subject in decline throughout the country, largely because ignorant parents simply do not realize the value that it offers to their children. The headmaster was pleasant and apologetic but informed me that I needed to start examining my options.

On Wednesday I was again summoned to the headmaster's office, this time to be issued an official written warning, a prelude to a disciplinary hearing. The school had a policy that every teacher needs to make their notes available to students electronically, and my notes were not on the server. I was devastated, knowing that I had in fact complied with this order. It seemed that they had been deliberately deleted.

On Friday afternoon, I was informed that many parents were complaining about me suggesting that I was making inappropriate racial comments, that I was too cavalier with my opinions, that essays took too long to be returned, and that I was not proactive enough in preventing cheating during tests. I knew these accusations were fallacious but could do nothing more than protest my innocence.

I started to receive anonymous hate mail in my staff pigeonhole; management expressed concern, yet nothing tangible was done to stop it. I began to fear going to work, feeling all the joyful anticipation that a sentient cow feels when entering the abattoir. I began to view my work environment with a new lens and greater clarity. These caustic experiences made me realize what a dreadful place this school was.

At this institution, learning was mired in the experience of antiquated practices, focused on marks for the sake of marks, treating curious young, minds as little robotic instruments whose purpose was to attain percentages for the school to use in their marketing. I began to feel as though I was collaborating in something evil. I needed to subtract myself from this toxic environment or lose my integrity.

Alison and I were both convinced that we had done nothing wrong in our professional capacities, but that this was an orchestrated campaign of psychological terror. We both dreaded going to work every day, fearing that we would be summoned to defend some imaginary offense. At least we had each other.

The final straw came the next Monday. I had finished teaching and decided to go home early. When I got to my car I found that one of my tires had been slashed and graffiti had been drawn on the rear window. A large circle, dissected by a dotted line, had been painted in red lipstick or crayon. it was near impossible to remove, simply smudging when I wiped it. I was furious, blaming a maladjusted student when I noticed a black Mercedes-Benz with tinted windows parked about thirty meters away, outside the campus gate.

Fishing inside my truck, I grabbed the wheel spanner and was about to confront my tormentors when the passenger door opened and an enormous beast emerged. This man was even larger than the brute who had punched me a few days earlier. I looked around to see if there was anybody capable of helping me because if I had to fight this monster, I would certainly need assistance. I was all alone; not even the security guard was present. He strolled toward me with catlike confidence until he stood beside me, a little too close for comfort.

I was an athletic, well-coordinated man, and at six-foot-two inches and two hundred and ten pounds of tight muscle, I was normally capable of defending myself, but I felt small beside this juggernaut: he was at least three inches taller than me, forty pounds heavier and twenty years younger. His dark glasses and black suit made him even more intimidating. Without saying a word, he reached into his suit pocket and pulled out a bottle of pills, which he shook vigorously. Now I understood; the graffiti was a crude drawing of a pill—a tablet! Placing a heavy paw on my shoulder, he smiled disarmingly.

"I would like to help you with the tire, but I don't want to get my suit soiled." I decided to risk a retort.

"You're a real brick." He looked at me uncertainly, not sure if he had heard me correctly. He smirked: "You need to go to a pharmacy and get those tablets, or you may need stronger medicine," he warned.

"Remember, prevention is better than the cure—much better." He chuckled, delighted by his own wit.

"Don't be patient," he added, "or you may become one."

"Thanks for the advice." I tried to ignore him and started changing my ruined tire, but my heart was pounding as I watched him amble back to his car, very pleased with himself. When I drove away some time later, I slowed down as I reached the Mercedes-Benz, tempted to show them the finger. As I drew level, the driver's window rolled down, revealing the familiar tanned face of my former interrogator. He waved slowly as I passed by. Drawing away from the Mercedes-Benz, I saw its lights flicker in my rearview mirror as it edged onto the road in leisurely pursuit.

When I arrived home, Alison was already there and she was beyond consoling: someone had slashed her tires too. It was apparent to me that our discomfort was simply being escalated in stages, and it would not be long before there was physical damage done to one or both of us.

I returned from work the next day to find the black Mercedes-Benz parked in my driveway. This time Alison was not at home and I invited the men into the house, reasoning that they were probably familiar with it anyway. I tried to be as casual and friendly as possible, but the tension was palpable. To their credit, the men, whom I assumed were with the State Security Agency, reciprocated. They were polite and even inquired about my health and my work. They eased my tension, but they never identified themselves. It did not take long for the older, tanned man to get to the point.

"Mr. Savage, you and I both know that your precious collection was not stolen. You and I both know that we will be seeing a lot more of each other until that collection of yours is found. I can promise you now, that this will never end. Don't think of yourself: think of your pretty little girlfriend. Does she really deserve to live like this? Make this easy, give us the collection and all of this will go away. You can get on with your life if those little ornaments miraculously reappear: we won't ask questions. I'm sure your girlfriend's health is important to you. I'm sure that you wouldn't want her to become more stressed. Think of her." His cryptic comments and veiled threats were not lost on me. I decided then and there on a course of action.

My decision was validated later that afternoon when Alison arrived home, teary-eyed and distraught. Wiping her tears away and gathering her dignity, Alison told me that she had had a similar conversation. Two individuals had confronted her and issued her with an ultimatum. Either the collection would reappear, or her boyfriend's health would deteriorate very rapidly. They were targeting our weak spot: each other.

74

I did not think that Alison could take much more of this, and quite frankly I knew that I couldn't either. I feared for Alison's safety and my own sanity. We sat on the comfortable couch in my living room and I hugged her long and hard. I think she believed that I was hugging her to console her but, truth be told, I probably needed to be hugged more than she did. There we were, two individuals literally entwined with one another, rocking gently in each other's cathartic embrace. This persecution simply had to end.

I sat Alison down on the veranda as the sun was setting and made a proposal to her. It was not marriage that I suggested.

"I think that you and I need a holiday," I said speculatively. "We have never been away together, and I think we need a break from all this unpleasantness. I think we need some relaxation time together. Besides which, I would also like to get some answers."

"I would like that," Alison responded, the relief almost tangible. "Where are you thinking of going? It would be wonderful to get away from all these prying eyes for a while. I think that every move we make is being watched."

"Actually, I want to go back to Kataza. I would love you to see the place where I grew up. I know that you will love it; it's absolutely beautiful—like you."

She tightened her grip on my hand. "Thank you."

"I don't want anyone else to know where we are going. I know that our emails and internet activity are being monitored, so what I suggest is that we make a booking for a camping site in Botswana. Whoever is watching us will be able to see that we are going away for an innocent holiday. Once we are in Botswana we can cross the border at the Plumtree border post, which is far more relaxed than Beitbridge, and we can stay at a hotel in Bulawayo for a week or two. I don't think anyone will be any the wiser."

"We may as well be hanged for a sheep as for a lamb," Alison reasoned.

"I'd rather be hung like a horse," I joked. Alison allowed herself a small smile.

"I'll let that one slide." she riposted. "Do you think that they will allow us to leave the country?"

"I don't see why not, particularly if they can see dates of entry and departure. If we only book for two weeks, it should reassure them that we intend to return."

"I'm not so sure that I want to," said Alison seriously.

"There's one small caveat," I apologized. "Would you mind if we invited Professor Cameron to join us?"

"The cunning linguist?" Alison japed with little humor. "Why do you want him with us?"

"When we get to Kataza I want to look around the old walls. If we are lucky enough to find anything else then I would like to have an expert on-site. I promise you that we will still have plenty of alone time. I just think that it would be invaluable to have someone with us who can give us advice and tell us what is worth keeping and what is not assuming, of course, that we find anything at all. I just want to be prepared for any eventuality."

Alison considered my proposal seriously, possibly a little disappointed. "Actually, I think it's a very good idea. But if we are going to ask the professor along there must be no possible connection between us and him. I will invite him, but I think it would be prudent for him to fly to Harare and then drive down to Bulawayo from there. If there is any connection between him and us, we won't be allowed to go. At least if he is going to Harare, there is a plausible reason: he could be going to see his colleague at the university."

"I agree. Maybe he could book his flight for a couple of days before we leave and his return flight for a couple of days after. Then the timing will seem a little less suspicious," I added.

Alison returned from work the next day and informed me that she had not spoken directly to Professor Cameron, but had used Tabitha as an intermediary. She still had not met the man. His name was Bryan and he was a relative youngster, only forty-five. Both Alison and I are in our fifties. Alison allowed herself a wry smile. Apparently, Bryan was as excited as a puppy with a bone: he thought it a huge adventure. We were a little more cautious.

I felt both relief and excitement. I was going to see Kataza again and Alison would be with me. My two great loves together. Accordingly, we started to make the necessary preparations. We bought camping gear, hiking gear, and bush clothes. Anyone observing us would have been convinced that we were going on a short camping trip. In fact, we were jumping out of the frying pan.

PART TWO

CHAPTER 13
SEPTEMBER 23, 2015, 9:20 AM:
BULAWAYO

To his few friends he was known simply as Gumede. To the assemblage of men seated before him, he was known by his *nom de guerre*: *umCwabu*, the chameleon. A special place is reserved for the chameleon in Bantu beliefs: it is believed to be the messenger of the ancestors and is much feared because of its ability to see in different directions at the same time and for its ability to change color. The chameleon is always a harbinger of bad luck and Gumede had chosen this name as a deliberate comment about the superstitions of his heritage. Even though these men all knew each other by reputation, this was the first time that they had assembled together in one room.

Sitting in a comfortable leather couch was *Inhlathu*, the python, whom everyone recognized as one of the top-ranking generals in the military and as one of the possible candidates to eventually succeed Mugabe as president of the country. In this setting, he did not look as omnipotent and imposing as he did on television. In fact, he looked rather pitiful; he obviously felt nervous, vulnerable and exposed, as did they all.

Beside him sat *Mpisi*, the hyena. *Mpisi* was instantly recognizable as a prominent professor of African history. There too was *Ilinqe*, the vulture, a prominent businessman and *Iganyana*, the wild dog, a prominent politician. *Ululwane*, the bat, was a judge in the Constitutional Court and was reputed to be a close friend and confidant of Mugabe; he was another whose name had been linked to higher honors.

Gumede surveyed his 'apparat' with unconcealed pride. It had taken him many years, and much patience, to accumulate incriminating evidence against each of these luminaries with which he could guarantee their subservience. He knew that none of them liked him—few people did—but he was certain of their resentful loyalty. Before him sat the unsmiling figures of *Iqaqa*, the polecat; *Ikhanka*, the jackal; and *Isikhova*, the owl. These were all-powerful and respected men and, when the time came, they would all endorse him as their leader and master giving him an unassailable control of the country. But they did not know that yet!

Gumede had started gathering damning evidence against his potential rivals when he had been promoted to chief of police in 1995. At the time, he was engaged in a lucrative enterprise selling ivory and rhinoceros horns to a large Asian syndicate. He became aware that a rival "businessman", whom he now referred to as *Ikhanka*, had stumbled onto the identity of his second-in-command, now deceased. *Ikhanka* was collaborating with an ambitious young judge and together they had hoped to eliminate Gumede's enterprise and establish a monopoly of the notorious trade in death. Using his position within the police, Gumede had instituted a covert investigation into both men.

As each believed themselves to be invincible, they had both become a little too casual and were easy pickings. The judge had been offering benevolent rulings for a price, and he became the first of Gumede's hostile acolytes, soon followed by *Ikhanka*, whose poaching activities and foreign accounts were diligently recorded and archived.

Gumede had spent many torturous hours deliberating and had eventually decided not to expose these individuals but to manipulate them through blackmail and fear. For their part, they were grateful that Gumede never demanded pecuniary reward from them; instead, he demanded their reluctant support, endorsement and the occasional favor. As each of them performed their favors for Gumede, further compromising themselves, his dossier on each of them grew and grew. So began Gumede's stellar ascent to power.

Gumede had summoned his cabal together with an express purpose in mind. He wanted each of them to know who else was beholden to him and to realize the truly terrifying extent of his 'circle of gratitude'. Now none of them would ever dare to challenge him, knowing the resources that he could mobilize against any opposition. It was a truly masterful maneuver. To maximize the impact, he had deliberately arrived late, wanting to demonstrate his command—his power—and to drive home the fact that he was completely in charge.

"Good afternoon gentlemen," barked Gumede as he stood in the doorway. "Don't get up," he instructed, emphasizing his authority. None of the group attempted to rise, although a couple of them managed feeble smiles; the others simply gazed dispassionately at him. *My subservient minions, how I despise each and every one of you*, Gumede thought to himself.

"Gentlemen, I have called you all together because we have urgent business to attend to."

"What could be so urgent that I have had to cancel important state business to be here?" asked the politician, resentfully. Summoning all his courage he spoke without considering the repercussions of his words; an act of pure bravado: "I am tired of being told what to do. How do I know that you are not simply bluffing? These 'dossiers' that you claim to have may not even exist at all," he smirked smugly, issuing a clear challenge to Gumede.

Gumede strode forward and stood above his challenger. "You know it because I have revealed information to you about your nefarious activities that you know to be true. What you are really questioning is not my knowledge of your larcenous doings, but whether or not I have been meticulous with my records and whether or not I have kept proof of the crimes that you know that you have committed.

"Many years ago, it dawned on me that simply storing knowledge and files on a computer would be very risky. All anyone would need to destroy evidence would be to destroy the computer. So, I have copied my files on to external hard drives and those external hard drives are hidden in places inaccessible to you. Should you want to test my resolve, I must warn you that every other man in this room would make it their priority to destroy you because if they didn't, I would make it my priority to destroy them. The information that I have about your illegal activities would be more than enough to earn you the death penalty. As for me, I have a great deal of money in a great many countries. All I need to do is choose a country to live in and then release information to the press. Now, do you want to continue this conversation or are you going to do as I instruct you to do?"

By this time, Gumede was leaning down toward his frightened adversary so that their faces were almost touching, and the obstinate lackey was staring into the obsidian black of his eyes.

"I am with you," the politician acquiesced meekly.

Gumede smiled. "Good. Now listen to what I have to say."

The other guests were suitably intimidated by this show of strength and leaned forward attentively to listen to Gumede's instructions.

"I am not a patient man, yet for many years I have bided my time and waited for the right opportunity to act. Slowly and carefully, I have accumulated information and, in so doing, I have gained an unwitting team. You, gentlemen, are that team. You will be committed to my cause because you have too much to lose should you not be. For my part, I will reward your loyalty, however reluctant, by making you all very wealthy, very respected, and very, very powerful." Gumede had their undivided attention.

"Gentlemen, the time to act is now. The old man Mugabe is running out of time; the economy has almost ceased to exist and the party is fracturing. We are constantly hearing succession talk, and as one person gains influence and appears to be the natural successor to Mugabe, so another denounces and replaces him. Mugabe has seen to it that anyone who becomes too popular with the people is quickly removed from office. Over the last few years, it has become increasingly apparent that his trophy wife (the young typist thirty years his junior) Grace is destined to become the next president. I simply cannot allow that to happen."

"How do you propose to prevent that?" inquired the judge, curious.

"Look around you," Gumede instructed him. "Sitting in this room is the next cabinet of the country. We have a Minister of Justice, a Minister of Internal Security, a Minister of Defense, a Minister of Education, a Minister of Economic Affairs, and a future Deputy President. We also have in our midst a future Supreme Court Justice. Gentlemen, what we are going to do is launch a coup d'état."

CHAPTER 14

Toward the end of September 2015, Alison and I drove to Bulawayo. We left Randburg just before 8 o'clock in the morning. It was a long drive, fraught with unwarranted tension. I think we were both nervous, anticipating problems: we had to go through four different customs checks, and we were worried about being apprehended. We needn't have worried: the customs officials at Mafikeng were efficient and courteous, both on the South African and Botswana sides of the border. We stopped at Gaborone and Francistown for refreshments and a bite to eat before reaching the border between Botswana and Zimbabwe. Unlike my experiences at Beitbridge, the border post between South Africa and Zimbabwe, this was a refreshing breeze. We were ushered through with broad smiles and encouraging words: "Enjoy your stay in our beautiful country." Alison and I were both relieved.

Bulawayo was much as I remembered: it still had the old Victorian charm. But there was an air of decay about it; it was run down, there were potholes in the roads, some of the old buildings needed a coat of paint, and the sidewalks were swarming with hawkers. The streets of Bulawayo are exceptionally wide; wide enough to turn a span of oxen. This meant that from the pavement on one side of the street to the pavement on the other side, you could fit in eight lanes of traffic! In the center of the street were the glorious flamboyant and jacaranda trees, adding streams of color and shade. We found our way to Gray's Inn and booked in under Alison's name—as Mr. and Mrs. Turner. We were both tired, but still did a little bit of window-shopping and sightseeing, simply to familiarize ourselves with our surroundings. Then we had a pleasant meal, watched some television, and went to bed.

Even though I was desperately anxious to see Kataza again, I wanted Alison to connect with my past and to be able to identify with it. So, we spent the next day exploring. We did some shopping and sightseeing in Bulawayo; we visited the Museum of Natural History, and we had lunch at Centenary Park and admired the large fountain. Lunch consisted of fresh doughy bread, grapes, cheese, and fruit juice. We ate it sitting on the lawn under the shade of the old cycads, enjoying the all-pervasive scent of the 'yesterday, today, and tomorrow' bushes. It felt good to be home.

Lying next to Alison, propped up on one elbow with grapes in my other hand, like a Roman patrician in his villa, I made a confession to Alison: "There's something that I have not mentioned before. There is an old friend of mine whom I would really like you to meet. In fact, he is a lot more than an old friend: I used to think of him as the brother that I never had. Would you mind very much if we drove out to Esigodini tomorrow, and I can introduce you to him?"

"Sure." Alison sounded enthusiastic. "I would love to meet your old friend. Tell me a little about him; why do you call him a brother?"

"You know that I am an only child," I explained. "Growing up at Kataza could have been very lonely, were it not for Mzali. Mzali is the son of my dad's old foreman. When I was just a little lad, it was Mzali who took me under his wing. He is about two years older than me, and it was he who taught me about life and the bush. We were inseparable. We used to play soccer with the other kids, on a field that was largely compacted dirt, clumps of grass, and paper thorns, and then we would go off together, sometimes just the two of us, and sometimes with a couple of other kids, and we would build little forts, practice our stick fighting, and explore the countryside. I was always welcome in his home, and he was always welcome in mine."

"I'm surprised," Alison reflected. "Didn't your parents object to you bringing a Black kid into your home?"

"Not at all; and his parents did not object to him bringing a white kid into their home. In fact, I can vividly recall Mzali's mother giving me a good solid smack on a couple of occasions. It did not matter to her whose son I was. If I was in her house, I had to behave according to her rules. I do not know if my parents ever knew, but if they did, they would probably have congratulated her. I was a naughty little kid," I remembered with a smile.

"Nowadays, that would be considered abuse," mused Alison.

"I know," I agreed. "I think we've become soft. I know that discipline can be misapplied, but I never felt abused. When my parents gave me the occasional hiding I always knew what it was for, and I always knew that I deserved it. I know that my parents took no joy in it, but they felt that it was appropriate and needed. Quite honestly, I feel the same way. A child needs clear boundaries. My parents certainly never dwelt on my misdemeanors. I remember crying for half an hour or so, regretting what I had done wrong, and then going through to the lounge. I remember my dad always used to say to me, 'Are you okay chap?' and he was genuinely concerned. Then I would apologize, and we would get on with our lives again. But I had learned my lesson. I would rather get a hiding, then the issue is dead and buried, than be locked in my room hour upon hour in disgrace, while I am continually told that I am a bad person and the issue lingers like a foul smell. Get it over and done with!"

"I agree." Alison was lost in thought, and I think she was recalling a few hidings of her own.

"I remember being caught drinking when I was at boarding school," I continued. "I got caned six of the best. My dad reprimanded me, but I think that secretly he was quite pleased. I think Dad always respected people with gumption; he wanted a son with spirit. Not that I was ever allowed to drink at home," I quipped.

"Well, he certainly got one," Alison praised. "So, you were drinking at school, yet you hardly ever touch alcohol now."

"Truthfully, I wasn't drinking the booze; I was selling it to the prefects."

"Ah! Bribery and corruption in the lowest places," Alison laughed. "You really were a delinquent."

"Actually, I saw a gap in the marketplace. I was just being entrepreneurial and enterprising," I corrected her, appealing to the economist in her. "I was simply showing initiative."

She snorted with mirth. "I hope you know that you are rambling. Get back to the point.

So Mzali's mother treated you in pretty much the same way that she treated her own son: love and discipline. How did your parents react to Mzali?"

"I think my parents realized that I needed companionship and that it was healthy for me to be able to play and relate to other kids. The only other kids for miles and miles were the workers' children. Mzali was always welcome in our house.

"There were times when we went through to my bedroom and listened to music, read comics, and talked about girls. Occasionally, Mzali would have lunch or dinner with us, and my parents treated him as they would have treated any other kid, white, black, brown, or puce! I know that they both liked Mzali, and part of that was because my dad depended on and trusted his father."

"But didn't he feel uncomfortable? Surely there was some social vertigo; a poor Black kid in a rich white kid's home and the white kid's father employing the Black kid's father?"

"I don't think so," I responded, not completely sure of my answer. "At least I hope not. My dad treated his workers well. He respected them, and they respected him. He paid them well, looked after them, and housed them. They would always come to him for advice, be it about finances, health, or matrimonial disputes. He was their chief, for want of a better word.

"I never heard my dad raise his voice to any of his workers. I can recall seeing Dad, sitting on an overturned bucket next to a fire with some of his workers, eating sadza with his fingers. He was never afraid to meet them on their own terms and he never believed that he was intrinsically better than any man. I think that they respected that.

"I believe that Mzali liked and respected my parents; he certainly never behaved as if he was uncomfortable. He was always very quick to voice an opinion and was not shy to play around in front of them, or to push me around, or to disagree with their opinions."

"If you were so close to Mzali, why is it that you are only now telling me about him?" Alison inquired.

"It is a sad story. My parents sent me away to an expensive boarding school, an oasis of culture in an intellectual desert, while Mzali went to the local secondary school to receive a cursory education. After I was about thirteen years old, I only ever saw Mzali during my school holidays."

"That must have hurt him," Alison empathized. "It must have driven home to him the fact that, despite your friendship, you were not equal; you were from different social backgrounds. It must have emphasized the inequalities and the injustices of the country. He would probably have felt it very deeply because he had been part of your world. I think it would also have made your parents seem patronizing and condescending, tolerating him in your home, acting as though he was an equal, yet in fact, you were miles apart socially. I think he would have thought that the social divide was caused by the accident of birth: race." It amazed me how perceptive and intuitive Alison was. She had hit the nail on the head.

"I think my parents felt a little guilty. But I was their son and got preferential treatment. They could certainly have afforded to pay for Mzali to be educated at an expensive boarding school, but that would have set a precedent; they would have been expected to enroll every child of every worker at an expensive boarding school; that they could not afford."

"But Mzali must have been devastated and disappointed," Alison stated.

"You're absolutely right," I agreed with her. "When I was about sixteen and Mzali had just finished secondary school, he simply disappeared. One day he was at Kataza and the next day he was gone. I think that there was a great deal of anger simmering inside him. He must have felt that the system was wrong and unjust: which it was. Anyway, we heard through the grapevine that Mzali had joined ZIPRA."

"Hang on, sweetie," Alison interjected. "You will need to give me some context."

"I'm sorry," I apologized, realizing that the history was unfamiliar to Alison. "Let me put it in perspective."

"Eloquent brevity," Alison instructed me with mock severity and a wry smile.

"I'll try," I promised. "In the 1960s, Western society was in transition and new ideas were percolating to the surface; ideas of racial and gender equality, and a more egalitarian society. Britain was divesting itself of its colonies, including what used to be Rhodesia and is now Zimbabwe. In Rhodesia these ideas, combined with aspirant nationalism, were gaining traction. In a sense, we were also a minuscule part of the Cold War being played out on the larger stage. Rhodesia was ruled by a white minority government and two major Black liberation movements emerged: ZANU, the Zimbabwe African National Union, led by Mugabe and representing the dominant Mashona tribe, and ZAPU, the Zimbabwe African People's Union, led by Joshua Nkomo, and representing the smaller warrior tribe, the Matabele. Later on, a third, but less significant, liberation movement was added to the conundrum, and that was the United African National Congress, the UANC, led by Bishop Abel Muzorewa, who was also of the Mashona tribe."

"You sound as if you are reciting a textbook," Alison interrupted, smiling sweetly. "I hope your lessons are a little livelier." She winked provocatively, having fun at my expense. I smiled weakly: "I'm sorry. I know it's a little dry, but I need to lay out the bare bones and facts in order to simplify understanding. By the way, I have wonderful memories of listening to the band of the Rhodesian African Rifles in this park. I particularly enjoyed their rendition of 'Sweet Banana', the regimental marching song." Alison smiled broadly and moved her right hand in a circular motion: "Hurry up and get to the point." I tried to obey.

"ZANU had a military wing called ZANLA, the Zimbabwe African National Liberation Army, and ZAPU had its own very efficient military wing known as ZIPRA, the Zimbabwe Independent People's Republican Army. ZAPU was almost entirely Matabele and they were damned good soldiers. They were trained in Russia and they really did know their business. The old Rhodesian Army regarded Mugabe's rival ZANLA forces with contempt and disdain: they were trained in China, and most of the training was political indoctrination. They were very brave with women and children, but they were not good soldiers.

"The Russians did not focus on political indoctrination. They focused on military matters and remember, the Matabele are a very proud warrior nation. They are of Zulu stock and actually defeated the Zulu in battle, led by Mzilikazi."

"So, you and Mzali were on opposite sides in the war," Alison observed astutely.

86

"I suppose we were, although I never saw any actual combat when I was in the military," I replied. "I have often wondered why it is that Kataza was only attacked once in the war. That was one time too many, I know, but we were in a hot zone and it could, and should, have been far more. I have a sneaking suspicion that Mzali may well have had something to do with that. I do not know, but I like to think that is the reason. I do know that he earned himself quite a reputation and was highly respected in the organization. Perhaps he tried to protect us. On the solitary occasion that we were attacked, it was by a notorious psychopath by the name of Gumede ..."

CHAPTER 15
CUTBACK:
JUNE, 1977: KATAZA

Sweat poured from my forehead and from my chest as I came to a halt, gulping for air, but feeling rather pleased with myself. I had just run eight kilometers through the bush in twenty-six minutes: a personal record. As I slowed to a walk, I felt for the padlock keys in the pocket of my running shorts and unlocked the new security gates that now encircled the homestead. Our two Rhodesian ridgeback dogs, Caesar and Cassia, were waiting at the gate for me, their tails wagging. The security fence was designed to offer some psychological protection from guerrillas and terrorists should we ever be attacked, but I resented it as it seemed to separate us from the farm and its people.

Walking into the garden with the two dogs beside me, I stumbled into another of Dad's recent—and annoying—innovations: sandbags! With the war escalating, Dad was determined to keep us safe and had taken precautions which both Mom and I felt were extreme and unnecessary, and which detracted from the beauty of the homestead. The old majestic house was now invisible to the naked eye as Dad had decided to surround it with a thick wall of sandbags, two bags wide, and stretching up to the gutters of the roof, the only part of the homestead that remained visible. A small alley, about three paces wide, separated the sandbags from the homestead, giving it the impression of a miniature castle. I thought it looked a little like how the walls at the far end of Kataza must once have been when they were still intact.

Another of Dad's annoying contrivances was the sandbags which now peppered our once rolling lawn. Dad thought it prudent to have rows of sandbags, three sandbags high and three sandbags wide, radiating out from the corners of the homestead and from the sides of the house. Each of the sandbag mounds was placed about ten paces in front of the previous one, and each was slightly to the right of the one behind it. This meant that each line curved to the right like the blade of a scimitar. They were a scar on the face of the garden, interrupting the sweeping flow of the sea of lawn. But they were necessary, and we had made the most of a bad situation by planting leafy bulbs around each ugly grey mound.

Dad had explained his reasoning thus: "If we are ever attacked, we cannot stay in the house, cooped up, crowded in, and easy targets. An attack is likely to be short, sharp, and intense. They will probably rain mortars upon us, and we do not want to be indoors when that happens. They are also likely to fire a rocket or two at us, which is why I have copied the farmers in Mashonaland and built a fortress of sandbags. Once again, we are better off if we are outdoors, but we cannot afford to be exposed when we are outside, and we need to be able to respond if they shoot at us. We can take cover behind these little sandbag mounds. If we are attacked at nighttime, our sight will be impaired, so we must return fire by aiming at any muzzle flash we see. As soon as we return fire, we will have exposed our position; we will need to roll to the right and leopard crawl to the next mound of sandbags. They will shoot at our muzzle flash, so we need to have moved away from that spot. As we fire and move, we will constantly be changing position and advancing toward them, possibly unnerving them. Any contact is unlikely to last longer than about five minutes, because the sound will carry, and the neighboring farmers will use the Agric-alert radio system to summon the District Commissioner and the police reservists. Reinforcements will be here within half an hour at the most, and our assailants will know this. They are not stupid people and they will have planned their attack to be quick and efficient. They will want at least a twenty-minute head start on our reinforcements, aware that they know the bush well, are excellent soldiers, and may well have tracker dogs. If we can resist for just five to ten minutes, we should survive." He was a wise man, my dad!

Coated in a film of sweat, which was rapidly caking, I went and sat at the plastic outdoor table that had been placed under one of the magnificent bushwillow trees. Mom appeared from a gap in the wall of sandbags with a beer mug full of freshly squeezed and sweetened orange juice, and sat down with me, the two dogs lying contentedly beside me.

"How was your run?" Mom asked as she took a sip from the beer mug.

"It was great, thanks Mom," I huffed, as a fresh wave of sweat started to flow and I felt the excited blood course through me. "I pushed myself hard today and I feel really alive."

"That's good," replied Mom as she patted Cassia, who responded with a mighty wag of her tail and an enormous burp. Just then, the Land Rover chugged into view leaving a cloud of dust behind it. June is the middle of the dry season, meaning that the lands were parched; the air was dry and the soil loose. Everything seemed to be coated with a layer of dust and I longed for the rainy season to wash away the dirt and bring new life to the plants. While I appreciated the bleak and austere beauty that winter brought, I far preferred the green of spring to the brown of autumn and the heat of summer to the frigidity of winter.

"Hi chap," Dad greeted me cheerfully, as he seated himself next to Mom, giving her a kiss on the forehead as he did so: "Hello Gorgeous."

Mom reached for his hand and gave it a small squeeze. It felt as though all was right with the world now that Mom and Dad were talking again. Mom stood up.

"I'm going to go and fetch you a beer," she said to Dad, giving him a pat on the shoulder. As Mom disappeared behind the sandbag wall and entered the homestead, Dad turned to me.

"I see that you have just got back from a run," Dad discerned. He looked at me analytically, as though sizing me up, "and I tell you what, that wiry frame of yours is starting to put on some fairly meaty muscle— you're starting to shoot upwards. I think you're going to be a fairly big and scary guy in a few years' time! It must be those loaves of bread and the three helpings of dinner that you eat every day," he said with a hoarse chuckle. "You're eating me out of house and home."

I was thinking of a witty retort when Mom reappeared with Dad's beer. He too was sweating, and there were rivulets of moisture cutting through the dust encrusting his berry-brown face. Dad drank half the beer in one mighty, thirsty gulp and wiped his mouth, just as the phone rang.

"I'll get it," he said, as he lit his cigarette and brushed his khaki shorts, causing little puffs of dust to appear. It was now about 5 o'clock and early evening, as I watched Dad march wearily toward the house, his cigarette glowing as he took yet another hit of nicotine. I followed Dad into the house, wanting to have a quick shower and to get changed into clean clothes. As I was pulling off my green running vest, I overheard Dad on the phone.

"Hello Lionel," said Dad. "How can I help you?" A brief silence ensued as Dad listened intently to Lionel Wilson, the local District Commissioner. "I see. Thanks a million, Lionel. Forewarned is forearmed. Keep well."

I pulled on a clean shirt, went through to the kitchen, and cut some dried cabanossi, which I then carried out to the garden table. We never sat on the veranda anymore as it was enclosed by sandbags, and I spent as much time in the garden as I possibly could because the house was always in Stygian semidarkness, requiring us to switch on the lights whenever we were inside. Frankly, the homestead was a depressing place. As I sat down with Mom and Dad, placing the bowl of cut cabanossi in the center of the table, Dad spoke: his voice was gentle, reassuring, and very concerned.

"Chap, that was Lionel Wilson on the phone. He says that a group of about seven terrorists has been spotted on the Robinson's farm and that they are heading in this direction. Lionel thinks that this may even be *umCwabu* and his men, in which case we must be properly prepared. They probably won't attack us, but we need to be particularly vigilant tonight and over the next few days. I am going to go down to the compound now and make some arrangements with the staff. I want you to stay here with your mother and keep her safe: always keep your rifle in hand, stay indoors for now and, if anything should happen, get the dogs into the bathroom where they will be safe and where they will not get in our way."

"How are we going to keep the people in the compound safe?" I asked Dad, worried.

"I'm going to make absolutely certain that every individual is inside the compound. Then we will make sure that every adult male does sentry duty in shifts throughout the night—and for the next few days if necessary. I have a few old claymore mines hidden away which we will place around the village, and I will show Henderson how to use them and how to disarm them. I will collect them in the morning and set them up again tomorrow evening. I know that we are not allowed to arm Black civilians, but I'm not prepared to leave my people unprotected. If all else fails, I will tell the community to flee into the bush and to make their way to the cattle dip as a rendezvous point. I will also tell Henderson to phone me if they are in trouble. I don't know if I can do any more than that."

I did not sleep well that evening: it was not because I was afraid, but because I was excited, almost wishing for something extraordinary to happen. Be careful what you wish for, you may just get it! It was nearly 2 o'clock in the morning and my eyelids were starting to droop as weariness caught up with me. I was jolted back to reality by a muffled sound: 'Thwap'. It sounded as though a bird, or a large bat, had flown into the sandbag wall. 'Thwap'; 'Thwap'. It was the sound of bullets thudding into the sandbags. Then I heard the crack of gunfire and the sound of something exploding behind the house. 'Whump'…; mortars! The explosion was quickly followed by three more. They overshot their mark. Suddenly the dogs exploded into the room bristling for a fight and barking furiously. As I lunged to my feet, grabbing my Uzi as I did so, Dad rushed through, hastily pulling on his khaki shorts.

"Get the dogs into the bathroom and put out an emergency call on the Agric-alert; then I want you to stay with your mother in the passage. Lie down flat on the floor and keep the door open; if anyone comes through the house I want you to shoot them. Aim for the largest target: the chest. If it is me returning, I will call out to you."

With that, Dad went back into the bedroom, picked up his trusty shotgun and filled a massive pouch with shotgun shells. I knew why Dad was selecting his shotgun in preference to a rifle. The 'shot', ball bearings, spreads out over a distance, improving the chances of hitting your target. Where precision shooting was not the priority, the shotgun was always his weapon of choice.

Dad sprinted toward the living room and disappeared into the darkness of the night. I quickly did as Dad asked, but Mom and I would not allow Dad to fight alone; we were all in this together. As I followed in Dad's footsteps, there was an almighty explosion as a rocket plowed through the far end of the sandbag wall, narrowly missing the homestead. Then we heard the 'kaboomph' of Dad's shotgun; he had fired both barrels at once, and I assumed he was aiming toward where the handheld rocket had been fired from.

Cautious and concerned, I crept into the alleyway between the sandbags and the homestead. I crouched in the massive hole made by the rocket and began crawling up the cavity of spilt sandbags, which provided excellent cover and allowed me to see into the garden. It was a dark night, and I could only dimly discern Dad's shape, lying motionless behind a mound, hidden by plants. Bullets were thudding into the sandbags and the ground around him. He was pinned down: trapped! All thoughts of personal safety vanished, and I sprinted to the nearest pile of sandbags, desperate to help Dad.

Like Dad, I had a keen eye and a steady hand; I was an excellent marksman: a sharpshooter. As a new wave of bullets splattered into the ground around Dad, I could see three or four muzzle flashes, which were all clustered close together. These terrorists were all together on the raised ground about one hundred meters from the homestead, allowing them to shoot down at us from above. I aimed my Uzi toward these muzzle flashes and went ballistic.

I suppose adrenalin got the better of me and I emptied an entire magazine in their direction. I don't know if it was my imagination, but I distinctly heard a bullet slapping into flesh. I discarded the empty magazine and rammed another clip into the Uzi. The hail of bullets ceased, and now Dad was annoyed!

He hurtled toward the next mound of sandbags and let rip, firing the two barrels of the shotgun in close succession. He kept going until he reached the end of the garden. As he reached the security fence, the halogen security lights went on. They were mounted on the corner posts of the fence and were designed to provide a screen of intense light that would illuminate the countryside beyond them while protecting anyone behind them from prying eyes. Looking back toward the house, I could vaguely discern that Mom had overcome her fear and was kneeling in the gap between the sandbag walls. She was grasping a pistol in two hands and firing toward our attackers. Good for her!

"Yvonne, get back in the house!" Dad yelled, an edge of panic in his voice.

"Bruce, I want you to stay where you are until we are sure that we are safe," Dad instructed me insistently. The clamor and chaos were gone, and now we lay in the garden and waited. An eerie silence enveloped us, and it was only when the sounds of the night returned that we started to relax a little. The insects, the birds, and the frogs began to recover their voices and we, our composure. Still we waited! It was only when the vehicles of the police reservists screamed up to the security fence that we unraveled ourselves and went inside with one of the reinforcements, presumably the man in charge.

Inside the house, Dad and I found Mom sitting on a settee in the lounge, pale and trembling, while two excited dogs charged around the living room, jumping onto chairs, and venting their pent-up energy. Dad sat next to Mom and put his arms protectively around her.

"Are you all right, Yvonne?"

Mom said nothing; she was traumatized and in shock.

"Would you like me to stay with you?" one of the police reservists asked, concerned.

"No thanks, Jim. I think we are safe now and that we need some time to be alone," Dad answered, knowing that Mom needed company and reassurance.

"Okay then," Jim grunted, reluctant to leave. "We are going to conduct a sweep of the area and will return here when we are satisfied that you are safe. We will be back soon."

"Please, will you go down to the compound and check on the workers? Make sure that they are safe," requested Dad.

"Sure thing," Jim gave Mom a concerned look but said nothing as he turned and departed the homestead. Dad gave Mom a squeeze.

"I'll be back," he insisted and walked through to his study. Mom stood up and gave me an almighty hug, squeezing so tightly that I could hardly breathe.

"I am so cross with you," she scolded, "and I am so relieved that you are all right." And as she spoke the words, the tears flooded out of her. "You bloody idiot. You could have been killed!"

"I'm sorry Mom," I responded contritely. Trying to deflect attention away from my indiscretions, I praised her bravery. "You were magnificent Mom, and if you had not switched on the security lights, things might have turned out differently. You saved the day!" As I spoke the words, Dad returned from his study with three generous measures of brandy. Immediately recognizing my ploy, he collaborated with me, trying to add a little levity while also praising Mom.

"For the female of the species is more savage than the male," he joked. It seemed to work, and Mom responded by raising her middle finger. We all smiled. Dad placed the drinks on a coffee table, walked up to me, and gave me a firm hug before shaking my hand.

"Thanks, Bruce; you saved my life." Dad's eyes were brimming with tears. "We should all be dead now; their plan should have worked. What they did not include in their calculations was that a fifteen-year-old boy would be home during the school holidays."

Dad looked me squarely in the eyes: "No. Not a fifteen-year-old boy—a fifteen-year-old *man*." Without saying another word Dad reached for the glasses and handed Mom and me a brandy. Dad was finally giving me a drink! He smiled at me.

"Savor it and drink it slowly, because we are not going to make a habit of this."

About an hour later, the police reservists returned, just as the first pale-lilac-blush of morning light was washing away the night. Dad and I walked out to the police vehicles, Mazda utility vehicles with Browning machine guns mounted at the back, as the reservists milled around the garden, patting the dogs, and enjoying the scenery and cigarettes. I walked up to the police vehicles to admire the machine guns, only to notice that one of our assailants was lying on the ground, chained to the chassis. He was dying. Dad looked down at the luckless man before him, overcome with remorse. This remarkable man, who refused to kill any animal, had been put in the invidious position of having to take the life of another human being. I heard Dad mutter the immortal words of the Hindu deity Vishnu: "Now I am become death." He turned and walked away, focused on the ground in front of his feet.

The doomed man gazed up at me dispassionately, his face contorted with pain, and his breathing labored; the stench of death wafted over me. The metallic smell of blood and the fecal smell of a punctured colon prevented him from dying with dignity. His emotionless stare made me realize that we were not enemies to him, merely obstacles. I felt compassion and pity for him, even though he had tried his damnedest to kill me and my family. Now he was dying, and there were no great causes left for him to fight for or to die for. He was perforated with shotgun pellets, and I watched helplessly as his life leaked out in a crimson pool and his eyes lost their glossy sheen and turned to marble. I knelt beside the man and held his hand in mine as his spirit slipped away into oblivion. Death is dirty, grimy and, infinitely sad; death lasts a very long time. The memory of that dying man still haunts my dreams and my nightmares.

*****

A couple of days after the attack, as my school holidays were drawing to a close and I was due to return to boarding school, Dad invited Mom and me to join him on a walk to the dairy. I suppose we all needed companionship as we dealt with the deep issues of life and death. I think that Dad needed to talk and that he wanted to advise me, give me direction in life, and make sure that I was not mentally scarred. As we walked along the dirt road toward the dairy, he placed a comforting arm on my shoulder and Mom held my hand. I think that they both were worried about me; after all, I had experienced that which no youth should ever experience.

"I hope the experiences of the last few days will not distract you from your examinations. Your whole life is ahead of you, and the direction that your life takes will depend, in part, on your grades. Your Mom and I want the best for you. You need to think long and hard about the future and how you want to spend the rest of your life. You're a gentle soul at heart, but you have nerves of steel and you are very stubborn. You're a man of integrity, but you do not like to bend or compromise, and this could work against you. You need to choose a profession where these qualities are valued. Never lose sight of what is important in life and choose a career that will provide you with joy and satisfaction. Your career should stimulate you, enliven you, and nourish your soul. Otherwise, it is just a job and you are simply working for the salary."

"Find a good woman and make sure that your life is filled with love, companionship, and a touch of passion, Mom added wisely. "Family is more important than friends."

"Ah chap, I hope that life is kind to you," Dad said sincerely. "Remember that what matters most in life is character. Qualities of integrity, loyalty, kindness, and compassion are the qualities that truly make a man. Violence, anger, and confrontation are always the resort of lesser people."

Mom started to wax philosophical, assaulting me with sage advice. "Always seek contentment over fun, laughter over tears, wisdom over knowledge, knowledge over ignorance, comfort over luxury, permanence over insecurity, and stability over thrills."

"Always cherish the right things in life: nature, good people, and family. Never be afraid to say what needs to be said, but say it calmly: never shrink from confronting injustice, never compromise your principles and avoid malcontents," Dad added softly, not wanting to be outdone.

As Dad added his own words of wisdom, it dawned on me that I had become a conduit as my separate parents expressed their own separate aspirations fears and wishes. This counseling session had turned into a competition between them. At that moment, I wished that they had their arms around each other instead of me. These two lovely people were disconnected, and I was their only link to each other. I realized with hollow sadness that these dear people were drifting irreconcilably apart. I knew then that this would be the last time that we would all be together as a family.

CHAPTER 16

Alison was rapt with interest as I reminisced.

"What an awful experience for you to have gone through," Alison commiserated. "It's interesting that you don't blame your old friend for having fought against you; instead you believe that he kept the wolves at bay. I think it is wonderful that you want to reconnect with Mzali after all these years. Do you think that you will still have much in common?"

"I don't think that people ever really change. Mzali's character will be basically the same as it always was, although molded a little by experience," I responded thoughtfully. "We have a lot of shared experiences, and our lives have followed similar patterns since last we saw one another. We are both teachers and we both have some experience of the military. I'm sure we would have a great deal to talk about."

"Even though you were enemies?" asked Alison.

"Mzali and I were never enemies," I corrected her. "We may have fought for different armies on opposite sides during the war, but he was always my friend. Even though we were in different camps, we had a lot in common: both the Rhodesian Army and Mzali's ZIPRA forces were fighting a common enemy: Mugabe. Although they committed the occasional atrocity, as did every army, they preferred to engage the Rhodesian Army in actual combat, unlike Mugabe's lot who avoided combat, depending on terrorizing and torturing defenseless civilians to ensure compliance. Nkomo's ZAPU party sought an independent, or at least an autonomous Matabeleland, hoping to occupy Matabeleland after the election and to defend its independence through conventional warfare. Their ambitions all focused on what would happen *after* independence and majority rule, hoping to stave off Mashona dominance. Mzali's men were of a similar mindset to the Rhodesian Army; they were real soldiers."

"It sounds as though you admire the Matabele," Alison observed.

"I do. They are a very proud nation and honest, hardworking people. Unfortunately, history has not been kind to them."

"In what way?" Alison inquired.

"Like the Rhodesians, the Matabele people were also betrayed by the British at the ballot box. If it were not for British subterfuge and betrayal, Mugabe would never have come to power."

"You are starting to tread on thin ice when you criticize the British," admonished Alison playfully. "Remember that I have some British ancestry."

I laughed. "I love you despite your genetic limitations."

Alison smiled sweetly as she extended her middle finger. "Tell me about this British cunning," she commanded.

"To do that I'll need to provide a little context. After being recruited into the Rhodesian Army, I was stationed at the Rhodesian military headquarters in Harare. It was while I was there that I came into possession of a top secret document. In fact, I will need to confess my criminal past to you…"

CHAPTER 17
CUTBACK:
MARCH, 1980.

Smoke stung my eyes, and my clothes were saturated with the smell of it. Robin Delport and I had been burning documents for a solid two days. Just as we seemed to be making headway, someone else would appear and throw more documents onto the enormous stack before us. I felt like Sisyphus performing his never-ending punishment for the amusement of the gods.

We were in a small courtyard in the middle of army headquarters, and I was still acclimatizing to my new surroundings. A few days earlier, I had been at the School of Infantry, the Rhodesian equivalent of Sandhurst Academy, training to be an officer. Of the many candidates who had endured officer selection, only eighty had been chosen and I was one of them. My uncle, a military man himself, had offered to accommodate me, and now I was rubbing shoulders with all the influential Rhodesian military commanders. Not that any of them ever noticed me; I was an impressionable young lad who shined their shoes and served them coffee: an invisible man. My one reward was that I had been promoted to second lieutenant—for what little it mattered!

Lieutenant Colonel Sykes, one of the most powerful men in the country, needed a bodyguard, a minder, and I had been recommended for the job, largely because our bush war was drawing to a conclusion, and officer training had become a redundant exercise. He was a kindly and avuncular man, despite his serious expression and his lofty position, and I remember him with fondness.

Robin and I shared an office on the opposite side of the corridor from Lieutenant Colonel Sykes so that I was instantly available should he need me. He was disabled, and one of my functions was to wheel him from place to place. Another of my functions was to censor military communications and press releases, protecting the ignorant public from uncomfortable truths. Now that Robert Mugabe had won the election and was to be inaugurated as the first president of Zimbabwe at the beginning of April, there were even more truths that needed to be destroyed, hence the frantic burning of endless documents in two 44-gallon drums.

A friendly face appeared in the doorway. It was Captain Sally Yates. "Hey Brucey boy, you are wanted down the corridor," she smiled.

"Thanks, Sally." On the parade ground and in public it was "Yes Captain, no Captain," but in private she allowed the formality to slip, probably because she was a friend of my uncle. I threw another armful of secret documents onto the fire and watched them slowly ignite before heading down the corridor to Lieutenant Colonel Sykes, fearing that I may have incurred his wrath for some imagined offense. Tempers were short, and patience was frayed that day. His door was closed, so I knocked.

"Come in."

I walked in and stood rigidly at attention in front of his desk. He looked up at me as he placed a document on his desk.

"I want you to take the contents of that cabinet," he instructed, gesturing absently toward a large filing cabinet, "and I want you to burn everything that's in there."

He looked away and started to read the document again, looking very perturbed. I walked over to the filing cabinet and started to take documents out of their folders, trying to make as little noise as possible. I collected an armful of documents and took them through to the courtyard for destruction. When I returned to the office for another load, Lieutenant Colonel Sykes was leaning forward in his chair, deep in contemplation. Earlier that afternoon he had been locked in a meeting with General Walls and General Hickman and when they emerged from the boardroom they had all looked grim. Something had angered them!

"What are you going to do when you are released from the army?" Lieutenant Colonel Sykes asked absently. I looked at him, surprised that he was asking me a personal question. I snapped to attention.

"I will be going to university, Sir," I responded. He looked at me thoughtfully, scrutinizing me.

"At ease," he instructed. With my legs slightly parted in a more comfortable stance, and my arms behind my back, I still felt uneasy.

"Sit down," he commanded me, waving me toward a chair at his desk. I sat.

As I sat there, silent and stiff, he gazed at me thoughtfully. The intensity of his stare made me uncomfortable.

"Are you all right, Sir?" I asked.

"No, I am not," he responded, grouchy. He had obviously been weighing up the consequences of confiding something important in me.

"You deal with confidential information daily, and you strike me as a fairly intelligent young man. Read this and tell me what you think." He slid a document across the desk toward me. The document was stamped 'Top Secret' and contained the minutes of a congressional hearing in the USA from the time of the election. The document was interesting reading. It outlined the British opinion that any elections in Zimbabwe-Rhodesia would probably be won by Bishop Muzorewa, the incumbent president, and that Joshua Nkomo of ZAPU would win the entire Matabele vote and come second.

According to British intelligence, Robert Mugabe and his ZANU party would come in a distant third and be relegated to relative obscurity. This would not sit well with other African states, as Muzorewa was regarded as a compliant puppet of the Western powers, and Robert Mugabe was the hero of Africa and the champion of the liberation movement. Due to the Cold War, Britain was anxious to maintain positive relationships with African states and needed Robert Mugabe to have greater influence in the new government. The document outlined a British plan to subvert democracy in the country by allowing a blatant disregard for the Lancaster House Agreement which stipulated that Britain would take control of the country in the buildup to the elections and that all the warring parties would be confined to barracks.

The British were aware that Mugabe was transgressing these rules and that untrained youngsters, *mujibas*, were presenting themselves to the British monitoring forces to be confined to barracks at the assembly points while hardened veterans roamed free, terrorizing the population with impunity now that Muzorewa's army was incapacitated. What was particularly disturbing about this document was that it was written long before the election process and was a deliberate plan to sabotage democracy to suit a political agenda. What was even more disturbing was the fact that Britain was collaborating with the USA in this process. Britain tacitly condoned murder, mutilation, and mayhem, disregarding people's lives, and ignoring their suffering. The worst excesses of the bush war were perpetrated under British tutelage in the run-up to the election.

"This is political dynamite, Sir" I stuttered uncertainly. "This proves that the British are guilty of interfering in the democratic process and suggests that Mugabe would never have won these elections without the complicity and intentional negligence of the British."

"You're very astute," he complimented me. "We have not been defeated by Mugabe. We have been defeated by malicious British interference and Muzorewa's childlike naivety. This is not a defeat for Rhodesia and white minority rule; this is a defeat for all the people of this country and for democracy." He looked directly at me.

"What do you think of our esteemed leader, Bishop Muzorewa?" The question made me uneasy, as Muzorewa was technically our commander in chief.

"I believe he is a very good man, Sir, in that he is a decent human being. But he is a weak leader. He is tepid and uninspiring."

Lieutenant Colonel Sykes smiled grimly, obviously agreeing with my diplomatic assessment.

"He is a flatulent man," he said dismissively, "full of hot wind, and absolutely no substance."

He shook his head as he unburdened his opinions upon me. "I cannot believe that we will soon have to welcome Mugabe as our president. Just a year ago we had this war completely under control. With Muzorewa's men added to the Rhodesian Army, we had taken control of the ground and our external raids into Mozambique had shattered Mugabe's forces."

"Excuse me, Sir; what do you mean by 'controlling the ground'?" I interrupted.

"It simply means occupying the villages and maintaining a constant presence in the countryside. Effectively, being able to protect people from insurgents and preventing the enemy from operating there," he explained patiently, before continuing undeterred.

"The raid at Chimoio alone resulted in the destruction of nearly a third of Mozambique's economic infrastructure. Mozambique had instructed Mugabe to leave the country. Victory was assured and Muzorewa snatched defeat from the jaws of victory. He agreed to attend the Lancaster House conference and to hold new elections, throwing a lifeline to the vanquished Mugabe. He was seduced by promises of Western recognition and the dissipation of sanctions; he was seduced by his own vanity, wanting all doubts of his popularity with the people to be dispelled. He was warned, repeatedly, not to open the door for Mugabe and to risk his presidency, but he refused to listen.

"When Muzorewa first came to power after our internal settlement, the elections were free, fair, inclusive, and peaceful—64 percent of the country voted, with Muzorewa getting 67 percent of the votes. It was a massive endorsement of the democratic process and, of Muzorewa himself. Muzorewa was hoping to accomplish a similar victory in our most recent elections, and he probably would have, were it not for British interference." Lieutenant Colonel Sykes was visibly irritated by the incendiary report, feeling that he had been personally duped and betrayed.

"What will you do now, Sir?" I asked timidly, crossing a boundary and asking a personal question of my superior officer. He did not appear to mind.

"I may possibly retire on my British pension and live a life of anonymous obscurity in a dull grey country, hoping for the sun to shine and for the occasional glimpse of blue skies," he responded with a hint of self-pity.

"We are on the wrong side of history, and future generations will not judge us kindly. The canvas of history is colored by the artist and only interpreted by the observer. Fate will not smile on us. We believe we are right, but we are not. Democracy is a flawed process—it allows for rule by the mob. We have been betrayed by the British and undermined by the idiocy of Muzorewa.

"I am proud of many things that we have brought to this country: education, industry, agriculture, commerce, and prosperity. But this war has sullied us. We constantly talk about the crimes and brutality of the terrorists, yet we have committed equally brutal and barbaric crimes. I will be glad to walk away from this war. Our focus was always on the wrong thing—communism—when it should have been concentrated on nationalism and inclusiveness." His diatribe was unfocused and tinged with bitterness.

"I wish you well for the future, Sir," I said sincerely. As I spoke the words, I leaned forward and handed the top secret document back to my commanding officer.

"You too, son," he replied. He did not take the proffered document.

"You can keep it if you want to," he said, with a frown. "Just try not to be caught with it. I have the original document in safekeeping. You have been burning documents for the last two days, many of them far more incendiary than this one; you can keep it as a souvenir of your time in the military. After all, what does it matter now? It doesn't reflect on *our* conduct. The game is over, and the scoreboard shows that we have lost."

"Thank you, sir," I responded gratefully, smiling broadly. He smiled back and his portly face lit up briefly.

"Go and burn some more history," he instructed. "Dismissed."

That afternoon I left army headquarters feeling conspiratorial and nervous, with a top secret document in my possession hidden under my shirt. About a week later, Mugabe was inaugurated as the first president of an independent Zimbabwe; I was released from the service and allowed into the University of Cape Town on short notice, well into the academic year. It was the end of a gallant Ivanhoe era. The final curtain had fallen; the last act of a forgettable play had drawn to its conclusion; and the inglorious cast of an inglorious performance was about to disperse toward their uncertain futures, floating like debris on a turbulent sea of change. The audience was not applauding.

CHAPTER 18

"I'm sure Mzali would love to hear of your illicit activities and to read that document," smiled Alison, as she shifted into the shade of a cycad tree and popped the last of the grapes into her mouth. "It's still gathering dust in my garage," I reassured her.

"Have you seen Mzali since then?" asked Alison cautiously.

"No, but I kept getting rumors of his activities through the grapevine. His dad was still working at Kataza, and the last time I was up there I was told that Mzali had qualified as a teacher and was at Esibomvu Secondary School, close to Esigodini. It's funny, but Dad never spoke of Mzali again after the attack on Kataza. I think Dad felt betrayed, but I also think that Dad understood Mzali's reasons and sympathized with them."

"So, how do you know where Mzali is now?" Alison queried. "He may well have left the school."

"The internet," I said triumphantly. "I did a Google search and, believe it or not, Esibomvu Secondary has a website! Not only is Mzali still there, but he is now the headmaster. Good for him!" I was genuinely pleased for him.

"Have you contacted him yet?"

"No. I've had a look at the school timetable on the internet. He is now on holiday, and he lives on the premises. I thought that we could take a risk and assume that he will be home tomorrow. I would love to surprise him after all these years."

CHAPTER 19

Esibomvu Secondary School was far larger than I had anticipated. It was a sprawl of neat buildings, immaculately clean but deserted for now. I could picture the school during term time, infused with life, hordes of kids milling about and running around. But for now, it was a soulless place. Spotting a gardener, I asked where I could find Mzali Sithole. I was given flawless directions: straight ahead, the house at the end of the avenue.

Alison and I drove up to Mzali's house, and I was impressed by the garden: arum lilies, gladioli, hydrangeas, a large white stinkwood tree, and the ubiquitous 'go away' birds. I had a feeling of déjà vu. I knocked on the door tentatively, hoping that Mzali was home. It took a minute or two, but eventually the door opened.

"Hau!" Mzali could not believe his eyes. I could see the recognition taking shape in his mind, wrestling with his disbelief.

"I don't believe this," he celebrated. He appeared overjoyed and struggled to contain his emotions. He hugged me spontaneously. "How are you? It's been so many years." It was a poignant moment for both him and me.

"How are you Mzali?" I asked. "You're looking well."

"So are you." He scrutinized me carefully. "Hau, but you have grown old," he laughed, "and you are still very ugly!"

"I know," I replied. "But at least I am not as old as you."

"No. But I'm Black—we never look old. Come in, come in," said Mzali, ushering us into his home. The house reflected his personality; it was neat and tidy, the furniture was unpretentious, but comfortable; there were indoor plants, giving it life; and some brightly painted, life-size guinea fowl carvings which hinted at his quirky sense of humor. I introduced Alison and Mzali to one another, while Mzali seated us.

"Congratulations Mzali," I said. "You've done really well for yourself." Mzali went through to the kitchen to brew tea: Twinings Earl Grey.

"Thank you," he replied. "It's been a struggle, but it's been worth it. How are you? Tell me about your life."

I summed up my life story in two minutes, telling him that I was a teacher and that I lived in Randburg.

"How is your dad?" I asked.

"He is well, thank you. But he is old now. He left Kataza a long time ago and stays on the communal lands in Filabusi. I was very sorry to hear about your dad; he was a very good man—and I am sorry to hear about Kataza," Mzali commiserated. I knew he was sincere.

Mzali still looked much as I remembered him; a little older and wiser, but still the same ebullient man. It was invigorating to once again be chatting with him. Alison took an immediate liking to Mzali and he to her.

We spent an hour or so talking about our lives, our loves, our interests, and our work. In short, we were filling in the blanks, getting to know one another again, and catching up with years of absent news, as old friends do meeting after time apart.

At one point, I went into the garden to admire the view and, as I looked back toward Mzali's house, I noticed him and Alison talking animatedly. Alison looked up and saw me; her face lit up with a broad grin, and she waved to me. Mzali turned around and waved too, and as he did so they both laughed in unison. They were talking about me. When I went back inside, both Alison and Mzali were in high spirits.

"You've done very well for yourself, Bruce," Mzali congratulated me with a smile. "You are obviously very lucky in life; it is amazing that someone so lacking in talent and looks as you are could end up with a girlfriend as beautiful and intelligent as Alison."

I pretended to be offended. "My talents are numerous! How do you know that Alison is intelligent?"

"Because she has listened wisely to all the profound advice that I have offered, and a very intelligent person knows to listen carefully when they are in the presence of true genius."

Alison smiled and shook her head while I laughed heartily. "You haven't changed one bit. You are still as delusional and pompous as ever. How could someone so dim-witted ever become a headmaster?"

"Luck and bribery," he admitted.

Both Alison and I wanted to see more of Mzali, so I asked him if he would permit us to treat him to dinner the following evening. He agreed to meet us in Bulawayo. As we were preparing to leave, Alison excused herself giving Mzali the opportunity to confide in me.

"Bruce, I want you to know that I always loved your family and I did not join ZIPRA to harm you. In fact, I think I helped to save your dad's life!"

"Mzali, you don't have to explain yourself to me. I understand. If I had been in your position, I would also have joined ZIPRA. How did you save Dad's life?"

"Do you remember that all the combatants were confined to barracks in the run-up to the elections in 1980? A base was established for ZIPRA just down the road from Kataza, on the old Edward's farm on the banks of the Ncema River."

I remembered it well because we used to drive past it on the way to the village: a handsome old thatched farmhouse that was barely visible from the road. I also remembered it being converted into a battle camp.

Mzali continued: "We were based there for over a year and, after years of fighting, it felt good to be safe. But we soon got bored. The men wanted action, and discipline was hard to maintain. We were frustrated, and we hated the thought of Mugabe ruling us. We rebelled. Do you remember the Entumbane uprising?"

I told him that I remembered it well. After independence and Mugabe's victory in the elections, ZAPU was relegated to a subservient and irrelevant position, which they resented; nearly two years after 'independence', the ZIPRA troops were still confined to barracks. The restless ZIPRA troops, stationed in the Bulawayo suburb of Entumbane, eventually lost patience and attempted a coup d'état.

"Well," Mzali continued, "we had plans to attack Kataza first and then move on to Bulawayo. Our commander, Masuku, was close friends with Gumede, and Gumede desperately wanted revenge. He had attacked Kataza during the war and he had failed. Gumede convinced Masuku that we should attack Kataza, that it was a symbol of white colonial rule. He poisoned Masuku's mind against the Savage family. I went and spoke to Masuku. I pleaded with him and told him that your father was a good man, a kind and wise man. I reasoned with him and I cajoled him: I told him that we could not afford to waste time with Kataza when our comrades needed us in Bulawayo. Eventually, I convinced him not to attack Kataza."

I thought Mzali may well have been seeking redemption, asking, but not begging, for my forgiveness, or for my understanding at least.

"Mzali," I responded sincerely, "I owe you a massive debt of gratitude for saving Dad's life. Thank you. What you do not know is that you saved my life too…"

CHAPTER 20
CUTBACK:
FEBRUARY, 1982: KATAZA

Home for the holidays, I sipped my coffee and gazed out over the garden and into the bush as I reclined in my chair on the veranda. Gone were the mounds of sandbags. The lawn was a tranquil ocean of green, stretching toward infinity, interrupted by patches of bright cheerful color: flotsam on the sea. It was wonderful to be home at Kataza, peaceful and serene, so far removed from the upheavals, demonstrations, and political angst consuming South Africa that I was becoming alarmingly inured to. With the sandbags removed, the imperious old homestead was once again revealed to the light. Normality had returned to Kataza. Well, almost; Kataza seemed emptier and lonelier without Mom.

Caesar and Cassia were lying beside me on the cool terracotta tiles, hoping for me to take them into the garden and to throw sticks for them to chase. It was nearly time for their regular playtime: four o'clock in the afternoon. When they were younger, they loved chasing sticks and then forcing me to run after them to retrieve the sticks from them. Now that they were older, their muzzles tinged with grey and their hips stiff with age, I think that they played simply because they believed that it gave me pleasure. As I was steeling myself for some rough and tumble with the dogs, the phone rang. It was Lionel Wilson, still the District Commissioner.

"Hello Bruce," he said, surprised to hear my voice. "Are you still at Kataza for the holidays?"

"Hello, Mr. Wilson. Yes, I am. These holidays are nice and long; the academic year does not start again for a few weeks' time."

Lionel Wilson loved to talk, but today he did not have time for idle chitchat. Something was wrong.

"Bruce, is your dad around?"

"No, Mr. Wilson. He is still out on the farm dipping cattle. Can I give him a message?"

"Please Bruce." His voice was tinged with trepidation. "I have just received a call from the police. One of their informants has warned that the ZIPRA forces down the track from Kataza intend to attack Bulawayo either later today or tomorrow."

"Don't worry, Mr. Wilson," I reassured him, "we are well stocked. We don't need to go into town for at least another two weeks."

"I'm afraid there's more to it than that, Bruce. It seems that these men have been living close to Kataza for over a year and have come to regard it as symbolic of all that is evil about European colonialism. Before advancing toward Bulawayo, they want to take a short detour and obliterate Kataza. They regard it as a 'whetting of the spears' to initiate the young warriors into battle, giving them confidence and bloodlust before advancing toward Bulawayo. Your dad needs to evacuate Kataza because it is certain that it is about to be attacked and you stand no chance against five thousand soldiers and Russian tanks."

My blood ran cold as the stunning reality of his words sank in. I had to find Dad and I had to find him soon. A multitude of thoughts raced through my mind: the workers would need to be moved to safety; we had to protect the cattle; we needed to make sure that the dogs would be safe; we could not allow the homestead to be destroyed. But the first order of business was to find Dad.

"By the way, Bruce," Lionel Wilson added, "we have fewer than ten men at the police station. We have decided to suspend services until this fracas is over: normal transmission will be resumed as soon as possible," he quipped sourly, frustrated by his inability to intervene.

"Thanks, Mr. Wilson," I said softly.

"Good luck, Bruce," he replied, the concern evident in his tone. "I hope to see you at the clubhouse soon. Perhaps we could have a game of tennis and enjoy a drink together afterward." With that he put down the phone and contact with the outside world was severed.

With the sun low in the sky behind me, I jogged through the bush toward the cattle dip, fearing that Dad would have already left. It took me ten minutes to get there, and almost all the cattle had been dipped. As the last of the cattle plunged into the dip and thrashed to the other side, the herd was busy being rounded up. Indignant and confused, the lone cow joined the herd, saturated. As the four Matabele farmhands started to muster the cattle, Dad noticed me. He was aside from the cattle, chatting to one of the young men and sharing a cigarette with him when he looked up.

"Hi Bruce," he beamed. "You're just in time to avoid the manual labor."

"Punctual as always," I responded. "Your taunts are just water off a cow's back *Madala*." The farmhands smiled politely to themselves when I referred to Dad as 'old man'. With that, one of them cracked a bullwhip and the herd started to move forward, each of the men taking up their positions to prevent any of the cattle from straying off.

"Do you want a lift home, or do you want to run back?" Dad asked me.

"Actually Dad, we need to talk. I have some important news."

"Climb in," Dad instructed me, as he stepped into the Land Rover and positioned himself behind the steering wheel.

The Matabele herdsmen were chanting a soft soothing song to the cattle, calling each of them by name as they slowly wended their way forward. As we rumbled slowly back to the homestead, trying to minimize the dust behind us, I could hear the plaintive lowing of the cattle growing fainter and fainter as they ambled back toward the dairy.

The day loomed to a close. By the time we got home, the sun was setting, a glorious apricot gold, and both Dad and I had digested the ominous news. We examined our options: we could seek refuge in Bulawayo, which was the obvious choice, or we could brace ourselves for a fight. Dad politely suggested that I drive to Bulawayo and that he stay at Kataza, but we both knew that this was unacceptable to me. Still, Dad had tried! Our primary concern was for the workers. We could not abandon them, yet our presence alone was a magnet for the ZIPRA soldiers; by staying at Kataza we were drawing the enemy toward us, endangering the village. Eventually, we decided that we would stay and fight if necessary, nobody was going to drive us away from our home, but that the workers needed to be in a place of safety.

So we took a quick trip down to the village to inform the workers of the news. Dad advised them that the wisest course of action would be for them to post sentries to give them advance warning of any imminent threat, and for the entire village to flee to a predetermined rendezvous point, the dairy, if in any danger.

One of the young men spoke out: "Boss Ian. Boss Bruce. This is our home too, and we are all family. We want to stay with you and fight these men. Please let us help you."

"Thank you, Thomas," said Dad, so quietly that his voice was almost indistinct. He placed his hand on Thomas's shoulder and addressed the entire village.

"Thank you all for your concern, but this our fight and our decision. You must protect your families; keep them safe."

"You all need to stay together and make sure that nobody goes missing. If any of the men are with Boss Ian and me, then the village will be weakened and you will be less able to fight," I added. Reluctantly, the young men agreed.

Dad and I believed—fatuously—that we were valiantly standing up for what was right, and that fate would somehow protect us from harm; that good would triumph over evil. We were incredibly foolish. We knew that we were going to be attacked by an insuperable enemy, and we knew that we could not win: we accepted that. In truth, we had decided to accept death, albeit subconsciously. Death, without surrender: death, on our own terms.

When you accept death, all fear disappears, and all anxiety dissipates. There is something liberating about embracing the possibility of death without actively seeking it. With the acceptance of the final truth comes honesty and an unburdening: all secrets are revealed, and no truths are judged. It is what it is: what will be, will be.

Dad and I made our preparations: Dad unpacked the gun cabinet and I whipped up some sandwiches; we had not yet eaten, and neither of us felt hungry. We decided to wait in Dad's study, where we surveyed our arsenal: Dad's shotgun, two FN rifles, and an Uzi submachine gun. We had ammunition in abundance. Thankfully, the government had not yet insisted on farmers surrendering their weapons! Ironically, the Agric-alert radio system had long since being discarded.

We assumed that any assault would be a full-frontal attack, counting on the sheer weight of numbers and firepower to overwhelm us, but we also realized that they could be subtle, and decide to use snipers, wanting to preserve the old homestead. We decided that we would await our fate in darkness; that we would never allow them a clear shot at us; and that all noise would be muffled; we kept all the curtains drawn and crawled below the windows. We wanted Kataza to appear to be deserted.

Sitting there in the dark of Dad's study enveloped by silence, our senses were heightened, and the adrenaline was pumping as we anticipated a bloody confrontation. Caesar and Cassia seemed to instinctively sense that something was off-kilter and lay quietly together on their dog cushions, hardly moving the entire evening. For a time, Dad and I played chess by the dim light of a solitary candle, but we soon tired of it because we could hardly distinguish between the white and black pieces; nor could we concentrate. We were restless and impatient.

I decided to resume my intimate relationship with the FN rifle by stripping and reassembling it in the dark while Dad timed me. I remember that I got my time down to twenty-seven seconds: a personal record.

"I know it sounds strange, seeing as they want to kill us, but there is a part of me that feels sympathy for these guys," I admitted to Dad. "They fought for their independence hoping for an autonomous Matabeleland, which was denied them, and have been betrayed at the ballot box. They have been cooped up in barracks for two years and have seen one master replaced by another. I don't blame them for being frustrated."

"Unfortunately Bruce, that is one of the perils of democracy: the tyranny of the majority. The Matabele have been bullied by the ballot; less numerous should not mean less worthy. All too often, democracy tends to be ruled by the ignorant; a qualified democracy, allowing only educated

111

people to vote, might be wiser for Africa, but that would cause other problems. The obvious solution to ethnic disputes would have been a federal system and the devolution of power, preventing one ethnic group from ever subordinating another. But, in their wisdom, this solution was denied by the parties at the negotiating table. It seems that this option was perceived as a prelude to national fracturing and eventual fragmentation. The problems of Africa would have been reduced if federalism had been adopted more widely and enthusiastically."

"A little like what has happened to our family," I remarked absently, realizing as I uttered the words that they might be hurtful to Dad.

"I'm sorry Dad," I apologized. "I didn't mean to sound critical."

"Don't worry chap. You are right. The family has fractured and you are now the only link between Yvonne and me. It's very sad, and I know that I am to blame. Every day I think about what I could have done differently to keep the family together. When I came home from the farm, I would sit and talk about cattle and crops when I should have shown more interest in her concerns. The stress of the war did not help our marriage either." Dad was battling with that most corrosive of emotions which seeps insidiously into every facet of life: guilt.

"To be honest Dad, I don't know if that would have helped. You were a good husband, and you're a great father and friend to me. I think that you and Mom simply drifted off in different directions and there was very little that you could do to change that. Mom needed to be closer to friends and society, she is a sociable person, while you are more comfortable with your own company and need to be in the bush, away from society." My attempt to reassure Dad with anodyne words was cold comfort to him; no amount of reassurance on my part would rekindle the marriage.

As we sat together, enveloped in the charcoal darkness of the study, Dad and I confessed our fears, our failures, our disappointments, our longings, and our ambitions. The fact that we struggled to see one another aided our emotional purging; it was as though each of us was talking to our inner self. We had always been honest with one another, but this deeper transparency, without judgment, helped us to know one another more intimately and to establish an element of trust that went beyond familial bonds. Now we were blood brothers, willing to fight, to suffer and die for each other. Now we were equals.

As we sat there waiting, sounds became amplified and shadows were magnified. Every rustle of grass was a soldier; every shadow was a monster. Dad and I were continually going from room to room and peering through the curtains into the darkness beyond, seeing nothing. Every now and again one of the dogs would react to a sound by raising its head and pricking up its ears. That would be our signal to patrol the perimeter fence. Dad would stay on the veranda armed with his shotgun while I would ferret around the edges of the garden peering into the bush. At a given signal, Dad would switch on the old, reliable halogen security lights, hoping to blind and dazzle any would be intruder and allowing me to see into the wilderness beyond. Nothing.

As the sun rose in all its amber glory, it dawned on us that the anticipated attack would never come. Still, we remained vigilant, just in case we were wrong. It was only when Dad tuned into the BBC and heard about the Battle of Bulawayo, that we allowed ourselves to relax. It occurred to me that Bulawayo was aptly named 'place of slaughter'. Apparently, the ZIPRA forces had advanced on Bulawayo anticipating an easy victory only to be confronted by the old Rhodesian Light Infantry, now assimilated into the new Zimbabwean Army. The ZIPRA forces were slaughtered. It is ironic that one of the greatest ever victories of the Rhodesian Light Infantry came when protecting Mugabe and his ZANU party whom they had fought against for fourteen long years.

The danger was over, and we had survived—yet we had done nothing. Despite the inactivity, this was one of the most meaningful moments of my life. What was significant for me was that we had confronted our fears, Dad and I together, and we had been prepared and willing to die for what was worth protecting and for each other. For me, it was not the fight, but the willingness to fight that mattered. Dad and I now knew each other's mettle and it was steel.

CHAPTER 21

When Alison and I got back to the hotel Professor Cameron was waiting in the lobby. A short, slightly built man with a wild mop of brown hair, his clothes spoke to his personality; despite the heat, he wore a blue-grey tweed jacket, baggy khaki pants, a light blue cheesecloth shirt, and leather sandals. In his left hand he gripped a worn leather briefcase. He had a curious idiosyncrasy: he seldom made eye contact as though he was constantly embarrassed, a mendicant gaze. I got the impression that he was mentally removed, settling into reality briefly and then wandering off on a tangent, permanently distracted. For all his oddity, or perhaps because of it, I took a liking to him.

"Did you enjoy your trip, Professor?" I asked.

"Yes, yes—very interesting. Please, call me Bryan." He shook my hand, but his eyes were on Alison. Then he gazed at the ceiling before surveying the carpet. I looked at Alison and she looked at me, smiling. This was going to be fun.

Adjourning to the lounge, it soon became apparent that he lacked artifice and was simply socially awkward; there was a gormless innocence about him, both amusing and disconcerting.

Oblivious to social mores, Bryan made a valiant attempt at polite conversation. Fixing his gaze firmly on my drink, he struck.

"So Alison, Tabitha informs me that before you met Bruce you had not had sex for five years."

Never before had I seen Alison at a loss for words, but Bryan's comment left her wide-eyed and slack-jawed. Laughing, I squeezed her hand beneath the table offering moral support. Rebounding from her astonishment, Alison erupted with delight, hugely entertained.

"You're right Bryan, Alison was very rusty when we met—there were cobwebs." With a mighty guffaw, her eyes dripping from laughter, Alison punched my shoulder.

"Speak for yourself!"

Bryan shifted his eyes to above Alison's shoulder. "Your penis is truly fascinating."

I gawked, surprised. Oblivious to his faux pas, Bryan continued unabated. "It is normally referred to as a betyl and suggests a culture with fertility rites."

114

Relieved, I realized that he was talking about the ancient phallus. "How so?" From the corner of my eye I could see that Alison had turned away, trying hard to suppress her laughter.

"We had assumed that because it is ivory that it would be elephant tusk, but we were wrong; it is carved from hippo tooth. The date is also interesting, somewhere between 870 and 930 CE, placing it at the genesis of the Mapela Hill culture. Quite extraordinary!"

Regaining her composure, Alison intervened. "Tell us about the script on the tablet Bryan."

"It was tricky to decipher. I had difficulty recognizing it because it is a bastardized version of Ge'ez, an ancient language used by both Phoenicians and Arabs from Saba. Once I discovered that, the tablet was easy to translate."

"What did it say?"

"They are a diary of sorts, speaking about a young man's daily life and recording the activities of a small community including mundane facts about gold yields, harvests, and personal interactions. If it was inscribed in the same era as the hippo tooth was carved, then it would have been created during the Abbasid Caliphate, long after the dusk of the Sabaean civilization."

CHAPTER 22

A crescendo of silence engulfed the room like a muted tsunami. The enormity of Gumede's words and the insanity of his proposal were beyond comprehension. It was the general, *Inhlathu*, who broke the silence, desperately trying to articulate his confusion.

"This is preposterous," he whispered. "It is impossible."

"I agree," interjected the history professor, *Mpisi*, nervously brushing imaginary debris from his pinstripe Armani suit; a neatly folded triangle of a yellow silk handkerchief protruded from his breast pocket. "No one has ever dared to attack the old man. For one thing, he is far too well protected and for another, too many people depend on his largesse and patronage for their political livelihood; he is far too popular. No government that comes to power by attacking the old man will ever have the support of the people. We would be inviting the military to intervene. The country would descend into chaos and there would be looting and pillaging throughout the nation. We would be pariahs with a bounty on our heads. No. It is too risky!"

The businessman, *Ilinqe*, expressed his opposition to the venture with extremely colorful language. Having delivered his angry diatribe using every expletive imaginable, he concluded by stating: "There is no way that we can possibly stage a coup d'état." He gazed around the room, bristling with hauteur: "I assume that 'silence is consent?' It appears that we have consensus and that the decision is 'No'."

Gumede's eyes narrowed, his cheek muscles tightened, and his teeth clenched. He would not tolerate insubordination or insolence. Trying hard to conceal his anger, he put on the mask of a reasonable man. He knew that he had to acknowledge their fears and to dismiss them with logic rather than rage. He knew, too, that this was the moment of truth, and that if he did not convince them now, then all his ambitions would simply fade away into oblivion. Speaking in a softly modulated voice hardly more than a whisper, but dripping with authority, he attempted to reassure his coven of conspirators.

"Gentlemen. We are all Africans; the warm, red blood of Africa flows through our veins. We are brothers. Western ideas and foreign ideologies are not for us; we have our own traditions. Democracy is only useful when it suits our purpose and here it does not. So please

116

believe me when I say that your opinions in this matter are of no consequence to me. Democracy is rule by the ignorant, the poor, and the meek. The old man recognized that four decades ago. We need to be bold and to take control of our destiny now, while the fruit is ripe for the plucking. The country and the party are both in decline; the politicians and the people are swimming in a sea of uncertainty. This is the time to act decisively. The rewards if we do are immeasurable." Gumede scanned his coven critically, looking for any signs of doubt or dissent. He could see that they were all unconvinced. He needed to be more forceful.

"You are all forgetting the fact that your options are limited. Your fortunes are now inextricably entwined with my own. The information that I have on each one of you is so scandalous, so criminal that you dare not reject this proposal. But fear not, I have no intention of being branded a criminal. If all goes according to plan, it will be Mugabe's loyal cronies who are blamed for his demise, and we will sweep to power on a wave of popular consent. You will all be embraced as heroes, protectors of the revolution, while the old guard will be flushed away and labeled as traitors. We will not bring chaos; we will restore order and we will be celebrated as saviors. Gentlemen, my plan is simple, but brilliant."

CHAPTER 23

The next evening, our third day in Bulawayo, we met Mzali and Bryan at Friar Tuck steakhouse on Josiah Tongogara Avenue. Mzali arrived in his black dress suit, complete with a charcoal silk tie, which was tied in a perfect Windsor knot. I complimented him on his wardrobe.

"Sartorial splendor," I exaggerated. Bryan had donned a dark blue tweed jacket and khaki trousers, while Alison looked magnificent in an elegant malachite-green dress and emerald earrings. My plumage was less spectacular wearing jeans and a short-sleeved blue shirt. I ordered a beer for Mzali and a Cinzano and lemonade for Bryan, while Alison and I both enjoyed a Jack Daniels and ginger ale.

We were settling into our seats and Mzali was becoming familiar with Bryan, when a troupe deposited themselves into the booth beside ours. From the outset, they were far too noisy and too flamboyant for my taste. The most vocal was a sleek, slender woman with flawless cinnamon skin and beautiful almond-shaped eyes, trying to chase away the years by dressing like a teenager. Her companion was a stout lady whose body was barely contained by her dress which threatened to burst with any sudden movement. Both women wore short, tight fitting skirts, hugging their bodies and inhibiting movement.

The slender willowy woman had selected a bright red outfit and a scarlet leather jacket bestrewn with metal studs, while her companion was wrapped in a bright yellow dress which shimmered as she walked, clumsy in her high heels. The dress contrasted sharply with her ebony skin. They both wore blonde wigs and a little too much makeup, looking ghoulish as their eyes scanned the other patrons to see who was watching them. The slender woman had a sheen of golden glitter on the tawny skin of her arms and neck and revealed a beautiful blue butterfly tattoo on her left shoulder when she removed her glossy leather jacket.

There was something rather sordid and sad about their behavior, mutton masquerading as lamb, but in essence, it was a primal sexual display, like colorful birds spreading their feathers to signal their willingness to procreate. Although crude, it was effective.

They were accompanied by two Black gentlemen in expensive suits and gaudy jewelry. The slender woman's companion was a proudly muscular young man who obviously spent much time lifting weights. He was noticeably uncomfortable. Used to having women fawn over him, admiring his physique, he was now expected to be subservient.

In a voice as astringent as carbolic soap, she was berating him for his lack of manners. He had neglected to open the car door for her and had walked into the restaurant before her, provoking her ire. From what little we could discern, it seemed that he had the rather unfortunate name of "Damned Idiot"! He looked embarrassed. On a primal level, she was projecting dominance like a mantis that kills her mate after procreating. As she spoke, deliberately demeaning her companion, her predatory eyes evaluated the patrons. Even this was a sexual display.

"What on earth does he see in her?" I speculated incredulously.

"Do you really want me to tell you?" Alison asked mischievously.

I laughed. "You filthy creature! That's why I love you so much. I love you for your mind." Mzali was grinning from ear to ear: "Hau, Mziki. You haven't changed." The ice had been broken, and we settled into pleasant banter. Alison and I sat side by side with Mzali facing me and Bryan facing Alison. It wasn't long before Bryan and Alison were engrossed in conversations about ancient lands and trade systems. When the waiter brought the menu, I noticed that all the prices were expressed in American dollars.

"Isn't it tragic that this country now has no currency of its own, yet at independence, its currency was worth twice the American dollar?" I asked.

Mzali agreed wholeheartedly: "This country has been cursed with one economic calamity after another compounded by hyperinflation, ineptitude, and corruption. The banking system has collapsed and most of the population is unemployed. Companies are closing every day. Crime is rampant and infrastructure is deteriorating. This is a dystrophic state; everything is winding down," he lamented sadly.

Alison's ears pricked up at the mention of economics. "I think the root cause of the economic disaster is Mugabe's fear of Western economic imperialism, Coca-Colonization. He is right to fear foreign exploitation, but his fear verges on paranoia and has colored his political thinking to the extent that he has destroyed the country by trying to protect it from foreign governments and corporations: a self-fulfilling prophecy."

"He has also seen other African countries bankrupted by their excessive debt repayments to those instruments of Western policy, the International Monetary Fund and the World Bank," interjected Bryan.

"Mugabe is correct to be cynical about Western motives, but you cannot protect a nation by ignoring the realities of the world and trying to trade on your own terms with larger and more efficient economies, many of which are megacorporations," Alison added. "Since World War II, American foreign policy has been conducted according to the spurious notion that capitalism and democracy go hand-in-hand, which is not necessarily true. At best they coexist, but capitalism tends to thrive in dictatorships which provide a stable, predictable marketplace. The Americans have always projected the illusion that they are the disciples of democracy, but it is not democracy that they fight for; they are the apostles of capitalism. America has supported some of the most despicable dictatorships in the world and they all have one thing in common: capitalism."

The garish gaggle in the neighbouring booth was becoming annoying, their dialogue increasingly intrusive and distracting. The woman with the butterfly tattoo continued to berate her muscular appendage, while her accomplice seemed overly anxious to impress, criticizing, correcting, castigating, and condemning her own companion in a shrill, shrewish voice. He was silent and sullen, painfully aware that he was incidental. It was clear that these men were purely decoration and would be discarded as soon as they entered the nightclub for which they had all dressed. Both women secreted insincerity from every clogged and powdered pore. The tattooed woman's companion had been conspicuously silent, unused to not being doted on, but was gradually becoming more assertive as irritation grappled with embarrassment, and the alcohol suffused his bloated veins.

"I think one of the big disconnects in modern world politics," Alison raised her voice to compete with the neighboring table, continuing to lecture her fascinated audience, "is that the Western nations perceive the world very differently to both China and Russia, their principal geopolitical rivals; the West has promoted free enterprise, despite their own subsidies. With the collapse of communism, this new trend of globalization has gathered momentum and has accelerated incrementally. Western politics are always informed by financial interests, whereas Russia and China are still largely nationalist in the way they conduct themselves, and their economies are subordinate to the state. I think that Western governments are driven by their corporations. What we are seeing is nationalism versus globalization; pragmatism versus populism; and informed decisions versus ignorant suppositions. Quite honestly, I think the Americans get annoyed when they do not get their own way. One of the ironies of all this is that America, the paladin of democracy, is driven by corporate interests and corporations do not conduct themselves in a democratic way: they themselves are dictatorships. The employees do not elect their chief executive officer, and the employees never have any say in corporate decisions."

I agreed wholeheartedly. "Ever since 1944 and the Bretton Woods Conference, the world has been governed by corporate globalization, loosely aligned megacorporations, with the mutual interests of profit and power. They have financed presidential elections, ensuring that the president is a slave to many masters. The International Monetary Fund and the World Bank were installed as tools to implement political and corporate policy to combat the pernicious threats of communism and nationalism using dollar diplomacy. These huge corporations control the oil, banking, car manufacturing, military, and intelligence sectors, as well as the media. Their enormous contributions to presidential campaigns ensure that they control the president and that democracy is a sham: a narcotic for the masses.

"America accuses the Russian government of managing the media. How ironic, when in America, it is the media that manages the government! I think that Western governments find it difficult to relate to people who are not motivated by money."

"In which case, you would be an enormous enigma to them," Alison complimented me.

Bryan wanted to have his say too. "Let's not forget that when the Soviet Union collapsed, the West made certain fiscal promises to Russia; promises that have not been kept."

"I bet the British were involved," I teased. Alison extended her middle finger. Bryan examined the ceiling, grinning benignly.

"I agree with what Alison has said," he stated, still staring into space. "There is another irony here, and that is the fact that America claims to be a haven for individualism, the home of the rugged cowboy, yet it has always been the territory of the 'robber barons', the very antithesis of individualism."

"Of course," Alison perceptively observed, "the whole perception of right and wrong, good and bad, is perpetuated by the megacorporations of Hollywood, which epitomize the American dream. After World War II, the 'dream factory' inculcated the idea that Americans had almost single-handedly defeated the Nazis. All the villains were blonde-haired, blue-eyed, emotionally stunted Germans and, as the Cold War gathered intensity, it was the avaricious and corrupt Russians who were the evil enemy. As the Cold War abated, and apartheid became the issue of the day, it was racist Afrikaans thugs who were stereotyped as the dim-witted menace to society. Now, of course, it is Arabs and Muslims who are painted as the great insidious threat to humanity, mindless fanatics intent on blowing up everything that is good and right. And, of course, that means the American way of life. It's so simplistic," she despaired.

By now our neighbors were becoming positively annoying, neither caring nor noticing that they were embarrassing the other patrons. Trying hard to ignore the increasingly heated exchanges, and to not lose patience, we were subconsciously talking louder simply to be heard.

"Yes," Mzali added loudly. "The Americans can only see things in simplistic, self-serving, terms. They all see themselves as the persecuted cowboy, valiantly standing up for all that is moral against insuperable odds." Mzali laughed, "Ironically the cowboys tended to be illiterate foreigners who were employed as cowboys only because no 'decent' person wanted the job!"

"The solitary hero standing up for all that is good and right: that is the American perception of their identity. It is the individual against a corrupt and evil system. The modern-day version of the cowboy is the Superman myth: the well-intentioned loner fighting injustice. Wouldn't it be wonderful if the Americans could just consider the possibility that they may, perhaps, possibly, be wrong?" Bryan observed.

"If you want to arouse the American public give them pornography and politics," Bryan added atonally. "Bread and circuses."

"I think that they are the same thing," I noted cynically. "Porn stars and politicians are both prostituting themselves; they are both performers of a sort."

"Ah," Mzali smiled, "but the women of Lobengula Street will not perform for any price, nor will they perform any perversity." Alison smiled grimly.

"Politicians will prostrate themselves to the mammon of popular approval and perform any unpalatable or undignified act simply to remain exposed to the public," Bryan added, his eyes focused on the back wall.

"Especially if they are British," I added acidly. Once again, Alison smiled sweetly and extended her middle finger.

Emboldened by beer, and tired of being belittled, the muscular man beside us finally snapped and started shouting obscenities at the slender woman. The other man looked away, embarrassed. The restaurant manager was hastily summoned, and he warned the party to behave themselves to no avail. Exasperated, he summoned the security guard who looked bewildered. An insult later, Mr. Muscles slid out of his chair with a steak knife loosely grasped in his right hand, arguing with the security guard as he casually waved the weapon about. He was probably unaware that he was still holding the knife, but Mzali reacted quickly. Mzali slid out of our booth and took two quick steps toward the melee. With one fluid, deft movement, he gripped the man's left wrist and squeezed into the nerves with his thumb, causing him to drop the knife. Mzali then grabbed the man's right wrist and twisted it behind his back. With the thumb and first finger of his left hand, Mzali gripped the man's shoulder muscle and squeezed into the nerves, incapacitating him. As

Mzali marched the man passed us, with a minimum of fuss, I could hear Mzali whispering reassuringly into his ear.

"Let's go outside and get some fresh air," Mzali murmured. "I feel for you, and I don't blame you for being angry, but this is neither the place nor the time to cause a disturbance. Come with me my friend, the night air is very calming."

We were all tremendously impressed with the decisive and unobtrusive way that Mzali had dealt with the situation. As Mzali escorted the man outside, I went and spoke to the lady with the blue butterfly tattoo, telling her that it was probably better for everyone if she and her friends remained seated for a while until they had simmered down and regained their composure. The manager agreed.

Now that the distraction had been removed, once Mzali returned we continued to enjoy the conversation and the company and allowed ourselves the comforting indulgence of an Irish coffee. Bryan, though, was beginning to dim.

"I must say," he drawled, "I'm finding this all a little complex for this time of day."

"It's not complex at all," Mzali interceded. "If you want to understand politics, stop thinking of all the complicated issues and try to imagine countries as children in the playground."

"What age are these children?" Bryan queried with a sardonic smile.

"Young kids, anywhere between the ages of six and eleven," Mzali astutely suggested. Alison and I were curious, our attention fixed on Mzali as we waited for him to explain his reasons. He obliged happily.

"Kids of that age will tend to form simple social groups, just as adults are part of more sophisticated social structures. Alliances and rivalries will form, and children, like nations, will compete for resources: the sandbox, the best toys, and the slide."

"I like your analogy," Alison remarked. "The essence of all genius is to be able to simplify the complex."

I looked at her and thought that in her case it was probably true. I knew that Alison had the ability to make complex theories seem easy. By now the drinks and the dollars had been flowing relentlessly, and we were all starting to feel a little drowsy.

"I have found this absolutely fascinating," said Alison drily, "but I'm afraid that I need to get to bed. I hardly slept last night. Bruce kept me up all night."

"What you mean is, you kept me up all night," I corrected her, laughing.

Alison enjoyed the double entendre. "If only that were true, but there were far too many lapses."

It had been an interesting and entertaining evening and I had certainly enjoyed the conversation. We may not have solved the problems of the world, but at least we had identified some of them!

Before we left, I pulled Mzali aside and told him that Alison and I wanted to go out to Kataza the next morning. I asked him if he would like to join us. He was delighted but concerned.

"Hau," he responded predictably, "it has been so long since I've seen Kataza. I would love to see it again. But I must warn you, Kataza is not the same place that you remember. The farm is no longer functional, and its new owners are not nice people. If they see you on the farm they will be very angry. You cannot go to the farmhouse. If you want to visit Kataza they must not know that you are there. I'm sorry."

As we were preparing to leave, Alison asked Mzali a random question. "I know this it is impertinent of me, Mzali, but have you ever been married?"

Mzali took some time to answer and I noticed his eyes glaze with tears for a brief moment.

"I was once," he told her sadly, "But not any longer."

"Why?" asked Alison innocently. Mzali did not answer Alison directly. Instead, he focused his gaze on me.

"After the Entumbane uprising, Mugabe wanted to punish us Matabele," Mzali spoke softly, choosing his words carefully. I could see that he was trying to control his emotions. "He organized a campaign called Gukurahundi. His notorious Fifth Brigade was trained by the North Koreans and led by Comrade Shire, a man so vile that he made vultures vomit. For a year and a half, he waged war against us, against an unarmed civilian population, killing men, women, and children.

"I had a wife, Lucy, and I had a little daughter, Busisiwe. She was only five years old. I was teaching at Esibomvu at the time, and Lucy and Busisiwe were staying at Filabusi. The Fifth Brigade arrived in the afternoon and they killed the entire village, including my wife and my little girl."

There were no tears now, too much time had passed and too many tears had been shed, but it was obvious that Mzali was still distraught by the memory of his wife and child's deaths. The United Nations had condemned the campaign as genocide. Up to thirty thousand innocent people were killed because of their ethnicity—and this from a man who had claimed he was fighting to get rid of racism. African leaders either ignored it or applauded it: after all, Mugabe was an international hero, a liberation icon, and these Matabele mothers were rebels. The Western democracies simply ignored the mayhem with profound indifference.

There was nothing I could do to console Mzali apart from allowing him to seek solace in silence. The three of us sat quietly until Mzali broke the silence and asked if anyone wanted another drink.

"I know that words cannot bring any comfort, Mzali," I apologized, "but I am very sorry. The Fifth Brigade committed horrible atrocities, I've seen it with my own eyes…"

CHAPTER 24
CUTBACK:
DECEMBER, 1983: KATAZA

The ripe smell of fresh cattle dung infused the air and I loved it! Some of the city slickers I knew expressed disgust when I admitted to liking the smell, but it was earthy and clean and reminded me of home. And cow dung was a useful commodity: it was used as flooring, and dried cowpats burned like peat. Dad and I were together in the bush, each with a hiking stick in case we startled a snake, and I was using mine to push back some branchlets obstructing me. We were both laughing, I cannot remember why, when our talented cook Fasika's panic-stricken voice caught our attention.

"Boss Ian, Boss Bruce, come quickly."

"What is it, Fasika?" asked Dad, studiously avoiding stepping into a cowpat.

"I have just received a phone call for Edward. It was from his wife living in his home on the communal lands near Gwanda. She has been badly hurt and Edward needs to get to her quickly. Please, will you help?" said Fasika as he reached us, gasping for breath. Edward was the gardener and had worked on Kataza since before I was born; he was virtually family.

"Of course we will. What happened to her?"

"I don't know. I handed the phone to Edward and he is very, very anxious, but will say nothing except that she is hurt and needs help. Something has also happened to his son, but she won't say what."

When Dad and I got back to the homestead, Edward was sitting in a chair on the veranda as the tears flowed down his face. He was so upset that he could hardly speak and needed to be helped to the Land Rover. Leaving Fasika to look after matters while we were away, we sped off toward Gwanda, about sixty kilometers south. Gwanda was a bustling little town, but Edward's home was in the little village of Gwakwe, approximately twelve kilometers west of it.

Edward hardly spoke as we hurtled closer and closer to the communal lands. What little we managed to glean from him was disturbing. Edward knew very little about what had happened but

126

apparently, the notorious Fifth Brigade had paid a visit to his little village. The Fifth Brigade had been formed for the express purpose of punishing the Matabele for having challenged Mugabe in the Entumbane uprising. It was composed entirely of members from the Shona, the traditional enemies of the Matabele, and sought to reinforce the notion that the Matabele were inferior and subservient to their new Shona overlords. The Fifth Brigade was led by Comrade Shire, a despicable excuse for a human being, and had been trained by the North Koreans.

About five kilometers before reaching Gwanda, we were stopped at a police roadblock. These policemen were heavily armed and were all sporting AK-47s. One of the policemen ordered all of us to step outside of the vehicle and we were body searched. Something serious must have happened at Gwanda. The policeman then ordered us to produce our identification documents. Luckily my passport was in the glove compartment, but the policeman nearly had a hernia when he saw that I was a South African citizen—as I always have been. Only recently a couple of ex-Rhodesian soldiers, now serving in the South African Defense Force, had been shot and killed near the border, so tensions were high.

"You're a South African spy! I am going to arrest you," he shouted, shoving me against the Land Rover. I suppose I must have looked the part: I was young, tanned, fit, lean and well muscled, and I had a crew cut.

Dad intervened, alarmed that things were getting out of control. "This is my son Bruce. He is a university student from the University of Cape Town, and he is home for the holidays. We have a farm near Esigodini. Please radio the police at Esigodini; they know Bruce and will tell you that Bruce is just a student."

The policeman glared at me suspiciously, but he called the police in Esigodini. They must have reassured him because he calmed down somewhat but still wanted to know why we were heading toward Gwanda. We told him that we were simply passing through Gwanda on our way farther south. He seemed to accept our explanation and allowed us to move on. By now we were all hypercautious, fearing what we would find at Gwakwe village.

Almost a kilometer south of Gwanda, Edward directed us to turn to the right onto a small track. It was almost impossible to drive along the track as it was bestrewn with large rocks and small weathered valleys had been cut into the ground from countless rainstorms; we had to inch our way forward. Our first indication of trouble ahead was the inordinate number of crows perching in the acacia trees; crows are carrion birds and enjoy feasting on meat. Then there was the fact that the sky was filled with swirling spirals of vultures, indicating death and lots of it.

About six kilometers from Gwanda, we noticed for the first time the rancid smell of rotting meat. At first, I thought that it must have been a dead animal but then the first of the corpses came into view. The body of a young man had been meticulously arranged so that he appeared to be sitting peacefully on the ground leaning against a rock. He looked perfectly at ease until I noticed the cavity where his stomach had once been. He had been disemboweled and had been dead for some time because his entrails had already been eaten. The stench of putrid flesh was unbearable, assailing the nostrils like a lungful of ammonia. It was repulsive.

With macabre humor, some soulless idiot had raised the corpse's right hand and tied it into place so that he appeared to be waving. The face was partially eaten by predators and the eyes were missing, leaving nothing but vacant sockets. Upon closer inspection, I could see that his foot had been shot off, leaving jagged white bone protruding from his tattered trousers and, where had once been red flesh, there was now green, rotting meat: even the predators would not eat that! But the flies loved it. There were flies all over this poor forgotten man and his leg was seething with them. It was then that I noticed a cardboard sign in his left hand. It was a small sign, written in uncertain letters. It said: '*Pambire* Mugabe. *Pambire* ZANU': 'Long live Mugabe. Long live ZANU'. I glanced at Edward and his face was white with horror, fearing for his wife and son.

A little further down the track were more corpses. This time, two bodies had been deliberately placed on the branches of a small acacia tree. They must have been there for a couple of days at least because the smell was indescribably terrible and they had been feasted on by birds. It was obvious that these bodies had been positioned along the track as a visual message to the local people not to ever challenge the government and as a statement of the government's omnipotence.

The rest of the journey to Gwakwe was harrowing; we passed several more corpses and had hardly a breath of fresh air, so pervasive was the stench of death. None of us said much, except the occasional incredulous mutter of "Oh my God," or "I can't believe this." There were no words to express the horror, disgust, and contempt that Dad and I felt. It must have been much, much worse for Edward.

When finally we reached the little village of Gwakwe it was as though we were entering an apocalyptic vision of hell. Mangy and skittish dogs slunk nervously from hut to hut, obviously severely traumatized. This was a large village of nearly a thousand homes, yet it appeared to be deserted. Still the stench of death persisted; there were rotting bodies close by. Some of the homes had been razed to the ground, leaving nothing but smoldering embers. All the remaining homes were pockmarked with bullet holes.

"Where is your house, Edward?" Dad asked. Edward pointed ahead. His home was a relatively large three-bedroom house which he had built himself on the other side of the village.

We found his wife, Lilith, in the living room, sitting stiffly on the sofa without moving. She hardly acknowledged our presence, besides glancing in our direction. Dad and I allowed Edward and Lilith their privacy, and we went outside to allow them to talk. Dad and I walked along the solitary dirt road that split the village into two halves and, as we walked toward the end of the road, the abhorrent smell of death and decay grew stronger and stronger.

Some two hundred meters beyond the last house, we came across a nightmarish sight: scattered randomly around a clearing which had been a rubbish pit were dozens of mutilated bodies in various stages of decomposition. They were all male, ranging from small children to old men. Litter covered many of the corpses while plastic bags and bottles vied with bodies for the attention of the flies. They were swarming implacably around this death pit. The humming sound of countless flies was the funeral dirge for these invisible victims of barbarism. In one instance a corpse, apart from the others, had been picked clean by ants and vultures and the bones were bleached chalk-white by the sun. My mind was numb with shock and disbelief. Dad and I did not linger long; we needed to get away from the carnage. We were both silent, speechless as we struggled to comprehend the senseless suffering and slaughter; words were redundant because we were sharing the disgusting experience and thinking the same thoughts. I could barely imagine the grisly barbarity that had transpired here and feared for Lilith.

Ashen faced, we walked away from the clearing and as we left, I felt acidic bile rising in my throat and blood-red thoughts. I was as angry as a harried hornet. At that moment, I could happily have killed the perpetrators of this crime. Worse still, I could probably have tortured them to death: no pain was excruciating enough, and no dying long enough for these filth. When we arrived back at Edward's house he was still with Lilith in the sitting room, and tears were pouring from his eyes as he sobbed uncontrollably. He looked up at Dad, his eyes pleading for help.

"My son, my little Petrus, is dead. They killed him. They stabbed him. What did he do wrong? He was a good boy, and now he is gone forever."

"Bruce, please make us all some tea," Dad instructed me, wanting time alone with Edward and Lilith. Obediently, I went through to the kitchen and made some tea, taking my time to do so. When I returned to the living room I poured us all a strong cup of black Darjeeling. No one was interested in the tea though. Dad grasped Edward gently by the hand and pulled him to his feet.

"Come with me, Edward," said Dad soothingly. "Let's talk outside."

Dad and Edward moved out into the yard. Dad's voice was hushed and compassionate, while Edward's was charged with emotion as he railed against the injustice and brutality that had been meted out to Petrus and to Lilith. Every now and again his voice would break, and I would hear him sobbing. I tried to console Lilith, but did not yet know what had happened to her and was of little use. Any words that I spoke would be trite, meaningless and condescending. Instead, I put my arm around her and pulled her close to my chest. At first, she was rigid with suspicion, but after a few minutes she relaxed, wrapped her arms around my chest, and cried.

The journey back to Kataza was thoroughly unpleasant as no one had anything to say: we were all mute with emotion, locked in our own private thoughts. Dad drove Edward and Lilith to the workers' village and helped them to Edward's house. The entire community greeted us when we got there and rallied around Edward and Lilith, providing what comfort they could. Neither Edward nor Lilith ever returned to Gwakwe.

Back at the homestead Dad and I poured ourselves a beer and sat on the veranda. Somehow the world was not as pleasant a place as it had been that morning: it was tainted and tarnished.

"What exactly did Edward tell you?" I asked Dad.

He took a deep breath. "Apparently, a detachment of the Fifth Brigade drove into the village four days ago. The little village was going about its daily business when these bastards rounded up the entire community. They separated the men from the women, making the women watch as they simply opened fire on the men. The Fifth Brigade was shouting threats, '*bulala upapa, bulala gundwane*: kill the flies, kill the rats,' as they mowed the men down like animals. They simply butchered these innocent, harmless people. Some of the men tried to run away, but they were bayoneted to death. That was the fate of young Petrus, barely eight years old and hardly capable of comprehending what was happening. Lilith witnessed the death of her own son. As they bayoneted him, the fifth brigade was screaming, '*gufa, gufa*': 'die, die.' Lilith was powerless to help him.

"By now all the women were petrified. One or two of them tried to run away, but they too were shot. Having slaughtered the men, these "indomitable warriors" systematically raped the women. All the women, except the very old and the very young, were repeatedly raped in the street. Young innocent girls, still playing with their dolls, were raped."

By now Dad's voice was starting to quiver with emotion as he struggled to suppress his anger. He stood up and walked into the garden to calm down and, for the only time in my life, I saw Dad crying. He stood with his hands on his hips as the tears flowed, and then he went and sat on the grass beneath a tree with his back to me. I could see him breathing deeply as he lit a cigarette and stared into the wilderness, trying to regain his composure. It was at least four cigarettes later that Dad returned to the veranda.

"I'm sorry Bruce," he apologized. "I don't know what came over me; this whole incident has gotten to me."

"Don't apologize. I feel it too, and I don't know the full story yet. Would you like another beer?"

"No thanks. I could do with a stiff Jack and ginger: a little more Jack and a little less ginger than usual, please."

When I returned with our liquid fortifications we sat in silence until Dad was ready to continue.

"Poor Lilith was raped over and over again—as were many of the women. When the scum had finished their 'duties' they took some of the bodies with them so that they could place them along the road, like billboards to advertise their power. When these 'men' left, Lilith found her son and carried him into the bush to bury him. Then she and some of the other women made their way to the clinic at the Mtshabezi Lutheran Mission, about four kilometers away from Gwanda. The clinic became a temporary refugee camp for dozens of traumatized and brutalized women, all needing medical assistance. The Lutheran Brothers looked after Lilith and the other women for three days, but Lilith was unable to make phone calls or communicate with the outside world, which is why it took so long for Edward to get the tragic news."

"I'm shocked," I admitted. "I knew that something terrible must have happened to Lilith, but this is simply disgusting. Both she and Edward will need a lot of care and help. How does anyone cope with something so tragic and so personal?"

"What's worse, Bruce, is that Lilith blames herself. She has been violated, victimized, and abused beyond belief, yet she is filled with shame and remorse. She is ashamed of being raped and will not talk about it, as though she has done something wrong. She feels that she has lost her humanity and has been permanently defiled. For the rest of her life, she will blame herself for having been raped, and she will live with the images of her son's death indelibly imprinted on her mind. She will never recover: at best the damage may be managed, and she can resume some semblance of a normal life, but she is forever changed. So is Edward."

Rape is the most heinous of all crimes; it is a violation of the soul, of the inner self, and the wounds never heal completely. There is no emollient for the damage done. Rape is not an act of lust; it is an act of violence, attacking the very core of the victim's identity. In recent years, the United Nations has declared the institutionalized rape of women because of their race or ethnicity is a calculated attempt to dilute the ethnic gene pool and is therefore attempted genocide. Dad and I bore witness to that fact.

Sitting on the veranda, shocked by what we had seen that day, Dad and I were desperately trying to make sense of a world turned upside down. All that we knew and trusted had been thrown into doubt. Even during the war, there was at least an understanding of what was driving people to fight and to kill, but this senseless massacre was like stepping into another reality where nothing made any sense and all logic was irrelevant.

"I can't understand the depths of depravity that some people are capable of stooping to. It's like swimming in a sewer. How can anyone get any satisfaction from killing defenseless people? How can anyone justify these actions?" I asked, dumbfounded. "I really cannot understand it."

"Neither can I, Bruce," Dad reassured me. "There are times when my faith in humanity is sorely tested. There are times when I believe that humanity is a disease, destroying nature and all that is good. These cowardly people are missing something vital in their character. In a way, they are to be pitied: they have no soul."

"I'm afraid I will never feel pity for cowards who can do what we saw at Gwakwe. There are monsters amongst us: more than we imagine" I dolefully discerned.

"These despicable creatures are committing genocide, wiping out entire communities simply because of tribal enmities and hatred. What makes it easier for them to commit these atrocities is the fact that they have been indoctrinated to think of their enemies as vermin, polluting society. It becomes much easier to eradicate people when you stop thinking of them as human beings—as blood, bone, and brawn—and to start thinking of them as an infestation. When people are brainwashed to abstract other people, to dehumanize and deconstruct them, portraying them as 'flies' or 'rats', then they are performing a useful, sanitary service by ridding the world of something noxious. Throughout time, people have always found a way to rationalize the most barbaric and inhumane acts, while preserving a sense of righteous indignation and moral superiority. Humankind's capacity to fool itself is virtually unlimited." Dad's uncharacteristically cynical words resonated with me.

"When too much power is concentrated in the hands of too few people the temptation to abuse it is too seductive." I mourned quietly.

"Well said, Bruce," Dad congratulated me without enthusiasm. "There is an old Cherokee legend that claims there are two wolves fighting for dominance within the spirit of every person: the white wolf and the black wolf; the wolf of purity, love, and compassion, and the wolf of evil, hate, and destruction. The question is asked: 'Which wolf will triumph?' The answer is: 'That wolf which is fed the most'."

Dad looked at me intently, his sorrowful eyes moist with sincerity. "Feed the white wolf."

CHAPTER 25

Colleen Noble had always felt like an outsider. Beautiful and ambitious, she had always been driven by money. Possibly it was because she had no real friends and no permanent attachments, nor had she ever. Or possibly it was because she was one of the few mixed race people in Bulawayo. The biracial community was a community apart—lacking a defined identity—neither Black nor white.

Single, still, at the age of forty, Colleen had never experienced the joy of truly caring for another person or of having that love reciprocated. She had no children and had no responsibilities to anyone but herself. She was a survivor, as was her lover and patron, for whom she now waited impatiently. He had warned her that he might be late, saying he had an important meeting to attend. As the minutes dragged by, her trepidation built. If the meeting had gone well, she would be treated like royalty; if the meeting had gone badly, she would be treated like dirt. Life with him was a lottery. And, as she bolstered her spirits with another gin and tonic, she noticed his shiny black BMW roar into the driveway. She quickly fortified her nerves by gulping what remained of her drink. He burst into the room triumphantly, beaming from ear to ear.

"Hello *sithandwa sami*," he exhorted. Relief washed through her: it was very seldom that he called her darling. The meeting must have gone well!

"Gumede," she exulted, "How good to see you. How did your meeting go?"

"As I anticipated. Our future is looking very bright. In fact, the future is so bright that soon the entire country will be at my feet," he confided. "Tonight, we celebrate!"

"What about your wife? Surely they will be expecting you home soon?"

"My wife can wait. She thinks that I am still in a meeting. Besides which, I do not owe her an explanation. Please do not trouble me with thoughts of her: she is inconsequential."

"Can I get you something to drink?" Colleen asked, hoping that tonight she would be taken to a fine restaurant and have the opportunity to display her jewelry.

"Yes, please," Gumede replied, as he deposited himself into the luxury Italian settee.

Colleen returned with Gumede's whiskey and sat down on the settee beside him, the dutiful mistress. Theirs was a relationship based on mutual need and devoid of love or affection. As she sat there, patiently waiting for him to initiate conversation, he marveled at her beauty. What a wonderful trinket she was! Glowing with self-satisfaction, he admired his possession. Colleen was an exotic, heady blend of East Asian, Bantu, and European genes: her almond-shaped eyes, high cheekbones, and perfectly formed, full lips betrayed her East Asian lineage. Her hazel eyes were offset by flawless satin skin and a glossy mane of raven-black hair. She was a living, breathing aphrodisiac!

Colleen recognized the growing signs and now knew exactly how Gumede intended to celebrate. A shiver of fear coursed through her veins. How desperately she loathed this man, and how deeply she loathed herself for needing him. Still, every dog will have his day, and she was using him as much as he was using her—and use her he often did. One day she would be free of him and he would pay a price for the way he treated her. For now, it was expedient to tolerate him, but she had grown tired of being treated like a whore even though she felt like one.

Gumede had been generous to her, helping to finance her computer business and her lavish lifestyle, but he had made it abundantly clear to her that she was indebted to him and that there were virtually no limits to what he would demand of her as payment. For his part, he admired her pliant morality and her flexible body. Colleen was the outlet for his pent-up anger: she was a necessary tool and would allow him to do things to her that his wife would neither understand nor tolerate. Together they were perfect for each other—the sadist and the masochist—and their carnal activities were violent and tempestuous.

"I think it is time for you to model that lace underwear that I love so much," Gumede said lewdly.

"Why don't we sit and talk for a little while longer?" Colleen responded blandly, trying to delay the inevitable.

"I would prefer some horizontal conversation," Gumede growled ominously.

Assuming Colleen's approval, but not really caring, Gumede gripped her wrist and dragged her through to the bedroom where he pushed her onto the bed. Lying supine and inviting, she slowly and provocatively undressed for his viewing pleasure, secretly cursing every passing moment. As she lay naked and exposed before him, he marveled at the seductive swell of her pert breasts, her lean muscled legs, her perfumed skin, her carefully groomed pubic hair, and her blue butterfly tattoo. He was going to enjoy himself tonight; he could not wait to ravage her loins.

Colleen gazed up at Gumede, strangely aroused by the anticipation of his 'celebration', yet fearful of its consequences. She knew from past experiences that afterward, she would lie exhausted on the bed, listening forlornly to Gumede drive away, as she nursed her tender and battered body. That she would be consumed with self-loathing for having endured his depravity, and guilt for having enjoyed it. She knew that her own desires were inconsequential to him—that she meant nothing to him—and she consoled herself with the rather pleasing thought that she would exact her revenge. She had a copy of his precious hard drive!

CHAPTER 26

Alison, Bryan, and I met Mzali in Esigodini shortly after 10 o'clock in the morning. He was sitting waiting for us in the Queen Bee restaurant. We had all chosen similar gear: khaki shorts, loose-fitting flannel shirts, and hiking boots. Earlier in the morning, I had packed sandwiches and fruit juice in a picnic hamper, and we had two thermos flasks full of coffee. Always organized, Alison had gone to Lancaster's Pharmacy and bought medical supplies: plasters, mercurochrome, antihistamine cream, and such. She wanted to be prepared for any contingency. I had done some planning of my own and had brought spades, trowels, and canvas bags.

I thought it prudent to approach Kataza from the north rather than its southern entrance, so I decided to use a back route. We drove past the Coulson's old farm and I wondered what had happened to them and where big Alistair was now. We turned left onto the old Bushtick road, driving past Colin Martin's old farm Ponderosa. He had probably been a fan of the old television series Bonanza. The road grew progressively worse. It had obviously not seen a grader in years. I was thankful for the fact that I had rented a 4x4 Toyota Land Cruiser.

Eventually, we reached the northern extremity of Kataza. Three Fingers kopje pointed imperiously to the sky about two kilometers in front of us. Even though this was mildly unfamiliar territory to me, I still felt like a prodigal son returning home. I was elated. Driving parallel to the old boundary fence, we came to a rusty gate and turned toward it. Mzali opened the gate for us, and I drove through it and stopped the vehicle. Alison and I both got out of the car, and I bent down and kissed the ground: Kataza.

"Home at last, home at last, thank God Almighty, home at last," I recited. Alison could see that I was overjoyed to be back. She put her arm around me.

"So, this is Kataza," she said admiringly. "This countryside is absolutely beautiful."

I think there were tears in my eyes, but I cannot remember. We drove along the stony track for another ten minutes or so, edging closer and closer to Three Fingers kopje until the track petered out and we could go no farther. The bush here was dense, but I felt comfortable in it, inhaling the familiar herbal aroma. We gathered our kits and started navigating toward Three Fingers kopje. Every now and again Mzali, Alison, and I

ANDY STEWART

would need to wait for Bryan. Every plant, rock, and insect aroused his
curiosity. I started singing the old Clint Eastwood song: "I talk to the
trees, but they won't listen to me." Alison and Mzali laughed. We had
all grown fond of Bryan's idiosyncrasies.

It took us the better part of half an hour to finally reach Three
Fingers. I had only been there once or twice in the past; it was simply
too far from the homestead. It was even larger than I remembered it—
massive and majestic. We found a clearing on the northern side of the
kopje, so that the kopje lay between us and the old homestead, shielding
us from prying eyes. The four of us sat down beneath the shade of an
old rhus tree, enjoying our surroundings and a cup of coffee. We sat for
another ten minutes or so, and then negotiated our way through the
boulders and the bush toward where I remembered the walling to have
been. I did not know how familiar Alison or Bryan was with the bush,
so I gave them a friendly warning.

"Guys, just remember to keep your eyes open. This place is alive
with snakes, scorpions, and spiders. Be particularly watchful for cobras
and puff adders. Also, remember that this place gets the occasional
itinerant leopard, and there could well be baboons about. If you see
anything dangerous, do not run. Stand dead still and give Mzali or me
a missed call on the cell phone."

I made sure that we all had each other's cell numbers, and that we
had reception, which we did. On that cheerful note, we scurried and
stumbled around looking for the old wall. Predictably, it was Mzali who
found it. It was hardly perceptible, it was so overgrown with bushes.
We all reconnoitered, pacing from one extremity to the other, to
familiarize ourselves with it. The visible portion of masonry was about
a hundred meters long. I was looking for any sign that the earth or the
rocks had been disturbed, forlornly hoping to discover where Thabani
and Senzo may have been digging. I was to be disappointed; it had been
too long ago.

I did not know where to start, so we mentally divided the wall into
four sections and each of us was allocated a portion. We started
excavating the ground in our sections. By now it was about 12 o'clock,
and the strenuous activity meant that we were all sweating profusely. It
was about 35° Celsius and the air was dry. After about half an hour of
unrewarding scouring and digging, we sat together and ate some
sandwiches. I felt despondent: I had thought that we would simply
arrive at the site and find a treasure trove of trinkets neatly stacked in a
pile waiting for us. This was going to be hard work.

Alison was impressed with the walls, even though they were only a
couple of feet high: "Look at how wide these ruins once were," she

138

exclaimed. "This wall must be two meters wide. That means that the height of the building must have been quite impressive."

"What I would like to do," I informed her, "is to try to get some idea of what this must have looked like in its heyday. I think we should climb up the kopje and look at this from above imagining where this wall would once have gone. I'm pretty sure that the tablet was not found here."

Alison looked up at the precipitous kopje. "That is one hell of a climb," she stated factually, with a hint of trepidation in her voice.

"It is, isn't it," I enthused. "Come on, you will enjoy this."

Halfway up the kopje, we found a suitable rock to perch on and we admired our wounds. Both Alison and I were covered with scratches from all the bushes, branches, and deadwood. We looked down on Mzali and Bryan waiting at the bottom. They appeared minuscule from this height, two little ants scratching at the earth. The view was stunning.

I clutched Alison's hand. "Let's go around to the other side of the kopje. From there we will be able to see my old home."

Another fifteen minutes of scrambling up and around rocks and we were seated on an exposed slab of granite. In the distance, we could just discern the faded green roof of the old homestead. Surveying my domain, I felt like the king of the castle. Kneeling gracefully in front of me was my loyal subject, Kataza. From this giddy height I felt all-powerful and serene, yet at the same time, I felt humble and insignificant: a confusing cocktail of emotions. I was swimming in the grandeur of Kataza and absorbing the ambient energy.

"Isn't this wonderful?" I asked Alison rhetorically. "There's something else I would like to show you if I can only remember where it is," I said, searching the recesses of my memory.

"Take my hand," I told her as I stood up. Together we clambered a little further around the kopje until we came to a little rock wall and there it was!

"I'm so glad that I remembered where it was," I exclaimed as I pointed to a beautiful Khoisan painting. Alison was mesmerized.

"This is amazing," she remarked, examining a small painting of an eland being hunted by three men. The eland was depicted in ochre and the men in ox-blood red. If you looked long enough, they appeared to move.

"Whatever happened to these people?" Alison asked.

"They were eventually pushed away and out of this land," I said. "As the Bantu migrated south, the Khoisan people were driven out and now the remnants of the Khoisan remain in the Kalahari Desert, hunting in just the same way as in this painting." We admired the painting a moment longer, before returning to the apex of the kopje for one more glimpse of Kataza.

"I think that this must be one of the most wonderful moments of my life," Alison whispered respectfully.

We sat together, holding hands. Neither of us spoke, not wanting the moment to end. But it had to end. After about ten minutes, when we had paid our respects, we went back to the other side of the kopje trying to speculate where the wall may have led. We surveyed the landscape, scrutinizing every detail of the topography.

"Remember, all of these ancient ruins were built to a circular design," I told Alison.

"If we look at the curve of the wall and then extrapolate, it would have extended toward that little granite outcrop."

I pointed to a small kopje in the distance. "It would have flowed away from that, and then connected with that slightly larger group of rocks over there," I speculated, realizing that it would have been a fairly large enclosure.

We both made a mental note of the trees and rocks that lay close to where we thought the ancient wall would have run. Clambering down the kopje was as hard as climbing up it had been. Often our feet would slip on the loose earth and rocks, and it was hard to maintain our balance. There were times when we were almost horizontal, resting on our hands, sliding feet first down portions of the kopje. When we had landed at the bottom, we found Mzali and Bryan, describing to them where we believed the old wall would have been.

We all traversed toward the small rocky outcrop of granite, noticing here and there flat square slabs of granite that could well have been from an ancient wall. There was a small, misshapen tree at the top of the outcrop, tenaciously gripping the rock: a sentinel surveying the scenery. We explored every inch of the ground but could see no evidence of any digging. I saw a discolored rock and picked it up—an orange and black centipede rowed frantically away. We reached the small outcrop but, once again, there was no evidence of any walling. By this point, it was about 3 o'clock in the afternoon and I think that we were all feeling disheartened, bereft of hope.

"Why don't we come back tomorrow?" I suggested.

"I think that's a great idea," said Alison. "I think I need a bath and a bandage."

"I'm willing to come back every day for as long as it takes," Mzali promised. "If those little boys found something here, then there must be something else waiting to be found. We just need to explore a little more. We have obviously looked in the wrong places but the right place is close by."

With those encouraging words, we packed up and made our way back to the vehicle. I enjoyed the trip back to Bulawayo. I felt satisfied and content having seen Kataza again.

CHAPTER 27

Donald Swanson was one of the few men who actively intimidated Gumede. Tall and well muscled, he was fastidiously dressed, yet without affectation. He had an aura of power and an easy self-confidence. He treated Gumede with a patronizing tolerance that verged on humor. As they sat together, alone in the dimly lit comfort of a private lounge in the Churchill Arms hotel, it was Gumede who looked ill at ease as Swanson reclined comfortably in a leather armchair, brandishing a Cognac in his left hand and a Cuban cigar in his right.

"Tell me, my friend, how are your plans progressing?" Swanson spoke softly, his sonorous voice a gravelly baritone with a distinctly American accent.

"We are almost ready to take control. Only a few minor details still need to be taken care of," Gumede responded subserviently.

"What details? Tell me about this plan of yours, so that I can be very careful to distance myself from them, and whatever incendiary event you have planned," Swanson insisted with calculated indifference.

"We had originally planned to explode a bomb at Harare Stadium where Mugabe is scheduled to deliver a speech next month. But the security is too tight, and then I was invited to attend the speech myself."

"It would be very inconvenient for you and your plans to be president were you to be blown to bits," Swanson commented dryly, the hint of a smile on his face. "So, what do you plan to do?"

"In a few days' time, Mugabe will attend a rally near Lomagundi, northwest of Harare. The stadium there is very small and sound equipment will need to be transported from Harare and installed on-site. The plan is to fill the speakers with explosives and ball bearings."

"Making a gigantic claymore mine," Swanson mused. "I like it. It could work … and, of course, it will make a very clear statement. How do you intend to get the speakers through security?"

"The security is complacent and the equipment is very seldom checked. The speakers themselves will appear untouched and operate normally. Security would have to open them up to discover the bombs and they are very unlikely to do that. The bombs themselves will be detonated by a remotely controlled radio," Gumede explained, desperate for approval.

"Do you trust the people who will be making these bombs? How loyal are they to you? What is preventing them from reporting you to the authorities?"

"I trust them implicitly. As you know, I have created a network of loyal functionaries who cannot afford for me to fail; it would mean the end of their careers and possibly their lives. A police captain, loyal to me, has been tasked with the job of getting the bombs in place. He, or one of his intermediaries, has approached one of the sound engineers and ensured his cooperation by holding his wife and daughter hostage and an explosives expert has already inserted the C4 and ball bearings. Another of my loyal servants has been tasked with providing security for the event, so I am very confident that the sound speakers will not be inspected," Gumede proudly explained.

"You seem confident, but remember this—you have tried before and failed," Swanson stated.

He was referring to an incident some months previously. Grace Mugabe was notorious for firing her chefs. Aware of this, Gumede had arranged for a promising young chef named Gideon to be employed in the Mugabe mansion in the exclusive Harare suburb of Borrowdale. The unfortunate young man had been tasked with poisoning Mugabe and had taken some considerable time to summon up the courage to do so. But he was motivated by the fact that his family was being held hostage and had eventually acquiesced. At the last moment, he had a crisis of conscience, or perhaps he reasoned that his family would be slaughtered anyway, regardless of his actions. The young man confessed to his crime before any damage could be done, and he was sent to languish in Chikurubi prison, lamenting his actions.

"This time I have taken additional precautions," Gumede reassured Swanson. "I have ensured that at least two sound engineers are involved and they both have families. I have also made sure that the seating has been independently compromised. Nothing can go wrong!"

"Well, I hope for your sake that you are right. There is a great deal at stake here, and the people whom I represent will not take kindly to failure," Swanson warned ominously. "How do you intend to take control once Mugabe is eliminated?"

"I have manufactured incriminating evidence proving incontrovertibly that Mugabe's loyal followers were not very loyal and that they planned and executed his assassination. I have the military and the police in my pocket. They are simply waiting to unveil the evidence and arrest anyone of influence who remains loyal to Mugabe. They will be denounced as traitors and I will be hailed as the one man who remained loyal to Mugabe. I will be praised as Mugabe's protégé and friend, the defender of all that he stood for. The people will accept me with open arms," promised Gumede, smugly satisfied with his own duplicity.

"As will the world, my friend. We will have our friendly dictator and the markets will be stable, predictable, and productive; as the economy prospers so will you and your friends," predicted Swanson. "Have you put any thought yet to the legislation that I recommended to you?"

"I have delegated that particular task to a judge on my payroll. As soon as we are in control, the Indigenization Act requiring all companies to be owned by Black citizens will be repealed. Foreign companies will be free to operate in the country unhindered and corporate taxes will be lowered. Foreign companies will be allowed to repatriate the bulk of their profits."

"This all sounds really swell," Swanson drawled, "but this ... intervention ... of yours is public and messy. While it is so simple that it may work, it is also crude and violent. It makes me uneasy: there are too many loose ends." Swanson smiled at Gumede, challenging him to respond. Like a petulant child being scolded, Gumede justified himself.

"I think it is a good plan, but I'm not stupid; if this fails, no one will be able to link it to me." He glared at Swanson defiantly.

Swanson chuckled inwardly, knowing that he was rubbing raw nerves and delighting in teasing this illiterate, violent man who was so adept at manipulating others but so naive in the world of corporate power politics. Swanson responded with tolerant contempt.

"Assuming your little 'nostrum' fails—as I suspect it might—do you have a contingency plan?"

Gumede knew that he was being mocked but could not quite figure out how. He responded with churlish annoyance; Swanson's arrogance was irritating him. He was not used to being subordinate. "My men in the military are ready to act. Their patience is reaching its limit, and they have endured the taunts of Grace Mugabe for too long. She has manipulated her senile husband to promote her own agenda, and she is poised to pounce on the presidency. My men have too much to lose, too many vested interests, to allow her to succeed."

Swanson looked on patiently, waiting for Gumede to get to the point.

"Should my plan fail, the time will come when the military will intervene and stage a coup d'état, entrenching their influence, which is rapidly being diluted by that ambitious woman. They will intervene in the name of democracy, and will gently push Mugabe to one side, using his age and infirmity to excuse his gullibility. Grace will be denounced as a traitor. Our coup d'état will appear as a benign intervention to restore free institutions and prosperity to Zimbabwe. It will be embraced by world opinion and be accompanied by celebrations."

Swanson interjected: "And the people will believe that they are being liberated from captivity. Instead, the ropes will be more tightly wound. I love it! It is so twisted—so very Western."

Gumede grinned, grateful for the approval.

"Tell me, my friend," Swanson continued, "I'm curious. This contingency plan of yours is far more graceful than your preferred plan; why do you persevere with an assassination attempt?"

Gumede paused before answering, grateful to be taken seriously. "My preferred option allows me more personal control and will avoid elections and world scrutiny. It also affords me more leverage to control my puppets when they stand on the podium and preach about justice; it is far more certain in its outcomes. Although the military intervention will be more readily endorsed by the people and by foreign powers, it is riskier as there are too many uncontrollable permutations and my leverage will not be as effective with the military in charge. There is a risk that I will lose control of the situation. Besides which, for all my blackmail, many in the military are still loyal to Mugabe and may balk at deposing him. I prefer to make their choice simple."

Swanson smiled. "I see your point," he acknowledged. "Let me offer you some free advice. When you play with the military you're not playing with a tame animal; you are swimming with crocodiles. When you swim with crocodiles, you're likely to be consumed. Be careful."

Gumede looked contrite, almost apologetic, as he digested Swanson's cautionary words. Swanson had become bored and drew the briefing to an end. "Well then, you seem to have all the bases covered. On behalf of those that I represent, I wish you good luck. It only remains for me to salute you: Hail to the Chief."

CHAPTER 28

We returned to Kataza the next morning, arriving there earlier than the previous day. The countryside was reverberating with the sound of birds, and we noticed a small herd of impala grazing contentedly. It reassured me to know that the game animals were still around. Kataza used to abound with impala, zebra, wildebeest, kudu, and the solitary little duikers. It probably still did. A little surer of our bearings now, we headed directly to the small outcrop with the gnarled and twisted tree keeping guard, protecting its benefactor. It looked like an enormous bonsai, grotesquely beautiful. Wild crinums clung desperately to the crevices in the granite rock, and one of them was in flower, looking remarkably like a dark pink St. Joseph's Lily. All around us were the ubiquitous go-away-birds. We explored all day without any luck. By nightfall, we were hot, sticky, and despondent.

"Maybe we should accept that there is nothing here," Alison speculated. Once again, it was Mzali who refused to give up.

"This is an ancient place. She is not going to surrender her secrets until we have won her trust."

I thought Mzali's metaphor rather appropriate. We needed to keep looking and remain focused and positive. In the spirit of optimism, I made a rash suggestion.

"Alison and I have camping equipment back in Bulawayo. Why don't we camp here and, if we haven't found anything in two days' time, we will reconsider? Even if we do not find anything, we can at least enjoy a little camping trip. After all, Alison and I did plan to go camping."

"I love the idea," Alison said.

"So do I," added Bryan, surveying the distant horizon.

"It's settled then," Mzali announced enthusiastically. "Tomorrow we sleep in the bush."

It had been many years since I had last slept at Kataza and I looked forward to spending a couple of evenings under the clear star-lit night sky.

*****

That evening Bryan, Alison, and I stocked up on supplies. Mzali had told us that he had the requisite gear, but we would need to buy some

146

equipment for Bryan, and that we could only do the next morning. As soon as the shops opened, Alison and I bought a camping bed, sleeping bag, portable lamp, a flashlight, and whatever else we thought was necessary. Alison, bless her, bought Bryan some chocolates and a rose. When I asked why, she smiled.

"So that I can place them on his bed before he turns in; welcome to Hotel Kataza." Now that we were properly prepared, we drove out to Esigodini again to pick up Mzali.

One of the first things that we did when we got back to our familiar spot at Kataza was to erect the tents and establish a proper campsite. This was going to be our home for the next couple of days, and we wanted it to be as comfortable as possible. There were three tents in all, and we positioned them in a triangle, all the doors facing in toward each other. At the center of our campsite, we dug a hole and built a circular wall of rocks around it. This was where the campfire would be. Alison then placed our portable camping chairs around this hole in the ground. Our lodgings looked comfortable and domestic. A short distance away from the campsite, we dug a shallow pit and piled the sand to one side, leaving a spade embedded in it. This was to suffice as our temporary latrine. Once we felt settled, we all made our way back to the walling.

We searched all day but found nothing. At about 4 o'clock, we returned to our campsite. Mzali and I went to collect firewood, and we were careful to collect only dry wood. We did not want to advertise our presence, so we wanted wood that burned with as little smoke as possible. Every now and again Mzali would check the wood that I had collected, and he would throw away the odd couple of branches, admonishing me severely for not having selected the right wood and for having forgotten which timber burned with smoke and which did not. Even now, he was still preparing me for the real world. At last, he was satisfied with the wood that we had collected and we returned to camp triumphant.

We spent a thoroughly pleasant evening huddled around the campfire. Mzali had brought a galvanized iron pot, a witch's cauldron, and we cooked a delicious stew with rice which we followed with bowls of yogurt. There is something hypnotic and magnetic about a fire, drawing you in toward it, and it evinces conversation. We talked for hours, never loudly, and, when there was a lull in the conversation, we listened to the orchestra of the bush surrounding us. We made coffee to which we added healthy measures of brandy, and the conversation seemed just a little more mellow. I noticed Alison sneak into Bryan's tent while he was pouring himself another tipple of coffee. I presumed that she was preparing his bed for him. We washed the dishes and went to bed. Just as Alison and I were crawling into our sleeping bags we heard Bryan call out to no one in particular: "Thank you."

We unraveled ourselves at the first pink blush of dawn. Breakfast was a quiet affair, as we all took time to wake up properly. It was the coffee, more than the scrambled eggs, which I needed. Strangely enough, I felt wide awake. The air seemed cleaner and crisper out here in the bush. I felt healthy, vibrant, and alive, a feeling amplified by the ambient life. Like me, the bush also seemed to be invigorated, with the early morning birds a fountain of feathered activity and the sound of insects announcing their presence was both reassuring and uplifting. I think the others must have felt the same way because everyone seemed to be in the best of spirits. Mzali was his usual hale and hearty self, exhorting us all to get up and get started. Even Bryan seemed unusually focused and refreshed.

We made our way to the site of our excavations and settled into a pleasant rhythm of digging, kneeling down to clear the earth like dogs digging for a bone. Our cheerful bonhomie was gradually diluted by our failure. We became increasingly exasperated and short-tempered and, by about 10 o'clock, we were all thoroughly despondent. How quickly the mood had changed. We all clustered together for a cup of coffee, seeking solace in each other's company.

Sitting next to me on the granite rock, Alison leaned over and whispered in my ear: "I want you to come with me. There is something I would like to show you." We excused ourselves from the company, explaining that we would be back shortly. Alison took my hand in hers and led me back to Three Fingers kopje.

"What is this all about?" I asked Alison.

"Just wait," she said. "I want to take you back to the vantage point we had the other day. Perhaps this is a waste of time, but I want to conduct a little experiment."

We scrambled up the mountainside, constantly wary of snakes and scorpions, until we reached our private retreat. Sitting down, alone with Alison, I felt that I was somehow abandoning Mzali and Bryan who were now back at work, digging furiously and forlornly at the base of the old rocky outcrop. From here, their efforts seemed even more futile than ever because they were so removed from us.

"I think we need to look at this from a completely different perspective," Alison said to me.

"Well, we are certainly in the right place," I replied, admiring the wonderful view.

"We were asking ourselves the wrong question when we were up here last time," Alison informed me. "We were trying to imagine where ancient builders would have built their city and where the old wall led to—which is the obvious question to ask. What we should have been asking is 'where would two young kids want to play?'" Alison pondered.

It was so typical of Alison to think outside of the normal parameters and to want to get a new outlook on the problem.

Alison and I surveyed the countryside below in silence, imagining that we were two little kids playing truant. Perhaps we were, I thought, considering our situation. We scanned from left to right and we both pointed simultaneously to a small kopje, overwhelmed with boulders and vegetation.

"There!" we exalted in unison. The kopje was well removed from where we were searching, but it was redolent with opportunities for exploration and excitement. At its base, there was a confusion of large boulders and it was surrounded by a seemingly impervious lattice of tangled trees and vines. Feeling energized once more, Alison and I slipped and slid to the base of Three Fingers, constantly trying not to overbalance. When we reached Mzali and Bryan, we were both out of breath but our sense of purpose had been renewed. Alison explained to Mzali and Bryan that we needed to look elsewhere, in the distant kopje.

"But it's a waste of time," Bryan protested petulantly.

"Well, we might as well waste our time over there as waste our time over here," Alison rebuked him. Bryan smiled apologetically: point taken.

We trudged across to the little kopje and as we approached, I could see the spirits of Mzali and Bryan visibly lifting. The closer we got, the more obvious it seemed that this would be a wonderful place for kids to play in. I think that it brought out our own inner child because we also wanted to explore and allow our imaginations to run wild. But unlike little kids imagining castles and kings, we were actually looking for signs of an ancient civilization. This kopje was not as small as the outcrop, but it was a great deal smaller than Three Fingers. It was only about forty meters high, but all around were forbidding boulders and trees.

We decided to circumnavigate the kopje so that we could get some idea of where to start looking. One side of the kopje was particularly attractive because it was not too steep, and about halfway up its side there appeared to be a small cave, partially hidden by undergrowth. We were not sure but the black spot, about half the height of a man at the base of a rock, looked as though it might be the entrance to a rock shelter. We scrambled up the side of the kopje in single file with Alison leading the way. I went behind her to catch her or to soften her landing should she fall. Besides, the view was magnificent.

As luck would have it, it was indeed the entrance to a cave and I imagined that it would have been the perfect place to hide from any attackers or intruders. At some point, this had been a leopard's lair, and it was littered with old leopard scat. The pungent, musty smell was particularly prevalent. Chivalrous to the end, I offered to enter first and Alison was visibly relieved. I cautiously and carefully insinuated myself inside the cave, finding that it opened up a little allowing me to stand upright. It was small, about seven paces deep and four paces wide. The others clambered in behind me, and we admired the little retreat.

Alison took command: "Now what we have to do is to try to imagine where someone would hide something that was really important to them," she instructed with authority.

We all looked around, trying to imagine a secret hiding place within this secret hiding place. I gravitated toward the far end of the cave and, kneeling down, started to loosen the earth which appeared to have been packed down. To the left of me, I noticed a spot where the soil seemed looser and I crawled over and resumed my scratching. It did not take long. There was a cavity in the rock and it appeared that a small stone enclave had been deliberately fashioned. But whatever was once here had now gone. I think that I had rediscovered the place where Thabani and Senzo had found their treasure trove.

Mzali grabbed a trowel and began digging frantically into the hard-packed soil around the edge of the back wall. About twenty centimeters down, he struck gold: literally. There was a large 'thunk' as his trowel struck rock. It was a slab of granite that had been carefully placed over another cavity. Inside the cavity lay a wealth of gold bangles.

Encouraged by this, I started digging next to this little trench and, sure enough, there was another trove beside it. Inside this ancient security safe lay three flat rectangular objects, each of them carefully wrapped in what appeared to be tanned leather. The brittle vellum was well-preserved, as though it had been hermetically sealed.

We excavated as much as we could, but we had exhumed all that the cave had to offer: there was no more. Overjoyed with our efforts and our discovery, we sat around the entrance, congratulated one another, and enjoyed a cup of coffee. I suppose a purist would consider our actions as profane vandalism, ransacking a valuable archeological site, but the exigencies of our situation dictated our course.

As we sat on the side of the kopje, the sweat dripping off our brows and our smorgasbord of treasures laid out in front of us, our exhilaration dimmed: we could not help but wonder what events had transpired here so long ago that these few random treasures were buried in a remote and hidden cave, away from the main dwelling. It was most curious. It was Alison who voiced what we were all contemplating.

"Why were these artifacts buried here?" she speculated. "And why are there so few of them?"

"I have no idea," Bryan said. "It's almost as though they were hidden in a hurry, with no foresight or proper planning."

"Perhaps the answer lies in the oral tradition of the Bantu people," Mzali suggested cautiously. "I remember sitting next to the fire at night listening to my grandfather tell me the stories of my ancestors as I listened, transfixed. Those stories echo the tales of Credo Mutwa who claims that when the Bantu migrated south from central Africa, they came upon an evil people below the Zambezi River."

Alison looked at me and smiled, her beautiful blue eyes twinkling: she knew that she and I were both aware of this rendition of history.

"This brown-skinned race from foreign climes enslaved the indigenous Khoisan people and the Bantu, exploiting them mercilessly in their gold and copper mines. These heretics worshipped demons and had no compassion for human life, engaging in human sacrifice. The Bantu people massed against these godless people and destroyed them. All vestiges of their culture were deracinated and no reminder of them was left. Where possible, the walls of their cities were torn down and their culture erased from history and from memory. All that remains of them are hoary tales to frighten children," Mzali concluded philosophically.

Mzali's myth conjured up a mental movie, and I imagined an event from eons ago: a horde of coal-black Bantu warriors, their skin glistening, adorned with ostrich feather headgear and armed with shields of hardened hide, their assegais glinting in the searing sunlight, attacking a poorly defended outpost of Phoenicians. In my mind I saw slaves, both Khoisan and Bantu, rejoicing as their malicious masters were butchered. Amidst this carnage I imagined a man, dressed in robes and adorned with gold jewelry, hastily snatching up whatever he could and sneaking to the cave for refuge from the onslaught. Knowing that death was imminent, either immediately through the blade, or eventually by starvation, this man hastily hid his cargo—all the remaining proof that he had once existed.

While he was hiding, the enraged Bantu army physically tore down the walls of the town and scattered the rocks. They ransacked the records, destroying every vestige of this evil culture. The surviving enemies were killed, slaughtered, and their bellies eviscerated to release the spirits trapped within according to Bantu tradition. I returned from my mental reverie and saw Alison looking at me with a quizzical expression: I must have appeared to have been in a mild trance, so engaged was I with my imaginings. I smiled apologetically and she grinned.

"Welcome back," she said, obviously amused.

I suppose we all had our own private thoughts about how and when these artifacts had been hidden. So much time had passed between then and now that it forced us all to confront our own mortality and to consider how little time we had left to live our lives. It struck me forcefully that life needs to be embraced, without hesitation, because it is ephemeral and can be snuffed out in the blink of an eye. It also occurred to me that our daily concerns are trivial when viewed through the telescope of time. We are all condemned to become ancient history and to be entirely forgotten like dust in the desert.

Returning to camp with our trophies, I felt particularly victorious, perhaps even sanctimonious. I felt that I had somehow vindicated myself and that our journey had all been worthwhile. It may sound melodramatic, but I felt as though I had been on a quest and had somehow found the Holy Grail. I think that Alison may well have felt the same way judging from her satisfied expression. Yet, I felt a sense of responsibility because I had initiated our odyssey all that time ago in Randburg when I had introduced Alison to the clay tablet. I was the progenitor of this adventure and now I felt justified.

We did not allow ourselves the luxury of procrastination or complacency. As soon as we arrived back, Alison sat us all down in our tent and she carefully placed the three leather-bound packages on her camp bed. With infinite care, she gently unfolded the friable leather revealing three immaculately preserved clay tablets, each covered in clear script that looked virtually identical to that on the tablet which Dad had bequeathed to me. Alison was doe-eyed with wonder and amazement while Mzali glared at the tablets, ruminating darkly as though a vestigial ancestral memory had awoken from its slumber, instinctively recognizing the tablets as incredibly ancient and evil.

"Professor," Alison instructed, "you're up. It's time for you to take center stage and strut your stuff." She smiled expectantly. She picked up one of the clay tablets and handed it gently to Bryan.

"What does it say?"

Bryan looked at her with confused indignation. "I have absolutely no idea," he protested. "I cannot read this script. The most I can do is tell you what type of script it is. If you want me to translate it I will need to take it back to my study where I have my books and notes. I need to compare this with other translations and the basic dictionary of the script that has been compiled."

Alison, Mzali, and I were stunned. We looked at him with incredulous incomprehension. It was for this reason that Bryan had been invited to join us and, now that he was needed, he was of no help at all. I was overwhelmed by the absurdity of the situation and started laughing: failure on the brink of success. Alison was a little less amused.

"But Professor, you knew that this is why you were here, to translate the clay tablets if we found any!"

"I thought I was here to tell you whether any artifacts were valuable and if the clay tablets had writing on them or not," Bryan defended himself indignant.

"But we could have invited anyone along to do that!" Alison fumed impulsively, her bile rising. "In fact, we didn't need anyone at all to do that. Bruce or I could have done that."

Bryan was obviously hurt and rejected, and I did not want him to feel that he was not wanted.

"Come on, Professor. How valuable are these gold bangles and these clay tablets?" I invited him to exercise his expertise, offering him the opportunity to redeem himself.

"They are valuable," he said with intensity, grasping his opportunity gratefully. "I think that the clay tablets in particular could rewrite history."

I was not convinced that they were as important as that but did not want to argue the point as Bryan needed his pride.

"I think that we should store these valuables in the car," Alison said with feigned optimism. "We need to keep them safe."

I think she needed a little space of her own in order to calm down. After all, this was still a productive and happy day. Alison and I packed the clay tablets into an old, large biscuit tin and wrapped the gold bangles in a pillowcase. We carefully placed the treasures into our rucksacks and walked silently to the Land Cruiser which was parked a little distance from the campsite underneath a magnificent old tree that protected it from the sunlight.

"I'm so sorry," Alison apologized. "I really didn't mean to put a damper on the day. It's been absolutely wonderful; it's just that I am incredibly disappointed in Bryan. It would have been the icing on the cake to have been able to read what is on the tablets."

I gave her a consoling hug. "Don't worry. I still love you. I quite agree with you. I was also hoping that Bryan would be able to read the tablets, but it does not really matter. Perhaps the suspense will be good for us. We have something to look forward to: another mystery to solve!"

Alison stopped walking, placed herself squarely in front of me, looked me steadily in the eye, and gave me a long hard hug: "I adore you." At that moment I was quite convinced that this was the best day that I had ever lived.

The sun was already beginning to set, and what a magnificent sunset it was: blazing saffron, gold, and orange. The sunsets at Kataza had always been glorious, perhaps because of the dust in the air, Dad and I had often speculated. The mood in the camp was buoyant and we cooked steaks and potatoes wrapped in tinfoil on the grill; we were particularly generous with the brandy in our coffee afterward. When there was a lull in the conversation, I stood up to replenish Alison's drink.

"I think I would like a particularly stiff one," she insinuated. I poured her another drink and the two of us disappeared into the tent to celebrate: very tenderly and quietly.

CHAPTER 29

We woke at the first flush of sunrise, the euphonic sound of birds cajoling us to action. When Alison and I emerged from the tent, we found that both Mzali and Bryan were already awake and had started cooking breakfast.

"Hau, it's good of you to join us. What kept you up so late?" Mzali asked seriously; then he started laughing.

"I must apologize," Mzali said to me, "You're not old, you only look old. You two are like teenagers when you get together."

"I hope that teenagers don't do what we do!" I joked.

"Seriously Mziki, this is a good woman. Alison is good for you, and you must hold on to her."

"I know Mzali. I'm not going to leave her; I only hope that she will stay with me. I don't want her to get bored with me," I responded fearfully, my anxiety revealed.

"Why would she get bored?" Mzali asked.

"My life as a teacher is deadly dull," I answered truthfully.

"It probably is," Mzali told me, "but remember, she is also a teacher and her life is probably just as boring in her eyes. Together you must create your own excitement and, if you care for her and show interest in her, you will stay together." I was grateful for his wise and reassuring words.

We sat down and ate a hearty breakfast of bacon and scrambled eggs, which we washed down with strong, sweet coffee.

Now that we had accomplished what we had set out to do, I felt it incumbent upon me to at least try to say hello to some of the old workers who had been so good to me. I wanted to see how they were, how many of them were still working at Kataza, and I felt a sense of obligation not just toward them, but to Dad as well. He would have been disappointed had I not inquired after them. In a sense, it was a filial duty. Quite frankly, I would have been disappointed in myself if I had not tried to see them: after all, I loved these people and was concerned for their well-being. I was also concerned for the well-being of Alison and did not want to attract unwelcome attention, placing her in jeopardy.

"Alison honey," I said to her, "I really want to see if some of the old staff are still here and, if so, how they are doing. Do you mind if Mzali and I sneak across to the old living quarters? It will take us a fair while to get there, but I would hate to leave Kataza and not know."

"You must go," she said compassionately. "But I would really like to come with you. I would love to meet some more of the people who you grew up with. I'm sure to hear some embarrassing stories about you as a child." Her glee was undisguised.

"I'm sorry," I said regretfully. "It is simply too risky. I'm not convinced that I should be doing this at all, for fear of placing you and Bryan in danger. If Mzali and I do go, then we must go alone." Reluctantly, Alison agreed.

It took Mzali and me a long time to get to the little community, so concerned were we to avoid detection and so nostalgic at seeing places barely remembered. When at last we did get there, we decided to stay hidden behind a tree until we recognized a familiar face: we had no idea whether war veterans were living here or not. Eventually, the formidable presence of Miriam came into view, and Mzali called her over to us in a hushed voice.

"*Conjane* Miriam," he greeted her, his joy a pleasure to behold.

"*Conjane* Mzali," she responded, and then she beamed as she recognized me.

"*Conjane* Mziki," she squealed with delight. "*Eish*, it is good to see you. How are you?"

"I'm well, thanks, Miriam. How are you?" I asked.

"Hau," she said angrily. "Things here are not good anymore. All the old workers have left: Kataza is not making any money now. The new boss and his manager know nothing about farming. The manager sits all day at the house and drinks beer, while we try to survive. Have you seen the cattle?" she asked sharply.

Mzali and I had passed by some of the cattle on our way to the village and were disgusted by the neglect. These animals had obviously not been getting the correct feed and were covered in ticks: they had not seen a cattle dip in years. These were prizewinning cows, and now they were emaciated, reduced to skin and bone. I told Miriam that we had indeed seen what was left of the cattle.

"How are your two boys?" I asked, remembering their young faces well. She shook her head.

"Hau," she said, "those two boys left here long ago. There is no work here anymore. They went to Bulawayo for a while, but could not find work there either. Now they have gone to South Africa and have a lucrative business transporting people between Bulawayo and Pretoria in a minivan."

I was pleased for the two young men: they had always shown initiative, and it was good to know that their enterprise was paying off.

"How are you doing, Miriam?" Mzali pressed her.

She gave him a disparaging look. "When the war veterans arrived here, they were full of their own importance: pompous and pretentious. Once a week they would take the children away from their homes and into the bush for a *pungwe*. They would tell the children not to listen to their parents and that Mugabe is the savior of this country. The minds of our children were poisoned against us."

I knew that this was common practice and that these *pungwes*, or night vigils, were used to indoctrinate malleable young minds, as they had been in Cambodia with such devastating genocidal consequences.

"Our children were taken away from us and they were taught that all white men are evil, especially the Savage family. We were all told that your family became rich off our work and that you did not deserve to have anything anymore. We were told that we had been used and exploited, but that those days were over now. We would work for the new owner, and we would become fat and wealthy." She lamented: "Look around you. Where is our wealth? These people do not know how to farm and have allowed everything to go to waste. Look at us: we are now just subsistence farmers, wondering where our next meal will come from." There were no words that I could offer to console her, so instead, I hugged her.

Mzali and I did not want to leave without having one last look at the old farmhouse. We made our way toward it, cautiously. When we reached the old wire garden fence and looked inside, we were appalled. The elegant old homestead was on her deathbed; she had been criminally neglected. The paint and the plaster had chipped away, exposing bare brick beneath, and the roof was filled with holes where the tiles had lifted. The rolling lawns were gone, replaced by tattered vegetable beds and maize. The birdlife had gone too, replaced by chickens: meals on the move. Looking through my binoculars, I could see two gentlemen sitting on the veranda enjoying a beer in the same place that Dad and I had shared our last meal together at Kataza. It was all terribly sad. Mzali and I had seen enough and made our way back to camp.

There was a somber atmosphere that evening as we ate dinner, Mzali and I mourning the demise of that elegant old lady, the homestead. We mourned too for the workers who had been promised so much and to whom so little had been delivered.

When we woke up the next morning, Alison and I both wanted to go back to the cave, simply to satisfy ourselves that there was nothing left to find. When we told Mzali were we were going, he told us that he and Bryan would join us later in the morning; he wanted to replenish our stock of wood so that we could cook lunch. Mzali mused that we should leave later that afternoon. Both Alison and I agreed with him.

Alison and I explored the kopje and cave thoroughly until we were convinced that we had unearthed all its secrets. Making our way back to camp, I noticed a thin thread of smoke snaking sinuously into the air.

"Oh no," I said to Alison, "this is exactly what we didn't want."

"I hope we have not given our presence away," Alison concurred. We picked up our pace.

We were too late. When we were a couple of hundred meters away, a cloud of dust, the sound of vehicles screeching to a halt, and angry voices alerted us that all was not well. Cautiously, Alison and I crouched low and made our way to a rock about fifty meters from the camp which we hid behind.

"Why on earth did anyone light a fire?" Alison pondered.

"I can only presume that Bryan must have wanted a cup of tea or coffee and that Mzali wasn't yet back with dry wood. Bryan must have found some wood and started one."

This was an explanation, but it could not excuse the naive carelessness. Peering out from behind the cover of rock, Alison and I witnessed a frightening spectacle. In retrospect, it was so horrific that it all took place in lurid slow motion. About eight young men leaped from the back of a pickup truck, shouting and brandishing pangas. Bryan stood up to greet them with a bewildered look on his face. The leader of the posse walked up to Bryan and slapped him hard across the side of the face, and pushed him. Bryan fell backward in a tumult of flailing legs and arms. He slowly gathered himself up but was now surrounded by angry men. One of them hit him hard in the face and there was a gush of blood. Even from this distance, I could tell that Bryan's nose was broken. It was then that fate intervened in the form of Mzali. He was magnificent and incredibly brave. We heard a roar of indignation and Mzali burst into the camp, a pile of dry wood in his arms.

"Stop this," Mzali yelled. The young men were taken by surprise and calmed down a little as they reassessed the situation. Like an ebony lion protecting his cub, Mzali stood in front of Bryan, daring anyone to attack. Mzali dropped his load of wood and, waving his arms at them, he gestured to the young men to step back. The leader of the pack stepped forward, shouting at Mzali with his panga raised in the air, ready to strike. Mzali stood his ground. He placed his hands on his hips and started to berate the young man. What he said was indistinct, but a few words drifted across to Alison and me.

"ZIPRA ... mujibas ... good man ... leave now." The leader seemed placated, but not completely satisfied. The young men around him were mumbling, but it appeared that an agreement had been reached, however unpopular.

"Mziki," he shouted, "come out. It's safe."

Alison and I emerged from our hiding place and made our way across to the camp. I extended my hand to the young jackal and, by implication, to his entire pack.

"Hi," I said. "Bruce Savage."

The young man looked at me with anger and barely concealed contempt. He slapped my hand away, an act which the pack obviously approved of, judging from their encouraging remarks.

"Ten minutes," the young man said sourly.

I demurely began to pack the cooking utensils, while Alison went across to Bryan to tend his wounds. I think it was a subconscious act of defiance on her part, to show that she would pack after she had taken care of more important business. She sat the confused professor down and knelt in front of him, dabbing mercurochrome on his face.

"Are you all right, Professor?" she asked, the concern apparent.

"I'm fine, thanks," said Bryan. "I'm afraid I was a little foolish"

"Don't worry, everything will be all right," Alison reassured him.

Mzali was busy getting the tents down, and I went across to help him.

"Thanks, Mzali," I said sincerely. "You were magnificent there. I don't know what would have happened to Bryan if you hadn't intervened. I think they might have killed him."

All the time that we were packing up, we were constantly being harangued. Insults, jibes, and questions bombarded us from every side:

"Why are you here?"

"Get out of here, you colonialist scum."

"You still think that you own the place?"

I did not respond, knowing that if discretion is the better part of valor, then silence is the better part of wisdom: it is impossible to reason with unreasonable people. I knew that they were enjoying this; it made them feel masculine and dominant and, from my point of view, they were. Sullenly, we made our way back to the Land Cruiser, Alison holding Bryan as we walked. My final farewell to Kataza was ignominious as I left in disgrace, my pride battered. As we left with our proverbial tails between our legs, the pack of angry young men was on their feet, shouting at us and wishing us anything but well. Silently, I said my goodbyes knowing that I could never return.

CHAPTER 30

We drove back to Esigodini, feeling disconsolate, and hardly a word was spoken. Alison was fussing over Bryan, and I think he secretly enjoyed the attention. When we dropped Mzali back at his home, I walked inside with him and thanked him once again for having saved our hides. I promised him that I would see him again before we left Bulawayo, and he told me that he looked forward to that. Alison, Bryan, and I drove back to Bulawayo with our precious cargo safe on the back seat. I felt particularly desolate, knowing that I had seen Kataza for the last time, and regretting the fact that I had left in disgrace. It felt like the end of an era. I now know how gutted Dad must have felt when he had left Kataza and his family to their respective fates.

It was about midday when we reached Bulawayo and we all wanted to freshen up at the hotel. Alison and I had a shower and scrubbed the dirt and grime off ourselves before getting dressed in fresh clothes. We decided that we would unpack the Land Cruiser later, but that we needed a drink and some time to sit quietly by ourselves and reflect on what had happened. We invited Bryan to join us, but he declined. I think that he also wanted some time to himself, as he had suffered the worst of our ordeal. Perhaps he was simply allowing Alison and me to be alone. Shame, I felt sorry for him but decided not to insist.

Alison and I drove to the Hillside suburb to sample the food of a secluded bistro that had been recommended to us. It was a quiet garden venue and there were only a few patrons, which suited us well. We did not feel like company or crowds. We ate a little food and we drank a little drink before we decided that it was time to make our way back to the hotel. Alison and I decided that we should leave within a day or two now that the purpose of our holiday had been achieved. As I was paying the bill, the thought came to me that our excursion was somehow incomplete without a visit to one of the magnificent ruins that had so occupied our thoughts for the past weeks.

"Alison honey, I know that we need to leave fairly soon but why don't we take an excursion out to Khami Ruins tomorrow morning?" I suggested.

"That sounds wonderful," she replied. "How far away are they?"

"They're close by, about fifteen kilometers northwest of Bulawayo. If we get there at about 10 o'clock, we will be able to wander around the ruins, have a picnic lunch, and still be back by about 2 o'clock in the afternoon."

"That's great," Alison said enthusiastically. "I think we should do our packing in the afternoon and leave the day after tomorrow. I feel a little uneasy with those tablets lying vulnerable in our rucksacks. I think we should get them to a safe place sooner rather than later." I concurred.

When we arrived back at the hotel, I sought out Bryan and found him enjoying a drink and the afternoon sun at a table close to the hotel's swimming pool.

"How are you feeling, Professor?"

"I'm starting to feel a little better, thank you," he responded with a naughty smile. "It's amazing how well these Pimm's cocktails are going down! Very therapeutic!"

"Professor, Alison and I are going to go out to visit Khami Ruins tomorrow morning. They really are a sight worth seeing—the architecture is simply spectacular. Would you like to join us and we can all enjoy a picnic together?"

"I really would have loved to join you," Bryan responded, "but just half an hour ago I phoned a colleague of mine, Professor Sibanda, who lectures at the nearby university. He is a professor of African history and I am now curious to learn more about these antique civilizations. I am hoping that he will be able to educate me a little."

"Bryan, we will be back by about 2 o'clock in the afternoon. Why don't you meet Professor Sibanda sometime after two? That will still give you plenty of time to chat with your colleague."

"I'm afraid that he has a rather busy schedule, and the only time that he was prepared to meet with me was between 9 and 10 o'clock and even then, reluctantly," Bryan apologized.

"I would have thought that he would make time to see an old friend."

"Actually, he and I have never met. I think that he has agreed to meet me as a professional courtesy, professor meeting professor."

CHAPTER 31

The Bulawayo Museum of Natural History is situated next to Centenary Park at the southern entrance of Bulawayo. It is an imposing circular building, and it was at the entrance that Bryan waited for his colleague in academia. Professor Sibanda arrived at precisely 9 o'clock and sauntered over to Bryan, his immaculate attire hinting at his sexual proclivities: he obviously considered himself suave and urbane, but simply looked prissy. He was adorned in a pinstripe Armani suit and a neatly folded triangle of purple silk handkerchief protruded from his breast pocket; he had on a mauve silk shirt and dark purple tie. His shoes were as shiny as a mirror and there was hardly a crease in the leather. Gold studs were embedded in his ears; an expensive gold watch adorned his left wrist; and he wore a gold and onyx signet ring on the small finger of his left hand. It was his right hand that he now extended to Bryan.

"Good morning, Professor," Sibanda said, his voice surprisingly deep, as he shook hands with Bryan. His grip though, was weak and effeminate.

"It's an absolute pleasure to meet you, Professor," Bryan responded gleefully.

"How can I help you?" Sibanda asked politely.

"Thank you so much for agreeing to meet with me, Professor," Bryan replied. "In recent weeks I have developed a great curiosity about the marvelous and intriguing ruins in this country and I have read voraciously all that I could to get a greater understanding of their history. I am only in Bulawayo for a few days and thought it would be a wonderful opportunity for me to meet with an expert on the topic. I realize that it is probably an inconvenience for you, but I do appreciate your taking the time and trouble to chat with a fellow professor."

"It is no trouble at all," Sibanda reassured Bryan. "I enjoy every opportunity that I get to boast about our wonderful African heritage; after all, it is a professional courtesy."

"Professor ... " Bryan began, only for Sibanda to hold up his hand in interruption.

"Please, call me Enoch."

"And you can call me Bryan," proffered Bryan with an appreciative smile. "Enoch, when were these ruins built, and by whom?"

"You say that you have already read on the topic, so I will assume that you know the conventional truth. The most famous of these ruins, Great Zimbabwe, is thought to have been built around 1250 CE, at approximately the same time that the Renaissance was beginning in Europe. But the ruins at Great Zimbabwe are not the oldest; they are simply the largest and best known. The oldest of the ruins yet discovered lies just two kilometers from the Limpopo River, at Mapela Hill. The Mapela Hill complex is now believed to have been constructed as early as 950 CE, just as Europe was emerging from the Dark Ages. Mapela Hill was a contemporary of the Bambandyanalo site, which is very nearby. Related to the Mapela Hill complex is that of Mapungubwe, just below the Limpopo River, which began in about 1100 CE. These centers were Iron Age sites and traded extensively with contemporary Asian cultures.

"As the climate changed and became drier after about 1300 CE, the culture shifted north toward Great Zimbabwe. Great Zimbabwe fell into decline roundabout 1450 CE and was replaced by the Khami culture, which included the ruins at Dananombe and Naletale. The Khami civilization traded extensively with the Chinese and Portuguese but was conquered by the invading Rovwi people in 1683. The city of Khami was abandoned, but the Rovwi occupied both Dananombe and Naletale until they themselves were displaced by the invading Matabele just more than a century ago. So you can see, Bryan, that the Bantu people have had a sophisticated civilization for over a thousand years."

"What do you say to the suggestion that African oral tradition denies this, and claims that the ruins are so old that 'they were built when the stones were soft'? And to the suggestion by Credo Mutwa, himself a tribal elder and custodian of tribal tradition, that it was 'white people from across the sea' who built these ruins?" Bryan asked, aware that he might be treading on dangerous ground.

Professor Sibanda tolerated the question and answered with good humor, chuckling. "My dear Bryan, these fantastical utterances were made by people desperate to please their white colonial masters. Less subservient oral tradition is quite clear: it was the Bantu people who built these ruins."

Bryan wanted to elicit as much information as he could. "What was being traded with these foreign cultures?" he asked.

"Great Zimbabwe was providing gold and ivory and receiving beads and porcelain. There were probably a great many other products that were traded, but they were possibly perishable and did not survive the test of time," Sibanda explained. "The later Torwa culture that is responsible for the Khami complex is presumed to have traded mostly with East Africa," he confided proudly.

"How is it that we have such precise dates for these structures?" queried Bryan. "What is it that has been dated?"

"As you know, Bryan, we can only carbon date organic material. The bones of people found buried around these sites have given us accurate dates as well as ash deposits, preserved edibles, and, in the case of Great Zimbabwe, a timber beam used in the construction of the complex to bolster the masonry. We have also been able to establish fairly exact dates for the pottery by comparing it to the styles and types of pottery in use in the country of origin." Professor Sibanda was in his element, obviously enjoying himself.

"Furthermore, the absence of conflicting evidence is also instructive. Absolutely nothing has been found at any of the sites to suggest alternative dates or origins."

"So, if new evidence were discovered that conflicted with these dates, it would not render present evidence invalid, it would simply mean that these sites had been occupied before the dates suggested by existing evidence?" Bryan sought clarity. "Particularly as the stones themselves cannot be dated."

"I suppose your logic is correct," admitted Sibanda cautiously, "but these sites have been exhaustively examined and absolutely no evidence that contradicts this view has ever been discovered while the evidence to support this view is overwhelming."

Sibanda looked troubled. "Tell me, Bryan, is there a reason for this line of inquiry? I'm beginning to suspect that your probing is not as innocent as I had first thought. Your questions all tend to lead in a particular direction."

"I must apologize Enoch, but yes, there is a reason for my slanted line of questioning. As I mentioned earlier, I have done a great deal of reading, and I am not entirely convinced by the current narrative. As you have suggested, it tends to rest on the absence of evidence to the contrary. I feel that the present evidence is inconclusive."

Sibanda's attitude altered visibly. "Professor Cameron, it has been interesting meeting you, but I am afraid that I need to get back to the university. I'm not prepared to discuss your racist insanity. Enjoy the rest of your stay."

Bryan was taken aback by the rapid change in attitude and Professor Sibanda's temperamental outburst. "Enoch, what would you say were I to tell you that I have spent the last few days on a farm not far from here and that I have in my possession conclusive proof that these ruins were built by Semitic people?" Bryan spoke without thinking, childishly seeking one-upmanship to deflate Professor Sibanda's hubris. He immediately regretted his words, but it was too late. Professor Sibanda lost patience.

"I would say that you are lying and that you are a fraud. I would also say that whatever evidence you think you have will be easily refuted as a ploy by racist colonialists to discredit our proud history. It will not withstand academic scrutiny. I warn you to be careful, Professor; what you are preaching is a heretical gospel and I have powerful friends in high places. I am now returning to the university, and I suggest that you return to wherever it is that you came from."

With that, Sibanda turned on his heels and walked away, not bothering to look back. As he walked, he reached into his pocket and grabbed his cell phone.

CHAPTER 32

Gumede sat at his massive mahogany desk, his open laptop resting on the scarlet leather inlay. He reclined comfortably in his green leather desk chair and surveyed his enormous office, a testimony to his success. Three large leather settees dominated the conversation area, and between them lay a Persian carpet. Like all the other fixtures in the room, the solid coffee table was constructed from expensive wood. The room was surrounded by specially installed bookcases, filled with collectible books, none of which he had ever read: appearance is always more important than mere substance. His gaze returned to the graphic scene unfolding on the screen of his laptop. He was growing impatient. When would this fool arrive? Already he was twenty minutes late. Just then, there was a loud, insistent knock on his door. Bitter and embarrassing experience had taught his secretary that it was prudent to knock before entering this room. Swiftly lowering the lid of his laptop, Gumede responded.

"Come in," he bellowed. His secretary opened the door, allowing a scruffy old man to enter gingerly, his hands clasped tightly together. He had made an effort to impress Gumede by donning his only suit, but the threadbare clothing served only to denigrate him; the old grey cloth, made shiny by time, was worn through, and the sleeves were far too short.

"*Conjane Baba,*" the old man said, as he delivered a short, subservient bow, deliberately avoiding eye contact with Gumede. That would be considered rude. Gumede did not stand up; he had only just closed his laptop. Nor did he invite the old man to be seated; the hierarchy needed to be preserved.

"*Conjane,*" replied Gumede curtly. "What can I do for you? More to the point, what can you do for me?"

"*Baba,* I think you'll be pleased with the news that I bring you," said the old man hopefully.

"Let me be the judge of that," Gumede snapped. "Give me your news. Can you not see that I am a busy man?" Gumede asked, gesturing toward his computer, the lid of which was not quite closed. At least the sound was muted.

"Yes, *Baba,*" he meekly agreed. "Yesterday some intruders were discovered on the farm Kataza. Some of the older workers recognized Mzali and Mziki. There was a lady with them and another white man whom they called 'Professor'. We gave this man a beating and we threw them all off the farm," he boasted proudly, expecting to be congratulated.

"What were they doing on the farm?" Gumede enquired brusquely.

"I don't know *Baba*, but they were looking around the old walls."

"Why did you not phone me? Why did you need to travel all this way to see me in person?" asked Gumede, knowing full well that his informant was hoping to be rewarded with cash, so scarce at this time. Before the old man had a chance to answer, Gumede's phone rang.

"Excuse me while I take this call," Gumede instructed. "It is probably important state business," he lied, wanting to keep the old man in awe of him. He stroked the screen of his cell phone and placed the phone to his ear. "Gumede," he said and paused to listen.

"Ah! Professor Sibanda. How good it is to hear from you. What can I do for you?" Gumede listened with rapt intensity, occasionally shaking his head.

"Professor Sibanda, thank you for this information. As luck would have it, I have an old man in my office with me right now and his story corroborates yours. Don't worry; I will attend to this as soon as I have an opportunity." Gumede turned to the old man, returning his cell phone to his pocket.

"This information that you have brought me is more important than I had initially thought it would be. Thank you. Have a pleasant ride home," said Gumede dismissively. He fished around in his left trouser pocket and hauled out his wallet. Carefully selecting an old creased banknote, he handed it to the old man, who took it in his right hand while his left hand held the right wrist in the traditional Matabele way. The intention was to show that the gift was so heavy and important that the right hand, the clean hand, needed assistance. In this case, the gift was indeed great: 100 US dollars.

"*Niyabonga Gakulu*: Thank you very much," said the old man, scarcely believing his good fortune. "Mister Bed, you're a very good man."

Gumede smiled to himself as the old man departed the room. It had been many years since anyone had called him by his first name: Abednego.

166

CHAPTER 33

As Bryan prepared for his meeting at the Museum of Natural History, Alison and I wended our way toward the picturesque Khami Ruins. The journey was short, pleasant, and rewarding. We were the only visitors that day, allowing us free rein to explore the exquisite ruins unhindered and to allow our imaginations to run wild.

The Khami complex was a series of ruins built on and around small kopjes that overlook a river below. We admired the magnificent architecture and the stone patterning built into the walls. Khami is still well-preserved and the quality of the masonry is superb, exceeded only by that at Dananombe and Naletale, although Khami is more extensive than either. The solitude was overpowering, lending pathos to these sculpted marvels. It was a privilege being there alone with Alison as I desperately wanted to spend time with her. She was entranced by the ruins.

"This is absolutely stunning," she said, as we sat to gather our energy, having spent nearly two hours exploring. "Can you imagine what this place must have looked like in its prime, with all its many people going about their daily business?" I imagined the ruins as they once must have been, intact and pristine, with contented people going about their daily lives of tilling the fields and raising their families. It was a pleasing thought.

"It's awe-inspiring," I said admiringly. As we sat together, appreciating the silence, it seemed to me that the quietude added an aura of mystery to the venerable ruins.

"Why don't we find a more comfortable place to have our picnic?" I suggested. I wanted to find the most beautiful spot possible to maximize the ambiance. As we walked slowly around the ruins, Alison noticed that a 44-gallon drum that served as a garbage bin had been overturned and there was litter strewn everywhere.

"How disgusting," she remarked. "It is unacceptable that people come out to a glorious venue like this and vandalize the place!"

"It wasn't people who did that," I chuckled. "It was honey badgers."

"What is a honey badger?"

"It is an adorable, mischievous little creature about the size of a Staffordshire bull terrier, but with much shorter legs," I replied hesitantly, trying to find some form of comparison to which Alison could relate.

"The honey badger is highly intelligent, has an insatiable curiosity, and is one of the few wild creatures with a real sense of humor. They are incorrigible scavengers and probably raid these garbage bins every evening. They are also amazingly tough and resilient, and there is no predator that will willingly attack them. The honey badger is brave beyond belief: it will attack buffalo, leopards, and even lions if necessary. When it attacks, it does not attack as other predators do, targeting the throat or the soft underbelly—the honey badger goes directly for the groin."

Alison laughed: "Like an angry woman."

I chuckled. "Absolutely."

It was refreshing to see Alison relaxed and enjoying herself.

"This tough little guy will take on animals much bigger than itself, and it will prevail. If it is wounded in the process, its metabolism is so evolved that it will survive wounds which would be lethal to other animals. The honey badger is virtually immune to all snake poison. If it is bitten by a venomous snake such as a cobra, black mamba, or puff adder—which would be fatal for most animals—the plucky little honey badger will go into a cataleptic state and will lie comatose on the ground while its body deals with the toxins. After an hour or two, it will get up, shake itself off, and carry on as normal."

"You really admire them, don't you?" asked Alison fondly, giving my hand a little squeeze.

"I really do. They are tenacious and irrepressible."

Eventually, we found a site suitable for our picnic and I laid out a large blanket for us to recline on. I had wanted this occasion to be memorable and had provided a picnic of gourmet delights. I had bought a magnum of perry, which Alison loved, to complement the smoked salmon, smoked marlin, camembert cheese, pickled cucumbers, tinned artichokes, and waterblommetjies. I had brought two loaves of rye bread, butter, lemon juice, and a pepper grinder. But that was not all. Secreted away in one of the compartments of the picnic box was a beautiful ring, which I had bought some months before. I had decided to spurn convention and ignore diamonds, choosing instead something more appropriate for Alison: something with real character and personality. I had chosen a silver ring with a topaz stone which perfectly matched her beautiful blue eyes.

The meal was delicious and the company delectable. My heart started to pound, and the adrenalin surged as I mustered the courage to ask Alison my momentous question. As my hand sought out the ring, my cell phone started ringing insistently. I tried to ignore it, hoping that the ringing would cease, but Alison intervened.

"Are you going to answer that?" Alison drawled lazily. It was Mzali.

"Mziki," Mzali intoned, his voice tinged with apprehension. "I'm afraid that I have bad news."

CHAPTER 34

"What's the matter, Mzali? What's wrong?" I asked, my anxiety levels mounting.

"About an hour and a half ago I had a visit from the police. They were polite but insistent. They wanted to know why we were all out at Kataza yesterday, and they wanted to know why you are back in the country. It seems that someone from Kataza recognized you and has informed the new owner of our intrusion. Guess who the new owner of Kataza is?"

"I have no idea Mzali. Who is it?" I asked, without caring about the answer.

"Gumede," Mzali said, pausing for the fact to sink in. My blood ran cold: I was stunned.

"I had no idea that he owned it," Mzali continued. "It seems that he got his revenge after all, kicking your father off the property. But he is now incensed, and he wants to arrest you for trespassing. You must be careful, Mziki, this man is powerful. He is a rich man and he is a minister. I know that he used to be the deputy minister of law and order, the police, but I do not know what portfolio he now has.

"There is something else that you need to know, Mziki. When Gumede attacked Kataza all those years ago, it seems that his left knee was shattered by a bullet. Apparently, his leg was amputated, and he now has a prosthetic leg. The police were asking many questions about you. I think that he has a lot of hatred toward the Savage family and that this may become a personal and private matter between Gumede and you.

"Beware; this man still has a lot of influence with the police; he has a nest of vipers at his beck and call."

I knew Gumede from reputation only but, from what I'd heard, he was a man completely innocent of any redeeming virtue.

"Thanks for the warning, Mzali. I'm not sure that we have done anything wrong though. He has no reason to arrest me. At most, we were simply trespassing. Why are you so concerned?" I asked cautiously.

Mzali responded with a question. "Where is Bryan now?"

"I'm not sure. He had an appointment with a Professor Sibanda this morning, but that would have ended hours ago. He is probably at the hotel sipping his Pimm's cocktails and admiring bikinis by the pool. Why do you ask?"

"Because the police were asking many questions about what we had found at Kataza. They went on and on, asking what evidence we had discovered. They do not know that we have clay tablets, but they do know that we found something significant. I'm sure that neither you nor Alison would have mentioned that to anyone and I know that I haven't, which means that Bryan must have said something to someone. It also gives Gumede an excuse to arrest each one of us."

I silently cursed the good professor.

"Shame, I feel sorry for him; he is a lovely human being, but he simply does not understand social conventions or human nature," I despaired, exasperated by his naiveté.

"Bruce," said Mzali, using my first name for the first time in years. "I feel in the marrow of my bones that Gumede will contrive to arrest you, but I think that I may have bought you some time. The police asked me when you were leaving, and I told them that you and Alison wanted to stay here for another week. I also told them that I did not know where you were staying and that I believed you were lodging at a guest house. If I know Gumede, he will wait until the last moment to pounce on his prey in order to delay your departure and maximize the inconvenience to you. I think that you need to leave as soon as possible before that happens. I am also sure that he will now want to have you followed wherever you go. Be careful.".

"Thanks, Mzali, my friend. I appreciate the warning. I think Alison and I will leave the day after tomorrow." An ominous feeling of foreboding flushed through me. Once again, I would be leaving what I loved with a dark cloud looming above me.

"By the way," Mzali added as an afterthought, "I have some gossip that might interest you. In fact, it may even help you. When the police left my house, I phoned Miriam back at Kataza wanting to warn her that one of her people cannot be trusted. She was upset, and it was she who told me that Gumede is the new owner of Kataza. She mentioned that her niece, Priscilla Maseko, owns a computer business in Bulawayo and that Priscilla has a business partner by the name of Colleen Noble. It seems that Colleen is a good looking woman and that she is good friends with Gumede: very good friends, friends with benefits. It also seems that she is a worried lady. Gumede has been helping to finance her and showers her with gifts, but she knows that he is losing interest in her. Her looks are beginning to fade and so is his interest in her. When he has completely lost interest in her, he will leave her for someone else. Miriam's niece, Priscilla, always wants to be the center of attention and has a loose tongue. Wanting to impress Miriam, she told Miriam that Colleen Noble has protection to ensure that Gumede does not abandon her. I do not know what this protection may be, or if this information is of any use to you, but apparently the protection is comprehensive; in Miriam's words, it is huge. I have a nasty feeling that you may need protection of your own."

"Thanks, Mzali," I responded gratefully, "but I don't know what I can do with that information. I think it best that Alison and I get back to the hotel and start packing."

"Mziki, you don't fully understand," Mzali said impatiently. "I know this man. You cannot ignore him. He is going to come after you. I promise you that you are going to need protection of some sort. I have a friend from my days in the military. His name is Mandla and he has agreed to meet you at the hotel this evening. It is 2 o'clock now; I suggest that you get back to the hotel before 5 o'clock."

CHAPTER 35

Mandla was all that his name suggested: strong. He was tall, lean muscled, and charming, and he exuded an aura of menace.

"What line of work are you in?" asked Alison innocently, trying to gauge his character. He smiled in a roguish, enigmatic way.

"I am a … businessman," he said cryptically. I believe that I read him perfectly: he was a military man who throve on adrenaline. He was proficient, precise, intelligent, and a lone wolf: part predator, part puppy—mostly predator.

We were congregated around an isolated garden table, the farthest removed from the hotel swimming pool. The sun was preparing to set, painting the evening sky with wild, lurid slashes of purple, pink, and mauve. The whole gaudy scene seemed so melodramatic and conspiratorial that it seemed ridiculous; I desperately wanted to laugh if only to dilute the tension.

"Would you like a drink?" I invited Mandla.

"Yes please," he said with a smile. "Ginger ale would be refreshing. Thank you."

"Would you not prefer something a little stronger?" suggested Alison.

"I never drink alcohol: it dulls the senses." This was another clue to his character: Mandla was a man who liked to be in control.

"Once again, I would just like to apologize and to say how sorry I am to have placed us all in this predicament." Bryan's contrite apology was unnecessary. We all knew that he had no way of knowing that his innocent words would have had any repercussions. You cannot blame a man for actions without malice.

Alison reached out and held Bryan's hand, silently consoling him. "Don't worry Professor. We know that you meant no harm."

Looking pointedly at me Alison suggested a way forward. "What matters now is that we deal with the situation. I know that Bruce wants to leave, but I am inclined to agree with Mandla. I think we need to know more about the protection that this woman claims to have."

Mandla interjected: "Mziki, I know that you simply want to leave and get Alison to safety, but I think that Gumede will have you arrested at the border. I am prepared to bet that the border crossings have already been placed on high alert. You are already engaged in a game of cat and mouse, only you don't realize it yet. At the moment you're a low priority and he is probably enjoying the thought that you are unsuspecting of an ambush. That would appeal to his sadistic sense of humor. If you had something that threatened him, it would change the nature of the game. You are already in his sights and he is simply waiting to pull the trigger. If you really want to protect Alison, you will get a weapon of your own with which to fight back."

"What we need to do now is to figure out what this protection might be and where it is secured," Mandla continued confidently. "We know that Colleen is in the computer business, so it would seem logical that her insurance is related to computers. It would also seem logical that this insurance is information—dirt on Gumede. If her protection is information, then it is unlikely to be cumbersome documents. It would need to be stored on a computer."

"A desktop computer or a laptop would be too vulnerable," I surmised. "A computer could easily be found and destroyed. If it is information that we are looking for, then it is undoubtedly stored on something small, compact, and portable."

"It must be on either a thumb drive or an external hard drive," Alison interjected. "If she has a lot of information about him, then it will almost certainly be stored on something with more memory: an external hard drive."

Mandla smiled. "We are making progress. See. This is not difficult. Now we need to get a better idea of where this object might be hidden."

"Well, we know that she owns a computer business. Perhaps it is located somewhere at her place of work?" Bryan speculated tentatively.

"No." Alison was emphatic. "I think that Colleen is a fairly intelligent lady. She would not hide it anywhere so obvious. If Gumede were ever to doubt her loyalty that would be the first place that he would search. And, were he in any doubt, he would probably burn the business to the ground.'" Mandla obviously had an opinion of his own but was observing our debate with detached amusement.

"I know it is also an obvious place," I suggested, "but she may well have hidden it in her house."

Alison smiled. "Colleen is a woman who likes to manipulate people. I think she would hide it somewhere that would allow her to have deniability—where someone else could be blamed for her duplicity. From what we have been told Priscilla, on the other hand, is a lady who enjoys drama and wants to be perceived as important. The two women are business partners, so I am pretty sure that this evidence will be somewhere in Priscilla's home. If not, it may be with Colleen, but I doubt it."

"Well done!" Mandla congratulated us. "It seems that we now know what we are looking for and where to look. What else do you suggest we do?"

Alison smiled. She was really enjoying the mental challenge.

"Well, if we are to have leverage of our own then we need to make copies of the external hard drive. We would probably need to have at least two copies, as insurance. That means we would also need a computer from which to copy it. None of us has a computer with us, and none of us has enough money to buy one."

"Never fear," Mandla reassured us. "I have a laptop that we can use."

"Now we need to find out where Priscilla lives," Bryan informed us.

"No problem," said Mandla. "Tomorrow morning at 9 o'clock I will go to their computer shop and I will buy two external hard drives, each having two terabytes of memory. I think it only fitting that I spend some money at their shop. Don't worry about the cost; that will be between Mzali and me. Later in the day, I will discreetly follow Priscilla home. She will lead me to her house."

Alison smiled disparagingly. "Men are so stupid," she chuckled. "Always over-complicating simple things."

She turned her back to us and summoned the waiter. "Waiter, please will you bring me a telephone directory?"

CHAPTER 36

Both Colleen and Priscilla owned houses in the exclusive suburb of Selbourne Park, adjacent to the Ascot Shopping Center. I arranged to meet Mandla at the shopping center at 9:30 in the morning. That would give Mandla time to purchase our external hard drives, assuming that Colleen and Priscilla opened shop at 9 o'clock. I had never committed a criminal act before, yet here I was preparing to burgle someone's house. The fact that I only intended to copy information and not to deprive someone of their possessions was small consolation: I knew that I was doing something terribly wrong. Although Bryan agreed with our course of action, he did not want any part of it and decided to spend the morning at the hotel. Alison insisted upon being involved, not wanting me to bear the burden of guilt alone. She was to be our driver and agreed to sit and wait for Mandla and me in a small coffee shop.

Mandla arrived shortly before 9:30, dressed in jeans and a comfortable cotton shirt, and clutching an expensive ostrich leather briefcase. "Equipment," he explained, and together we strolled the short distance to Priscilla's grand home: she had done well for herself. I was hoping that Priscilla did not own dogs, and was relieved to find that she did not. Her house was spectacular, a veritable mansion. There was hardly any traffic on the street, probably because most people were at work, and Mandla and I did not look conspicuous, making it easy for us to quickly climb over the six-foot wall into Priscilla's yard, where we hid from potential observers. Skirting stealthily around the house we found a window, the latch of which was loose, and we managed to enter without damaging anything. Fate was kind to us because Priscilla obviously felt safe enough not to need an alarm system, nor was there any sign of a domestic worker: we had her home at our mercy! Once inside Priscilla's sanctuary, we reconnoitered the rooms to gain an understanding of where Colleen might have hidden an external hard drive. The possibilities were endless.

"Don't waste your time looking at anything that is portable," Mandla instructed me. "To hide something in the back of a television set or in the innards of a radio, for example, would not be terribly bright. Even a settee or a dining room table could be lifted up and carried out by burglars—particularly in a quiet leafy suburb like this."

"Where do you suggest that we start looking?" I whispered. Mandla laughed.

"Why are you whispering?" He was amused, being more used to this sort of activity than I. "There is no one around to hear you. Unless you start playing loud music, we are perfectly safe for now."

"Answer my question," I insisted.

"It is as important to know where not to look," Mandla replied patiently. "Looking inside drawers and cupboards is unlikely to yield dividends. Neither would the toilet cistern be productive; the chance of moisture seeping into the hard drive would be too great. Were I to hazard a guess, I would say that it is probably hidden in or behind something that is a fixture. If there is a built-in safe in the house it would also be too obvious for someone with Gumede's resources."

As he was saying this Mandla was busy opening his briefcase. He whipped out a long flexible metal tube, explaining that it was an arthroscopic probe with a camera, similar to that used in medical procedures, allowing doctors to see inside their patients without being too intrusive. He adroitly attached the tube to his laptop computer.

"Come with me and have a look at how this works," Mandla urged. We walked through to the kitchen and Mandla placed the laptop on one of the kitchen counters. Then he switched on the arthroscopic camera and inserted it through a hole behind the built-in kitchen cabinets. A perfect picture of the back of the kitchen cabinet appeared on the screen of the laptop.

"It might not be prime time viewing," chuckled Mandla, "but it serves a useful purpose. Mziki, why don't you go and have a look around the rest of the house while I am doing this?" As I was about to leave the kitchen Mandla gave me some useful advice.

"Mziki, look for anything that appears out of place. Look to see if there are fingerprints on the ceilings or the walls; try to establish if there are false backs to any of the cupboards, or if any of the floor tiles look loose. Let me just say, for the record, that there is a good chance that we will not find anything here. It is possible that the hard drive could be hidden in the garage, or in Colleen's house, or in any number of places. But this is a good place to start."

With those less than encouraging words, I went to explore the rest of the house, employing a more critical eye than before. After about half an hour of fruitless exploration I made my way to the bedroom—which was so tidy that it was antiseptic—and I noticed that the ventilation brick above the window appeared loose and that the paint around it was slightly cracked. Standing on a chair, I inserted my fingers into the holes of the brick, as if it were a bowling ball, and managed to wiggle it free. I put my hand into the empty void and felt around, but I could feel nothing but loose grit. I needed a torch.

As luck would have it, Mandla was well prepared and had a small halogen torch in his briefcase.

Making my way back to Priscilla's bedroom, and feeling guilty about violating her private space, I peered into the cavity. The outer wall was solidly constructed and was two bricks thick. There was a tiny space between the bricks of approximately two centimeters and wedged tightly into this space was a mass of brown paper. I managed to get the end of my knife behind the package and to slowly ease it toward me until I could get a grip on it. I hurtled down to the kitchen, taking the stairs three by three, and presented my trophy to Mandla.

"This is either beginner's luck or you were born to be a criminal," he teased me, delighted. Sure enough, wrapped inside the brown paper was a hard drive, which we attached to Mandla's computer. There appeared to be only one folder on the hard drive and it was simply entitled 'G'. When we opened the folder, it was as though we had opened Pandora's Box; there must have been at least thirty other folders inside. We clicked on a couple of these and inside each was dozens of photocopied letters, a collection of copied emails, scanned documents, and video clips incriminating the person whose name the folder bore. This was conclusive evidence that Gumede had been obstructing justice and blackmailing prominent persons.

There were two folders that intrigued me. The first bore the letter 'A' and proved to be incendiary. It outlined Gumede's plans to stage an insurrection and detailed his connection with powerful foreign dignitaries and corporations. The second folder was labeled 'Secret' and was even more explosive: it contained information linking Asian business interests with prominent South African government officials, to the extent that these interests were intruding on governance and the cabinet. In short, it entailed the sort of 'state capture' that Gumede himself had achieved.

This file also included damning evidence, mostly from large European corporations, about corruption and self-aggrandizement in a great many government tenders, including arms deals. Mandla was horrified, and for the first time since I had met him, he started to look edgy and uneasy.

"Mziki," he whispered reverently, "this is bad news. This is the sort of information that countries go to war over, that people pay millions of dollars to conceal, that people kill for. I don't like this at all. I think we need to copy this quickly and get out of here as soon as possible."

Mandla inserted our two hard drives into the available ports and immediately started to copy the information.

"There is so much information on here that this could take a while," he warned me. "Let's make some coffee and enjoy Priscilla's hospitality." The files took almost an hour and a half to download, and I was concerned that Alison would be worried, so I phoned her. I had given her express instructions not to phone me as I did not want her to be complicit in my crimes, but I now believed that she needed to know the reason we were taking so long to get back to her. I felt vulnerable and conspicuous and told her that Mandla and I would not meet her in the coffee shop as planned, but that I would send her a message when we were leaving and would meet her at the car. I wanted to get as far away from Priscilla's home as I could, and I wanted to do it quickly.

When the information was safely downloaded, I wrapped Colleen's hard drive in the brown paper and returned it to its hiding place, taking care to replace the ventilation brick as carefully as possible. Then Mandla and I removed all traces of our presence, washed the coffee cups and returned them to their cupboards. We left the way that we had entered: through the window. What I failed to notice in my eagerness to leave, was that one of Priscilla's neighbors was standing immobile behind the translucent screen curtains in her own bedroom window and noticed Mandla and I departing. She was concerned and phoned Priscilla.

CHAPTER 37

It took Colleen and Priscilla fewer than thirty minutes to close their shop and get to Priscilla's house. They were greeted in the driveway by Priscilla's agitated neighbor.

"They were professionals," the neighbor insisted. "They did not appear to be in a hurry, they were careful to close the window, and they did not appear to steal anything. One of them was a white man. He was tall, about six feet and two inches, he had blonde hair, he was tanned, and he is about fifty years old. The other man was Black and was even taller than the white man, and he was also at least fifty years old."

Rather than easing Colleen's anxiety, this information served only to heighten it: there was only one thing in the house that she was concerned about, and it did not need to be stolen to cause irreparable damage to her.

"The hard drive, Priscilla," she shrieked, beside herself with angst, "Gumede has stolen the hard drive."

The two ladies rushed inside the house and sprinted as best they could up the stairs and into Priscilla's bedroom. As soon as she looked at the ventilation brick Priscilla noticed that the cracks in the paint were slightly more pronounced than when she had left the house that morning. Colleen grabbed a chair and pushed it against the wall to allow her access to the brick, while Priscilla went to her stack of jerseys and found the length of thick wire which she had specially shaped to allow her to fish out the hard drive. As soon as Colleen had the hard drive in her hand it was abundantly clear that it had been tampered with: for one thing, the brown paper was torn, and for another, the extension lead was no longer plugged into the hard drive. This could mean only one thing: Gumede was not the culprit, and someone else had made a copy of her precious protection.

The implications of this were profound and took some time to register with her. Gumede himself was now at risk, and not by her choosing. She stood to lose her benefactor and patron, and she herself was exposed. If Gumede were to find out that she had copied all his documents he would be livid and there would be no limit to his rage. She now had a difficult choice to make: should she keep silent and live in fear, hoping that he never learned of her betrayal, or should she confess to him and hope for clemency? She could always tell him that she was safeguarding his interests and that she had made the copy as a spare, just in case his many enemies were to discover those drives that he already had. It was thin, but at least it was something plausible.

"You need to phone Gumede," Priscilla insisted. "You need to tell him that someone has copied your hard drive."

Colleen was gripped by panic and her mind was clouded by a multitude of thoughts all pressing for precedence. She could not think clearly. It now dawned on her that Priscilla, her closest friend, would never allow her to keep this secret. Priscilla sought thrills and admiration, but could not tolerate pressure. If she did not phone Gumede then sooner or later Priscilla would. Trembling, and aware that life as she knew it was about to change irrevocably, Colleen did the only thing that she could; she phoned Gumede.

CHAPTER 38

Conflicting emotions engulfed Gumede as he listened with horror to Colleen's confession, her voice as syrupy sweet as molasses. He knew that she was lying, weaving a web of plausible deceit, and she was going to pay a permanent price for her betrayal: a price that he himself was determined to exact. But for now, that would need to wait. Panic and rage vied for dominance within him as he summoned his secretary into the office. So distracted was he, that he forgot to close the lid of his laptop, exposing his secretary to the depraved scenes that had demanded his attention until just a few moments earlier.

"Get me the chief of police immediately," he shouted at her, needing someone upon whom he could vent his rage. As she left the room, disgusted and traumatized, he stood up and started to pace around the office, cursing as he did so. Gumede lurched clumsily forward: his bad leg always ached and throbbed in times of stress. He could not believe that all this information was now at large, and he knew exactly who was responsible: Bruce Savage, *umHedeni*.

While he waited for the chief of police, Gumede planned his response, and by the time the call came, ten minutes later, he had constructed a loose plan of action.

"*Ikhanka*," Gumede modulated his voice to conceal the panic welling up within him. "I have recently been betrayed by someone close to me and I have just received a report that Bruce Savage has a copy of the hard drive. As you know, that hard drive contains information which is damaging to me, to you, and to our future plans. I want you to set up roadblocks on absolutely every road leading into and out of Bulawayo—even the dirt roads. Every car leaving Bulawayo is to be searched, even if Mr. Savage is not in that car; find the hard drive.

"I also want your police to find out exactly where he has been staying. I know that he is with a blonde lady and a visiting professor. They are also associated with our old friend Mzali. I want you to send some men to Mzali. Find out if he has any knowledge of Mr. Savage's activities; find out if he knows where Mr. Savage may be and find out what it is that they found at Kataza. I want you to check every guest house and hotel in Bulawayo and within twenty kilometers of Bulawayo.

If necessary, you are to conduct house to house searches. These people must be found. Do you understand me?"

The chief of police was shocked—almost as shocked as Gumede.

"Yes Sir" he mumbled incoherently.

"You need to act as quickly as possible. I want this city quarantined within an hour. When you interrogate Mzali, make sure that you do not injure him fatally. I have an old score to settle with him, and now I can do it personally and with a legally valid reason: now he is an enemy of the state. I want to make sure that Esibomvu Secondary School will be advertising for a new headmaster before the end of the week."

CHAPTER 39

Mandla, Alison, and I did not return directly to the hotel; instead, we headed toward a remarkable little bistro named Déjà vu, which served the best coffee in southern Africa. I think that Alison and I both needed to be in tranquil, reassuring surroundings, and to drown our guilt with something comforting and warm as our anxiety subsided. I felt tainted and dirty, as though a treasured part of me had somehow been corrupted and I was no longer entirely whole: I had compromised my principles and integrity by resorting to criminality. I found solace in the logic that I had only done so to protect Alison and yet some vestigial reptilian part of my brain recognized that my actions had not been entirely altruistic and that I had also compromised Alison's principles by making her complicit in my actions; the fact that she had done so willingly and knowingly was small consolation. I was also terribly afraid: I was afraid of discovery; I was afraid for Alison; I was afraid for Mzali; I was afraid for my own safety: and I was afraid for my future with Alison. My sense of self had been thrown into doubt and I was consumed by uncertainty.

Even Mandla seemed perturbed, weighed down by the enormity of our discovery: the implications were immeasurable.

"Mziki," Mandla said quietly, "what is in those hard drives is dangerous information. Were Gumede ever to find out that you have it, he would do anything and everything possible to eliminate you. He would hunt you down and kill you. You must get out of here as soon as possible."

Alison had not yet seen what was on the hard drives and was still trying to comprehend what we had told her. It all seemed so farcical and unbelievable to her that she was still trying to wrap her mind around the sheer extent and reach of our explosive findings.

"There is one thing that intrigues me," Alison articulated. "You say that the folder labeled 'Secret' refers to state capture, corruption in government and a particular Asian business concern. A thought occurred to me as we were driving here, and it may be purely coincidental, but in the Marathi language of India the word 'secret' translates as *Gupta*."

"Well, there are many, many uncomfortable *Guptas* in that folder, believe me," I replied. "I don't know what we are going to do with these hard drives. This morning, before we raided Priscilla's home, I believed that they were simply leverage to get us across the border and circumvent our arrest: something that would make Gumede backup and retreat; but what we have here is something much more. I had been hoping that we could reach an accommodation with Gumede, but clearly that is impossible now. This is so massive that neither he nor anyone else mentioned in these folders will rest until the information is safely secured and we are eliminated. If Gumede ever does find out about this, we will have signed our own death warrants."

"Thank goodness he doesn't know," Alison reassured me. "Relax. Enjoy your coffee. Let's just sit and compose ourselves before we go back to the hotel. I think we should leave this afternoon."

"I agree, but how do we leave?" I queried. "We are all pretty sure that we will be arrested at the border, and these hard drives are no longer insurance. I had originally intended to phone Gumede were we to be arrested, and to use them as a bargaining tool, believing that the information would be incriminating in small personal ways that would be mildly embarrassing to the man, and that he would sulk a little, but that he would be prepared to relax his grip on us. This is earth-shattering. I cannot believe the sheer magnitude of this information."

"Miriam did say it was huge," Alison reminded me gently.

"I know, but huge is relative: I thought Colleen would have information about marital infidelity, an illegitimate child, tax evasion, or possibly an illegal overseas bank account; something more closely associated with Gumede's personal life."

"Mziki," Mandla interrupted. "I think I have a solution to your problem. You cannot leave this country by crossing at Beitbridge in the south or even at Plumtree to the west. I know that it will be a detour, but I think you need to travel north to the confluence of the Chobe and the Zambezi Rivers, where Namibia, Zambia, Zimbabwe, and Botswana all meet. There is a tiny border post at Kazungula where security is relaxed as they cater mostly for big-spending tourists. I have friends who work at that border post," he smiled knowingly, "…well, maybe not friends, but business acquaintances. I will phone these friends of mine and ask them not to detain you. They owe me favors, as I do Mzali, and they are not fond of Gumede." I now had some inkling of Mandla's business activities!

"Thanks, Mandla," Alison responded. "How far from here is Kazungula?"

"I suppose it is about three hundred kilometers," Mandla mused. "But you will need to take the rented Land Cruiser and leave your own car here; some of those roads are treacherous and you may have to deflate the tires when traveling on the dirt roads to get more traction in the loose Kalahari sand."

"What are you going to do Mandla?" True to character Alison was always concerned about the well-being of others.

"I'm going to go to the communal lands in Tsholotsho and visit my family. If they are asked, they will all swear that I was visiting them for the last two weeks." He smiled wanly. "In fact, I think that I should leave right now." With that Mandla stood up and opened his wallet to pay the bill.

"Don't you dare," Alison threatened him with a smile. "You have done enough for us already. Thank you."

I rose and shook Mandla's hand. "Mandla," I said, "thank you for everything that you have done for Alison and me. I am grateful. If there is anything I can ever do for you, please let me know. It has been an absolute pleasure meeting you." I meant every word.

"Likewise," smiled Mandla. "*Hamba Gahshle*: Go Well."

"*Shahla Gahshle*: Stay Well," I responded sincerely as he turned and walked out of our lives.

Alison and I decided to stay a little longer, not wanting to leave this refuge from reality. As we later found out, it was a propitious decision. As she held my hand in silence, her own hand appeared quite naked and underdressed. I felt frustrated, as though fate were conspiring against me; I never would find the right moment, the perfect moment, to unveil the silver and topaz ring that was still so lonely in our picnic basket. We each ordered another cup of coffee, which was doing little to calm me down, but I wanted to delay our return to the hotel for as long as possible. Besides which, even the sludge at the bottom of the coffee cup was tasty.

"Alison honey," I said, "thank you so much for helping us this morning. You really did not need to get involved in this debacle."

"It was a pleasure," she grinned. "It was quite fun acting like a spy. I enjoyed the cloak and dagger; at least I did until I found out exactly what you had taken. At least life is no longer dull and boring!"

I was delighted. "I don't think that I have ever been bored since first I met you," I confessed, exposing my vulnerability. "I think my greatest fear is that you will grow bored with me and that somehow I will fail to measure up to your expectations."

"You have added a healthy measure of gin to the tonic of my life," Alison reassured me with a broad smile. I was tempted to rush off to the Land Cruiser and find the ring which was still languishing there, when, once again, I was thwarted: my phone rang. Once again, it was Mzali.

CHAPTER 40

Mzali's voice was faint and feeble. Something was wrong!

"What's the matter Mzali?" I asked, fearing the worst.

"I have just had another visit from the police, and this time they were not polite. I'm afraid I am no longer as good looking as you remember me."

There was an edge of hysteria to Mzali's trembling voice, and I knew instantly that our lives were once again about to take an unpredicted course. I also knew that he must have been beaten and tortured while I had been sipping coffee, oblivious to his plight.

"What did they do to you?"

"These are inventive men," Mzali's voice quivered. "They have been using iron filings on me, and they have used electricity expertly."

I shuddered with empathy. By iron filings, Mzali was referring to tubes of cloth material, filled with iron filings, and then sealed. They were then used as a cosh, and were brutal in the extreme, breaking bones and rupturing organs beneath the skin, yet never tearing the skin itself and seldom leaving a bruise.

"I'm so sorry Mzali. What can I do?"

"Get out of this country right now. The police are coming for you and Alison. I know that Mandla helped you this morning because I asked him to. Someone saw you, and someone reported you to Gumede. He is incensed and will stop at nothing to get whatever it is that you have. Whatever it was that you found this morning has got him worried and angry. Mziki, I fear for you. Are you in the hotel?"

"No," I answered, desperately trying to collect my thoughts.

"Good. Do not go back to the hotel. They know where you are staying, and they will be waiting for you. I'm sorry Bruce, but I told them about the tablets," Mzali apologized.

"Forget about them," I reassured him, irritated by his concern for me and the tablets when he was so hurt. "They are ancient history. It's you whom I'm worried about."

"Don't worry about me," Mzali ordered. "I will survive this. But if you do not act swiftly I do not think that you will. At what time do you think you might have been spotted?"

"It must have been as we were leaving; that was probably about midday, perhaps a little before" I replied, fairly certain of the time. We arrived at Déjà vu at just after 12:30 and it was now 2:30 in the afternoon.

"This must be important for them to have acted so quickly," Mzali reasoned. "They arrived here at about 1 o'clock, and have only just left. These men seem determined and I am sure that there will soon be roadblocks on all the roads leading to Bulawayo. Act quickly. Protect yourself and Alison."

"Mzali, I will phone you back a little bit later. Get yourself to a doctor or, better still, get a doctor to come and see you. Hang in there." Ending the call, I delivered the bad news to Alison. Her face was riddled with concern.

"We must get back to Bryan," insisted Alison, succinctly weighing up the situation. We paid our bill and departed.

I drove slowly, not wanting to attract undue attention, and stopped the car about a block away from the hotel. There must have been a dozen police cars outside; I could hear sirens wailing, and I could see the blue police emergency lights flashing insistently. I thought about walking in and surrendering myself to the police, offering myself in return for the safety of Alison and Bryan, but I knew that Gumede would never allow Alison or Bryan to go free: They knew too much. I also knew that were Gumede to get hold of me that my life expectancy would be short.

Something stubborn inside of me refused to allow surrender and something dark within me wanted to punish Gumede. My fears for my own safety paled in comparison to my fear that Alison could be hurt. I also knew that we were now beyond redemption and had no recourse to the law: *personae non-gratae*. The legal system would never protect us from Gumede. The thought of Alison being raped or killed appalled me.

It was obvious now that Bryan was already in police custody, and that we could not go near the hotel. I was distraught and did not know what to do, who to approach, or where to go. I knew that there was nothing Alison or I could do to help Bryan now. At least he could argue that he was not with our party and had joined our excursion out to Kataza for curiosity's sake. He did not know that we had discovered any incriminating evidence against anyone and only knew that Mandla and I had been looking for information. I reasoned that Bryan was not guilty of anything, and that he might have an unpleasant experience with the police, but that he would eventually be released.

Reluctantly, I eased the car away and headed toward the old Essexvale road, which I knew was seldom used. Once on it, I drove onto a side road, stopping about two hundred meters down the track, hidden from any passing traffic. I knew that we had to abandon our plan to go north, but I had to think of another route to safety. I was lucky in that I react well under stress, and was thinking lucidly. I was able to detach emotion from the situation and reason with penetrating clarity; a plan was starting to form and take shape in my mind, but it was audacious and reckless. The more I considered it, the more rational it became, and I did not see that there were any other options. As I thought and plotted, planned and pondered, it occurred to me that Mzali was in just as much mortal danger as Alison and I were. I outlined my plan to Alison, and while she was thinking it through, I phoned Mzali again. Mzali answered immediately.

"Mzali my friend," I said, "I think I have a plan to get out of here. I also know that you are in danger and that your life is hanging in the balance. I think that you should join us, because if you don't, I don't think that you will live to see Christmas."

"Thank you, my friend," Mzali replied tepidly, "but no thanks. I know that my association with you will probably get me killed because that is the kind of man that Gumede is, but I am ready to see Lucy and Busisiwe again. I have led a full life."

Although I felt desperately sorry for Mzali, I was shocked by his mordant resignation. I needed to talk some sense into him.

"Don't talk nonsense," I chided Mzali. "Self-pity does not suit you: you are the headmaster of a school. Your children need you and your staff members need you. Besides which, you don't want me to spend the rest of my life living in guilt do you? I have a plan that can save us all." I obviously piqued his curiosity because he asked me what my plan was.

"I'll tell you that when I see you in person," I promised. "Can you get to the old Diana's Pool turnoff?" Mzali told me that he could, and I asked him to meet me there.

"Before you put the phone down Mzali, I have a favor to ask of you. Alison and I have not had time to stop anywhere for provisions, and we drove straight out to the old Essexvale road, which is where we are parked right now. Would you be able to stop and get some provisions for us all?" I enquired hopefully.

"Sure," he replied. "What do you need?"

"If possible, could you get about thirty cans of corned meat, as much clean water as you can carry, talcum powder, paraffin, candles, a couple of pangas, string, and some sweets; peppermints will do."

"I'll bring them," he promised. "Just give me a moment to write that down."

"Oh, and Mzali, I think you should do this quickly. Leave now. It won't be long before there are police roadblocks on every road in the province:

there might already be blocks up on the main roads. I can guarantee you that within an hour this place will be completely impenetrable. I'm pretty sure that the first roadblocks will be set up closer to Bulawayo, so we can still meet at Diana's Pool, but only if we hurry."

Diana's Pool was about halfway between Bulawayo and Esigodini and it was once a picnic Mecca. Residents of Bulawayo would often come out for the day at the picturesque natural rock pool. There was a small waterfall, more of a waterslide really, that fed into a large pool, and it was the perfect place for a family to spend an afternoon. I was pretty sure that it had probably not seen a visitor for nearly twenty years, but I could be wrong. More importantly, Diana's Pool was a gateway to the imposing, majestic, and virtually impenetrable Matopos Mountains.

*****

Removing his glasses, Bryan placed his book beside him on the bed and shut his eyes, hoping to fall asleep quickly. A little nap would do him good. As he was drifting off to sleep the sound of a key turning in the door snapped him back to reality. Before he could stand, three men burst into the room.

"Professor Cameron?" The man was attired in a black pinstripe suit and had a prosthetic leg.

"Yes," he mumbled. "What is this all about?"

His question was never answered as the other two men, dressed in jeans and T-shirts, gripped his wrists, twisted his arms behind his back and shackled him in handcuffs. Muttering protestations, a confused Bryan was led outside and hustled into an Audi sport utility vehicle which roared away toward the suburb of Famona en route to the airport.

"Where are we going?"

"Why are you doing this?"

"What have I done wrong?"

None of his questions were answered.

After about ten minutes of driving, they arrived at an innocuous-looking house and parked in the garage. Bryan was bundled out of the car and led inside to the kitchen. The heavy curtains were drawn closed, and he struggled to see until the lights were switched on, nearly fainting with shock when he saw the kitchen table. Spread across the top were a variety of instruments, none of which reassured him. There were pliers, knives, hammers, nails, and sealing tape. There was also a police rubber cosh and electric cables. Bryan felt light-headed as the blood drained from his face, and his heart began racing, fueled by adrenaline.

The well-dressed man shoved him into a wooden chair and his two colleagues got busy. Bryan was stripped naked and secured to the chair: he didn't bother resisting because he knew that it would be pointless.

"I don't understand. What is happening?" He looked at his captor, recognizing that this was an evil man, devoid of mercy and his heart sank farther.

When he was safely tethered, the horror began.

"Why are you in this country?"

"I came to see a colleague in Harare and then I wanted to visit the museum in Bulawayo."

Wrong answer! Electric cables were pushed onto the soft tender flesh of his groin and unbearable pain surged through him.

"Stop! Please stop!"

"Answer my questions honestly."

"We came to visit a farm near Esigodini hoping to find ancient artifacts."

"Did you find any?"

"Yes, we found some bangles and some clay tablets."

"What else did you find?"

"Nothing." Once again, unbelievable agony coursed through him. His vision blurred but he was still able to see the two torturers, smiling with delight.

"Your colleagues have taken something precious of mine. Where are they?"

"I don't know." Agony flooded him. "Please stop. I was going to meet with them later today. I don't know what they found. I didn't want to have any part of their burglary."

"So, you knew that they were engaged in criminal activity. What were they looking for?"

"I don't know." Bryan's hand was now cuffed to the table leg and one of his torturers gripped his left thumbnail with the pliers, pulling relentlessly. Bryan screamed in agony, but this only seemed to encourage his tormentors. He broke—rather, he shattered. Incapable of comprehending why he was being tortured and unable to bear the pain, he began sobbing uncontrollably. All three men laughed heartily: this was wonderfully amusing.

"Why were they engaged in criminal activity?"

Hoping for release from this nightmare, Bryan blurted out everything he knew—which was very little.

"They were trying to find information to protect themselves from a man named Gumede. They heard that one of his acquaintances had information to use against him, and they were afraid that Mr. Gumede would persecute them unless they had leverage against him."

"What did they find?"

"I don't know. I have not heard from them since early this morning." The man with the prosthetic leg lost patience and his temper. "You white bastard. You're lying! I want to know where you were going to meet them. You were involved!"

In a burst of rage, Gumede grabbed the police cosh, delivering an almighty blow to Professor Cameron's head, connecting him just above the right ear. Bryan died instantly.

*****

I drove cautiously along the old Essexvale road which eventually linked up with the main road between Bulawayo and Esigodini. Essexvale was the old name for Esigodini. I knew that we were taking a risk by traveling along this main artery, but I also knew that there were only another seven or eight kilometers until we reached the Diana's Pool turnoff. My gamble paid off, and we turned onto the dirt track that led to Diana's Pool.

I drove until there was a curve and a dip in the road, screening us from the main road. Alison and I got out of the Land Cruiser and started packing our rucksacks. I could see that Alison was confused; this was all happening a little too fast to make sense. She had not yet fully accepted our precarious situation. I needed to get her focused.

I set Alison to work, hoping that by giving her something to occupy her mind, it would allow her time to come to terms with our unfortunate reality. "Alison, honey," I said in a soothing tone, "We need to ignore anything that is too bulky or too heavy; we can only take the bare essentials with us, Mzali is bringing some food and water. We will need basic medical equipment, sleeping bags, the collapsible tent, and some clothes: preferably hard-wearing, and preferably khaki, green, or brown. We do not want to be wearing bright orange clothes. Oh," I added as an afterthought, "we will also need tea bags, sugar, powdered soup, and some basic cooking utensils. Pack some matches too."

We were still busy sorting and discarding our luggage when Mzali arrived, looking grim. His face was a welter of bruises and cuts, his lips were swollen, and his right eye was almost closed shut with swelling.

"Hello again Mzali," I greeted him. "Are you all right?"

"I'll be okay," Mzali reassured me without conviction.

"Are there any broken bones?"

"No, I don't think so," Mzali diagnosed, prodding his chest. "My ribs are sore, but otherwise I'm still healthy."

"You were wrong, your looks have improved substantially since this morning," I joked, trying to add some levity to the situation. He tried valiantly to smile, but it obviously hurt him and he grimaced instead.

"Hi Mzali," Alison greeted him. She examined his wounds: "My, they have done a job on you," she commiserated, trying to disguise her shock.

"I'll survive," Mzali reassured her dolefully.

"We will all survive," I promised emphatically, not truly convinced of my own words.

"Come Mziki," Mzali instructed, "tell me about this fine plan of yours."

"Let's go back to the car and get comfortable," I suggested, "and then I will outline the plan of action."

We settled ourselves in the car, and Alison turned on the radio. It must have been shortly after five o'clock in the evening, and we were just in time to hear the tail end of the news broadcast. The broadcaster was announcing that a visiting professor had been mugged and robbed in Centenary Park earlier that afternoon. The police reported that he had died of his injuries. We all looked aghast, scarcely believing what we had just heard. It was now clear that Gumede would go to any lengths to catch us. Sanity is seldom an absolute and Gumede's was obviously a darker shade of sane, poised on the precipice. Alison was horrified.

"I can't believe it. It was only the day before yesterday that we were at Kataza, and only yesterday morning that we were at Khami; this afternoon we were sipping coffee with Mandla, and this morning Bryan was alive and well. What on earth is going on?"

"One day a rooster; the next day a feather duster," I responded heartlessly. It was not intended as a joke, but a reminder of our own mortality. Alison squinted at me with disgust, misinterpreting my intention.

"Are you serious? This is not the appropriate time for jokes."

"I'm sorry," I apologized contritely, "but I am not joking. I think we need to be mindful of the fact that we are in great danger."

"What I don't understand is how this is all happening so quickly," Alison puzzled, bemused.

"I know. This is not the sort of news that would normally be broadcast. We must assume that Gumede is sending us a warning. Only three people were intended to hear that broadcast and they are all sitting in this car," I said mournfully.

"If Bryan is dead," Mzali accurately assessed, "they will be searching for us in earnest, and they cannot admit that we have sensitive information; they will have to focus attention on the tablets." As if to validate Mzali's observation, the news broadcaster started to announce the last snippet of news:

"In unrelated news, police are searching for three dangerous criminals, two white individules and a Black accomplice. These criminals are in possession of items important to the heritage of Zimbabwe, which were stolen from the Museum of Natural History earlier today. Their names are Bruce Savage, Alison Turner, and Mzali Sithole. A reward is being offered for any information leading to their arrest. Motorists are advised that police roadblocks have been set up on all roads leading to and from Bulawayo."

That, too, was a warning, but it was also important information: the police thought that Alison and I were still in Bulawayo. We had more time than I had thought.

"Tell us about your plan, Mziki," Mzali instructed me with contrived enthusiasm, his voice dull and listless.

"We all know that every road is blocked and that there is no way out of here," I began. "They think that we are like three birds trapped in a cage, but they have left the cage door unlocked. There is one place that they will not expect us to go, over there!" I said, pointing west to the Matopos Mountains. Both Alison and Mzali looked at me incredulously.

"You're insane," Alison reprimanded me sullenly.

"You can't be serious," Mzali said, appalled.

"Think about it. There is no other way out. If we cut across the Matopos we will almost be at the border with Botswana. I doubt that anyone will ever suspect that we are in the Matopos. They will patrol the roads, but they are unlikely to send a patrol into the mountains: it's too wild."

"There. You've said it yourself, it's too wild," Mzali pleaded.

"It's our only option," I stated. "We can do this; we have the supplies and the motivation. I know that it will be tough going, but it's not impossible. We can get beyond each and every kopje."

"No way," said Alison.

"I don't think that anyone has ever walked from one end of the Matopos to the other," said Mzali incredulously.

"I don't know of anyone offhand," I replied, "but I'm sure that someone must have done it at some time. Please, guys, think this through; this is the only way that we will come out of this alive."

Mzali and Alison were silent, analyzing the situation and weighing the options.

"What if we run out of food?" Alison asked.

"I'm sure that Mzali and I will be able to rustle up enough to keep us going," I answered.

"Hau," Mzali snorted contemptuously. "You've never killed anything in your life."

"I know that," I replied. "I'm proud of that. I have no intention of killing anything unless we absolutely need to. If it is a matter of survival,

I will kill, but only reluctantly. I'm sure that we have enough provisions to survive."

"What if we need to hunt?" Mzali asked.

"I will hunt if I have to," I assured him. "But you know that I have never had any time or sympathy for hunters. I simply do not understand how anyone can get any joy from killing an innocent, unsuspecting animal. If it is a matter of survival, I accept that."

"You say you're not a killer," said Alison, "but we have all that canned, corned meat in Mzali's car. Those animals died so that you could eat. Surely that makes you complicit; after all, you are paying good money for that meat and financing the death of those animals."

"Maybe so; I like meat and I am not going to stop eating it, but that doesn't mean that I have to go out and kill the animal myself," I replied. "Talking of canned meat, what gets me particularly incensed is canned hunting."

I was talking about the practice of rearing lions in captivity so that they are relatively tame and trusting. Big game hunters from America and Germany, propelled by an atavistic urge to slaughter, paid extravagant sums of money to shoot these magnificent beasts from the safety of a cage. They then returned home with their trophies and boasted of their masculinity and bravery. I reflected for a moment on the inhumanity of man, on the cruelty that makes men worse than animals, and likened these innocent lions to the gladiators of old. Both were born for one specific purpose: to die for the entertainment of others. Life is a precious commodity, particularly for the organism which is living it.

"Those are the worst sort of cowards," I said with venom. "They should be skinned alive and left in the sun. Even better, they should be given a stick and put into the same cage as those lions they bravely kill."

It is strange, the way that the human mind reacts to crises. The issue of survival, and the possibility of hunting and killing, had been raised, and I resented the thought of having to deprive another living creature of its life to sustain my own. I desperately needed an issue, any issue, to allow me to vent and purge my negative emotions: fear, doubt, and anger. This random, peripheral, issue allowed me an outlet to void the negativity—allowed me to think with greater celerity and to focus on the pressing issue of our survival. I believe that Alison instinctively understood this need, and she gave my hand an understanding squeeze.

"You see," Mzali said triumphantly, "there is a killer inside you; the right buttons simply need to be pushed."

"Let's focus," Alison chided us. "I'm willing to try this simply because I don't see any other option. What do we do now?"

I suggested that we drive onward to Diana's Pool, a distance of about twenty kilometers. That would probably be as far as we could go in a vehicle. The rest of our journey we would have to manage by walking. So, we got into our cars and we eased our way toward Diana's Pool. The road rapidly deteriorated, and about ten minutes after setting off, Alison and I heard Mzali hooting behind us. His car simply could not take any more abuse. We drove Mzali's car as far into the bush as we possibly could, away from passersby. I can still recall Mzali's standing next to his car, of which he was so proud, with tears in his eyes as he left it for the last time. I think it must have been at this moment that I knew that there was no going back. This was do or die.

PART THREE

CHAPTER 41

The Matopos is one of the last truly wild places on Earth: it is untamed, and parts of it are almost untouched by man. The Matopos is kilometer after interminable kilometer of enormous granite kopjes and as one ends, the other begins. In all, it is approximately three thousand square kilometers of massive kopjes, some of them hundreds of meters high, and each kopje a jumble of rocks and boulders clambering over each other. Some of these kopjes are "castle kopjes", huge blocks of granite so weathered by time that boulders perch precariously on the summit and roundabout it, like the crenellations on a castle. Some of these boulders have crashed to the ground and the base of those kopjes is littered with enormous boulders, the majority of them larger than a man.

Other kopjes have weathered differently, and these are the venerable "bald heads", smooth concave granite domes of immense size. The bases of the kopjes are fringed with tangled masses of vegetation which are often almost impenetrable. Because of erosion, the valleys between ridges of kopjes are incredibly fertile, and the vegetation is dense and lush. The golden grass stands as high as a man, and these valleys are peppered with magnificent old trees: mukwa, msasa, and lucky bean trees with their beautiful, scarlet flowers.

The Matopos is imposing and majestic, and there is a deeply spiritual quality to the place. Because it is so inaccessible, and because the habitat is so ideal, the Matopos abounds with animals. The stately sable, impala, and kudu roam around in small herds, and the Matopos is swarming with snakes of every shape and size, from pythons to puff adders, black mambas, and cobras. This veritable Eden has the largest population of leopards in the world because game is so plentiful and the kopjes so protective. If memory serves me correctly, the Matopos also has the largest concentration of birds of prey in the world.

I have never been in a cathedral, but I imagine that being in the Matopos probably had the same quality as walking into a Gothic cathedral for the first time: humbling and overwhelming. Whenever I have been in the Matopos I have been infused by a sense of wonder. The silence, the solitude and the majesty of these imperious, hallowed hills have always resonated within me, striking some latent primitive

198

chord. The grandeur and imposing size of the Matopos remind me of how insignificant man is, that we are simply caretakers for a brief moment in time, and that our tenure will fade and vanish. Yet the Matopos will remain, in permanent primordial splendor, a silent witness to the vanity of man. They have been around for eons and they will remain long after we have gone. Every tribe and every culture that has ever lived here has regarded these hills as holy and sacred: for good reason; there is a truly ethereal quality about them. It was into this dangerous, intractable, and unforgiving wilderness that we were about to venture.

With Mzali safely ensconced in the back seat, we crashed and bumped our precarious way toward Diana's Pool on a track that masqueraded as a road. When we finally got there, I recognized a clearing where the parking area had once been, overgrown now with tufts of grass and small bushes. I drove the car as far into the bush as I possibly could, and we disembarked and collected our rucksacks. We decided to discard the tent and many of our clothes, reasoning that they were unnecessary burdens. The hard drives we wrapped in cloth and Alison and I each took one, placing them in pouches on the side of our rucksacks. We also carefully wrapped the tablets and placed them in Alison's rucksack.

Diana's Pool looked tranquil and beautiful, devoid of litter now and restored to her former glory. The water flowed gently down the slope of the granite into the rock pool, and I remembered that the water was icy cold. Mzali, Alison, and I stood in front of Diana's Pool, our arms resting on the shoulders of the person next to us, contemplating the enormity of the vista before us and the magnitude of our undertaking. As I peered into the translucent pool and my ugly visage stared back at me, it struck me that this was no time for reflection.

"Every journey starts with the first step," I said, artificially cheerful. "All together now, right foot forward on the count of three. One; two; three …"

We all lurched forward together and leaped into the unknown; our perilous journey into the Matopos had begun.

We crossed the small stream below Diana's Pool and started across to the other side. We walked, scrambled, and climbed for another half-hour or so, until we decided that we needed to bivouac for the night. We found a suitable spot at the base of a small kopje and gratefully dispensed with our rucksacks. Mzali collected wood and we made some tea. None of us were particularly hungry so we all decided to forgo eating: I think our appetites had disappeared when we had heard of Bryan's fate.

Mzali sat apart from Alison and me, sullen and brooding. I could only imagine what horrors were traversing his tortured mind as I contemplated his ravaged face, still suppurating and seeping; his right eye was tightly shut, and the pulsing wound on his cheekbone was exposed and infected.

Correctly, I blamed myself for his dilemma. I had walked into his safe and dependable world and had taken all that he held dear. The edifice of his world had come crashing down, and he was confused and disconsolate. I think we were all struggling to comprehend our situation, but his plight was far beyond mine.

"Alison honey," I implored her, "Mzali needs attention."

Together the two of us tried to mend the physical wounds but, as always in life, there is no palliative for psychological wounds.

Alison applied a gelatinous antiseptic lotion to Mzali's cuts, covering them with plaster, but my feeble attempts to apologize and to console him were fruitless. He had retreated into a dark and dangerous place.

So much had happened in so short a time that we were all struggling to comprehend the rapidity with which our reality had shifted. We were so overcome with mental ennui and physical fatigue that we were careless. No one took watch that night and we took no precautions against predators. We were complacent and lazy. We were also lucky. We got through the evening unscathed, the three of us sleeping close together for imagined protection.

We woke up early the next morning, and as we sat around the small fire, I explained how I thought we should progress. I also made it clear that my memory was faded, and that none of my estimates were to be taken literally. I had spent some time in the Matopos when I was a youngster, but my knowledge of the hills was scanty.

"So far as I can remember," I said, "if we travel south from here we will come to Lumene Falls in about eight or nine kilometers. We then need to travel approximately southwest to Impu and Wabeyi kopjes, which is about fourteen kilometers. From there we will head due west to Khozi Hill, another nine kilometers, and on to Shashane Dam. That will be our biggest challenge because it is about fifty kilometers of hiking.

"At that point, we should emerge from the southern escarpment of the Matopos, and the worst will be over. From there we should skirt the western extremity of the massif and make our way to Ingwesi reservoir. That distance alone is about forty kilometers. Once we reach the Ingwesi reservoir we will be about thirty kilometers from the border with Botswana."

Alison shook her head in despair and disbelief.

"I can't believe we're doing this," she muttered to herself, cradling her chin in her hands.

Mzali put his arms around her: "One step at a time," he advised her. "Right now, we are in the middle of desolation, but a week from now you could be back in your comfortable home. We will all get through this," he encouraged her.

"Alison honey," I consoled her. "This sounds like a lot of walking, and it is, but we can do it. Just try and think of what the alternative is: certain death. A week from now this will all be over and we will have a wonderful story to tell our grandchildren."

Alison looked at me as though I was crazy. "You must be dreaming," she sulked and then she started chuckling cheerlessly. "What the hell, let's get started."

While Alison packed away the cooking utensils, Mzali and I repacked the rucksacks, taking care to give Alison the lighter load. The corned meat and the water comprised the bulk of the weight, and both Mzali and I knew that our load would become increasingly burdensome the more fatigued we became. I thought that I would try to phone Johan, just to let him know that we were in trouble, and perhaps the South African police could intervene on our behalf but, as I expected, there was no cell coverage out here: we really were on our own.

The first part of the journey was relatively easy as we traversed a relatively flat slab of granite for a kilometer or so, but within half an hour the weight of the rucksacks began to tell, biting into our shoulders and chafing with each step that we took. I could feel my skin becoming raw and the rucksack kept thumping into the small of my back, bruising my kidneys and making walking painful. Strangely enough, the rucksacks became less of a hindrance when we came to more difficult terrain. The constant climbing and descending meant that the rucksacks remained stable, but new physical tribulations beset us. Our knees began to take strain, unused to the exercise, and I could feel the tendons below my kneecap starting to hurt. Our breathing became increasingly shallow from all the exertion, and within another hour, our bodies were aching and our muscles were cramping. It was time to rest.

We had hardly said a word since we had left our Diana's Pool camp, so focused were we on the task at hand. It was Alison who had set the pace, and I was impressed with her fitness and her resolve. We sat down on the rocky ground to catch our breath, and I reminded Alison and Mzali that our biggest threat was dehydration: we needed to drink water regularly if we were to maintain our energy. I asked Mzali for the packet of peppermints, which I duly opened and rationed out.

"Here, suck on one of these whenever your mouth gets dry," I advised. "Try not to chew it, and your mouth will stay moist."

Once we had caught our breath, we set off again. I was filled with trepidation because I was already exhausted, and we had only just started our journey. I had to keep reminding myself that the first part of a long run is always the worst and that once a rhythm had been settled into, and the breathing became more regular, the easier it became. The key was to focus on the rhythm of breathing and getting into a metronomic cadence.

We climbed and we descended, kopje after tortuous kopje until our bodies were aching and our muscles were cramping. All the muscles in my body were rebelling, shrieking in agony, and my calves were cramping regularly. Every few steps I would need to bend down and massage them. Over and above that I was getting shin splints, the muscle membrane was starting to become inflamed, and I was taking shorter and shorter steps, in a perpetual limp.

Persevere; persevere; keep moving," I kept whispering to myself, urging myself to take just one more step—step, after step, after step, after step. The searing overhead sun was literally grilling us and our shirts were saturated with sweat. I was continually wiping the sweat away from my eyes, which were beginning to sting, and I could see that both Alison and Mzali were also starting to take strain, yet neither of them complained. Possibly they were made of sterner stuff than I.

We had been walking for about four hours, yet had only traveled about three kilometers, I guesstimated which was not surprising since we were constantly climbing and crawling up rocks and scrambling down slopes. It was difficult going, but we managed nonetheless.

"Let's stop and have something to eat," I said. "You guys must be exhausted."

"I thought no one was ever going to suggest it," Alison said with relief.

Mzali offered to prepare lunch, which meant opening a can of corned meat and issuing a fork to each of us. He appeared to have reconciled with his situation and was in better spirits, although I suspect that his wounds cut deep, and his calm attitude was more superficial than his physical injuries. I sat next to Alison and draped my arms around her.

"You are absolutely magnificent," I encouraged her sincerely. "You constantly amaze me. You are climbing up these mountains like a lovely little rock rabbit. Here you are, dressed in khaki shorts and you're still the most gorgeous woman I've ever seen. Where do you get all your energy from?"

"Thanks, Bruce darling," Alison said. "You're a dear. I'm afraid I don't feel attractive and I'm exhausted. I don't know if we can do this." Alison held my hand and squeezed, but she did not smile. "One minute we were in heaven, the next we were in hell."

"We are not in hell; perhaps we are in purgatory, but we are safe, we have each other, and we will get out of this. I promise you that." I was trying to keep her spirits buoyed, but I think I failed.

We ate our meal and set off again. This time I took the lead, largely because I wanted to set the pace and I wanted the pace to be slow: I was even struggling to keep up with myself! Rock after rock, step after step, and kopje after kopje we overcame. One moment seemed to blur seamlessly into the other, and I lost track of time; I was only aware of the sun shifting steadily to the west. Finally, at about 3:30 in the afternoon, we reached Lumene Falls. The little river which we had been following started to cascade gently down an escarpment, gathering momentum as the gradient sharpened.

The Lumene Falls is a series of short cascades, the water tumbling and gurgling merrily down from one little pool of water into the next. I had been here a couple of times in my youth, which now seemed so long ago, and I remembered it fondly.

We climbed down the rocks to below the waterfalls and walked along the riverbank, the shallow river widening below the falls. There was a little avenue of short green grass on either side of the river, separating the river from a phalanx of trees: a guard of honor. It was breathtakingly beautiful.

"I think we should camp here for the night," I said. "I think we've had quite enough exercise for one day."

I knew that I certainly had. We all needed to rest, and as we lay on the banks of the river, propping ourselves up with our arms, we admired the scenery and began to relax. I was convinced that we were safe from the police. My only concern was that we would be physically able to complete the journey. There was not a doubt in my mind that no one would come looking for us in this remote wilderness. I had neither heard nor seen a helicopter, and I took this as a sure sign that no one even considered that we would be here. I drank in the scenery, lapping up the beauty of the silver river shimmering silently into the distance like an iridescent snake, admiring the scarlet hues of a lucky bean tree, and appreciating the ancient cycads and tree ferns which kept watch over us. *This is a primeval paradise*, I thought to myself.

"This place is absolutely beautiful," Alison said admiringly. "This is like a wild Garden of Eden."

Great minds think alike! I caught a faint whiff of something sweet.

"Can you smell that?" I asked Alison.

"Yes, I can," she said. "It's sublime. What is it?"

"Wild thyme," I replied. "It's a rambling bush with white flowers. Sometimes they are blue, but the sweetest smell is from the pure white plants."

The three of us lay there together, composing our thoughts until I decided that it was time to come clean. I grasped Alison's hand, and together we waded into the cool water of the Lumene River. It was shallow and only came up to our calves, but it was so icy cold that my flesh tingled.

"Mzali," I said, "Alison and I are going to have a wash."

"Good idea," Mzali acknowledged. "I think I'll also get clean, but I want a shower. I'll go up to the waterfalls." He was obviously thinking of our privacy.

Alison and I waded downstream, hand-in-hand, until we came to a bend in the river where we could preserve our modesty. We undressed on the bank and waded back to the middle of the river. I cupped handfuls of the pellucid water and started splashing it over my body to wash away the dirt and the dust, and Alison did the same.

As Alison was rubbing the dirt off her legs, I marveled at her beauty. I started washing her body for her, particularly the part that she struggled to reach: her back. We sat down in the river together and helped one another to wash away the sins of the world. With Alison gently spooning water onto my face and caressing the dirt away, I felt as though she was somehow anointing me and forgiving me my indiscretions. Not a word was said, so comfortable were we with each other. As I stood up, with Alison beside me, shafts of early evening sunlight were lancing through the trees, and I felt like Adam in his kingdom, innocent and naked in an unspoiled virgin paradise, alone with my Eve. There was something surreal about the moment. Naked, I hugged Alison close and then held her at arm's length.

"I want you to know that I will never let you down, even if it takes my last breath. If need be I will carry you in my arms across each valley and over every mountain to keep you safe. I will never allow any harm to come to you. Please believe me when I say that you're the most precious thing in the world to me," I implored her. Alison looked me squarely in the eye, and then she held me again, her head resting on my shoulder.

"I am going to hold on tight to you," she whispered, "and I will never let go: I am going to enjoy every living moment with you." We stood there embracing in the middle of the river for a small eternity and then we slowly walked to the river bank together.

We got dressed and wended our way painfully back to where we had left the rucksacks. Mzali was already dressed, although not yet fully dry. Completing the metaphor of Eden, we noticed a snake, probably a cobra, slither through the grass toward the trees. We found a suitable spot for our sleeping bags, and I wished that we had a tent and camp chairs. But we did not, so we had to make do with what we had. We prepared a small fire and Alison heated a couple of cans of corned meat while Mzali filled a little can with water so that we could brew some tea. We were all going to have to get used to eating small meals. By the time we had eaten, the sun was setting, gilded gold and bronze, and we sat around the fire, massaging our aching thighs and our battered egos. My entire body felt sore: I had used long-dormant muscles which were waking from their lethargy and complaining bitterly about it. Every inch of every muscle was stiff and painful. Judging from all the whimpers, sighs, and rubbing coming from the other two, I believe we all felt the same way.

As we recuperated and relaxed beside the river, where the soil was moist, and the olive-green grass was soft and comfortable, a choir of frogs began to rehearse, celebrating spring and new life. At first, their voices were hesitant and tentative, but before long we were drowned by the operatic sound, our aquatic companions finding their confidence. The sound had a soporific effect, and although it pervaded the evening it was surprisingly soothing. Suddenly and immediately it stopped—something had disturbed them.

When sound ceases in the bush that is the time to be cautious. Within a few minutes, the musical feast began again, and once more we were engulfed in a crescendo of sound, each frog trying to outdo its rivals. The melodious frogs were offset by the high-pitched acoustics of the Cicada beetles and the intermittent accompaniment of the Crickets. We were assailed by a veritable orchestra of the wild. Eventually, the chorus subsided, and we were left to our solitude and our silence once more.

We sat together well into the evening, reluctant to sleep, fearing the dangers around us. We talked to distract ourselves from the real world, hoping to forget our problems if only for a short while.

Mzali took a swig of his hot, sweet Earl Grey tea and said: "I think that this is as close as anyone can get to true freedom."

"Ah," I responded, "true freedom is an illusion: like reality."

"What do you mean?" asked Alison.

"I simply mean that there is no such thing as complete freedom. Freedom always comes with a sacrifice."

"Go on," Mzali invited me. I think we all needed something to occupy our minds, and Mzali wanted me to talk, not really caring what I said, as long as there was sound to keep the silence of our thoughts at bay. I took the bait.

"We all think that freedom is simply about being able to do anything at all, without restriction, but this gives license to everyone to act in the same manner, which means that murder and robbery become legitimate. So, there must be rules to limit our behavior: laws. Then what good are civil liberties when you do not have the resources and the finances to exercise your choices? That means the government has a duty and an obligation to intervene: a good government facilitates educational opportunities, medical care, and pensions to protect people from their own neglect and from the fruits of their own avarice."

"I see where you are going with this," said Mzali, joining in the spirit of the exercise. "But it is no good having civil liberties and choices and having a government provide services to you if you simply remain ignorant and complacent. I think that true freedom lies in the ability to recognize that which is truly worth wanting. It is a psychological phenomenon."

I thought carefully about Mzali's observation. "I think I agree with you," I encouraged him, "but what you are saying has the smell of Communist thinking."

"It does," he agreed, "but it is a sweet scent, fragrant and pleasant." He smiled broadly, mocking me. I could see that his time in the Soviet Union had not been wasted.

"That's the wild thyme," I said, and he laughed quietly.

It was Alison who provided the *coup de grace*:

"Every society needs to have a constitution which celebrates personal freedoms and outlaws discrimination. But laws alone are not enough; society needs to function properly and the police force needs to be efficient enough to uphold the law. The laws also need to be gentle enough to protect the individual from over legislation, but tough enough to protect the individual from themselves and other people. It is amazing how swiftly people will sacrifice their civil liberties if they believe themselves to be threatened: unscrupulous people and governments manipulate this fear. But the most important aspect of true freedom is economic prosperity. Freedom cannot be attained in poverty. There is no dignity in destitution."

Here we were in the middle of nowhere waxing philosophical. It was glorious.

"I love this," I said. "I think that the greatest pleasures in life are cerebral." Ever the economist, Alison probed Mzali's mind.

"Tell me Mzali," Alison queried, "are you really a Communist?"

Mzali considered her question carefully. "I'm not a Communist in the sense that I support any dictatorship. Mziki here seems to think that I am a supporter of the old Soviet Union, but I'm not. In its purest interpretation, communism is the ultimate democracy: it is the opposite of tyranny. What I support is a system where everyone is well catered for and where all people have equal opportunities."

"That would make you a socialist," I interjected. "What about the proletarian revolution?"

Once again, Mzali thought before he spoke. "I think the proletarian revolution has already taken place," he observed, and no one even noticed. The proletarian revolution was achieved when everyone was allowed the vote: men and women, Black and white, rich and poor."

"I agree with you that communism is a beautiful dream, heaven on Earth, Mzali," the romantic in Alison unfurled. "But I'm not sure that it is attainable."

"I think it is attainable," I said, the idealist in me also surfacing. "But it is not going to come about through revolution: it will only ever come about through social evolution. People believe that capitalism and communism are incompatible enemies, but I do not think that they are. I believe that true communism will only ever be attained in a society which is incredibly wealthy and technologically sophisticated. Of course, that means that population growth needs to be curtailed. Communism will eventually emerge from capitalism. Communism is dependent upon capitalism, and the attainment of a communist society will not be despite capitalism; it will be because of it."

"I can't see that happening," Mzali said remorsefully. "Big business simply won't allow that to happen."

"I agree," Alison said, "just as the church has been prevented from interfering with politics, corporate interests should also be removed from the political arena and that includes not just big business, but also labor interests. We need to have restrictions on the operations of the stock market and on exploitative banking practices, neither of which were part of Adam Smith's Liberal vision of capitalism in the early days of the Industrial Revolution. The modern world is driven by debt and consumer credit. We need to return to a simpler, purer form of capitalism."

"Hau, this conversation is getting profound and philosophical. My head is starting to hurt," Mzali complained theatrically. I laughed; Mzali was right.

"I'm just trying to repair the damage that has been done to your mind after all those years of indoctrination," I joked.

"I was trained in Russia not China," Mzali corrected me.

"Even so, your mind has been polluted and poisoned by obnoxious ideas," I teased him.

"Of course, your mind is pristine and pure," Alison said with biting, sarcastic humor. We both knew that wasn't true.

"That's why you love me."

"That's why I like you," she corrected me. Her words lacerated my ego. She could see the self-doubt and disappointment that I felt and reached for my hand.

"I love you more than words can say," Alison said, reminding me of the old Leo Sayer song. I responded in kind.

"I love you twice as much tomorrow." As though to emphasize the point, we were once again serenaded by the philharmonic frogs; this time they sang a lullaby, coaxing us to get some sleep. We would need our strength and all our wits the next day.

CHAPTER 42

Our sleeping arrangements for the evening were the subject of much debate and concern: we were all worried about safety and wild animals. Eventually, we decided that we would all sleep together in a row beneath a suitable rocky overhang that we found. We decided that we needed to sleep in an upright position, leaning back on the rock for support: that way we would be protected from behind. We were all so tired that we knew we would have no trouble falling asleep. We had a large tin to bang on and frighten away any curious predator. Mzali and I then collected as much deadwood as we could find, particularly old branches, and arranged it and them in a protective semicircle around our sleeping area. We also filled the lid of the tin with paraffin and laid it next to the wall of branches, together with a lighter. The idea was to light the paraffin if there was danger and the dead branches would ignite—we hoped. We would all sleep with our pangas next to us, just in case a determined animal was not deterred by the fire and the noise.

"I'm not so much frightened by the leopards as by the snakes," Alison informed us.

"I agree," I said. "I'm terrified of snakes, but remember that most animals simply want to be left alone. If a snake decides to join us, it will be because it is attracted by the heat, and it should be easy to discourage at night. Snakes are cold-blooded and they would need to slither over cold granite to get here. They really aren't active at night. In fact, most animals will leave you alone if you ignore them; they will tend to warn you by hissing or rearing up if you get too close to them and they feel threatened.

"What scares me most is leopards. Leopards like to prey on baboons and they will regard us as large, ungainly monkeys; they will actively hunt us and the leopard hunts at night."

"What about hyenas?" Alison asked with a worried expression. She did not know it, but she was making me feel vulnerable and unsettled: I hadn't thought about hyenas and I dreaded them.

"Are there any hyenas around here Mzali?" I asked. Hyenas make me especially nervous: they are efficient hunters and they hunt as a pack.

They are incredibly powerful: the jaws of a hyena will crunch right through bone and they can easily bite your whole arm off. Add to this the fact that they look sinister—almost satanic. Africans associate them closely with witchcraft, as witches' cohorts, because their call sounds like evil laughter. The picture has been painted of the hyena as a cowardly scavenger, but this is a fallacy: often a cackle of hyenas will kill an antelope, and it is lions that will either wait around for their turn at the carcass or will drive the hyenas away. The hyenas will then slink, skulk, and sneak around the kill, waiting to get back at their own carcass. Because their hind legs are lower than their shoulders, they slouch toward their victims, making them appear wicked. In short, they are the epitome of all that is evil. Strangely, the closest living relative of the hyena is the sleek playful mongoose, and the hyenas are unusual in that their complex social structure is matriarchal: women rule!

"Probably," Mzali reassured me. Like leopards, hyenas also like to hunt at night. *This is getting better and better with every moment*, I thought.

"Don't worry," I said to Alison, "hyenas hate fire and noise, and if we remain vigilant we should be safe."

We decided that we would each act as a sentry for an hour at a time, and then wake up the next person on duty. Sitting side by side, with a wall of dead branches in front of us and pangas by our sides, I thought that we must have looked like three little monkeys sitting in a row: see no evil, speak no evil, hear no evil.

"What happens if we need the toilet," Alison asked. Trust her to remind us of practical matters.

"I'm afraid we're going to have to discard some of the social niceties," I apologized to Alison. "I know it may not seem terribly sanitary or civilized, but no one can break through the barrier of branches during the night: it is simply too risky. I'm sorry."

Mzali and I looked around for a bucket or a tin for us to use but could find nothing suitable. In the end, we resorted to building a small, circular stone latrine close to the branches and placed a pile of soil next to it to cover the evidence.

"I am so glad that we are all eating small meals," Alison said with disgust.

"I'm sorry Alison," I said, "but safety comes first. We are all adults and we all understand the facts of life. We simply need to understand the unpleasant necessities of the situation." Alison's sour expression showed that she may have understood, but that she was not charmed.

I decided to take first watch and decided that my shift would last for two hours, rather than the one hour that we had agreed upon, allowing the other two enough time to drift off to sleep. The first watch was uneventful, although I was constantly listening out for the high-pitched 'yip, yip, yip' of hyenas. I was relieved not to hear them and slept more soundly for that.

My second shift, early in the morning, was a little more disconcerting: I heard the occasional twig snapping, and the low grunting cough of a leopard that padded and paced softly around us, investigating the intruders in its territory. Perhaps it was simply curious because I never caught sight of it. It is amazing how the darkness of night can allow all kinds of imaginary terrors to surface and plague your thoughts, requiring all your self-control to simply stay still.

We all awoke at first light, hearing the harrowing, haunting cry of a fish eagle, so typical of the African bush. I felt refreshed, energetic, and alive, my unused muscles having responded well to the previous day's exercise, and I felt a little more limber and looser despite some lingering stiffness. Alison and I went down to the river together to splash our faces, and I was amazed by the plethora of Dragonflies skimming across the water; there were Dragonflies of every shape, size, and color, their translucent gossamer wings sparkling in the sunlight like the water, each with a lovely rainbow sheen. On our way back to meet Mzali, we noticed the distinctive pug marks of a leopard. My fears had been correct: we had had a nocturnal visitor and, judging from the number of prints, the leopard had been curious indeed.

We ate a little corned meat and drank some tea before packing our rucksacks and saying farewell to Lumene Falls. We had only walked a couple of hundred meters when I noticed a solitary marula tree close to the rocks on my right. It was pregnant with fruit, mostly unripe, but some of the small plum-like fruits were starting to turn yellow. It seemed that this Garden of Eden had its Tree of Knowledge after all.

"Have you ever tasted a marula berry?" I asked Alison, relishing the memory of the sweet taste.

"No," she replied, "but I have tasted the liqueur Amarula."

I marched her off to the marula tree and found a fruit that looked ripe.

"Try this," I suggested, "but be careful. "The skin is tough and waxy, and there is hardly any flesh. There is a big seed inside, and it is better to suck it, and appreciate the flavor." Perhaps this fruit was not yet fully ripe, because Alison's face distorted with distaste.

"This is really bitter," she grimaced, spitting the pip away in disgust.

"Everyone likes a little tart." I was trying to be amusing, but Alison ignored me, pretending not to have heard. She took a swig of water, swirled it around in her mouth, and spat it out again, trying to get rid of the foul taste. Perhaps there was a latent parable lurking in the incident: the forbidden fruit is only palatable when the time is ripe.

We made a lot better time that morning than we had the previous day, perhaps because our muscles had adapted, or perhaps we had simply committed ourselves to the task at hand. Although the going was tough, we were all in good spirits, and for some reason, the load felt lighter. Since Alison was the official trustee of the tablets, I did not want anything heavy in her rucksack for fear of damaging them, yet my own rucksack felt less heavy than the day before. After about four kilometers of walking, we came to a steep ravine and had to follow its course before once again reaching level land. We traveled about two kilometers farther and had reached the summit of one of the bald kopjes when we were confronted by a marvelous sight.

Below us was a small valley, resplendent with thickets of glorious msasa trees, their lambent spring leaves glistening, radiant in the midday sun. Some of the trees had golden leaves, others had red, or rust, or burnt orange. The result was a splash of glossy color, not unlike the colors so often associated with autumn. Unlike the autumn leaves, preparing to die and decay, these luminescent leaves were redolent of nascent life. It was spectacular.

A small herd of impala grazed languidly in the shade, and the valley was punctuated with stately mukwa trees, floating on a sea of bleached, beige grass. The castle kopje on the other side of the valley was tall, but not huge, and it was blanketed by a mass of undergrowth and rocks. As with all the kopjes in the Matopos, there was no way around it because its neighbors were so closely packed. The most energy-efficient way was to climb it at the shortest point. We descended carefully from the bald mass of granite and waded through the tawny, shoulder-high grass across the valley to the awaiting kopje. The impala sniffed the air, acknowledged our presence, and nonchalantly dismissed us.

Sitting safely under the shade of a large mukwa tree and in the shadow of the kopje, we brewed some tea and ate a few pieces of chocolate to replenish our sugar levels. While we were resting, I reflected on how much invaluable help Mzali had given, and how much he had sacrificed over the years. I had barged into his life once again, uninvited and unexpected, and he had welcomed me in like a prodigal brother. Now I had cost him his career, his car, and possibly his life. It also crossed my mind that if Alison had never met me she would be safe and happy, sitting in the security of her townhouse. I was overwhelmed by a sense of remorse and needed to expunge my guilt.

"Mzali," I said softly, "I'm grateful for all that you have done for me, not just in the last few days, but throughout my life: I mean it when I say that I think of you as a brother."

"Hau, Mziki," Mzali replied cheerfully, "I also think of you as a brother." He tried to dilute the serious tone: "But I am the older brother,

211

and you were always a big problem. You were always getting into trouble and I always had to look out for you."

"Hau, you were a naughty kid," he reminisced while chuckling to himself. I knew that, if anything, Mzali had been a lot more mischievous than I, but I didn't say so.

"Seriously Mzali," I said, "we never meant to treat you badly, or to make you feel unwanted. I realize now that we must have appeared to be condescending, but that was never our intention. Both my parents liked and respected you" Mzali digested my words for a minute; possibly he was mentally composing his response. "I loved your parents and I loved life at Kataza," he explained slowly. "It is just that when you went off to boarding school it made me resent you. Not you personally, but the unjust system that we lived in; not that anything has improved since then.

"I knew that you were a good person, but I also knew that I was just as capable as anyone else; yet you were getting a good education because you were white, and I was getting an inferior education because I was Black. I also knew that things would continue that way until we Africans got the vote.

"I imagined living in a white man's society, where everyone was prosperous and had opportunities, but with a Black government. I never imagined that this country would deteriorate and that there would be no opportunities for anyone unless they were connected to government.

"I did not fight to destroy Kataza, and I did not want your way of life to end. I was not looking for revenge: I was looking for justice. I simply wanted the same opportunities as you, and I wanted an end to racial discrimination. Now things are worse than they ever were before, and I am not convinced that we have ended discrimination. Racism and tribalism are the same thing, and the Mashona have been persecuting the Matabele ever since independence."

I tried to console him: "My dad never blamed you for leaving or for fighting on the other side. I know that he understood your reasons and that he sympathized with your cause. But we were caught up in the history of our time. We were white, and we were fighting for a way of life. That is why I supported Muzorewa: I wanted our way of life to continue, but I also wanted Black people to be a part of that. I never regarded myself as superior, because I knew it wasn't true. I know now that our actions were racist, and I accept that, and I apologize for that. We were wrong."

Mzali accepted my apology without saying a word, and we sat together in silence: brothers in arms. I did not know if I had cleared the air with him, but I felt better for having apologized: possibly I needed to say the words a lot more than he needed to hear them.

In a more somber mood now, we gathered our goods and made toward the Mtshabezi River and Impu kopje, which I estimated to be due west of us. Onwards and onwards, ever onwards, we plodded, pacing ourselves and preserving our energy as best we could. It was well into the afternoon when we finally reached Impu kopje, bald on the top, but with broken granite boulders and some sparse vegetation almost to the summit. There was a hut in the valley below the kopje and, not wanting to alert anyone to our presence, we decided to move on toward Wabeyi, hoping to reach there before sunset. It was another three kilometers away, and the terrain was rocky and uneven, but we arrived at Wabeyi just as the sun was setting. Wabeyi kopje was tall and steep, with a ridge of granite at the top that looked a little like a Mohican haircut. Just in front of Wabeyi stood a smaller kopje, and it was here that we decided to spend the night.

As we approached, there was a flurry of activity as we disturbed some little rock hyrax sun tanning on the rocks, the cute little creatures scurrying to the safety of whatever crevices they could find. In the last light of the day, we found a suitable place to rest and we cooked a welcome meal. We were all ravenous, and decided to splurge, eating two cans of corned meat each. It did little to satisfy our hunger.

That night we arranged ourselves as we had the previous evening, as though it were now routine, wishfully thinking that if it had worked for us before, then it would work for us again. It was a successful strategy and the night passed uneventfully, although we were constantly surrounded by the noise of nocturnal animals, and we worried about being discovered by one of them. Perhaps we were, but at least we were left alone.

As I drifted off to sleep for the first time that evening, I thought about how we had all developed a sense of camaraderie, and I was grateful for the fact that there was no bickering between us: it was as though we all accepted that we were dependent on each other. Of course, our situation was helped by the fact that we liked and respected one another. And, in the case of Alison, it went way beyond that.

The next morning, we set off at first light, moving toward Khosi kopje. We crossed the little stream that would later become the Tuli River and reached Khosi just after midday. It is an enormous kopje surrounded by dense undergrowth and on one side it had the appearance of a wave at its peak, with an almost vertical cliff. After refreshing ourselves, and allowing ourselves the luxury of a short siesta, we continued our hike across the Mtshelele River and toward Silozwe and Silozwane kopje, one of the most sacred kopjes in the Matopos. Although the going was still hard, we were now a little more used to climbing and descending, and our mood was buoyant. For the first time since we had left Diana's Pool our climbing was interspersed with conversation and cheerful chatter. We covered the ten kilometers to Silozwane in record time, arriving there just after midday.

Sitting on some rocks halfway up the kopje, we decided to boil some water for tea; we were busy eating chocolate to replenish our energy levels and congratulating ourselves on our progress when I caught the faint sound of distant voices floating on the wind. At first, I thought it might have been Mzali whispering, but he was busy savoring his chocolate. Alarmed, I looked across the valley toward the neighboring kopje, which I now know was Tebase kopje. There it was again: I could distinctly hear human voices, but I could not see any people. I rummaged through my rucksack and found the World War II binoculars that I had inherited from Dad, and placed them to my eyes. I looked to the left of the granite dome and there they were, five of them. I scanned from left to right and back again, and then I saw the diminutive figure of a San tracker, some distance ahead of his pack. I whispered urgently to Alison and Mzali.

"Come here guys and keep quiet." They intuitively sensed my caution and approached slowly and carefully.

"We've got company," I informed them, pointing to the figures on the opposite side of the valley. and handing Mzali the binoculars. Once again, the sound of human voices drifted across to us, the valley acting as a natural amphitheater. It struck me that these people might be Park Rangers, harmlessly tracking game. They were moving toward where we had previously been hiking, and were about to bisect out trial. The San tracker stopped when he intersected our trail and pointed across the valley toward us. They were tracking bigger game: us! It was now clear that this was a patrol, and they were hunting the three of us. Alison's face was a picture of panic, while I was angry with myself for having been lazy and cavalier with our safety: I had foolishly discounted the possibility that anyone would look for us out here in this forbidding wilderness and had taken no precautions to hide our trail.

Whispering, I said to Alison: "Don't panic. They may be hunting us, but they think that they have an advantage: which they do, but it is not as much of an advantage as they think. They believe that we are unaware of them and that we are unsuspecting easy targets: we are not! Look at them, they are sloppy and complacent."

Mzali nodded in agreement, but Alison looked confused.

"In counterinsurgency operations, there are a few rules that need to be observed," I explained. "Briefly, the basic rules are simple: shape, shine, sound, silhouette, smell, space, and movement. Make sure that your shape is broken up so that it is not obviously human: place some grass in your lapels and your hat and break up the outline of your face by smearing a few lines of mud across your forehead, your nose, and your cheeks. Do not be stupid about it and put an entire bush in your belt, just make sure it's enough to avoid you catching their attention.

"Make sure that any shiny objects are covered up: the glint of sunlight on metal or jewelry will attract attention. Make sure that you do not talk loudly, and if the enemy is close by, maintain a line of sight with your leader and only communicate using hand signals. Make sure that you do not stand above the horizon. Try and disguise any smell: to the sensitive nose, humans have a distinctive smell, and deodorant or perfume is unacceptable. We have some talcum powder, and we need to use some right now. When it comes to space, try to avoid regular spacing between individuals, because then they can pick you off by being able to predict when the next man will come into range."

Mzali nodded his head sagely in agreement. "All the mistakes that the Americans made in Vietnam," he added perceptively.

"Movement should be self-explanatory," I said. "Don't make sudden movements, and always move silently." I turned to Alison.

"Look at those guys over there," I instructed her authoritatively. "What are they doing wrong?" She examined them carefully, using the binoculars.

"Well, they are standing above the horizon, so 'silhouette' applies," she diagnosed triumphantly. "We can hear them talking so 'sound' also applies, and they are also guilty of 'shine' because their rifles are catching the sunlight."

"Good girl," I congratulated her. I then taught her some basic hand signals. I cupped my hand over my head to indicate 'gather around'; I held my arm out with my fist clenched to indicate 'stop'. I kept my arm in the same position but opened my hand to indicate 'approach with caution'. I pointed to my eyes with two fingers and then extended my hand in the direction I wanted her to look. Alison was a quick learner and internalized it all immediately. Mzali and I examined the landscape.

"I think we need to learn a little about the way these guys operate," I said to Mzali. It is amazing how quickly the mood can change: a few minutes earlier we had been happy, celebrating the success of the day, and now we were deadly serious, thinking about how to survive. Mzali was focused on our pursuers.

"I think the San might be the weak link," Mzali observed.

"Although he is probably the most skilled amongst them," I added.

Mzali nodded in agreement. As we watched them, the San tracker set off in pursuit of us, completely focused on our track. Both Mzali and I knew that there was no way on Earth that we were going to outrun or evade this little gentleman. Khoisan trackers are the best trackers in the world. The San people are brought up to be able to track the most elusive game in the most inhospitable terrain. Their skills have been handed down through the generations, and they can look at a leaf and tell you how long it has been lying on the ground by the rate at which it has dried. They have the uncanny ability to identify spoor where seasoned trackers see nothing at all, and they can tell you how old the animal is, if it is injured, if it is tired, how fast it is moving, what it ate for breakfast, and how long ago the track was made. So incredible are their skills that they are reputed to have a sixth sense, allowing them to communicate with animals on a telepathic level.

The little San tracker descended from the heights of the kopje into the valley below, intent on his task. The soldiers behind him followed lazily, laughing quietly and chatting amongst themselves as they all walked in a group together, allowing the diminutive tracker to outpace them. They felt secure in the knowledge that we were oblivious to their presence and were trusting the San to lead them to us. So focused on his prey was he, that the San tracker had started a slow jog toward us, his eyes fixed on our tracks. By the time he reached us, I estimated that he would be at least five hundred meters ahead of the soldiers: he was isolated.

Turning to Mzali I said: "Buffalo." He nodded in agreement. The Cape buffalo, so prized by hunters, is a large and strong beast with enormous horns. Normally docile, if wounded it turns into a bovine behemoth: it will run off for a distance, inviting itself to be tracked. It will then move in a large semicircle and double back on its own tracks, patiently waiting to ambush whoever or whatever is following it. When the hunter passes by, transfixed on the buffalo's scent or on its tracks, the buffalo will charge out of the underbrush and attack the unsuspecting transgressor. It attacks with an insatiable rage and, if its prey manages to climb into a nearby tree to escape, the buffalo will wait below the tree, for days if need be. We were now going to innovate and try the same strategy. We knew that our only hope was to ambush the San tracker and prevent him from ever linking up with the soldiers. Both Mzali and I perused our surroundings.

"I think that you and Alison should go and sit at the top of that ridge," I suggested to Mzali tentatively, pointing to a small ridge a little farther away. "When he gets to this spot he will just be able to see your heads, and if you and Alison talk quietly to one another he will think that you are relaxing and are unaware of him."

I pointed to a large boulder just behind me to my left. "I will circle around from here, back to that boulder, and if he is following our recent tracks he will walk straight past it, ignorant of my presence. Do you agree?"

Mzali nodded and walked with Alison to the little ridge that I had pointed out. I took a detour to my left and circled around to the rock, where I crouched down and unsheathed my knife. I became aware of my breathing, which suddenly seemed loud, as did the beating of my heart. I tried to take shallow breaths so that I would not be heard, and, luckily, I was not. As the little San walked passed me I stepped out from behind the rock, knife in hand. He saw me from the corner of his eye, but reacted too late. I clasped my left hand over his mouth and put the knife to his throat.

"I don't want to hurt you, but I will if I have to," I promised him. "Tell your friends to stay where they are. Tell them that you have spotted leopard tracks and that the leopard has a cub. Tell them that you want to make sure that they are safe and that the leopard is not here. Do you understand me?"

The little San tracker nodded vigorously in agreement, his eyes wide with fright. Cautiously, I removed my hand from his mouth, but pressed the knife firmly to his throat, and pulled him closer to me to remain hidden. The little San gestured frantically to the soldiers, waving them away, and shouted to them in the Matabele language. They stood immobile in the valley and then sat down to wait. No one wants to tangle with an irate female leopard protecting its young, and the bush here was so dense and the rocks so prolific that a leopard could easily attack you before you even knew it was there. I was not sure if our ruse had worked, but I had bought us a little time. I marched the indignant man up to the ridge where Mzali and Alison were waiting anxiously.

"Take off your clothes," I ordered. He looked at me, perplexed, trying to comprehend what I had just said. "All of them," I emphasized.

Alison turned away so as not to embarrass him, and he reluctantly stripped out of his ill-fitting uniform, revealing a traditional loincloth: the loose veneer of 'civilization' was sloughed off and discarded like dead, dry dross. Mzali now whispered in my ear: he had had an epiphany. Mzali made his way to a nearby tree and started peeling the bark off it. I now knew exactly what he intended. I do not know the English name for this tree, but the Matabele refer to it as *sihaqa*, the *q* being a click sound. Just a little bit of the bark in some lukewarm water produces a potent laxative. The potion takes about ten minutes to start working and has a distinctive, bitter taste.

Returning to our campfire, he placed the bark into the pot of hot water. I laughed to myself because he was putting so much bark into the water that it would incapacitate an elephant for a month. While we were allowing the chemicals of the bark to suffuse the water, we examined the San tracker's clothes while he waited there, expectant and bemused. We liberated his knife from him, and I emptied his water bottles, pouring the water into our own water canisters. By now Mzali's warlock potion was ready; Mzali stirred some sugar into it, and we siphoned it into the San's water bottles.

"The soldiers will think that the little San has had enough for one day and has simply gone away. His water is so precious that they will not allow it to go to waste. When they taste it, they will think that he has made a bush tonic for himself to give himself energy. They will pass it around from one to the other. They will all want some of his medicine," Mzali chuckled, imagining the outcome with unconcealed delight.

Turning to the San tracker, I started interrogating him: "Who do you work for?"

"The National Parks Board," he told me, adding that he had been told by his employers to help the soldiers.

"Are they soldiers or are they police?"

"They are police."

"Who is giving them orders?"

"Some politician has hired them, and the police force has allowed them to work for him. They are being well paid to find you." That was useful information: it meant that they were not acting in an official capacity, but were essentially hired mercenaries, working outside of the system.

"What is their morale like?"

"What does morale mean?"

"Are they happy doing this job? Do they have enough food? Do they have enough water? Do they like sleeping out in the bush at night? Do they argue with one another or are they all good friends?" I elaborated.

"They are not happy. They have been promised a lot of money, but do not know if they will be paid. They are running out of clean water, and they want to go home to their wives." That too was useful information, because it meant that they were reluctant players. They could be more easily dissuaded.

"There is one thing more that I want you to do," I instructed him, "and then you can go home, as long as you go directly home and do not join up with those policemen again."

"I promise you I'll go straight home," he said sincerely. "Thank you, thank you."

"I want you to tell those men that the leopard knows that we are here and that this kopje is a dangerous place. I want you to tell them to go around the kopje next to this and to meet you on the other side. Will you do that?"

He allowed himself a smile, knowing now that we had no intention of hurting him, and appreciating the trick that was about to be played on the policemen. He knew that we were buying ourselves another half an hour. He stood to full height, cupped his hands around his mouth, and shouted to the policemen waiting anxiously in the grass below the kopje. I watched them get slowly to their feet and grudgingly trudge to my right and away from us. We gathered our possessions and slid and scurried to the base of the hill with the San beside us. I then pointed west and wished him well. He stared at me thoughtfully, the gratitude glimmering in his eyes, and then he turned away and dutifully started jogging to the west, never looking back.

I placed his belongings, together with his water bottles, on top of a rock where I knew that they would be seen, and we started jogging to the west as well. Even though we had a head start on our pursuers I knew that they were fitter and faster than we were and that if we were to survive this, we would need to outsmart them somehow. I did some mental calculations and reasoned that it would take them half an hour to get to the tracker's clothes, another ten minutes to consume the water, and another ten minutes before they started feeling the effects of that water. We needed to make every minute count.

"Let's give them a run for their money," said Alison.

CHAPTER 43

We were so intent on eluding our pursuers and putting some distance between us and them, that we did not realize we were running into trouble. Mzali was slightly in front of us, and Alison and I were jogging side by side as we skirted the foundations of a large kopje. We were trying to avoid the heavy undergrowth, when we ran past some rocks and a stocky monkey orange tree, pendulous with fruit, straight toward a troop of baboons some fifteen meters in front of us.

Suddenly there was absolute bedlam as the baboons screamed the alarm in unison; a large male baboon walked menacingly toward us on all four legs with his teeth exposed. Baboons were shouting and screeching on the rocks and in the branches of the tree, whipping each other up into a furious frenzy and exposing their formidable teeth. The noise was unbelievable and the danger palpable. It was possibly the most frightening incident that I can recall.

We were intruders in their territory. A solitary baboon is frightening enough, having three times the muscle strength of a human being and being armed with long claws and canine-like teeth. A single baboon can easily kill a man, yet here we were confronted by about thirty of them, and they were angry. The irascible baboons advanced on us as we stood there in cataleptic horror. Mzali was standing slightly in front of me, and I gripped his collar as I stuck my hand out in front of Alison to hold her back. Thankfully, we were not too close to them.

"Walk backward, slowly," I commanded, hoping that it would work. "Don't look any of them in the eye, but don't turn your back on them: that will simply encourage them to charge."

Slowly and cautiously, we backpedaled, until we were well away from them, the noise gradually subsiding. We must have caught them on a good day, because I think that nine times out of ten we would probably have been torn limb from limb. Once we reached safety, the adrenalin rush wore off and my hands began to shake uncontrollably. None of us said a word for a minute or two, as we tried to control our fear. It was Alison who broke the ice:

"Well, that was fun," she said in her most flippant voice.

"I think we all need a change of underwear," I joked tremulously.

"Speak for yourself," Alison responded drily. Mzali was badly shaken as he sat on a rock bracing himself with his hands on his knees, breathing heavily.

"I didn't think I'd ever see you go white Mzali," I teased him, trying desperately to get control of my own emotions. He looked up at me, but he did not smile. That was far too close for comfort.

Every cloud has a silver lining, and our near death experience inspired Alison.

"I have an idea," she said. "Those guys are still following us, and they will follow us here. I want to try something to make sure that they come this way."

She started looking through my rucksack and found a candle and some string. Then she opened her own rucksack and took out a small mirror. She placed the mirror on a boulder and found a rock, with which she hit it, breaking it into four or five pieces. She placed the pieces of mirror around the candle and used the string to tie them tightly in place; then she asked me for my utility knife, with all its various attachments, and unfolded the screwdriver, which she used to bore a hole through the top of the candle. She threaded string through the hole, and we had a little ornament to hang from a Christmas tree.

"I hope that all holds together," she said with some doubt. We then hung her ornament from the closest tree.

"If lady baboons are anything like humans," she said, "then I'm sure they'll want to have a look in the mirror. If those soldiers are close behind us, they should see the light shining on the mirror."

I do not know if her lure ever worked, because we did not stay around to find out, although we did hear a distant cacophony of sound about half an hour later.

Careful to conserve our energy, we jogged rather than sprinted, but I knew that we would never outpace these fit young men; we needed some sort of diversion. I was struck by a preposterous idea, but we were so desperate to elude our pursuers that we had to attempt even the most ridiculous action. As we paused for breath, I asked Alison if she had any deodorant with her. She was perplexed.

"What do you want deodorant for?" she asked, bewildered.

"I have an idea which is worth trying even if it doesn't work," I explained. "The deodorant is combustible, and if it is heated, the canister should explode. I want to send these guys in the wrong direction; even if it slows them down just a little bit, it will give us more time to evade them."

My intention was to delay them and get them to waste precious time searching for the cause of the sound. Alison searched through her rucksack, and eventually found a small can of deodorant, which she handed to me reluctantly: this was her last vestige of personal hygiene. Gratefully accepting the deodorant can, I found a small tin, some paraffin, and matches.

While I was gathering the ingredients for our little surprise, Mzali was studiously scanning the landscape, looking for a suitable spot to place it. He decided on a small rock at a nearby kopje and we made our way there, hoping that we had enough time to lay our trap before our pursuers came into view. I dug a little hollow in the earth, using my hands, and then we made a small fire. I placed the deodorant can in the tin and was about to place it on the fire when Mzali restrained me.

"Put some sand in the bottom," he suggested. "The sand will absorb some of the heat, and it will take a little longer for the deodorant can to explode."

His suggestion made perfect sense. I did as he instructed while he and Alison kept watch. We then sprinted away, hoping that our ploy would be effective and gain us a few precious minutes. It must have been about five minutes later that we heard a loud 'BANG'! At least the plan had worked, although I do not know if it slowed the soldiers down much; I may have wasted more of our own time building the decoy than they spent looking for it.

Despite the fact that we were constantly on the run, every now and again I would crouch behind a rock and look for our pursuers through my binoculars, hoping for some respite and reassurance. We kept moving until the sun set, sometimes jogging, sometimes walking; but never stopping. The only thought that seemed to occupy us was to escape. We were moving fast, yet still they were gaining on us, moving inexorably closer. I knew that they had imbibed Mzali's potion because every now and again they would stop and wait while one or the other of them disappeared behind a rock or tree, but this was only slowing them down and delaying our demise rather than preventing it. I think we all felt doomed. The situation was quite hopeless.

As the last light of day started to fade, I looked through the binoculars and noticed that they had temporarily abandoned pursuit. They were not going to chase us through the night but were going to get some rest. I think they must have believed that it was only a matter of time before they caught us and that they could afford to get some sleep. They knew that we also had to rest: if we did not get some sleep too we would be so tired and exhausted in the morning that they would easily chase us down.

That night we could light no fires nor talk above a whisper: if we gave any indication of our whereabouts they could come and find us. We decided to wait and watch. The men hunting us were overconfident and took no measures to disguise their presence. They found a small cave halfway up a kopje that had a ledge in front of it like a little patio.

Many of the kopjes in the Matopos are punctured and perforated with caves; they are quite common, and this one was in one of the granite dome hills.

Mzali, Alison, and I talked about it, and we decided that we wouldn't simply be victims, allowing ourselves to be acted upon. I knew that we needed to be audacious and daring, remembering the adage "Fortune favors the brave." We knew that they were certainly going to catch us and that we were no match for them. We would either be captured or killed the next day: unless, of course, we managed to turn the tables on them.

Shortly after midnight the three of us started moving quietly toward the far side of the kopje which was now home to our pursuers. As quietly as we could, we climbed the far side all the way to the exposed summit, aided by the fact that it was a bright moonlit night. We stopped to collect our thoughts, hoping that we had not been heard. The posse was now below us, and we would need to get close enough to the sentry to disable him if possible.

I asked Alison to stay where she was, because it was the safest place for her to be, while I descended the kopje to the right of the cave, and Mzali descended to the left of the cave. I had to admire Mzali because I was scudding around and disturbing loose stones while Mzali crept cautiously toward his prey like a magnificent black panther: silent and lethal. I was awake and I was close to him, yet I could not hear a sound. We crept down the granite. Thankfully the surface was smooth and firm, allowing us sure footing. When we got to the ledge where the cave was we were slightly behind the sentry, who was sitting on a rock with his AK-47 cradled in his lap. The events of the day had obviously taken their toll because he had fallen asleep, and was quietly snoring as Mzali stealthily edged toward him.

Mzali crept right up next to the man and slowly bent down and lifted the AK-47 off his lap, and still he slept. Perhaps Mzali's potion had done more damage than I had given it credit for. Mzali switched the safety catch off and gently cocked the weapon. By this time, I had reached the opposite side of the cave entrance and, peering cautiously into the cave, I could see that everyone was asleep. Mzali placed the cold muzzle of the AK-47 to the sentry's head and the sentry reacted with panic and tried to stand up. Mzali used the AK-47 to push him back down and placed a finger to his own lip, signaling the sentry to keep quiet. Kneeling next to the man, Mzali whispered to him: "If you make any noise, I will kill you, and before your friends have time to reach their rifles I will have killed them too. Do you know who I am?"

The terrified sentry nodded.

"Then you will know that I mean what I say and that you have no chance at all," Mzali snarled with feline fury. Seeing him like this, I was glad that I had not encountered Mzali during our bush war: he was positively ominous.

"Stand up," Mzali ordered the sentry, and he then walked behind the guard into the little cavern, prodding him forward. The men slept on, oblivious to any intrusion.

"Light the paraffin lamp," Mzali ordered the sentry who duly complied.

The men woke up slowly, only to be confronted by their worst nightmare: Mzali with a rifle pointed directly at them.

"I want all of you to put your hands above your head and not to move at all," Mzali commanded. "Bruce," Mzali instructed without looking at me, "take all of their weapons from them."

I went to each of the four men in turn and took their rifles and whatever other weapons were lying about. Next to one of the men lay a rarity: night vision goggles; these men had been well equipped. I selected a rifle for myself and held onto the goggles, knowing that they would prove useful. The prey was now the predator, and the hunter was now the hunted: we had turned the tables on them.

"Collect their clothes Bruce," Mzali instructed me. I gathered all the clothes and all the sleeping bags and put them in one big pile at the side of the cave. Mzali insisted that every item of clothing be removed, even the underwear. The reason is simple, and it is psychological: there are few things more ridiculous than a naked man. It deprives a man of his masculinity, making him feel vulnerable, exposed, and humiliated. These men were stripped of their clothes, stripped of their pride, and stripped of their will to resist. No man wants to fight naked. Mzali addressed his captive audience.

"Do you all want to get home to your wives and children?" Mzali asked. They all nodded meekly.

"You will all live through this if you do as you are told," Mzali assured them, "but you will need to answer my questions fully and you must obey my commands. Is there anyone who disagrees with that?" No one disagreed.

"Where is the radio?" Mzali asked. It was next to the cooking utensils.

"Who is the radio operator?" One of the men raised his hand.

"What is your call sign?"

The man said that it was Zulu, Alpha, Romeo. Mzali crouched next to the man and ordered him to operate the radio so that we could learn what frequency was being used. It was no good trying to send a communiqué at this time of the night because it was unlikely that anyone would respond.

"Who are you in contact with?" The radio operator told Mzali that it was Gumede himself or another operator named Thando who used the call sign Alpha, Juliet, Bravo.

"When last did you have contact?" The radio operator said that it had been late the previous afternoon.

"Does Gumede know that we are here?" The answer was yes.

"Are reinforcements being sent?" The answer was no.

"Are your contacts expecting a call at a specific time?" The answer was 9 o'clock the next morning.

"What is your radio signal strength?" Mzali was told that it was weak and intermittent. Mzali squatted down in front of the men.

"I want you men to know that I'm taking a big risk. I know that I should kill you all now, but my friend Bruce does not like the sight of blood, so I will allow you to live for the sake of my friendship. But remember that you are in debt to us: we are giving your lives back to you. If you return to base with no clothes on, everyone there will laugh at you for the rest of your life, and wherever you work, people will laugh at you. To save your own reputation, I suggest that you go to a little village close to Gwanda or Balla Balla, that you buy yourselves some clothes, and that you never go back to work with the police. If you do, you must make up a convincing story. But that is your problem, not mine. We want you to move east, and tomorrow morning we will call your base and we will tell them that you were mistaken, that we were only German tourists, and that you have to escort them back to their bush lodge or else they will die."

Once we had all the information we needed, we poured some paraffin over the pile of clothes and set it alight. It burned brightly, making a magnificent bonfire. We stood the men up and marched them down the kopje, Mzali standing behind them and me standing to the side of them. At the bottom of the kopje we told them that we wanted them to walk east, toward Balla Balla, allowed them to put their shoes back on, and sent them naked and alone into the wilderness. We stood and watched them walk away in the bright moonlight, and then we made our way back to Alison.

CHAPTER 44

We did not sleep well that night. Perhaps the excitement of the evening's events occupied our thoughts, but our minds were overstimulated and would not switch off. Weariness eventually got the better of me, and I dozed off with the first hint of morning: the blackness of night was turning to a dull grey, distant trees were starting to gain shape, and the early birds were starting to announce the day: it was as though nature herself was stretching and gaining consciousness at the point I drifted off to sleep.

When I awoke with a start, the sun was already shining brightly, and Mzali greeted me with a cup of tea, which I sipped and slurped as Alison and I sat on the cave's patio and admired the stunning scenery. Mzali made his way to the summit of the kopje, radio in hand, hoping that the signal strength would be adequate to send his communiqué. He came back about fifteen minutes later with a satisfied look on his face.

"I think they bought it," he celebrated. "I told them that it was a false alarm and that we had only found three German tourists. I spun them a story: I said that the German tourists told us that they were staying at a bush lodge in the southeast of the Matopos and that they had gone for a short hike, lost their bearings, and did not know where they were. I told them that we would have to get the tourists back to their lodge and that three German tourists dying in the bush would not be good publicity for the tourist industry. I said that we could find no sign of Bruce Savage or his girlfriend, but that we would keep looking while we escorted the German tourists to safety. I stressed that you would have been mad to come out here. I also said that if you had come out here, then you would surely be dead by now. I think they believed me."

"Well done Mzali," I congratulated him. "I feel remarkably healthy for a corpse"

"And all the time I was doing this," Mzali chuckled, simulating the sound of radio static, and speaking through his closed fingers to muffle his voice. I could glimpse the child within him starting to surface.

At about 10 o'clock we set off on our journey again, heading toward the Sashane dam. We had deliberately divided our journey into sections and were focused only on achieving our immediate goal, making the undertaking less daunting and more manageable. Our hike was uneventful, if you can call being in one of the most beautiful places on Earth uneventful, but we were entirely focused on our destination and on each independent obstacle which confronted us.

It was now early October, and October in central Africa is suicide month, it gets so hot. By midday, we were sweltering in the searing, inescapable heat, and the sweat was running in rivulets down our backs, our sides, and our faces. At about 2 o'clock in the afternoon, the first delicate wisps of fluffy cotton-wool clouds began to form: by 4 o'clock, just as we were reaching Sashane dam, gigantic cumulonimbus clouds had closed ranks, the quartz-white clouds morphing into angry granite grey. These cathedrals of clouds looked remarkably like the Matopos hills, as though they were a celestial reflection of the kopjes below. The charcoal clouds were floating mountains of wrath, the leaden base promising to crack at any moment.

The threatening clouds were illuminated by occasional flashes of internal light, and as we looked for a place to rest and shelter from the rain, the first ominous rumblings of thunder announced a tropical thunderstorm. The first large drops of rain splattered down, heavy and ponderous, stinging my skin, and then the heavens exploded. The granite hills of the Matopos are laden with iron, which attracts lightning, and this can produce an awe-inspiring, but terrifying display of nature's power. Loud blasts of thunder pulverized the evening air, like cymbals crashing together, and bolts of lightning lacerated the sky, like snakes striking, accompanied by the sound of gunshots, as the electricity crackled and hissed in the night sky. Zeus was angry this evening.

We sought refuge beneath a large mukwa tree, but it did little to protect us from the torrential onslaught. Knees bent, our arms wrapped around our legs, we hunched forward to protect our faces from the pounding rain as we huddled together looking like three drowned rats. All we could do was wait for the storm to vent its rage. Thankfully, the storm only lasted for about half an hour, and the clouds went on their way looking for someone else to attack. In fact, for all its ferocity, the rain was not a punishment, but a reward: it was liquid life.

I looked at Alison, sitting there like a bedraggled little waif on a sidewalk, with a rucksack held above her head, vainly trying to protect herself from the rain. She looked adorable. I wrapped my arm around her and drew her toward me, pulling her tight against my body, and she snuggled into me to warm herself.

"You look so cute," I praised her. "You look like a miffed little puppy after a bath." She smiled and pulled me closer toward her.

"I feel like a little puppy," she said. "I just want to be stroked and patted."

I was happy to oblige. Mzali sat beside us and smiled knowingly at me before standing up to dry off.

"I'm going to look around for some dry wood," he explained, "but I think we will have to go without tea or hot food tonight."

We spent an uncomfortable evening together, cold and dreary, never quite managing to get dry, and we all pressed up against one another to insulate ourselves from the coolness of the evening breeze. We awoke in the morning to be greeted by one of those wonderful days that makes you thankful to be alive. The glassy waters of the serene Sashane dam sparkled joyfully in the crisp morning air; the air was crystal clear, the sky a pastel blue, the mellow sunlight was warm and pleasant, the grass was already greening, and colors seemed clean, bright, and sharp. What I appreciated most of all was the glorious musky smell of the African bush after the rain. We all felt refreshed and invigorated, like the wilderness about us.

Relieved that we had broken the back of our journey, but aware that we still had much to do, we set out toward the Ingwesi reservoir after eating a delicious breakfast, and we made good ground as the terrain became a little flatter. The countryside gradually changed, as the kopjes thinned and the valleys broadened, segueing to mopane woodland. We were still in inhospitable countryside, but the going was slightly easier.

At about 3 o'clock we had just reached the top of a small kopje and were sitting down to admire the panoramic view when some color caught my eye. Below us and to my left was a bright splash of scarlet, so typical of the new leaves of a msasa tree, and yet this swatch of color was only just higher than the granite ridge around it. It seemed strange, almost as though the tree was growing from a pit below the granite. My curiosity was aroused. I found the binoculars and stood up to examine the granite outcrop more closely. Looking at the granite mass from above, it appeared to be a circular caldera of granite with a hole in the center like a doughnut. This was not a kopje, it was far too shallow for that, and its circular shape made it look like a snake eating its tail. I decided to name it *Ntabanyoka*: snake hill.

"Guys," I announced, "I want to go and explore that little outcrop: there is something peculiar about it."

"We don't have time," Mzali said ruefully.

"Come on Mzali, be a devil," Alison chided. "We've been running for days on end now. We are not being chased anymore; let's just explore for an hour. It's not as though we are late for a meeting."

So we made our way down to the unusual outcrop of granite.

The granite rock was not high—only about three or four meters— but it was steep; nor was it large—it could only have been one hundred and fifty meters long and about one hundred and twenty meters wide—

yet we could distinctly make out the tops of trees that were level with the summit. There had to be space on the other side. We circumnavigated the mass of granite, the sides of which were almost perpendicular like a wall. On the south side of the granite, we noticed a gap in the rock, partially hidden by tall trees. Its sides were sheer, as though an entrance had been deliberately incised through it. This cleavage in the granite started almost at ground level: we could climb through to the interior!

We clambered up the mass of rock below the entrance and walked through the gap in the rock, only to be confronted by a veritable myriad of boulders and a tangled mesh of vegetation. The granite entrance was about thirty meters wide, which meant that the crater inside was about one hundred and twenty meters long and eighty meters wide. *This would be a perfect refuge for snakes or leopards,* I thought to myself. We pushed and pulled ourselves through the barrier of bushes, branches, and boulders, and stepped into a large clearing, where the grass was short and there were a few trees which had obviously grown tall searching for the sunlight. The interior was spectacular. There were large, ancient megalithic walls, resplendent with decorative rock designs at the top. These walls jutted out from the granite rock which had been incorporated into their construction. We all stood there silently in stunned disbelief.

"I think that we have inadvertently stumbled on to the Wall of God which the early explorers mentioned," I said in awe.

Matabele legend speaks of the Wall of God as one of the ancient megalithic structures so common in Matabeleland; they talk of it as a factual place, without doubting its existence. They inherited the legend from the tribes that came before them, who inherited it from the tribes that came before them, since legends began. The Wall of God is part of a panoply of myth and legend, but it is unusual as all the other cities have been found and identified, yet the Wall of God has not even though the Matabele have always stated that it is in the southern part of the Matopos.

"Think about it," I reasoned, "the granite outside and inside is almost straight, just like a wall. A wall always has an inside and an outside, and the actual walling is on the inside; this might once have been a small village, or perhaps even a religious site. Legend stipulates that it is in the southern part of the Matopos where the kopjes are higher and the scenery more grandiose. We have just walked from the southern parts of the Matopos and have not seen any ancient ruins at all. Perhaps the Matabele meant below the Matopos rather than south, and this is just below the most rugged parts of the Matopos. Perhaps the use of the word *God*, suggests a natural phenomenon rather than the work of man."

By now it was late afternoon and Mzali started gathering wood for a fire while Alison and I explored the ancient ruin, imagining the people who might have once lived there, and admiring the skill, the planning, and the effort that had gone into creating this fascinating wonder. At one point we disturbed an enormous cobra, which reared up for a moment in all its sinister reptilian majesty, before slithering away when we retreated. We did not have time to explore fully, but although we were not actively looking for any artifacts, we did find some gold bangles and iron arrowheads which we placed in a separate tin from our other trinkets.

It was not a large ruin but, judging from the size of the walls and the beautiful herringbone rock work, I like to think that it was an important place. Alison and I were so engrossed in our exploration that we didn't notice that Mzali had left us until he returned with a triumphant grin holding up two guinea fowl. We were famished and food was far more important to us at that point than arcane mysteries, so we sat down with Mzali and helped him to remove the feathers and prepare the birds for supper. We made a small spit and roasted the tasty birds as we sat around a roaring fire in the middle of an ancient ruin which no one had seen for centuries.

The ghostly platinum moonlight softly illuminated the ruins, conjuring up images of long dead people and my imagination ran wild, seeing wraiths haunting the dark recesses, wavering slowly as the wind shifted, pleading to live again. This eerie place had an atmosphere of dormant life waiting for resuscitation. Spectral slivers of silver filtered weakly through the trees and every shadow was imbued with plaintive spirits and phantoms, imperfectly resurrected. There was a strange feeling of dislocation, as though we had been transported to an earlier, simpler time. Somehow it was strangely comforting, believing that we were not entirely on our own.

It was a memorable evening, leaning against rock walls, warmed by the fire, feeling safe and secure, and enjoying each other's company. It still amazes me that through all our hardships, we never resorted to bickering or resentment.

As we sat there in the firelight I was leaning next to Alison, shoulder to shoulder, and holding her hand. She looked contented and peaceful, and I felt responsible and remorseful for causing her untold angst and anxiety.

"Alison honey," I said, "I am so incredibly sorry for having been the cause of so much misery. I'm sorry; I only hope that one day you'll find it in your heart to forgive me. I know that I can never take back time and undo what is already done, but I promise you that I will try to make this up to you."

"Don't be silly," Alison said. "I have never felt so vital in my life before. I have been happier out here, alone in the wilderness with you, than I have ever been before. I feel alive, truly alive." Alison looked thoughtful. "You know," she reflected, "I think this experience has made me appreciate you more than ever before. It has made me realize that I can depend on you in any situation, that you are reliable, that you will always be an optimist and see humor in the bleakest of times, and that you truly love me. More than anything else, that means a lot to me. You have been the glue that has held us all together and kept our spirits up. I knew that I loved you before we left, but now I feel it to the marrow of my bones."

I felt elated; to know that Alison loved me was all that I ever needed to hear. Her therapeutic words resonated melodiously to the core of my being.

"I love you too," I enthused. "You are my spiritual anchor in life. Why is it that we feel so good together?"

"Trust," Alison said. "No relationship can survive without trust. Of course, people need to be comfortable and compatible with one another, but I think that mutual respect and trust are the keys to any relationship. I know that I respect and trust you."

"And a little laughter helps," I said solemnly; "never take yourself too seriously."

"I am sitting here with two people who I respect and trust," Mzali intervened. "I suppose that I do love you both in a sense, but that does not mean that I want to marry you," he laughed, his mangled face contorting demonically in the firelight.

"I suppose there must be more to it than that: physical attraction plays a part," Alison said, giving me a meaningful glance and a knowing smile. "A relationship is organic, like a living organism, and needs to be nurtured and tended, lest partners begin to take one another for granted."

It seemed as though she was giving us both some wise and gentle advice; I reminded myself to always remember what a unique and wonderful person she was.

"You must plunge right in and immerse yourself in the relationship; there can be no lack of conviction, and there can be no lack of commitment," I added energetically; I spoke the words, but in truth, I was voicing my own internal monologue.

"I'll raise a glass to that," said Alison, giving me an appreciative glance.

"I am going to brew us something to drink," Mzali promised, thoughtfully giving Alison and me some privacy.

Alison and I sat in intimate silence together until Mzali joined us, carrying three mugs of steaming coffee.

"Where did you get the coffee from Mzali?" I asked. I had not tasted coffee for ages and was missing it. He grinned.

"I brought a small jar of Jacobs with me and was waiting for a special moment," Mzali confessed. "I think that this is that special moment."

Alison was in a philosophical mood, enjoying the safety of the sanctuary. "I'm sitting here in an ancient ruin," she said, highlighting the extraordinary setting, "yet somehow I feel that this is the only possible reality and that the outside world is an abstracted fantasy. It's a most surreal feeling."

"That's because this, this bush and this wilderness, is the real, natural world," I said. "The world of man, his cities and his constructs, is an artificial world. Here we sit with real people, people of substance and character, while other people go about their mundane and stressful lives. For all its horrors, what we have just endured has been exciting."

"I miss my home," Alison mused, "I miss my mundane life: it was safe, secure, and certain. I suppose I have mixed emotions because, on the one hand, I miss my dull and boring life, but on the other, this last week has been exhilarating, despite the trauma; or possibly because of it. But I have had enough of this now, and I want to return to normality. I want to go home.:

"I also want to get back to the safety of home," I replied, "but somehow I don't feel that I belong in the city: I feel like a stranger in a foreign land. I have never felt that I belong: my reality is Kataza, and all my life I've wanted to live isolated and apart, aloof from petty concerns. I have always wanted to insulate myself from reality."

"I've noticed that," Alison smiled sweetly, "but that is not a bad thing, provided that you're not hiding from life."

"I'm really happy with the life I've got, and it's good to be divorced from the problems of the world," I said; "It allows me my privacy and solitude and peace of mind."

"Yes," Alison agreed, "but you have spent much of your life lonely and alone. You're an oddity; you like people individually, yet you dislike humanity."

"I suppose that I have wanted to escape. The world I want is a serene and contented world. I have tried to recreate the world which I once knew at Kataza, and I look around me, and I despair for it. I see social decay, moral entropy, elastic principles, and spiritual atrophy: people are frantically running around in a pointless charade, trying to sate their hedonistic appetites, and so wrapped up in themselves that they are ignorant of the world around them. People spend their lives treading water, waiting for the tsunami of life to envelop and drown them. They are rushing everywhere, yet going nowhere and achieving nothing; their calloused souls have become diseased. Their values are warped and distorted: they excuse the inexcusable and defend the indefensible and justify barbarity as religion or culture or sport. The real social malaise is the loss of hope and faith: people dumbly accept social injustices, some of which are apparent, like poverty and starvation, but others of which are not so obvious, like excessive bank charges and unreasonable taxes. We simply resign ourselves to the fact that we are powerless in the face of an oppressive system. We surrender and we sacrifice our humanity on the altar of expediency."

"A cynic would agree with you," Alison interjected. "What you are expressing certainly resonates with me at times. Too many people are too eager to capitulate to social pressure and to compromise their morality. Society often has an antipathy toward truth and honesty. I get particularly disillusioned with those hypocrites who profess to be religious and will preach and pray about right and wrong, yet will meekly surrender their principles and refuse to stand up for their lauded values when under scrutiny; often they are so eager to be seen as 'nice' that they will desert decency. But there are always good people about, and often they are the people you would least expect to be dependable: the rough diamonds, with their rough language and their calloused carapace."

"The real problem is money," Mzali interjected. "Money is an addictive narcotic. Society is consumed by consumption. We live our profligate lives, convincing ourselves that we need unnecessary commodities, in constant competition with our neighbors and ourselves when that competition is redundant. We need to be satisfied with less; we need the wisdom to know what is worth wanting." Mzali smiled, reminding me once again of his wild ideas about freedom.

"We are all trapped in cages: cages of debt, cages of doubt, and cages of convention; we need to break the chains and escape from that cage," Mzali emphasized. "People live their lives vicariously, immersed in television, social media, computer games, or the internet and never venture into the real world: the physical world is experienced through osmosis, rather than truly enjoyed. For the youth of today, life is a dream, and it is never fully lived. At least our lives have been well lived."

"The world is filled with narrow-minded and needy people, all searching for approval, sucking those around them into the vortex of their angst," I added sadly. "Nowhere is this anxiety more manifest than in the bane of modern society: social media; I cannot understand its macabre fascination. I think that there is something intrinsically squalid about it: a desperate appeal for personal validation. There is something grimy, unsavory, and incredibly egotistical about inflicting the intimate details of your mundane life on those vacuous people who are bored enough to be interested.

"The truth remains that we are all secondary in the lives of others, and superfluous to all but our most immediate friends and family. Some people use social media to engage in cowardly gossip, slandering those who aren't present to defend themselves, and they believe this to be entertaining."

"This all sounds so bleak and depressing," Alison rued. "I am also cynical about social media because it is abused and misused, but I think it has tremendous potential to connect people and to effect instant communication and rapid transformation. I think that society and values are in flux as we transition from old traditional modes into a dynamic and promising new reality. I find the possibilities for change truly exciting.

"Just as technology is evolving, so too are our concomitant values; yet, at the core, human nature remains constant: fearful of the unknown, but naturally hopeful, caring, and decent. I look around me, and I see beauty everywhere. People may well be wrapped up in their own lives, but the human spirit is resilient and compassionate. Everywhere I look I see people helping other people, altruistic people volunteering for community work, donating money to the less fortunate, and trying to educate and uplift the downtrodden. I think there is a great deal to be thankful for and to admire: I think the human heart is caring and that humanity is moving in the right direction. Compare modern society to life during the industrial revolution; ours is certainly a superior world!"

"I agree," I responded, while Mzali looked on impassive. "I live my life the way I do because I want to surround myself with good people and the beauty of nature. My world is peaceful. The fact of the matter is that humanity is capable of glorious, wonderful acts and achievements—look at our art, medicine, science, and architecture— yet we are also capable of the most depraved and cruel behavior; I think it comes down to choices."

"Maybe your life is a little too tranquil at times," Alison observed solemnly. "You paint such a negative picture of the world, but I know that you're not a negative person, at least not in your private life. Your life would appear idyllic to most people; perhaps you have made it so. But you live apart and invite others in, rather than actively engaging in the world around you."

"You live apart because you are a dreamer," Mzali said affectionately. "You don't like to acknowledge reality, so you live in your castle and look at the world from a distance. Reality is uncomfortable and unpleasant because life can be cruel, and people can be spiteful and malicious."

"Yes, Bruce is an idealist, but that is one of the things I love about him," Alison defended me. I felt foolish, like a naive child, as Alison and Mzali discussed me dismissively.

"I don't run away from life," I insisted a little petulantly. "I am not trying to escape reality: I just want to live life on my own terms."

"You are your father's son," Mzali noted wistfully, recollecting Dad, alone in his blissful solitude at Kataza.

"Sometimes you need to compromise," Alison informed me.

"I'm not sure that I want to," I responded, sure that I did not want to. "You are both discussing my past, yet I have embraced change. Since Alison became a part of my life I have felt reborn and willing to welcome new experiences. I have always been selective about the company that I keep, preferring no company at all to bad company, and I am proud that I did not compromise before, because I would probably have settled for a lesser woman than Alison and dull mediocrity. My patience has been repaid, and now I am bound to Alison and I am a larger and more complete person than before."

Alison hugged me tightly. "Thank you. I feel the same way; the best things in life are always worth waiting for," she said softly and sincerely.

"Here we sit sounding terribly profound," Mzali said impatiently, "but we are simply talking trivial, meaningless nonsense; is life really so absurd and futile? Is there any purpose to it all in the greater scheme of things?"

"At the end of the day, I think that life has no meaning but the meaning you give it: we are all reaching out to one another, trying to connect," I said. "We all seek approval and validation, and yet we will only receive it when we give it to others. I like to believe in reincarnation, second chances, and I think that we are all here to learn to respect others and to embrace tolerance and compassion. That is how we connect, and that is how we evolve as entities."

Mzali was visibly irritated by the saccharine conversation and disengaged from the rather trite and pointless banter; he moved away from Alison and me and sat on a rock a few meters away, lost in sorrowful contemplation. He was drowning in thought and looked depressed. I could tell that he was struggling to suppress his emotions, consumed by a dark, brooding despair. I picked myself up and sat beside him, hoping to help chase his ghosts away.

"What is the matter, Mzali?" I asked.

"We have nothing here to entertain ourselves with, so we sit and we talk nonsense, but it does not change things: it is a waste of time. You and Alison have a life to go back to. You will return to your safe and comfortable lives. You two are running *toward* something; you have hope and a future. I am running *away* from something; I have no hope and no future. All that I have ever held dear is dead, and all sense of purpose has gone."

I had not considered his quandary before, and it disturbed me. He was right: Alison and I had been inconsiderate and insensitive. I sat next to Mzali and put my arm on his shoulder.

"Mzali, my friend, my brother, when we get out of this, I promise you that you will be able to start a new life—a better life. You will be able to stay with Alison and me as long as you wish to, or as long as you need to. You're not just a teacher, you are a headmaster, and people with your qualifications and your abilities are in short supply. You will find a good job and a good woman. You do not know what you are going back to, so it is not concrete to you, but I assure you that your life will improve. You will get citizenship because people like you are needed, and you deserve it." I fed him paltry morsels of hope, but they provided little sustenance. Alison seated herself on the other side of the Mzali.

"I'm so sorry Mzali," she apologized. "We have been talking rubbish to keep ourselves sane. You have sacrificed everything to help us, and we will not let you down. We will find you a great job and we will all be friends; this time next year we will all be together again, laughing about this experience and enjoying a few beers."

Mzali looked a little more hopeful, but we all felt a sense of false confidence: the future was too elusive.

CHAPTER 45

Already the little stadium just outside of Lomagundi was starting to fill up as the buses roared in and disgorged their eager contents. There was a celebratory, festive air as throngs of enthusiastic disciples ululated and burst into spontaneous dance in anticipation of listening to their idol speak. A temporary collapsible stage had been erected at one end of the small soccer stadium which normally hosted no more than a few thousand spectators, and the construction crew was working frantically to ensure that the seating was comfortable, that the hastily constructed roof was securely fitted, and that the sound system was in place. Portable generators were to supply power to the enormous Yamaha speakers that had been driven in from Harare. The people, the *povo*, needed to hear every word uttered by their political savior.

Sweat dripped freely from Angus Holdengarde's sun-creased face as he fought against time to make sure that everything was perfect when Mugabe arrived. He was pleased; the crew that had originally been hired to erect the stage had canceled on short notice, and he was glad for the extra income. Carpets were strewn across the wooden planks of the stage floor, comfortable seating had been neatly arranged in a semicircle, cold water was available, and the flower arrangements were all in place. Outside of the stadium, enormous tables had been laid out and a vast quantity of food was cooking as had been promised to the people to lure them to the rally.

Bread and circuses, as Nero plays his fiddle, thought Angus. All that remained was for the speakers to be connected and for the sound system to be properly tested. A tangle of wires was concealed under the lush red carpeting and portable steps had been placed at one side of the stage. Mugabe was now an old man, the longest serving head of state in the world, and he was not as mobile as once he had been. But he still commanded an audience! The constituency of Lomagundi was an important one, and the local people were anticipating a rare treat: not only would they see their venerable leader, Mugabe, but his wife and many members of the cabinet were also to grace them with their presence.

As two burly young men wrapped their muscular arms around one of the enormous Yamaha speakers and struggled up the steps, Angus heard an unusual sound: 'Thunk'. Thinking little of it, he directed the men to place the speaker at a 45 degree angle at the side of the stage. As they wrestled the speaker to the floor, Angus heard the sound again. Thunk'. Now his curiosity was aroused, and he walked over to the speaker. Nothing.

Grabbing the speaker, he gave it a good solid shake, and was rewarded: 'Thunk', 'thunk', 'thunk'. Alarmed, Angus sought out his toolbox and returned with his Phillips screwdriver. He carefully unscrewed the back of the Yamaha speaker and was puzzled to see a dozen ball bearings lying at the base. It was then that he noticed four massive rectangular blocks of what looked like grey-white putty, carefully placed north, south, east, and west of the actual speaker. Each of these masses was impregnated with hundreds of ball bearings. He noticed that the ball bearings had been pressed into the putty and then bound in place with masking tape. The heat of the day and the bump and grind of the journey had loosened the masking tape, the glue of which had partially melted, allowing some of the deadly ball bearings to drop from their perch. The putty remained firmly in place only because special chip board compartments had been screwed securely into the back of the speakers. Suspecting something sinister, Angus hastily summoned the security team. That is when pandemonium erupted.

"Seal the entrance," someone yelled. "Get all of these people out of here. NOW!"

"Everyone out!" another shouted.

"Warn the dignitaries!" someone else commanded.

One of them turned to Angus. "You'll need to get out of here right now," he directed calmly, but insistently. "It's a good thing that you had a mind to look inside these speakers. Well done!"

Feeling confused and overwhelmed, Angus made his way to the top tier of the stadium seating and looked out toward the Harare Road. He was just in time to see Mugabe's long cavalcade slow to an uncertain stop. Like a snake deprived of its prey, the cavalcade came to a halt, and then it turned around slowly and headed back into the maw of the dust cloud that it had created. At least the people would not be too disappointed: no one was going to abandon the meal.

CHAPTER 46

We slept well, our taut bellies full and our spirits uplifted. We ate a small breakfast and drank a cup of Mzali's coffee. Despite being pressed for time, our curiosity got the better of us, and Alison and I explored for a while, while Mzali browsed around outside the enclosure. We found nothing beside bangles, and I wondered where these ancient peoples had buried their dead. Surely not within this perimeter.

When Mzali returned, he mentioned that he had seen the remnant of a small wall nearby, so Alison and I went outside to investigate, aware that we did not have long to tarry. We clambered out of the entrance to the enclosure and walked toward an expanse of exposed granite where Mzali had directed us. As we approached, I heard a distinct hiss. That wasn't good! I grabbed Alison's arm forcefully and pulled her so that she staggered backward. There on the granite in front of us, lay a coiled puff adder, one of the most dangerous snakes in the world, perfectly camouflaged. It is a short but incredibly muscular snake. It can strike the full length of its body and is so lightning quick that if you are in range, you will be bitten. The bite can be deadly, the toxic venom causing your flesh to rot, and it can kill a person within a day or so. I remember one of my friends having to have his hand amputated in order to save his life. This puff adder was large, and perhaps it was the guardian of the gate because it certainly deterred Alison and me. We backed away before we came into its range, and we never did get the opportunity to investigate the area.

I would have loved to be able to have even more time foraging through the ruins, but there were far more important matters to consider. We were still wanted by the police and needed to get to safety. We left *Ntabanyoka* with some regret and headed south toward Ingwesi reservoir, arriving at the reservoir just before 3 o'clock that afternoon, exhausted once more.

Ingwesi reservoir is a large expanse of water, flanked by kopjes, and would be a wonderful place to visit with the right equipment. I imagined that it must have been brimming with fish, and possibly even crocodiles, although I doubted that. This was unfamiliar territory and I had no idea what wildlife there was: for all I knew there could be elephants or even lions in this flatter countryside. I assumed that there were probably leopards by the name of the reservoir: *ingwe* means leopard in the Matabele language. The reservoir itself was about five kilometers long, and we were forced to walk a little wide of the reservoir to avoid the kopjes. We made our way down to the spillway and followed the river downstream for another five kilometers. I knew that Botswana was now only about thirty kilometers due west and felt confident that we would reach there the next day. Both Alison and Mzali brightened up when I told them that we were so close to the border, and it was lovely to see the embers of hope rekindled and the sparkle return to Alison's beautiful cerulean eyes.

We headed west for a kilometer or so, before seeing a couple of huts and cultivated ground. Mzali suggested that we investigate whether anyone was there because we were out of food and short of water. As we approach the huts we saw an old, wizened man with grey hair sitting on a green plastic chair beside the entrance to a hut, and we approached him cautiously with Mzali taking the lead.

"*Conjane Umdala*: Greetings old man." The traditional Matabele salutation.

"*Conjane Baba*," the old man responded, regarding us with suspicion. We must have appeared a fearsome sight, three strange and dirty savages, each brandishing an AK-47. Alison and I waited together some distance away, as Mzali approached the old man and knelt beside him. They shook hands with one another in the traditional manner: grasp the palm, grasp the thumb, grasp the palm again. I do not know what Mzali said, but it must have been convincing because the old man started smiling and laughing, his desiccated face handsome with joy. He rocked in his chair and clapped his hands together before beckoning Alison and me to approach.

"You people are famous," the old man laughed. "They keep talking about you on the news," he enthused pointing to an old battery-operated transistor radio. There was no electricity here and batteries had to suffice. The old man stood up and shouted toward the fields. I spotted some greenery behind the huts which looked like a pumpkin patch.

A large lady emerged from the vegetable garden and waddled slowly toward us, wiping her hands on her long skirt. The old man asked her to make some sadza for us. Sadza is a maizemeal porridge, the staple diet in these parts. The woman spoke rapidly and loudly, giving the old man a piece of her mind, before smiling sweetly at the three of us and starting dinner. We were all extremely grateful, knowing that food was scarce and that they did not have much to give. While we were waiting to be fed, the old man poured us all some Chibuku and we were joined by half a dozen people returning from the fields. We were celebrities, and the old man got some good mileage out of parading us around like trophies for his friends. Our arrival there was apparently the highlight of his year. We ate a pleasant meal, the sadza moistened with goat stew and *marogo*: African spinach. As we sat around the fire, something was said about us: "*nuka sterek*" and everyone laughed; Alison asked me in a whisper: "what are they saying?"

"They are saying that we stink," I told her. We had been in the bush for the best part of a week, we had sweated profusely, we had not had the opportunity to wash properly, and we had seldom changed our clothes. We were filthy and our hair was greasy. We must have stunk to high heaven. That was our cue: I asked if there was any place that we could wash and was directed to an old hand pump about a hundred meters away. I let Alison go first, largely because she insisted fiercely, and then I got the opportunity to freshen up.

Looking around me, I noticed an old, battered Nissan pickup truck parked beneath an acacia tree some distance away. Here was a gift horse and I was not going to look it in the mouth.

I drew Mzali to one side and suggested that he should get the old man alone and ask him if we could use his car. Mzali knelt next to the old man and whispered in his ear. There was a heated debate before Mzali came and sat next to me again.

"He will allow us to use the car," Mzali informed me, "but he insists on coming with us. He thinks this is a great adventure."

Well, he has to have some way of getting his car back," I admitted. "I'm just a little bit worried about him getting into trouble. What if the police find out that he has helped us?"

"We have talked about that," Mzali said. He wants to help us. Remember that Mugabe has few supporters in this part of the country. I think he believes that this is his small way of striking a blow against the government. Anyway, he is eager and he is enthusiastic: besides which, how is anyone going to find out?" This was fantastic news and meant that our journey was almost over.

"I'm not so sure that he should drive," I said to Mzali. "I don't want to drive with any lights on, and I think we should use the night vision goggles."

"Good idea," Mzali said. He returned to the old man and there was another animated discussion before Mzali whipped out the night vision goggles. Our audience was enthralled, passing them between each other, accompanied by squeals of delighted amazement.

That evening as we sat with the old man and his consorts, Mzali asked why there were so few young people around.

"This ground cannot provide enough food for us," the old man explained. "There are no jobs, and there is no money. All the young people have left to try and find some employment in South Africa," he said with disgust.

I knew that droves of Zimbabweans were flocking to South Africa, impelled by the terminal decay of the economy, causing a major economic problem. The Zimbabweans were prized for their work ethic, and many South Africans resented their presence.

"But they need to be careful," I said. "If they are there illegally they will struggle to get the proper papers, and a lot of the local people will blame them for taking their jobs away."

"But it is the South Africans' own fault," the old man remarked spitefully. "We supported them through their struggle and now they must support us. The South African government claims that it supports democracy, but what did they do when Morgan Tsvangirai and the Movement for Democratic Change won the elections here and Mugabe refused to step down? They did not support democracy, they did not do what was right: they supported the liberation hero, right or wrong. They intervened and arranged for a power-sharing government, allowing Mugabe to persecute us again and to cheat in the next elections. Where are their principles? They abandoned us. Mandela would never have done the same: he was a good man; he was a wise man." Those listening nodded their heads in sad agreement.

Once the old man's entourage had returned to their respective huts, having consumed copious quantities of beer, he offered us the use of his beds. We took a short nap, having decided to leave at about four o'clock the next morning. That would give us time to reach the border before first light, and we could cross into Botswana as the sun was rising. We slept fitfully, but did manage to get some much needed rest.

There was an air of melodrama as we prepared to drive away, the woman being concerned about being left alone. We thanked her for her help, and Alison impulsively delved into her rucksack and produced a gold bangle. The woman was overjoyed!

We traveled on a terrible dirt road, trembling, lurching, and lumbering toward the border rather than droving. I was allowed to drive and it was a strange experience: the night vision glasses meant that I saw everything in shades of green, and it was difficult to distinguish potholes from rocks, which meant that we battered and barged our way forward. But at least we were not advertising our presence. We hardly ever eclipsed thirty kilometers an hour and reached the border at about 5 o'clock. The track made a right turn, and I could see that we had reached the mighty Limpopo River and that the road ran parallel to it.

We were profoundly shaken, but not stirred! I stopped the pickup truck and got out hesitantly to examine the river. The first rain had managed to replenish some of its resources, but the river was still nothing more than a little trickle, meandering lazily between sand and rocks. The banks of the river were about a hundred meters apart, possibly more. I knew that in a few weeks' time this river would look a little more imposing, but for now, it was a sand bed with intermittent puddles, waiting for water to flow down from the northern catchment area. I knew that the Limpopo River is home to crocodiles and hippos, and I scanned the river bed to see if any were about. I couldn't see any, probably because the water level was so low. They must have followed the waters south toward the ocean or north toward the Okavango Delta. Perhaps we were lucky and had just stumbled onto a part of the river that crocodiles and hippos did not like; I do not know.

I told Alison and Mzali that this was where we should cross, and as we were grabbing our rucksacks from the back of the pickup truck, the old man leaned down and produced some wire cutters which he handed to Mzali without a word. Then the old man got into the driver's seat and started barreling back toward his home. After about twenty meters he turned the lights on and accelerated away. I looked toward the opposite bank of the river and noticed a large fence. The thought had never crossed my mind that there would be a fence to surmount.

I handed the night vision goggles to Alison to wear, and it was her responsibility to lead Mzali and me across the river bed. We were not in absolute darkness and we could make out the occasional shape, but Mzali and I did depend on Alison's assistance. We were about halfway across the river when we heard the growl of a car engine. I thought that it must have been the old man returning for some reason and turned to greet him. I was instantly blinded by bright light as a mounted searchlight was switched on; I felt like a rabbit dazzled by the headlights of a car. Either one of the old man's friends had phoned the police, hoping to get the tempting reward for our capture, or the police had assumed that we would need to cross near here and were staking out possible crossing points: I have never found out.

"Stand still: don't move," a commanding voice shouted at me. "Get them," the voice said. "Watch out they are armed. Shoot them if necessary, but I want them alive!" I heard a flurry of activity as men jumped off the back of the truck.

"Run," I shouted to Alison and Mzali, and I pushed them away from me and took a few steps to my right. I wanted them out of the spotlight, and sure enough, the searchlight swept in my direction, keeping me in sight. I heard Alison and Mzali sprint toward the opposite bank, aided by the night vision goggles. I needed to distract the man behind the voice. Assuming that it was Gumede himself, I shouted to him.

"Is that old one leg? Is that Neill?" I taunted him. "Does your wife think you're limp?" I goaded him, hoping to provoke a mistake, playing for time. He did not take well to being mocked.

"Mr. Savage," Gumede snarled malevolently, "when I get you and take you back to Bulawayo, I'm going to inflict so much pain on you that you will beg for death. You will wish for only one leg. I have taken Kataza from your family, but that is not enough. Now I'm going to take your life!"

That was enough for me: I turned and ran as though my life depended on it. I turned my back on Gumede and ran directly to the opposite bank, scrambling up the steep sides and lying flat on the ground. The searchlight swept from side to side, trying to locate me. As soon as it went past me I picked myself up again and ran toward Alison and Mzali. As soon as it turned back toward me, I lay flat on the ground again. I could hear men searching clumsily for me and was grateful for the darkness.

"Just give me the hard drive and I will let you live!" Gumede's despair was instinct in his plaintive plea, railing quixotically against fate. He knew that his future was slipping away from him, just as we too were slipping away.

When I reached Alison and Mzali, they had cut a large hole in the fence using the wire cutters. Alison crawled through and then Mzali ushered me through before joining us. We were now in Botswana but we were not safe. I wanted to leave Gumede with one final reminder of me to taunt him one last time.

"By the way Neill," I bellowed into the night, "I was a young man when you attacked Kataza … and it was I who shot your knee off."

PART FOUR

CHAPTER 47

Weighed down by our rucksacks, we sprinted away from the border and the fence, never dreaming that Gumede and his drones would follow; but follow us they did. Looking back through the night vision goggles, I saw about seven men in hot pursuit of us. Mzali turned and fired a couple of random shots above their heads to discourage them, and our fire was returned, although the bullets went nowhere near us. Holding hands with Alison and Mzali, I lead us through the bush, giving instructions and pulling or pushing as we ran.

"Watch out Alison, there is a bush in front of you," I would say, pulling her to the side.

"Watch out Mzali, there is a hole in front of you," I would say, pushing him around it.

Darkness was our all. As soon as they had enough light to see by Gumede's men were sure to catch up to us. I saw a little light in the distance and headed toward it. When we reached it, the first soft, watery light of day allowed me to see that it was a small village and there was a police station. We slowed to a walk and placed the AK-47s into a garbage bin. I was hoping that there would be a policeman on duty, and there was: we woke him up. He had fallen asleep at his desk. I suppose that a small town like this would seldom see any serious crime.

"Help us. Please help us," I implored the policeman, who appeared to be groggy and confused. Then he saw Alison, and he sat up to attention and straightened his uniform.

"What's the problem?" he asked, alert now.

"There are armed bandits chasing us," Alison insisted, breathless. "They are Zimbabweans and they are shooting at us. They will be here any moment now."

The policeman stared at us incredulously. Were we serious, or was this some practical joke? He weighed up our appearance and decided that we were serious. He picked up the phone and summoned assistance. Holding the phone to his chest, he turned to Alison and asked: "How many of them are there?"

"A dozen," Alison exaggerated. He spoke into the phone again, telling his assistant to hurry up and to phone the police in nearby

Francistown. I knew that the police in Francistown would take a long time to reach us, and we would never survive a shootout.

"Do you have a vehicle?" I asked.

"Yes, I do," he replied. "Come with me."

He led us to the solitary road, and as we exited the police station, Gumede's men came into sight. As soon as they saw us they opened fire, and the policeman was galvanized into action. He unholstered his handgun and returned fire while the three of us crouched behind the police car. Our AK-47's were just a few meters away from us, lying in the bin, and I leaped toward it. It is a criminal offense to bear arms in Botswana, and I had not wanted us to run afoul of the law here too, but I was being forced to take my chances: rather a criminal than a corpse! I handed a rifle to the policeman and Mzali and pushed Alison behind a wall.

"Stay there," I ordered her. "Don't come out unless I say so, and if we get into trouble, get into the car and get as far away from here as you possibly can."

Crouched behind the vehicle, we returned fire, but needed better cover: a bullet will go right through the side of a vehicle and start to tumble, causing horrific injuries if it hits anyone.

"Is there a back entrance to the police station?" I asked. The policeman nodded vigorously, and I turned to Alison and told her to go around the back using hand signals. I then laid down covering fire, sending Mzali and the policeman back into the police station. Once inside, they covered me and we were now better able to hold them off. Gumede's men were persistent and determined. I can only assume that he had threatened them with all manner of punishment should they not return with our bodies. I wondered where he was, thinking it unlikely that he would have walked into Botswana on his prosthetic leg.

As we were crouching in the police station bullets started to smash into the wall behind us, and we returned fire. Our rifles were switched to repeat and we were firing two shots in quick succession, a double-tap followed by a pause, as we needed to conserve ammunition and to fire with accuracy rather than spraying bullets toward the enemy and hoping that something hit its target. For a few moments, we thought that we only had to contend with a frontal assault and were confident that we could at least keep them at bay. But fate intervened and the police officer, who had been phoned earlier, appeared on the scene. Foolishly, he drove his vehicle to the back of the police station and, as he was getting out of the car probably confused and bewildered, three of Gumede's men apprehended him. They had circled around to the back and were obviously hoping to surround us or to burst into the police station, taking us by surprise. They now had a hostage!

"Come out, Mr. Savage," a voice insisted. "If you don't, I will shoot this man."

"If you shoot that man you will have murdered an innocent civilian. What sort of soldier does that?" I shouted.

"He is not a civilian," the voice responded. "He is armed."

"What about my friends?" I asked hopefully.

"They can go home," the voice assured me. "We want you and we want the hard drive."

Alison was holding up remarkably well: she was keeping her wits about her and was demonstrating an amazing resolve, but I knew that were I to surrender she would certainly not be spared.

Turning to Mzali I whispered: "Left hook, right hook?"

Mzali nodded in agreement. The "hook" was a simple but effective counterinsurgency strategy. A contingent of men would divide themselves into two sections. The first section would confront the enemy head-on, laying down a barrage of fire while the second section would circle around in an extended arc until they were level with the enemy, who, hopefully, were still unaware of their presence. The second section would then charge the enemy from the side, over-running their position, while the first section ceased firing. You didn't want to shoot your own men!

I instructed the policeman to keep firing at the soldiers in front of the police station while I would lay down covering fire from the rear. Mzali was going to climb into the ceiling and knock a hole through the tiled roof; then he was going to come around from the side of the police station and overrun the enemy position; which is exactly what he did.

As Mzali burst around from the side of the building, I ceased firing. He caught them unawares as he ran at them from the side. As they were turning to fire on him, the captured policeman acted decisively: he grabbed his captor's weapon and fired, wounding his captive in the shoulder. Once again, Mzali was like a magnificent black panther, attacking with frenzied feline ferocity. Before they even knew what had happened, it was all over.

There were three of them in all, and Mzali and the policeman quickly secured them. Mzali left the policeman to watch his prisoners, while he and I returned to the fray, our odds substantially improved.

We managed to hold them off for about another twenty minutes, Alison using the policeman's handgun, before Gumede's men decided to fall back. It was not our marksmanship or our valor that saved our hides: it was the Botswana Defense Force. We heard the rotors of a helicopter in the distance, and Gumede's men turned tail and ran, hoping to get across the border before they were apprehended. They were here illegally and would be arrested.

With Gumede's men heading back toward the border, I turned to the policeman and thanked him. "We were chased across the border and had no choice but to bring the weapons with us," I told him. "If we are found with these rifles we will be in big trouble. Please, will you tell the police that these rifles belong to those soldiers? I promise you that we have not broken any laws, and only used the rifles to defend you and ourselves." He considered my request carefully.

"Okay," he conceded.

"You were fantastic," I told him. "Were it not for you we would all be dead now."

It may well have been flattery, but it was true. A little sincere praise can go an awfully long way. He was proud of himself, as well he should be. Not to be outdone, Mzali added his opinion.

"You would make a fine soldier," Mzali complimented him. "You are a brave man and we will tell everyone we meet how you saved us."

And then we waited to be arrested.

A police van arrived about an hour later, and we were hustled off to Francistown. I remembered Francistown as a small little trading village, but it had grown and now it was a bustling, vibrant town. We were taken straight to the police station and seated in a small interrogation room. We sat there for about ten minutes, waiting for someone to see us, and when the moment finally arrived it was a large and grim-faced policeman. He introduced himself as Captain Simelane. He was polite, but professional and got down to business straight away. He asked me why we were being chased, and I explained that it was because we had been caught trespassing on Kataza, which Gumede now owned, and that he had a personal vendetta against me and my family. I apologized profusely for being in Botswana illegally but explained that we had had no other choice. I explained that I was trying to protect Alison. I told him that Mzali had got caught up in this through no fault of his own and that he was being persecuted simply because he was my friend. I explained that another of our friends, Bryan, had been murdered by Gumede and that he would stop at nothing to get revenge for his leg. I was eloquent, and I was convincing, largely because it was the truth.

We are well aware of Professor Cameron's death," Captain Simelane stated. "We have captured seven bandits who entered the country illegally and attempted to murder one of our citizens. They face serious charges and will not be extradited to their country of origin. In Botswana, these transgressions carry the death penalty. We also captured a prominent Zimbabwean businessman and politician on Botswana soil. This is now a diplomatic and international incident, and there will be serious repercussions. These men confessed to having chased you across the border, and one of them claims to have been present when Professor Cameron was killed. He is telling us everything that he knows, from the time of his birth to the present day," Captain Simelane noted. "It seems that Minister Gumede is in hot water—boiling," he stated factually, without emotion.

Then he allowed himself a wry smile. "When the Botswana Defense Force found the minister he was crawling through the border fence: his face was in Zimbabwe, and his rear end was in Botswana, aiming toward us. Not knowing who he was, one of the men kicked his backside, and then pulled him back into Botswana. He is being detained and questioned as we speak, and both the South African and Zimbabwean governments have already been contacted. It will be difficult to sweep this under the carpet, and the Zimbabwe government will be embarrassed if one of its ministers is known to have committed murder and is being detained in Botswana while in the act of committing a crime. I suppose we could also charge him for gun running," Captain Simelane speculated.

He then emptied the contents of my rucksack onto the tabletop.

"When last did you have something to eat?" he asked, seeing that there was just one can of corned meat between the three of us. I told him that it had been the previous evening. He asked one of the policemen standing next to him to fetch us something. Then he emptied Alison's rucksack. He looked inside each of the three tins, opening the one holding the tablets first.

"What are these?" He asked, curious.

"Those are just curios from the gift shop in the hotel which we stayed at," Alison lied convincingly. He gave her a long hard look and placed them back in her rucksack. I think he knew exactly what they were, but I wasn't sure. He then opened the second tin, filled with bangles. He stared at Alison for a moment, and then he took one of the bangles and slipped it over his left wrist. He looked at Alison intently, challenging her to object. Perhaps he was trying to ascertain whether it was valuable or not. When she did not object, he took it off again and slipped it back into the tin.

"Keep it," Alison suggested.

"No thank you," the captain replied.

"No, really, I insist," Alison gently persisted. "It looks good on you; it suits you." The captain was delighted, slipped the bracelet back onto his wrist and admired it.

"I will be back a little later," the captain promised, flourishing his wrist. "Meanwhile, eat some breakfast and wait for me to return."

As he left, three welcome plates of bacon and eggs were brought through to us.

We waited, and we waited, and to their credit, the police did bring us a couple of cups of coffee, and they allowed us to recharge our cell phones. It must have been two hours later that Captain Simelane returned.

"This is your lucky day," he congratulated us. "The Botswana police are not going to press charges against you and you are free to go. But you have entered the country illegally: a customs official is on his way here to stamp your passports, and you are being issued temporary permits. You must be out of this country within three days. Customs officials at the Mafikeng border posts have been placed on standby, and if you do not report there within three days, a warrant will be issued for your arrest. All other exit points have been informed of the situation and have been instructed to usher you to the Mafikeng crossing, and not to process your passports. Do you understand?" We said that we did and thanked him profusely.

"There is one more thing," he intoned. "When you get to the South African side of the border, Mr. Savage will be arrested." I said that I understood and that I would willingly surrender to the police.

"I believe that you have something that they want," said Captain Simelane with a roguish smile, "but that is not my concern."

Turning to Mzali, Captain Simelane said: "I believe that the South African government understands your unique situation and that you will be allowed into the country." Mzali grinned sheepishly and looked relieved.

"Thank you," he said.

We hired a car later that morning after our temporary visas had been issued, and headed toward Gaborone and imminent arrest. When we were about halfway to Gaborone, an idea started to formulate in my mind.

"Alison honey," I queried, "how much money do you have?" She gave me a scathing look that told me it was none of my business.

"Why do you ask?" she inquired.

"Do you have any contacts at any of the universities overseas?" I asked. She could see where I was going with this.

"Yes, I do," she replied. "In fact, I have a good friend at Manchester University."

"Wouldn't you like to pay her a surprise visit?" I asked, chuckling, and then proceeded to outline my plan to Alison and Mzali.

CHAPTER 48

We arrived in Gaborone at about 3 o'clock that afternoon and drove straight to Sir Seretse Khama International Airport. It was a small, vibrant airport, and most of its flights were to South Africa or other African destinations. It transpired that it was only my personal details that had been forwarded to all customs posts; we managed to book Alison onto an Air France flight to Nairobi, but the plane wouldn't depart until 2 o'clock the next morning. Luckily, we were also able to reserve Alison a connecting flight to Heathrow Airport in London, where she would arrive the following evening.

Feeling a sense of relief, Alison, Mzali, and I found a small hotel to rest in and come to terms with the harrowing events of the last week. To be honest, so much had happened in so little time that it was all a blur; I did not even trust my own memory of days and distances, because memory is selective and can be self-serving, but the events were imprinted indelibly on my mind.

As we sat in the hotel, passing time and waiting for life to overtake us, I looked at my two closest friends.

"Well, here we are, safe and sound," I said, "rebels, rogues, and renegades: it is amazing that we survived the last week, but what I find even more surprising is that it has drawn us together and not driven us apart."

Mzali smiled: "That is because the whole is greater than the sum of its parts," he added. Alison, her arm around me, looked calm and analytical.

"I think the reason is that we complement each other perfectly. Between the three of us we constitute one entity; three personas, the doer, the dreamer, and the doctor, comprising one id or identity" I did not see the truth of that at the time, but in retrospect, I think that she was correct.

We spent a relaxed and lazy evening watching television. I was disconsolate. I felt as though a part of me was about to be amputated. There was a hollow abyss in my stomach, and the thought of being separated from Alison was gnawing at my soul. But it was vital that Alison get to England. We drove to the airport at midnight, allowing Alison time to report for her flight.

"Enjoy your flight," I urged her.

"Don't worry," she reassured me, seeing my distress. "I'll be back in a week or so, and this will all be over. I'm going to miss you."

As her aircraft took off, I remember feeling as though my soul was still attached to her and was being stretched and farther into a thin astral chord that would always connect to Alison.

Mzali and I spent the day lounging about in Gaborone. It was the next day that I received a call from Alison, who sounded ecstatic.

"I made it," she enthused. "I'm in London and I'm sitting here with my good friend Professor Haddon and a small team of excited academics. These tablets are historical dynamite; we haven't finished translating them yet, but we already know that they will change our knowledge of ancient history. Say hello to the team," Alison instructed me cheerfully, putting her phone on speaker.

"Hello," a chorus of happy voices greeted me, their accents distinctly British.

"Hi guys," I responded.

"I've got to go now," Alison apologized, "but good luck at the border with customs. I'm sure everything will be all right. I hope to see you in a few days' time." The thought of seeing Alison again was far more important to me than the revelations of arcane mysteries unlocked.

Mzali and I wanted to enjoy our liberty for as long as we could—we stayed in Gaborone until the last moment—but we knew that we had no choice but to report to customs before our temporary visas expired. When we finally did show, the Botswana customs officials were expecting us and we were rushed through hastily. They wanted to get rid of us like a foul smell, and we were almost dragged toward the South African side of the border.

When we got there, it was obvious that the Botswana customs officials had phoned ahead and informed South African customs that we were on our way to them. We were greeted cordially and taken to a little office. As we entered, I was horrified to recognize the tanned face of my old nemesis, the inquisitive State Security official who had made life so unpleasant for Alison and me. His expression was grim and foreboding.

Sitting next to him was a slim, middle-aged African woman, looking serious. The state security official introduced the lady as Precious Ndlovo, the deputy minister of internal security, and she greeted me politely without getting up from her chair.

"I'm irritated with you," she admonished, taking control of proceedings. "I have had to miss an official function just to come here and talk to you." I knew that this was even more serious than I had anticipated and my heart sank.

"You have no idea how much trouble this has caused," she continued. "Minister Gumede is being repatriated to Zimbabwe in disgrace, and I am sure that he will face criminal charges there. But they need to keep this entire incident quiet. The Zimbabwe government is insisting that you have stolen national treasures and they want them back: so do we!"

The state security man added: "Botswana might not have charged you and with an offense, but you are a South African citizen and we have every right to charge you ourselves. We are considering charging you with theft and smuggling," he said menacingly, deliberately trying to intimidate me.

"Give me your rucksack," he ordered, extending his meaty hand. I obliged, and he fished through my rucksack, finding nothing; then he searched Mzali's rucksack, finding nothing.

"Where are the tablets?" he asked abrasively. I smiled.

"Ah. That's a good question," I said. "You might have noticed that Alison is not with us. She is in London as we speak, and has already met with university academics. She tells me that the tablets contain information that will completely rewrite the history books."

"And as a British citizen, she is also considering pressing charges of her own. Those charges include the murder of Professor Bryan Cameron and the attempted murder of us three."

This news startled them: they had been certain that the tablets were with me and had not considered the possibility of Alison leaving with them.

"What is it that you want?" asked Ms. Ndlovo lazily, without real interest. That was about to change.

"I know that your focus is on the tablets," I said, "but once you have heard what I have to say, and once you have seen what I have to show, I think that you will agree that the tablets are fairly inconsequential. The tablets were merely a convenient excuse for Mr. Gumede to hunt me down. While I was in Zimbabwe, I came upon damning evidence against him and he is desperate to prevent that information from ever being revealed. Mr. Gumede has spent many years compiling information with which to blackmail people and I have in my possession a hard drive that you will find interesting. Alison has an exact duplicate of this hard drive, and she is making other copies as we speak. Alison will place the hard drive in a safety deposit box, and she is going to do the same thing with the tablets. Should anything untoward ever happen to any one of us that hard drive will be released to the British press. I think that you need to have a look at exactly what is on it. Pay careful attention to one particular folder entitled 'Secret'; you will find it interesting and unsettling."

I rustled through my rucksack and withdrew the hard drive, still wrapped in material. She looked at me warily as she took the hard drive. Without another word, she disappeared into an adjacent room with the state security official, emerging some twenty minutes later, worry etched on her face. She took a deep breath.

"I will repeat the question I asked you earlier," she said, her voice quavering. "What do you want?"

I felt pity for her as I had deposited political dynamite in her grasp, presenting her with a moral dilemma, and forcing her to choose between loyalty to her friends and colleagues and her own morality.

"You strike me as an honest person," I flattered her. "I'm not looking for a financial reward or for favors. I consider it a patriotic and moral duty of mine to give you this information. What you do with it is up to you, but there are a host of issues that need dealing with: some sort of purge is necessary. I know that you have only had a brief opportunity to look at what information is in those folders, but I can assure you that it could take years to deal with all the issues unveiled. Remember: to find the rot, follow the flies! I trust that you will do the right thing." She looked uncertain.

"Were this information to be released en masse the results would be devastating. It could topple the government, and no other political party is popular enough yet to govern with the consent of the people. It would unleash social discord on an unprecedented scale. The people would want to know why ministers have enriched themselves while the people clamor for social delivery, houses, electricity, sanitation, and running water. Foreign investors would flee the country, taking their capital with them. The economy would collapse, unemployment would rise, criminality would rise, and the country would be on the verge of ruin." I waited for a moment, giving Precious a chance to fully digest my ominous words. Knowing that I had her full attention and that I had now assumed command of the conversation, I proffered my opinion.

"This information can never come to light. It must never reach the public domain. If all these revelations are disclosed in tandem, there may well be a revolution. How the government and the party deal with this hard drive is up to them, but I think that this information needs to get to the right people, possibly the public protector: someone trustworthy and someone powerful enough to act on it. Each of the myriads of crimes detailed in that hard drive needs to be fully investigated, and the criminals need to be brought to justice. But this must be done over an extended time: slowly and silently, lest panic ensues. Be patient; you cannot rush."

Precious nodded demurely in agreement, mulling my words in her mind. She would need to make some momentous decisions, and she bore all the responsibility alone.

"You two have performed a great service to the country," she noted appreciatively, her voice decidedly flat, glancing first to Mzali and then to me, and allowing herself a wistful smile: "but how I wish that someone else had come in my place today." The state security officer bent toward Precious and whispered in her ear.

"Ah, yes," she said, "with all this unexpected news, I had forgotten." Her face softened as she turned toward me: "The tablets?"

"They don't seem all that important now, do they?" I said with a smile.

"No, they don't," she responded pensively. "But then again, even the small things need to be dealt with thoroughly."

"I have given the matter long and serious thought," I informed her, "and it seems to me that society is sometimes best served by keeping certain truths secret. As an academic, it offends my conscience not to unveil the historical truth, but sometimes the narrative is more important than mere facts.

"As it so happens, I also have a moral dilemma. I happen to like the present narrative that the Bantu people had a sophisticated civilization before the arrival of the Europeans, but it conflicts with what I now know. Yet I know what I know, and that is what is important to me. Sometimes we regret the truth, and I would feel a little sullied to see the history books rewritten and deprive the Bantu people of a source of great pride; particularly when the Phoenicians were barbaric people practicing slavery and child sacrifice. Although I would like it to be known that the Europeans were not the only people to have exploited Africa." I added as an afterthought. Precious nodded impatiently waiting for me to get to the point.

"I simply want my life back and to live without fear or interference. I know that there are people who would destroy my life to remove any trace of embarrassing truths, particularly when their academic prestige has been built upon facts that those truths would contradict. Those tablets will remain with the hard drives, in a safety deposit box, as insurance. I want to know that Alison's career will never be limited by politics, gender, or race and I want the same courtesy for myself.

"And then there is Mzali. He has sacrificed everything to help Alison and me. He was an exceptionally good headmaster and now he is left with nothing. I want to know that Mzali will get citizenship, and I want to know that his life can be resurrected. I want Mzali to be offered employment as a headmaster, and to be given a nice house to live in. I know that he will not be a burden to the state because he is an excellent person." I deliberately avoided Mzali's gaze, because all I was requesting was justice, and yet it might appear that I was being patronizing, offering what was not mine to give.

Precious and the state security man pondered my words and then disappeared together into the adjacent room. I could hear the two of them whispering animatedly to one another as Mzali and I sat together in expectant silence, our futures being decided for us. When they emerged, they were smiling for the first time.

"You have a deal," Precious said. "But there are conditions. If those tablets ever see the light of day, we will denounce them as fakes and you two as frauds." I knew that her harsh tone was playful and that she was simply trying to add humor to the bleak situation.

"Thank you," I said gratefully. "I agree and you can rest assure that I will never break this agreement."

"There is one more thing," I said.

"I think all your cards have been played," Precious informed me sternly.

"It is a small request and has no real bearing on matters, but I would appreciate it if I were allowed to keep the tablet and trinkets that started this debacle."

Precious allowed herself a resigned smile. "That's fine," she sighed in mock exasperation. Her tone turned serious again.

"Mr. Savage, Mr. Sithole," she said with sincerity, "on behalf of the government and on behalf of myself, I would like to thank you for this information. By the way Mr. Savage, you must never go into business; you are a terrible negotiator!" She laughed: "You could have asked for almost anything: you could have asked for money; you could have asked for power, privilege, or pecuniary gain, and yet, all you asked for was to be left alone. You are a most peculiar person, -- and you are an awful negotiator. But I am thankful for that."

"Don't be so sure," I corrected her with a chuckle. "What is important to other people is not necessarily important to me. After all, I did get exactly what I wanted, didn't I?"

"I suppose you did," she smiled. "Mr. Savage, Mr. Sithole, it has been a refreshing and unexpected pleasure meeting the two of you, but I now have serious state business to attend to," she said as she brandished the hard drive. "My colleague will see to it that you get home safely. Good luck!"

"You need some medical attention, my friend," the state security man said to Mzali, changing the subject. He called for a medic to attend to Mzali's face. I felt ashamed: we had spent so much time together that I had become inured to his facial injuries, accepting the unacceptable as normal.

We were offered a lift back to Randburg, and we accepted gratefully. The state security man introduced himself as Piet van Tonder and was remarkably amiable once we grew to know him. In fact, the trip back to civilization was thoroughly enjoyable. He turned out to be well educated, and a great conversationalist, so different from the impression I had of him as a ruthless thug.

*****

Mafikeng was about a hundred kilometers behind us when my cell phone rang. It was Alison.

"Hi honey; how are you?"

"I'm fine, thanks; relieved that we got through the border unscathed. Now we are on our way home, thankfully. How are you?"

"Excited," she gushed. "I have wonderful news. Your tablet has been deciphered and I'll be flying home in three days' time."

"You're right, that is exciting news. It'll be great to see you again."

"That's not the only reason that I'm excited. Is there a geographical feature near Kataza that looks like a rhino?"

What a strange question. I paused to think and asked Mzali if he could remember anything, putting my cell phone on speaker.

"What about that rock between the homestead and Three Fingers?" Mzali pondered. "We used to think that it looked a little like a sleeping hippo."

"You're right!" I exclaimed. "If there were a loose rock placed on the 'head', it would look like a rhino. That must be it. It's overgrown with trees. Why do you ask, Alison?"

"Well, there's reference to an ancient gold mine right next to the rhino, and we have surmised that it must be a geographic feature. It appears that there is gold on Kataza!"

I laughed. "Fate is unkind. All those years of living at Kataza, and we never knew we were on a gold mine."

"I've got to go now honey; I just wanted to know that you are safe, and to let you know that I'll see you soon. I miss you."

"I miss you too. I love you." Alison ended the call. Mzali and I looked at each other, amused by the irony. Then a thought struck me, and I thought aloud.

"The winds of change are gusting across Africa once more, Mzali. I don't know if you have any savings, but perhaps you and I should buy Kataza together? I believe it is looking for new ownership."

For the first time in days, Mzali grinned. "Wouldn't that be something? Me, an owner of Kataza! You and I as partners; I love it."

"It is a wonderful thought, isn't it?" I remarked. "It is just a pity that I don't have enough money saved. I hate to douse the pleasure of the moment, but Alison and I can't afford it."

Piet smiled: "Maybe I could lend you some money?"

KATAZA

It was late in the afternoon when Mzali and I arrived at my house in Randburg. We said our farewells to Piet and strolled down to my garden gate. As we approached, I saw my mother sitting on the veranda with Buddy and Jessie lying next to her in the afternoon sun. When the dogs saw me, they went frantic with delight; Buddy leaped so high with excitement that he licked my face while still in midair. Mom, bless her soul, had not wanted me to return home to an empty house. She was delighted to see Mzali, and he her. I made us all some coffee, gave some treats to the dogs, and we sat out on the veranda, regaling Mom with anecdotes and our implausible—but true—story

EPILOGUE

My story is told: I have exorcised my demons and purged my soul. I have ambivalent feelings: satisfaction and frustration, relief and regret. I am relieved that it is all over, but I have committed myself to silence and the truth will never be known. Was it all worthwhile? Well, my appetite for camping and canned meat has diminished, but I have some unusual ornaments and I have a lovely wife whose hand is now resting on my shoulder and who is reading these words as I write them, and who has just kissed my cheek!

She and I have matching gold wedding rings, forged from an old bracelet, and Alison has a stunning silver ring which compliments her azure eyes. Yes, it has certainly been worth it. I just wish that I could make the truth known to those willing to know. Were the truth ever to exposed, it would need to be presented as fiction; but then again, "truth is stranger than fiction." If the most convincing lie is wrapped in truth, then possibly the converse is also true. Perhaps I could present the facts as fable, and perhaps I should give my memoirs a name, and go back to where it all starts and ends: Kataza.

FOOTNOTE

Since the writing of *Kataza*, but prior to its publication, several events anticipated in the novel have transpired:

NOVEMBER 2017: President Robert Mugabe of Zimbabwe was deposed by his former protégé, Emmerson Mnangagwa. At 94, President Mugabe was the oldest and longest serving head of state in the world. Mnangagwa removed his mentor from power in a *palace putsch* as he was being increasingly marginalized and criticized by Mugabe's young wife, Grace. All indications were that Grace was being primed to succeed her husband as president, and she was building an enormous power base around herself, eradicating every threat to her ambitions.

Conspiring with military generals, Mnangagwa overthrew Mugabe, hoping to protect his financial interests and political influence. Mnangagwa's nickname is, *ngwenya*: the crocodile, because of his ruthlessness and the fact that it was he who sanctioned *Gukhuruhundi*, the genocidal massacres of the Matabele people. <u>Refer to the end of Chapter 27</u>.

NOVEMBER 2017: Comrade Shire, the man responsible for the *Gukhuruhundi* massacres when he was Commander of the notorious fifth Brigade, was appointed to a ministerial portfolio in the new, 'purified', cabinet. He has never expressed any remorse or regret for the genocidal atrocities committed on his orders. <u>Refer to Chapters 23 and 24</u>.

JUNE 2018: A bomb, similar to that described in *Kataza*, was exploded at a political rally in Bulawayo, in the preparations for new elections meant to validate Mnangagwa and his military machine. Two people were killed, and a number were seriously injured. The outcome of this marred election, which endorsed Mnangagwa, was criticized by all international observers, but accepted unconditionally by the African Union. <u>Refer to Chapters 27 and 45</u>.

2017 and 2018: The corrupt business activities of the Gupta family are currently being investigated in South Africa, and a host of prosecutions being prepared. The Gupta family is accused of having established a pervasive network of patronage which included the former president of South Africa, Jacob Zuma, and his son, Duduzane. Many government ministers and influential businessmen colluded in this "state capture" and are in the process of being brought to justice. Jacob Zuma is being prosecuted for a slew of crimes, ranging from the misuse of power to fraud and corruption.

Attempting to sanitize the family image, one of the Gupta businesses hired a British public relations firm, *Bell Pottinger*, together they created a marketing campaign denigrating white monopoly capitalism and portraying the Gupta family as paladins of Black economic empowerment. This marketing campaign was instrumental in fomenting massive racial tension throughout the country until it was exposed, although the effects linger. *Bell Pottinger* has since disbanded under a cloud of opprobrium and prosecutions are pending. Refer to Chapters 39 and 48.

NOTE: Former government ministers in Zimbabwe have previously been implicated in illicit poaching activities, and Grace Mugabe was accused of illegally aiding in the export of rhino horns to China. The Mugabe family is also rumored to have profited enormously from the vast Merange diamond fields, siphoning profits into their personal bank accounts, and paying members of the Central Intelligence Organization to retain their loyalty. Refer to Chapters 8 and 13.

The Matabele people remain marginalized, with no meaningful voice or political party to represent their interests.

www.ingramcontent.com/pod-product-compliance
Lightning Source LLC
Chambersburg PA
CBHW030247200626
46816CB00002BA/536